THE DEFECTOR

Charles Collingwood

Charles Collingwood was born in Michigan,
USA, in 1917. He went to Oxford as a Rhodes
Scholar after graduating from Cornell
University. When the Second World War
began he abandoned his studies to become a
reporter. Soon after he joined CBS and has
been a notable figure in radio and television
journalism ever since.
Collingwood has been Chief Foreign
Correspondent for CBS since 1964, has
visited South Vietnam on numerous
occasions and went to Hanoi in 1968. He now
lives in London when he is not on assignment.

First published in Great Britain in 1970
by Rupert Hart-Davis Ltd,
© Charles Collingwood 1970
First Sphere Books edition 1972
Reprinted June 1972

For Tia Luisa de la Bomba

Printed in Great Britain by
Hazell Watson & Viney Ltd,
Aylesbury, Bucks

The Defector
CHARLES COLLINGWOOD

SPHERE BOOKS LIMITED
30/32 Gray's Inn Road, London WC1X 8JL

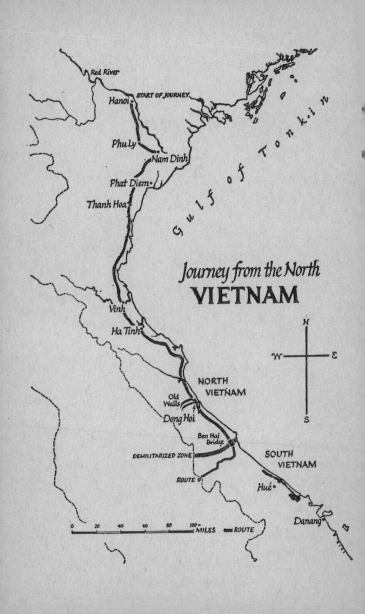

I

HANOI

1

I can wake up in Paris and think for a moment that I am still in New York. I have struggled from sleep in Prague and thought it was London. I have even got up in the night in some unlikely places and been sure I was home. But when I woke in Hanoi, I knew exactly where I was. In moments of danger and apprehension the instinct of orientation does not readily surrender itself, even to sleep.

I was wide-awake the moment I came to, and I knew at once that I was in the best suite in the Thong Nhat Hotel, that the bathroom was to my left, the door to the corridor over my shoulder, and the entrance to the sitting room at bottom left. It was four o'clock in the morning and pitch-dark, but a diffused anxiety had kept my faculties so sharp that I apprehended, if I could not see, the pale tent of mosquito netting around the bed and the propeller blades of the ancient ceiling fan slowly churning the moist night air overhead.

I lay there asking myself how I had got to Hanoi in the first place and how I was ever going to get out. I knew the answer to the first question but not to the second. It is always easier to remember how you lost the last hand than to figure out how you will win the next. I could not see how I was going to win with the hand they had dealt me. Or how I could throw it in either.

Sleep was impossible. Like most Southeast Asian cities, Hanoi is a noisy town at best. The peculiar contribution of the Communist regime has been to organize the din at the most unnatural hours. What had wakened me was the sound of the street cleaners outside my window—two women, one on each side of the street, shouting and gossiping to each other as they swept, the rhythmic sound of the homemade brooms punctuated by the shrill, birdlike cries of the North Vietnamese women. Then the trucks began to go by, creaking and clanking as though they were about to fall apart and blowing their horns in the night.

Unless you are used to it, four o'clock in the morning is an outrageous hour for such a racket. The people of Hanoi had obviously become used to it. You can become used to anything, and this had been going on since 1965, when the American bombing began. In those days most of the American planes came over by day. To keep crowds off the streets during daylight hours when concentrations of people would invite heavy casualties, the government had decreed that most business would be done at dawn, or dusk, or in the night. Thus everything got under way before first light—markets, stores, banks—so that people could do their shopping and run their errands in the protection of darkness. When daylight came, these things closed down, to reopen at dusk.

It had been a topsy-turvy arrangement even in 1965 because, as it turned out, the United States never struck Hanoi more than a glancing blow. Now, long after the bombing halt, the only reason to maintain this bizarre schedule was to remind people that they were still at war and that an unpredictable enemy might at any moment strike again.

The early-morning hours in Hanoi were no less hideous for that. It was impossible that the North Vietnamese enjoyed it much themselves; the instinct to sleep during the hours of darkness is a basic one. Visiting Western imperialists, however effete, could hardly be the only ones who preferred to stay in bed until the sun was up.

I wondered how many North Vietnamese were chafing against not only this early morning tumult, but the whole apparatus of wartime controls which still persisted even though the war itself seemed slowly drawing to an untidy conclusion. You could sense the regimentation everywhere. The whole place smelled of it. What you couldn't sense was how the people felt about it. People will put up with a great deal of control when the bombs are falling, which they resent when the bombs have stopped and peace seems around the corner. Reporters don't jump to conclusions, but it seemed to me that if the government of the Democratic Republic of Vietnam was not having problems on the home front, then the North Vietnamese were not human.

Evidently they were human enough to cause the government to run regular campaigns against complacency, bourgeois thinking, incorrect conclusions, laziness and the danger of falling into traps set by wily imperialist propaganda. The government even publicly denounced the generation gap, claiming that young people were listening to rock-and-roll music, wearing revealing clothes and generally being poisoned by imperialist culture. You could read too much into such campaigns, I supposed, but they didn't sound much like the old spirit of Dienbienphu. It would be interesting to know how deep that disaffection went and how high it reached. Did it really reach as high as Nguyen Van Thanh?

That made me think again of what I was in Hanoi to do. I didn't see how it could be done. The journalistic part was easy enough. That is my trade. The other thing wasn't my job at all, and I was very exposed, behind the lines in a garrison state positively hysterical about security. North Vietnam is not a landscape easy for a Westerner to fade into. With my round eyes, blond hair and six feet, I stood out in a crowd of Vietnamese like a black man at a White Citizens' Council meeting.

The worst thing was there was no one to help me. Pfeiffer had said I would be contacted. No one had showed. Unless it was Charlie. But Charlie couldn't have been put in Hanoi to help me. Charlie was going to be an albatross around my neck. What was Charlie doing in Hanoi anyway?

Across the street a loudspeaker started up. First it played a raucous martial anthem. Then the squawks of a woman counting out a cadence for calisthenics. Listening, I could pick out the sounds of at least two other loudspeakers in different locations. They must have set them up every few hundred yards. It was real Big Brother stuff. I wondered how many people still bothered to do their physical jerks at such an hour, keeping fit for the Fatherland.

I kneaded the wax balls of two ear plugs and stuffed them in my head. No help. I wished to God I had never come to Hanoi. I wished even harder that Charlie had never come.

II

BEFORE
HANOI

2

It began in Puerto Secreto. Puerto Secreto is an uncompromisingly picturesque little Mexican town on the Pacific Coast which for years has always been going to be the next Acapulco but remains a seedy, down-at-the-heel little resort that draws the kind of people who come there because it's cheaper than grander places. It's full of pot smokers, LSD trippers, failed poets, bad painters and loud tourists on package deals. It is also, in its crummy way, extremely beautiful, and I love it.

I had come to Puerto Secreto because I was tired. I was tired of wars, revolutions, invasions and student riots. Above all, I was tired of the International Broadcasting System, whose Chief Foreign Correspondent I am supposed to be and on whose behalf I had been going to South Vietnam three times a year, covering the Russians in Prague, the dust-ups in the Middle East, the colonels in Greece, the *événements* in Paris and every other damned thing that came along.

I forget now what it was that broke the camel's back— some ridiculous assignment when I hadn't even got my bags unpacked from the last one. Anyway, there followed an increasingly acerbic exchange of cables with New York, the upshot of which was that I id I was either quitting or taking a year's sabbatical leave of absence and they could jolly well

9

decide which. So they cabled back, take the year's leave of absence—unpaid, of course—and I sublet my house to a bad actor rich enough to pay the rent and came down to live in Puerto Secreto for a year.

It was an impulsive decision, taken partly out of fatigue, partly out of pique and largely out of self-pity. I have no idea whether I could have stuck it out for a whole year doing nothing. All my friends said I couldn't, that I'd go out of my mind if I didn't have something to do, and anyway it's immoral to do nothing.

As a matter of fact, after a couple of months of doing nothing I did begin to have a qualm or two, especially in the morning, when I was still completely sober and when I read the Mexico City English-language newspaper and saw how badly my former colleagues were covering stories I knew more about than they did. But I never had a chance to test my theory that I really could do nothing for a year, because I got this cable from Ned Bailey.

Now, I had known Ned Bailey for more than twenty-five years. We were passengers on the same ship, sailing in convoy to the invasion of North Africa in November, 1942. He was the most romantic-looking fellow you ever saw. Dark hair which he wore rather longer than was fashionable then, regular features of the Errol Flynn type and the same kind of dash. He had his uniforms made in Savile Row, a kind of amalgam of American and British military style, carried a swagger stick and could charm a bird out of a tree. He said he was a Psychological Warrior, but I learned soon enough that he was with the OSS.

We saw a lot of each other in Algiers. Shared a pair of sisters, as a matter of fact. Then I ran into him in Rome, where he had been dropped behind the enemy lines long before the surrender and ran a successful little intelligence and sabotage operation. I think after that he was in Yugoslavia out of Allen Dulles' and David Bruce's shop, but I didn't see him again until Berlin, where he was running some agents in the Soviet Zone. When I got married after the war, he came to my wedding, but well before that broke up—it seems a long time ago now—I lost track of him.

I gathered Ned had got out of the spy business and was doing some kind of international insurance work that took him all over the place. The next time I bumped into him was in the lobby of the Caravelle in Saigon around 1965. He said he'd come to write insurance on some big factory, right in the area of operations, which had arrived before the war and never been uncrated. I said it sounded a crazy risk to me, but he said that not only were we and the ARVN protecting it but that the Vietcong wouldn't touch it because they wanted it for postwar development when they took over. Anyway, he told me later he made a hell of a lot of money out of the deal, and as far as I know nothing ever happened to the factory.

Over the years we saw each other quite a lot, and I was always pleased because, as I have said, we went back a long way. I was pleased when I got his wire from Los Angeles.

J 234 UMX0719 ORDPDFZ
LOS ANGELES CALIF VIA NOGALES
WILLIAM BENSON
PUERTO SECRETO NAY MEXICO
CANT IMAGINE YOU ON SABBATICAL STOP YOU MUST BE UP TO NO GOOD AS USUAL STOP EYE LIKEWISE SO ARRIVING FRIDAYS FIVE OCLOCK FLIGHT TO LEND IMMORAL SUPPORT CABLE IF INCONVENIENT

NED BAILEY

For the next few days, I must say I looked forward to having old Ned down in Puerto Secreto. I knew everyone in town I wanted to know and had seen rather more of them than I wanted to see. A new face would be good for me. I knew him well enough to know he wouldn't overstay his welcome, and I thought we'd have a few days' fun and that would be that until we ran into each other at Annabel's in London or the Ritz Bar in Paris or some other place that was his style after I'd gone back to work.

I didn't have the slightest premonition.

I left the house a little early to meet Ned's plane, so I stopped off at Flip's place for a drink. Manuel, the bartender, knew I liked the Gordon's gin and not the Oso Negro, and he started mixing the martini as I came in the door; which is better service than you usually get in Mexico and the reason I keep going to Flip's in spite of the tourists in their Bermuda shorts and ankle socks.

I was looking at my watch to see whether I had time for another one when a couple of soft breasts were against my back and a couple of hard brown arms around my waist. I'd know them anywhere.

"Charlie, baby," I said, putting my hands around to squeeze her bottom and twisting my head for a kiss.

Her real name was Charlotte, but everyone called her Charlie, perhaps because she was all girl. They called her La Bomba for similar reasons. .

Charlie La Bomba was a character. Not always good news. She had tried everything in life, but nothing for very long. She was a natural rebel, an instinctive believer in lost causes, of which the cause most lost was her own. Nothing ever seemed to work out for her. Sometimes I thought she carried doom in her face. At least I could never imagine her as old. She had a kind of strength, though. A fierce insistence on her own private integrity which she defended at any cost. She often behaved outrageously, offending every right-thinking person. But she really didn't give a damn. Mixed up though she was, she was perhaps the freest spirit I have ever known.

La Bomba was also a very good-looking broad. She had a lovely live body, slanting green eyes and an Irish pug nose that kept her from being beautiful but made her merely awfully good to look at. She had an air of innocence about her that was curious considering the fact that she had slept with a large cross-section of the males in town. Quite often with me.

She was not a nymphomaniac and she was not a tramp. It was only that she liked men and she liked sex and if a man she liked thought it was important to go to bed with her, she didn't see why it was so important not to. But she never went to bed with someone she didn't like. I guess it really was that she felt the way a man feels about these things, which was all right with me, theoretically. Except that I cared about Charlie a lot, and sometimes I worried about her.

"I'd buy you a drink," I said, "but I've got to meet a guy at the airport."

"What kind of guy?"

"Your kind. He's tall, dark, handsome, trained to a hair and irresistible to women. They run up to him in the street and tear the buttons off his clothes."

"Then I'll go with you, and you can buy me a drink at the airport because Mexicana is always late."

So we drove out to the airport and the plane was late and we did have a drink and then there was old Ned. Handsome as ever, of course, although maybe let down a bit with the passage of years, but still in better shape than I was. Watching Charlie look at him, I was a little jealous.

"Billy boy," said Ned, looking straight at Charlie, "what is this you have brought to welcome the weary traveler?"

"A martini," I said, because that was not what he meant.

"I'm Charlie," she said.

"Charlie La Bomba," I added.

"La Bomba," said Ned, not taking his eyes off her. "Well, now, in Spanish La Bomba means a bomb, a pump and, in some places, a tart. Which are you?"

"All three. That's why they call me La Bomba."

"We'll get along fine," the bastard said.

And they did.

Charlie stayed for dinner that night, and she and Ned Bailey got along so well that I finally left them and went to bed. She was telling him the colorful, if somewhat expurgated, story of her life. I don't know whether anything went on between them except talk, but I suspected the worst, knowing them both. At least she had the grace not to be there for breakfast the next morning. I myself was not at my best at breakfast, being the least bit jealous, but Ned was bubbling over.

"That's quite a girl, that Bomba," he said.

"Yes, she's quite a girl."

"You know, we talked a lot last night."

"So I gathered."

"There's more to her than meets the eye."

"I'm sure you found it all."

"Look," he said, "you aren't sore, are you?"

"No, I'm not sore. But if all you wanted was to make a pass at a pretty girl, I don't know why you left Los Angeles."

"Oh, come on. She's more than just another pretty girl. She's a rare creature. She's an idealist, a child of nature."

"She's a nut. But I warn you, I'm very fond of her."

"I know, I know. Don't worry. She is kind of crazy, isn't she? Did she ever tell you what happened to her passport?"

"Yes, I know what happened to her passport."

La Bomba had got on some kind of pro-Castro kick a year or so ago—wanted to cut cane—and when she discovered her passport wasn't valid to travel to Cuba, she had mailed it back to the State Department in protest. Either they never returned it or it had got lost in the Mexican mails.

The whole thing was typical of her—wanting to go to Cuba, not going, making the silly gesture of sending back her passport and then not bothering to get it back. Now she couldn't go anywhere. I had always tried to restrain these sudden enthusiasms of hers, or at least to direct them toward something useful. There was one time when she was mad keen to go to North Vietnam to help Uncle Ho against the American imperialist aggressors. I told her Uncle Ho was too old for her and that, anyway, if she wanted to relieve human suffering, there was rather more in the South than in the North. Besides, she could get into the South and they weren't accepting American volunteers in the North that week.

I even had the International Voluntary Services send her all the papers so she could do some good works in South Vietnam. Nothing ever came of it, of course, as nothing ever seemed to come of anything in her life. That worried me. Not the IVS thing, but the lack of any direction or purpose in her life. Still, that was the way she wanted it, but she was wasting her life down in Puerto Secreto.

"You know, she's wasting her life down here," Ned said. "I'm going to send a cable today and fix it up about her passport. Then I'm going to find something for her to do. All that energy and idealism ought to be put to better use. Maybe I can help her."

"My boy, she is not called La Bomba for nothing, is she? You must have it bad. Ned, we've all tried to help her, but she doesn't really want help. She likes her crazy life here. She doesn't hurt anyone except herself. Don't try to reform her. She won't really thank you for it."

"I don't want to reform her. I just want to give her a chance."

"Ned, do me a favor and leave her alone."

He didn't say anything.

3 Ned didn't talk about La Bomba again until he left. After breakfast that morning we went out fishing in a boat I had hired. We went trolling up the coast beneath the jungle-covered mountains and among the rocks cut by the sea into arches until they stood out from the water like the great reclining figures of Henry Moore. Ned got a big dorado and I three sierra. We went into a little town at the mouth of a river and got the old lady at the little *palapa* restaurant to cook a couple of the sierra for us and gave her the other fish.

It was a great lunch, and we came home tired from all the sun and beer. After a shower and clean clothes we sat on the terrace with gin and tonics watching the quick and wonderful sunset in which these latitudes specialize. Ned started to kid me in a lazy way about my sabbatical.

"You can't stand a year of this," he said. "It will destroy you. It's too easy, too beautiful, the living is too good. You need the challenges and frustrations of work to keep you going."

"Like hell I do," I said. "Poor fellow, you're just a work-oriented bastard, numbed by generations of puritan propaganda into thinking that work is good for you, that it's the proper end of man. I tell you the proper end of man is so to arrange his existence that he doesn't have to work. I've managed to arrange it for just one year and, by God, I'm going to enjoy it."

"Not ever tempted?" he asked.

"Not ever tempted."

"Nothing would get you back before the year's up?"

"Nothing."

"No story you couldn't resist covering?"

"None."

"What about Vietnam?"

"Oh, come on," I said. "I've been covering Vietnam since 1960. I've made fifteen trips out there. I've walked through the rice paddies, heard the mortar rounds, taken the sniper fire, been up to the DMZ, listened to the generals, asked all the questions, got all the answers, tried to figure the damned thing out and am no wiser than when I started. No, thanks. Not for a while."

"That's *South* Vietnam?"

"Of course."

"That's what I mean."

"What do you mean, that's what you mean?"

"I was talking about *North* Vietnam. Suppose you had a chance to go to North Vietnam. Wouldn't you go?"

"Nobody's going to ask me to North Vietnam. They're too smart for that. These days they want people they can count on. Nice, fond, softhearted, softheaded liberals who will do their work for them. I've been around too long. I might introduce some complexity into the equation. No, they'll stick to the predictable notables and the rest of the protest marchers."

"But if you had the chance, wouldn't you want to go?"

"Oh, sure, I guess so. If I had the chance, I suppose I would want to go."

"Well," said Ned Bailey, "I think you're going to have the chance."

"Highly unlikely" was all I said, because there was some-

D.—2

thing in his voice that made me wonder. "What makes you think so?"

"Well, after all, you did put in a request to visit Hanoi last year."

"How did you know that, Ned?" I thought no one knew that except a couple of people at IBS. I *had* put in a request. I had once conceived the idea of doing a documentary on the history of Vietnam. It is ridiculous to try to understand a country unless you know something of its history, and, as far as I could see, neither the American military, the State Department, the press nor the American people had the first idea of what the two thousand years of Vietnamese history were about or how deeply the present conflict was rooted in the past. Vietnamese history became a preoccupation with me. I read everything in the only languages available to me— French and English. I talked to all the scholars—and found most knew less than I. I wrote a draft script and had even done some filming in the South. But since all of Vietnam's early history was in the North and since the documents and collections still in Hanoi were so much richer than those in the South, it occurred to me to try to get in there. So I wrote a rather fulsome letter to the Foreign Minister of the Democratic Republic of Vietnam explaining what I wanted to do, gave a copy to the North Vietnamese Mission in Paris and even showed a copy of my draft script to a Communist journalist who had been into the North and whom I knew to be friendly with them and asked him to put in a word for me. When I told IBS what I had done, they were furious. They had had applications in for strictly news purposes for months; and they feared I was liable to queer the pitch. So I forgot about it. But how did Ned Bailey know?

"I still have government connections, you know," he said.

"CIA?"

"Yes."

"I always thought that insurance business was phony."

"Oh, no. It's not phony at all. Perfectly legitimate. It makes a lot of money. Like that deal in Saigon. It also gives me an excuse to get around."

"Okay," I said. "What's going on?".

. "Well, we read a lot of their radio traffic, as you know. For the last couple of months your name has been cropping up all over the place. They've been running checks on you, asking their friends in the United States, England, Hong Kong, wherever they have friends, what they make of you. For instance, you showed a Communist writer in Paris a script of yours. He sent them a glowing report. Said you were a little naïve but good—knowledgeable and objective."

"That's what I wanted him to say. That was when I was still trying to get in."

"Well, it looks as though that's why you *will* get in. They don't know much about television, but they've been persuaded that it's the coming thing in the United States. Great force for molding opinion and all that."

I still thought I was an improbable choice.

"Then why don't they invite a real certified public-opinion-molder like Cronkite or Huntley or Brinkley?" I asked. "You can be damned sure they've all got requests on file, too."

"Because of that script, old boy. They think that anyone who is interested in their history can't be all bad. Anyway, all their other reports on you have been good."

"What do you mean, 'good'? I'm not on their side, you know. We do not see eye to eye. I hate the damned war, but I do not believe we should get out of Vietnam tomorrow at any price. If they've done any checking on me at all, they know that."

"Yes, I expect they know that, but I doubt if it bothers them particularly. After all, they've been talking for a long time in Paris with Americans who feel the same way."

"But, Ned, we aren't talking about a negotiation. We're talking about admitting an American reporter to North Viet-

·nam. In the nature of things, they would want someone who would reflect their view of the war. They see the war as an immoral act by the United States which we are waging against them with ruthless efficiency. A lot of Americans agree· with them. I happen not to. My own view is that this war is no more immoral than any other war, which isn't saying much, but that we have waged it with endless incompetence. I'm not just talking about the battlefield either. I'm afraid that we have managed, with the best will in the world, to demoralize South Vietnam to such a degree that they'll never be a viable society. I like the South Vietnamese. I'd like them to have their chance, which is what we started out fighting for. Now I'm afraid we may have blown it, but I want any peace settlement to give South Vietnam whatever chance we've left them. If we can get them that, now is the time to end the war."

Bailey apparently found my speech encouraging.

"Bill, you and the North Vietnamese may not be so far apart as you think, certainly not so far as to frighten them off. They may be rigid and doctrinaire, but they aren't stupid. As I read them, they have decided, quite rightly, that they are getting diminishing returns from the testimony of the fellow travelers and professional pacifists they've been letting in. That stuff doesn't pay off for them any more. They think they can get more mileage out of the witness of a professional reporter whom no one can accuse of being partisan. You know, the most effective piece of propaganda they ever made was to let Harrison Salisbury in, because the American people believed what he wrote."

"So now you think they want to try me?"

"That's what I came down here to tell you."

"Well, thanks for the tip. I'll believe it when I get the engraved invitation."

"Bill, I'm so sure about this that I'm going to ask you to do me a favor while you're there."

"No," I said..

I was to remember that night's conversation with Ned Bailey many times, not least while I was in Hanoi.

After that firm refusal, when I'd told him I had no intention of running errands for the CIA, we went inside. Ned got out the briefcase he had brought with him and took a long time rummaging around for the papers he wanted.

"Billy boy," he said finally, "you do me an injustice, you really do. You don't think I'd be foolish enough to try to sign you up to work for the CIA, do you?"

"What are you trying to do?"

"Just an exchange of information, a little trade, that's all I want to do. I tell you some things we know and some things we guess, and you keep your eyes open while you're there and then you tell me whether we're right or not. I'm not asking you to sell your soul. What do you think your soul is worth anyway?"

"Let's say $250,000. That's $25,000 a year for ten years. If it was for sale, that is, but it isn't."

"That's a bargain," he said with a sudden happy grin. "But I don't want your soul, just a little harmless information when you get back."

"I suppose you want me to count trucks in convoys, spot antiaircraft sites and identify the ships in Haiphong."

"Oh, no. That would be *spying*. Besides, we know all that. That kind of thing is not your job. All we want from you is what you'd try to find out anyway."

"In that case, why bother to come down here and give me this corny dialogue like a road-company Mephistopheles tempting Faust?"

"Because, Billy boy, I said I wanted to exchange information. I want to tell you some things you don't know, things that will help you do your job in Hanoi and, if you can verify them, will help your country, help end the war, help South Vietnam."

"Ned," I said, "I'll do anything to help my country, anything to help bring the war to an honorable conclusion, anything to help give South Vietnam a chance to go its own way. But I would be going to North Vietnam for IBS, not for the CIA. I'm just a poor working foreign correspondent with a job to do. Now, from that point of view, what's in it for me?"

It seemed to me that I had made a good point, but Ned just grinned again a huge grin as though I had played right into his hands.

"Bill," he said, "why don't you stop arguing until you've heard what I want to tell you? Then you can say yes or no. Okay?"

"Okay. But the answer will be 'No.'"

"Oh, God. Have it your own way. I'm not trying to compromise your precious integrity. I just want to convey a little background that will be useful to you. I don't know how much you understand about the hierarchy that runs things in Hanoi. Precious little, I suppose."

"Well, I knew Ho Chi Minh's role before his death. I once saw Pham Van Dong, the Prime Minister, in Geneva during the Laos negotiations. I know Giap runs the Army. I know Le Duan is the Party boss. I interviewed Le Duc Tho at the Paris talks. Trinh is the Foreign Minister. Who else? I met Dr. Thach, the Health Minister, at a medical conference in New Delhi, but he's dead."

"Pretty good. Did you ever hear of Nguyen Van Thanh?"

"No."

"He's the Minister of Postwar Reconstruction. Remember the name. And now," he went on, "how many of the top guys in Hanoi come from the South?"

"About half. Just as at least half of the government in the South comes from the North."

"Right. Now, do you think that there's such a thing as a Southern faction in the inner councils of Hanoi?"

"Well," I said slowly, beginning to see what he was driving at, "I've heard, like everyone else, of policy differences within the Politburo in Hanoi—differences on military strategy, attitudes toward China on the one hand and Russia on the other, differences on negotiating policy in Paris, that sort of thing. But I don't think anyone has suggested a split along North-South lines."

"We think there is one. It's not man for man, of course. Every Southerner in Hanoi doesn't take one view and every Northerner another. But we know there are profound differences of opinion on how the war should be pursued, how the negotiations should be conducted and what policy should be followed after the war in both the North and the South. They are split at least three ways, ranging from the Big Battalion, Keep-Up-The-Pressure strategy of Giap and Ho Chi Minh, through those who want to depend on less expensive guerrilla warfare, to those who want to make a deal right now at the conference table. It's all mixed up with ideology, age groups and all sorts of things, but our boys who specialize in these matters think they can detect a North-South division as well."

"There's a certain logic to it," I said. "I've always thought there was a difference between the National Liberation Front and the Northerners. Unification was always Ho Chi Minh's goal, and as soon as possible. The North has always wanted to run the whole of Vietnam; the NLF just wants to run the South. That's quite a difference. I can see how that same difference could be reflected in Hanoi itself, with the younger and more pragmatic elements taking what you might call a Southern line."

"We're pretty sure that's the way it is, and we think we know who the ringleaders are."

"Is Nguyen Van Thanh one of them? You asked me to remember his name."

"Yes." He pulled a paper out of his briefcase. "Let me

read you a little curriculum vitae on Mr. Nguyen Van
Thanh.

" 'Nguyen Van Thanh, born Saigon, March 9, 1926. Only
child. Parents wealthy, big landowners in Delta, controlled
office buildings, real estate in Saigon. Father high government
official, much in favor with French. Many rumors
about corruption. Family was not disturbed by Japanese
during occupation. Nguyen Van Thanh went through Saigon
school system, graduating from Lycée at 18. Schoolmates
say he already showed signs of sympathy with Nationalist
movement. In 1945–46 went to France, where studied economics at Sorbonne. Reported to have been brilliant student.
Engaged in no overt political activity but said to have frequently expressed his opposition to the crushing of the Vietminh Government in Saigon by the French in the fall of
1945. May have made Vietminh contacts in Paris. In October, 1946, received fellowship grant to study economics at
Cornell University. Lived at Telluride House. Said to have
been well liked. Nickname was "Jack Fan Tan." No reports
of radical activities. Returned to Saigon via Paris in January,
1947. Had angry scene with father, accusing him of being
puppet of French (this reported by father before his death
in 1961). Disappeared from home in March and joined Vietminh in *maquis*. Became platoon commander in following
year, eventually battalion commander. In 1953, Nguyen Van
Thanh apparently attracted patronage of Pham Hung.' "

Bailey looked up. "Do you know who Pham Hung is?"

"I don't think I do. He sounds as though he was important
in those days, though."

"He's important now. Since 1967 he's been in the South
running COSVN, which is the Communist high command
in the South. Pham Hung is an old associate of Ho Chi Minh
going back to the 1920s and '30s. He's also a Southerner and
an economist. Back in the Vietminh days he was Director
of Political Affairs in the South and then Director of Security

Services, their intelligence outfit. Very highly placed, you see. Well, apparently he took our friend Nguyen Van Thanh under his wing, and that established his credentials. Pham Hung put him into administrative jobs, where he excelled, took him North and as Pham Hung rose after the war, so did Nguyen Van Thanh. Let me go back to the dossier.

"'In 1955 Nguyen Van Thanh was given fairly high post in Ministry of Economics. His rapid rise began in 1957 when Pham Hung became member of Politburo. Participated in negotiations with Russians and Chinese on economics and aid. Named Vice Chairman of Agricultural Board in 1959. At 1960 Party Conference was elected member of Central Committee. In 1961, when Pham Hung was Acting Prime Minister, Nguyen Van Thanh became Deputy Minister of Economics. In 1966 named Minister of newly created Department for Postwar Reconstruction. As a practical economist and administrator is thought to have been increasingly at odds with party ideologues and hard-liners. Thought to have lost much influence when Pham Hung was sent South in 1967. May have barely escaped purge of officials in spring of 1968.'"

"Thanks, Ned," I said, "but that's almost more than I want to know about our friend Nguyen Van Thanh."

"Sorry if I'm boring you, but I want you to get the picture of this man—young, able, highly placed, a bit of a maverick and not completely trusted by his colleagues."

"I managed to absorb all of that."

"Well, I haven't told you the most important thing about him. He wants to defect. At least we think he does."

I whistled. My mind was working like a reporter's—that is to say, on the surface. What impressed me was the splash the story would make all over the world and the impact it might have on public opinion and public events.

"If a minister of the Democratic Republic of Vietnam defected, that could change a hell of a lot of things. It would embarrass the North terribly. They might need to soften their negotiating position in Paris. It could turn a lot of people against them. Good Lord, it might even break up the whole log jam."

"Take it easy," said Bailey. "I don't know about that. He's just one man, after all. Hanoi would do everything they could to discredit him. It might make them harder to get along with rather than easier. It would have some public effect, of course, and that would be a plus. We don't want him for that, though. We want him for intelligence. We've never had a defector at that level. You can't imagine how little hard information we get out of North Vietnam. As an insurance man, I can tell you that the life expectancy of an agent in the North is exceedingly brief."

He might be thinking of intelligence, but a political defector was big news to a journalist. "How did you ever find out that Nguyen Van Thanh was thinking of defecting in the first place?"

"That's a long story, which I would be shot for telling you. I can only say that we have a friend—from a country that would surprise you—who is also a friend of Nguyen Van Thanh. Sometimes our friend goes to Hanoi, sometimes he sees Nguyen Van Thanh, and then sometimes he gives us a guarded hint."

"That doesn't sound like much to go on."

"It isn't. That's why we need your help, Bill. I can't tell you how tough it is to get an agent in there. The whole society is organized to pick them up. The other day *Nhan Dan*, the principal newspaper—that's the kind of source we're reduced to using—anyway, *Nhan Dan* ran a story about this ten-year-old kid. A stranger in the village asked him for directions. Instead of telling him, the kid turned the stranger in to the police station. He was held up as a revolutionary hero and an example to all. I don't believe it was actually one of our men involved, but you can see the problem."

"Still, you've got plenty of Northerners in the South who have the accent and are familiar with local conditions. They ought to be able to pass."

"Of course we do, and we try to run them into the North, but they get picked up. They've been away from home too long. The Communists have developed a whole new language. They speak in slogans now. An American plane is not an American plane; it is a 'pirate-invader.' A farmer doesn't speak of filling his production quota; he talks of 'the-three-contracts-with-families.' Now, we put our guys in there, they speak with perfect North Vietnamese accents, their papers are in order, they've got a cover story, but by the time they've spoken five sentences people realize something's fishy and they're in trouble. It's a hell of a problem."

"And you think I can solve your problem because I'm going in anyway?"

"Look, Bill," he said earnestly, "if Nguyen Van Thanh goes south, it will be the biggest intelligence coup since World War II. A man in his position can tell us a great deal. He's an economist. He can tell us where they're hurting. He can tell us how Soviet and Chinese aid is being used. He can pinpoint the delays, the problems. He can tell us what the real policy debates are about and who is on what side. There's no end to what he can tell us. We're flying blind now. I can't emphasize strongly enough how important it is."

"Well, what do you want me to do? I can't go up to him and say, 'Mr. Nguyen Van Thanh, is it true you want to defect to the South?'"

"Good God, no. Play it cool, Bill. We don't want to get you thrown out. I'm pretty sure we can get a message to him in the next couple of weeks. All we'll tell him is that he can trust you. Then it's up to him. Don't stick your neck out."

"Well, Ned," I told him, "you've given me a wonderful story that I can't use and a responsibility that I don't want. On the other hand, if Nguyen Van Thanh chooses to disclose his intentions to me, I don't see how I can do anything but pass them on to you."

He was genuinely pleased. "Thanks, Bill. It's a real break for us to have you going in there. It can save us a lot of time."

The whole thing still didn't appeal to me a bit, but there was something exciting about it, at that. It's very flattering to be entrusted with a secret upon which the fate of nations might depend and to be involved with something that might make a difference between war and peace. The least bit scary, too. And I had an afterthought.

"But, Ned, even if Nguyen Van Thanh tells me he is willing to defect, you've still got to get him out of the country. How are you going to do that?"

"It's a problem. It's a real problem, but there are ways. There are always ways."

4

Ned Bailey stayed on another day, but he wouldn't talk much more about Vietnam. He wanted to see funny little Puerto Secreto, so I showed him the seamy side first—the beach where all the tourists go. When I first came to Puerto Secreto twelve years ago, the beach was still called Los Muertos after some forgotten battle where a lot of people got killed. Hardly anyone came twelve years ago, and those who did thought the name of the beach as good as any other. Then the town authorities changed it to Playa del Sol because they thought it would be good for the tourist trade. It evidently was because now it really does look like a battlefield, strewn with bodies and with an invasion armada of small craft offshore, steadily pumping out their heads into the water you swim in. Hepatitis Harbor, they ought to call it, or Amoeba Beach.

Nevertheless, it's a good place for girl-watching, a diversion for which Ned Bailey was nothing loath. An amazing number of pretty girls come to Puerto Secreto, and I'm afraid most of them go home disappointed. Sometimes you'll see a boy pick up a girl, but more often the boys pick up other boys. It's that kind of place. This is hard on the girls, but the girls are still not hard on the eyes.

We had a drink at Bill Wulff's place on the beach. I asked

for gamma globulin but settled for a Bloody Mary. It was very satisfactory watching that expanse of creamy flesh on the beach slowly turning pink in the sun. We talked of other girls in other places and how the latest crop of German girls was so great while the French had gone off a bit although the Italians were as fine as ever.

Then we went into town and Maxie at the Mexicana office canceled someone off the next day's flight to Los Angeles and put Ned down for it. We ambled through the market, which, to me, is always one of the best things in any Mexican town. All the vivid fruits and vegetables are piled up the way Tamayo used to paint them, the bandanna handkerchiefs in a thousand patterns are hung out like the leaves of some exotic tree, the caged birds sing, the junk jewelry glitters, the serapes smolder with color, and the people look as though they had stepped out of a picture by Diego Rivera.

Ned needed some bathing trunks, so we walked through the town to Xavier's shop, and he bought four pairs in violent Mexican stripes. It really is a pretty town. In some artless way, the houses sit just right. The sun has toned down the bright Mexican colors until they are just right, too. Of course, the Americans are trying to ruin it, but Mexico is a very resistant place. The Spanish tried to ruin it, the French tried, and a lot of Mexicans have done their best, too. But it survives, and I think it will survive the Americans as well.

I decided we'd better try out the new trunks on a beach that hadn't been spoiled by people. We stopped at the place where they broil chickens on a spit, got one, picked up some *bolillos*, the good Mexican rolls that are hard outside and soft inside, laid on a couple of bottles of cold white wine and were off. We drove out of town and around the bay to a place where there is nothing but beach for miles. Not a soul, except the odd Mexican walking or riding by, God knows where to. It's the kind of beach that must have brought people to Puerto Secreto in the first place, but people are strange; once two or three are gathered together, they want to stay gathered together and are unhappy if they find themselves alone.

"Better than the mob scene at the Playa," I said.

"Much better. Remember that beach outside Algiers where we used to take the girls and then go to sleep in the cedar forest? It's like that, only there aren't any cedars."

"Or any girls." Then I thought of Charlie and half-wished we'd brought her along. But we hadn't and Ned had seen quite enough of her anyway. We swam and ate our chicken and drank our wine and talked about the old days. Funny how men who have been in a war together always get nostalgic about it, no matter how miserable they had been, telling each other the same old anecdotes over and over again. I wondered whether twenty years from now middle-aged men would find themselves reminiscing happily about Vietnam.

"Ned, do you really think they'll ask me to go to Hanoi?"

"Think so," he said drowsily. "Pretty sure."

"Then there are lots of things I'd better start doing. I'll have to get some books and background together."

"Plenty of time. Mills grind slowly out in Hanoi. No hurry. Any more wine left in that bottle?"

It was a wonderful afternoon. Most of the time I could even forget the Hanoi business, though it lay in the back of my mind all the time. It's always that way when you start a new assignment. You sort out what you know and then start up in alarm at all you don't know. You wonder what you ought to take, whom you ought to see, what books you should read. Your mind never stops, at least mine doesn't. There may be some correspondents who step into each new situation secure in the confidence that they will unravel it in a moment or, that if they don't, they will be able to make it sound as though they had. Not me. I always start out with the gloomy foreboding that I will never find the key to unlock the mystery, that I'll be taken in by the people whose job it is to take me in, that I'll be caught out in some ignorant mistake, sound like a fool and generally fall on my face. It's better when I get there, but before I start for a new place I'm always half-convinced I'm going to make a mess of it. Only half-convinced, of course. Otherwise I'd never go anywhere.

"How long do you think it will take?" I asked as we drove home.

"What will take?"

"This Hanoi business."

"Oh, I don't know. A month, I guess. Maybe six weeks depending on what you have to do when you get back."

"When do you think I'll get the formal invitation?"

"Stop worrying, Billy boy. A week, two weeks, three maybe. I have an idea their plans are fairly well along. Don't worry, they'll let you know."

That night we finally got a few things straightened out about the Hanoi trip. We had watched another sunset and had had a few more drinks and I thought Ned Bailey was past making sense, but he suddenly became very business-like. He didn't even "Billy boy" me.

"Now, not a word of all this, Bill," he said. "You can't tell anyone. Not your best friend, not your girl, especially not your office. I don't mean just the Jack Fan Tan business, I mean the whole thing. It's all got to come as a surprise to you. Don't even suggest to anyone that you may be going away for a trip. Just wait and when you get the word, move fast."

"I had figured that out for myself."

"Well, if your friend George Mannering back at IBS News got even an inkling, he'd be sending cables, setting up briefings, dropping hints, and it could blow the whole thing. I promise you, it wouldn't take much to derail this whole express."

"I read you loud and clear. Now, suppose something does go wrong, what do I do? Do I get in touch with you, do you get in touch with me, do I have a contact somewhere?"

"Yes. You'll have to go to Phnom Penh and go in from there on the ICC courier plane. Someone will meet you in Phnom Penh."

"How will I know him?"

"Don't worry, he'll know you."

"Listen, Ned. I'm not one of your agents. A lot of people know me. I want to make damn sure anyone I talk to comes from you. Can't he wear a red rose in his buttonhole or something like that?"

"All right." He looked around the room for a minute, his eye settling on the pre-Columbian figures I had arranged in a cabinet. "You're interested in archaeology, right? My man will come to you and say, 'Are you interested in archaeology?' You will say, 'Yes.' He will give you a card with an address and you go to the address. He will fill you in on anything you need to know and do anything that has to be done."

"What's his name?"

"You don't need to know his name. He'll tell you anyway."

"What about visas, Ned? Don't I have to have a visa for Cambodia? Sihanouk blows hot and cold on American journalists. Right now he's blowing cold."

"Bill, quit worrying, will you? You act as though you never made a trip in your life. You don't have to tell the Cambodians you're a journalist. You aren't going to write anything there anyway. Tell them you're a tourist and you didn't know you had to have a visa. They'll issue you one at the airport. Then go to a hotel and lie low."

"What about the North Vietnamese?"

"Oh, Bill, come on. You do just what you'd normally do. You go to the North Vietnamese Embassy in Phnom Penh, or you send them a note, and say how delighted you are to be going to Hanoi and when would it be convenient and do you need any documents, and then they fix it up. What's the matter with you anyway? Has being in Mexico made you forget what it's like to go out on a story?"

"I'm sorry, Ned. I'm a worrier. I'm always like this. Besides, I've never worked for the CIA before."

"Well, forget about that right now. You're not working for the CIA. You're going in to do a job for IBS and when you're in you do that job. If you see your old friend Ned Bailey when you come out, that's nobody's business. Seriously, Bill. No cloak-and-dagger stuff. Don't start asking questions about Jack Fan Tan the minute you get off the plane. Just go about your business, but keep your eyes and ears open. Whenever you're in doubt, remember you're a reporter and think of IBS and not the CIA."

"I guess that's good advice, but remember, I'm going in absolutely cold. I don't know anything about North Vietnam. You say I can't tell my office. Can I at least have them send me some books?"

"No. I'll send you any books you want. What would you like?"

"Anything about North Vietnam. Better send me Doug Pike's book on the Vietcong. And Jimmy Cameron's book. He went to Hanoi. Send me his book. And Buttinger's *The Smaller Dragon*. And Bator's book on Geneva. And Devillers. And Wilfred Burchett. And Paddy Honey's stuff on North Vietnam. Paul Mus, I guess . . ."

I was just getting started, but Ned said, "Bill, for Christ's sake, you'll never read all that. Most of it's out of date anyway. Trust me, I'll send you down some things that might be helpful. Come on, let's have another drink."

He grinned at me. "Are you always like this? I mean, you're acting like some kid about to sit for an examination."

"You're damned right, I am. Every time I go to a new place it's exactly like an examination. I've got to answer a lot of questions, even if they're only the ones I ask myself.

And the more I know before I start, the more likely I am to come up with the right answers."

"I always thought you were the assured, self-confident type without a worry in the world, carrying all before him, always getting to the right people, always getting the inside stuff. The beau ideal of a foreign correspondent, that's what I thought you were, and here you are, as nervous as a cub reporter going out to cover his first traffic accident, wanting to make sure he gets all the names spelled right."

"Well, now you know," I said.

Ned was so tight when he went to bed that I set the alarm for half an hour earlier than necessary because I was sure it was going to be a struggle to get him moving and out to the plane. But when I got up, he was already packed and on his second cup of coffee. A very well-organized fellow in his deceptive way.

Naturally, we got to the airport early. A lifetime of broadcasting has given me a fixation about time. If you're a businessman, you can always be five minutes late for an appointment. If you're a writer, you've always got a little leeway, whatever your deadline is supposed to be. But if you're a broadcaster, when that light goes on, you've got to be there. If it goes on at 7:30:45 and you aren't there until 7:30:46, you might just as well have stayed home. So I'm a little early for everything, especially things like planes that don't wait around for you. Hell, I even get to cocktail parties on time.

So we had time to spare. Ned kept saying things like, "Well, let's say good-bye now. No point in waiting around here. Nothing's drearier than an airport."

And I kept saying, "Certainly not. You don't think I'd abandon a pal in a place like this? What kind of a host do you think I am?"

But he kept on about why didn't I go home, and he kept looking around as though he were expecting someone. "Just casing the joint," he said when I asked him whom he thought he would see here. "Why don't you go home?" he said again.

"Let's have a drink," I said. "You haven't had a margarita since you've been here. Mexican national drink. No tourist should be without one. Brings the color back to your cheeks. Restores the tired brain. Improves your disposition. You're grouchy as hell this morning. We'll get them to open up the bar."

So we had a margarita and the salt on the glass tasted good at that hour of the morning, not to mention the tequila. Ned kept looking around and claiming he wished I'd go home.

They didn't call the flight until after the second margarita. I didn't know about Ned, but I was feeling a lot better. He was getting his briefcase and his *bolsa* and his gate pass all together when the door of the ladies' room opened and out bounced Charlie La Bomba and ran up to us with many a hearty kiss and warm embrace.

"Where are you off to?" I said.

"Oh, just to Mazatlán for a couple of days."

"Same plane goes to Mazatlán?" Ned asked in surprise.

"Yes," I told him. "They pick up your tourist card there."

"Well, glad of the company," he said to Charlie. "So long, Billy boy. Don't forget what I told you."

"I love you, Bill," said Charlie.

And off they went. I went out and waved as they got aboard and waved again as the plane pulled away. It wasn't until they were airborne that it came to me. Charlie wasn't going to Mazatlán at all. Ned Bailey was taking her to Los Angeles. They'd arranged it all. That was why he was trying to get rid of me and why he kept looking around. She had been hiding in the ladies' room the whole time, hoping I'd get out of there.

"Well, the son-of-a-bitch," I said aloud. The bartender took one look at me and put another margarita on the fire.

5

I am not ordinarily superstitious and I do not believe in omens unless they actually hurt. I mean, if someone knees me in the groin, I will accept that as an omen that I am about to feel distinctly unwell. The way Ned Bailey took Charlie La Bomba away from me hurt, and I came to see my whole encounter with him as a bad omen for the Hanoi expedition. In the days that followed their departure I found myself thinking of ways to get out of the thing.

The simplest way, of course, would be to wait until I heard from my New York office and then tell them I didn't want to go—oddly enough, I had ceased to doubt that I would get an invitation. There were a hundred excuses I could make—I was still tired, which was true; I was writing a book, which was not true; I was fed up with Vietnam and the war, which was true up to a point; I was sick. There were any number of ways to turn them down.

But I knew I wouldn't do it. It was like the escalation of the Vietnam war itself. Theoretically, you could always pack the thing in. Practically and emotionally, the reasons for going on always seemed a little bit stronger, if only to prove something to yourself about yourself. I could understand exactly how our government, proving things that didn't need to be proved, had let the whole thing blow up out of all proportion. Not that my going to Hanoi was any kind of an escalation except of my own war with myself.

Of course, what I was going to do I knew how to do, and that was part of why I knew I was going to do it: to prove to myself that I still could. If you let it, everything in life becomes a test. That's why I had got so tired and taken the year off in the first place. But now I knew I was going to measure myself against the test of Hanoi. One thing was sure, though: I wasn't going to knock myself out for Ned Bailey, Jack Fan Tan or no Jack Fan Tan.

The books from Bailey arrived quickly. They are the only things the Mexicans don't hold up in customs while they decide how much they can extort from you. There was also a bland, brief bread-and-butter note which mentioned neither my trip nor Charlie. I spent the time sitting out on my terrace, reading the books and steeping myself again in Vietnamese history and trying to memorize the current cast of characters in Hanoi, insofar as anyone knew anything about them, which wasn't much. I only found Nguyen Van Thanh mentioned twice, once in a list of officials who came from the South, the other time just in a list of officials.

It was probably because I was consciously thinking so much about Vietnam and unconsciously regretting so much leaving Puerto Secreto that it occurred to me how very much alike the two countries are. It's not just the climate, or the look of the land, although they are very often similar. Or the thatched native houses, which are the same, stick for stick —I have a drawing by Miguel Covarrubias of a hut in the Isthmus of Tehauntepec which might just as well be one in Quang Ngai. The likeness goes deeper than such things.

The people are of the same stock, to begin with. The aboriginal inhabitants of North and Central America were Asiatics who migrated across the Bering Strait until the end of the last Ice Age, when the waters flooded out the land link. The Mexican Indian is stockier than his Vietnamese relative and not so finely made, but their common primal origin is stamped in their faces, their bearing and, I suspect, in the working of their minds. I say I suspect that, because one thing the Vietnamese and Mexicans share is an absolute impenetrability to Western understanding. They do not think like us, or see the world like us, or themselves in the world like us. And just when you think you've begun to understand them a little, to reach them a little, you discover that you have not at all, but only that the mystery is greater than you had supposed.

The two peoples have a good deal in common. Each has been marked by two things which left ineradicable scars. The first was rape, violation and subjection by a foreign power. The second is geography. Both Vietnam and Mexico have a huge, powerful, culturally contagious nation to their north. To remain Vietnamese when you are next to China, Mexican when you are next to the United States, is a desperate national preoccupation. As that old rascal, Porfirio Díaz, said, "Poor Mexico. So close to the United States, so far from God."

All this has given both Vietnamese and Mexicans a marked xenophobia, a distrust of foreigners and an aptitude for violence. They know they cannot live without foreign influence, but they want to choose *which* influence. Sometimes they choose wrong. Sometimes, of course, the foreigners choose for them. That is their tragedy, although each people has shown itself perfectly capable, like any other people, of concocting its own tragedy.

It's very easy to carry this sort of comparison too far, but it seemed to me that Mexico was, in some ways, not the worst place from which to embark on an expedition to North Vietnam.

The invitation from Hanoi was a long time coming. One day, about three weeks after Ned Bailey's visit, Fran Tremear, the local real estate lady, came skidding up in her jeep.

"Bill, someone from the telephone office just came by to say there's an urgent message to please call your New York office at once."

"Oh, God," I said, because, as far as I knew, there were only two telephones in Puerto Secreto, one in the official telephone office and the other in the Hotel Océano. Alexander Graham Bell used to get his calls through faster than you could on either one of them.

"Wait a minute, Fran, and send a cable for me."

I scribbled one out, saying, "Telephones impossible please cable," marked it "urgent" and gave her the money.

Then a little later a neighbor, Herb Benfield, knocked on the door.

"Bill, I was passing the telephone office, and they stopped me to say you're supposed to call New York."

"Thanks," I said, "but I've just told them it's quicker to cable."

Two more people came by, so I sent another cable. Finally a kid from the telephone office itself arrived and said they were holding an urgent call for me. They won't quit, those IBS people, I thought, and went into town with him.

Of course, they weren't holding the call at all, and the girl at the switchboard gestured at the crowd of little brown people waiting for the adventure of talking to their relatives on the other side of the mountain and the clutch of tourists waiting to call home to see if little Junior had got over the croup, and said, "*Dos, tres horas para usted.*"

Dos, tres horas, hell. I went over to the Océano and had Pura put in the call while I waited at the bar. After *dos horas* I was getting pretty tight by the time Pura came in to say, "No good, Beel, there is a storm in the mountains and the line to Tepic is *rompida.*"

I went to the Telégrafos and sent a long, drunken cable

to New York to the effect that I had wasted a whole day trying to phone them, that I'd never touch a telephone in Puerto Secreto again, and that if they wouldn't cable me, I wouldn't do whatever it was they were calling me about. I wasted a lot of words. It cost a fortune and I saved the receipt for my expense account.

The next morning at breakfast, when I was on my third cup of coffee, there was another knock at the door. The cable, surely. But there stood a large Mexican policeman with an enormous .45 strapped to his waist. He looked menacing. All Mexican cops look menacing to me. If there is one rule about living in Mexico, it is this: never fall afoul of the law. No gringo has ever got anything but a home-town decision down there.

"Señor Benson," he said, politely enough, "I have come to escort you to the office of the chief of police where there is a telephone call for you from the Central Intelligence Agency."

My first thought was Ned Bailey. It was all off. I didn't know whether I was relieved or disappointed. My second thought was that something had happened to Charlie. My third thought was that maybe he was going to marry her. My fourth and fifth thoughts were, Goddamn him anyway. If the Puerto Secreto police think I'm in trouble with the CIA, they'll make my life here hell. If they think I'm working for the CIA, it will be worse.

The police chief's office was full of detectives, all festooned with military hardware, all lounging about in various attitudes of repose, exhausted, I supposed, from their strenuous efforts in rounding up the hippies for deportation if they found marijuana on them. That seems to be their main job. The chief himself was the only one in the bunch who looked as though he could detect a cough in a tuberculosis sanitarium.

Sure enough, there was a phone on his desk and it was off its cradle. I asked after his health, begged a thousand pardons for putting him to such trouble on such a busy day, and said there must be some mistake, that it couldn't be the CIA since I had not the pleasure of their acquaintance. He said he was very well, hoped I was equally so, that it was always a pleasure to receive me in his humble office, and that it was certainly the CIA, they had made that very clear.

"*Bueno, bueno,*" he said into the phone in Spanish. "We have found Señor Benson and brought him to the instrument. He is here."

I took it, went through the operator in Tepic, the operator in Mexico City, the operator in the United States and got ready to read the riot act to Ned Bailey. Instead, I found myself reading it to George Mannering, the news chief at IBS. He was as pleased as a Boy Scout who had just got a merit badge for woodcraft.

"I knew I'd get you, Bill." He was laughing, the damned idiot. "I figured if there was any kind of phone in Puerto Secreto, the chief of police would have to have one. So I just told him to arrest you and bring you in to talk to me."

"Very clever, George. But did you have to say you were the CIA? They'll think I'm some sort of international spy. Looking for defense secrets at the Piano Bar. They'll have a tail on me for the rest of the time I'm here."

"Well, I hope you won't be there very long. That's why I'm calling you."

"Why the hell didn't you cable as I asked you to?"

"Too important to trust to the cables, old boy. This is very big stuff."

"Okay," I sighed. "What is it?"

"Hanoi," he said. "They want you to go to Hanoi. You remember that application you put in last year? I don't know why they accepted yours. Everybody's got applications in— every network, every newspaper, every magazine, every free-lance. We gave them a list of three names and yours wasn't even on it. I don't know why they chose you."

"You're very flattering."

"No, no, no! You've got me all wrong. It's just that you're on your sabbatical and we didn't want to disturb you. You're perfect for it. You're our Chief Foreign Correspondent. You know South Vietnam. You covered the Paris Peace Talks. You're the only one who knows anything about Vietnamese history. Maybe you can do that documentary after all. You're the ideal man. No one else in the world can do the kind of job you'll do."

He was lathering me up pretty good, which is his specialty. An awfully nice guy, though. But I thought I'd better put on a show of reluctance.

"George, I may be the greatest thing since the wheel, but I haven't said I'm going. I've just begun to settle down here. I'm still tired and I'm out of touch. Send someone else."

"Ah, Bill, how could you turn this down? It's the opportunity of a lifetime. You'll win every award in broadcasting. Can't you see it? The first network correspondent into Hanoi! Don't worry, kid, we'll make it up to you. Besides, they won't take anyone else. It's you or nothing. How soon can you go?"

So, eventually, I said I would go. If I chartered out of Puerto Secreto to Mexico City, the next day I could catch an Air France plane that paused in New York and went on to Paris, where I could pick up their round-the-world flight that stopped in Phnom Penh. There were still a lot of details, though.

"What crew do I take, George? Can I have Tiffin and Morley from London, or Masraff from Paris?"

"No crew, I'm afraid, Bill. That's part of the deal. They don't trust cameras. We've got to use someone acceptable to them. A man named Muller. He's pretty good. We bought some of his stuff for that documentary on Red China, remember? He does good wörk. He's already in Hanoi, shooting background stuff."

"Black and white, or color?"

"Color. We'll have someone meet your plane in New York and give you all the stock you'll need."

"Well, have him check it through to Phnom Penh, will you? I don't want to have to hand-carry it."

"Done. Give me a call from the airport and I'll fill you in on anything new."

"Okay. And better get the research people to make me up a file on everything recent about North Vietnam, the Paris Peace ·Talks and anything else you think I ought to know. I'm ignorant as hell. The local English-language paper is not what you would call comprehensive."

"You shall have it. And, Bill, thanks a lot. I knew we could count on you."

"Well, don't count on anything until you see what happens. Good-bye, George. I'll call you from Kennedy."

I thanked the chief of police, who had been there listening all the time, although, as far as I knew, he didn't have any English.

"It wasn't the CIA after all," I said. "Just my office in New York. The initials are similar."

He smiled a fellow conspirator's smile, as though only those of us who had to wrestle with the dark forces of international intrigue understand the need for these little evasions and white lies. He gave me an *abrazo*.

"Vietnam," he said knowingly.

"Yes." He couldn't help but have gathered that much.

The police chief ushered me out of his office as though I were James Bond, and, to tell the truth, I felt a little that way myself.

The first thing I did after I left the police station was to go out to the airport to arrange the charter. They didn't have anything on the field, but they raised operations in

Guadalajara on the radio link for me and asked them what was available there. I couldn't follow the Spanish through the static, but the man on my end could.

"Twin Beech," he said. "Okay?"

I groaned. Plug, plug, plug all the way to Mexico City.

"Is that the best they've got?"

"All they got."

"Okay, then."

More static. "He can be here in two hours."

"Make it three. I haven't packed yet."

Static. "He says all right in three hours. But be on time. He wants to be back in Guadalajara tonight. Got date with girl. You pay cash, he says."

"*Muy bien. Muchas gracias.*"

I went to the bank, drew enough pesos for the flight, stopped at the taxi rank in the Plaza, told a driver named Calixto to pick me up at the house in two hours and fifteen minutes, which was cutting it pretty fine, went home, put the car in the garage and locked it, told the maids I was leaving for a month, got out my Gucci suitcases and started to pack.

I hate to pack. You'd think I'd be used to it by now, but I'm not. I pack badly and I usually take the wrong things. This trip I couldn't afford mistakes. I probably couldn't even find an extra pair of socks in Hanoi. So I figured it all out with some care.

I put out two dark summer-weight suits, the best I had. One thing I'd learned a long time ago is that when you are dealing with officials in any Southeast Asian country except the Philippines, you wear a suit. If possible, a dark suit. And a tie. You dress like that because they dress like that. It may be only a formality, but they set store by formalities. It is also a mark of respect, like addressing someone by his proper title. Whenever they go to a hot country, most Americans seem to think they are in a resort and go around in espadrilles and loud sport shirts. This is not calculated to make a favorable impression on a cabinet minister or even a bureaucrat, grade three. He does not think he is in a resort. He is in his office, dealing with his great responsibilities, of which you are one of the least, and he dresses according to his rank and dignity. If you are a visiting American, it is best to return the compliment.

So the first things I put out were my two best and darkest lightweight suits. Each had the little ribbon of the *Légion d'Honneur* sewed in the lapel, and that was a good thing, too. If the North Vietnamese were anything like the South Vietnamese, there remained a kind of love-hate nostalgia for the French they had driven out, and an American with the *Légion d'Honneur* might be somehow more worthy of respect than one without it, although they would never admit it.

Then I put out the right shirts, the right socks, three very sober ties and a pair of plain black shoes. So much for the formalities. For the informalities, I took a seersucker suit, a linen sports jacket, three pairs of slacks and all the plain-color, half-sleeved summer shirts I could lay my hands on.

I would be going out in the field. In one drawer there was a bush-jacket suit, which had become a kind of uniform for the IBS correspondents in South Vietnam. The little Chinese tailors on Tu Do would make them up for you in a day. They are practical, with lots of pockets, tough enough for rough country and right for the climate. Also, I decided, all wrong for Hanoi. A little too much of the uniform about it, a touch too military. I wanted to be a very unmilitary-looking American in Hanoi. Instead, I put in three pairs of khaki trousers, some wool socks, a pair of desert boots for walking if it was rough and a pair of moccasins if it wasn't. I also folded up the thinnest raincoat I had. If I remembered rightly, in North Vietnam this would be the time of the *crachin,* the period between the rainy season and the dry season, when it doesn't really pour but it spits, as they say. It would also be hot and I sweat a lot, so I took all the handkerchiefs in the drawer.

Into my toilet kit I threw an extra pack of razor blades. The local variety were sure to be terrible. I put in two cakes of Floris soap. I knew all about soap in underdeveloped countries. I went back to my suitcase and found room to squeeze in two rolls of toilet paper. I knew what that would be like, too. I took two bottles of Milibis-with-Aralen for malaria and amoeba. Some Dexamyl for the hard days when I would need it. Checked to see there were enough aspirins in the kit. Then I made a drink. The hard part was over.

Next, I unzipped the old Olivetti and made sure the carriage was locked for traveling. Found a new ribbon in case I needed it. Got plenty of copy paper and carbons. Looked in my briefcase to make sure I had enough passport pictures—everywhere you go in Southeast Asia you need documents and every document needs pictures. I still had about twenty. More than enough. I said my passport number out loud and then looked at the cover to be sure I still had it memorized. I had. I went through the inoculation records I keep in the back of the passport with a rubber band. Everything was still good except cholera. Damn. I'd have to get it at Kennedy. Paris would be too late. If the shot wasn't twenty-four hours old, some little clerk in Phnom Penh might give me an argument. I didn't want any arguments in Phnom Penh. The Mexican tourist card was inside the front cover of the passport, which is where it was supposed to be. I didn't want any arguments in Mexico City either.

Only one thing more. The floppy bag I carry with me on the plane. The pockets in the divider are full of every damned thing—bottle openers, corkscrews, paperclips, ball-point pens, five or six different kinds of foreign money in separate envelopes so that at least I have tipping money and taxi fare in the place I'm most likely to go, addresses, telephone numbers—all kinds of junk. Sometimes even I am surprised at what I find in there. I put into this bag two books on Vietnam and a novel, half a bottle of Scotch which would get me through the night in Mexico City, my briefcase and an old orange alpaca cardigan sweater I wear on planes because it's more comfortable than a jacket. After all that, there was still room in that old bag. I'll never find another one as good.

I had another drink and tried to remember whether I had forgot anything. Of course I had. Toothbrush. I put in the one I'd been using and a new one. Also another tube of the Selgine salt toothpaste, which is the only kind I can use in the morning without throwing up. God, how I hated packing. I didn't remember James Bond ever having trouble packing. Just a few things in the heel of his shoe, the old Beretta, and he was off.

Calixto arrived on schedule, and I was at the airport five minutes before I had said I would be. The plane was already there, and the pilot couldn't wait to get started. He was a good-looking young fellow, and I guessed he really did have a date in Guadalajara that night. *Muy macho*, as the Mexicans say. He also knew his business, had his courses and radio frequencies all written down, and we whipped out of there in a hurry.

I love looking down at Mexico from a small plane. Bill Spratling taught me that years ago and how to look at what you see beneath. I thought again how much Mexico resembled Vietnam, except you don't see any signs of recent operations. You can't fly over South Vietnam without seeing the patterns of shellholes, the swaths cut by bulldozers or the marks of defoliation. Otherwise a lot of the country we flew over looked the same. Although in my state of mind I might have felt the same way if I were flying over Iowa.

In Mexico City, the plane was turned around and airborne by the time they got my bags into the terminal. I went to the unfashionable hotel I stay in because they take better care of me than they do in the gaudier places, and got George Mannering on the telephone. I would have liked to have got him out of bed, but the time difference isn't that great and he was only eating dinner.

"Anything wrong, Bill?" he said anxiously. "You're still going, aren't you?"

"Sure. Just a few things I want you to do for me."

"Whatever you say."

"Money," I said.

"Oh, don't worry about that. I put you back on payroll as of yesterday."

"Money for the trip. Better have someone meet me at the airport with a couple of thousand. Make it twenty-five hundred."

"How do you want it, traveler's checks?"

"No. Green. They probably never saw a traveler's check in Hanoi. Get me fifteen hundred in hundreds and the rest in twenties, I guess."

"Done. You'll have to sign for it, of course."

"Of course. And George. My cholera shot has run out. Can you fix it with the public health people to stab me and validate it at the airport? Otherwise I can't get into Phnom Penh, let alone Hanoi."

"I'll fix it. Anything else?"

."Just one more thing, George. First-class. I'm booking the tickets first-class all the way."

"Well . . ." To do him credit, Mannering hesitated for only the slightest beat. "Well, I suppose that in view of what you're doing for us, it's the least we can do for you."

I knew then that they really were grateful. At IBS, third-rate comedians travel first-class, actors, singers, cameramen travel first-class—for all I know, the bloody bookkeepers who seem to be running the company these days travel first-class. But not correspondents. A correspondent may have to fly all night, hunched up between a squalling Indian baby and its mother on one side and a protuberant German businessman on the other, and start covering a complicated and sometimes dangerous story an hour after he lands, but he must travel tourist. Only by the most special of special dispensations does he ever get a first-class ticket. Old George was grateful. He was telling me how grateful he was.

"Really hate like hell to interrupt your sabbatical," he was saying, "but you're the only one. No one else could do it the way you'll do it. It'll be a great feather in your cap. . . ."

He went on and on about how I was the greatest correspondent since Richard Harding Davis or maybe Thucydides. It embarrassed me and I hung up as soon as I could. It was the only thing I didn't like about Mannering—the pregame pep talks and fulsome praise. On second thought, though, I realized I didn't really mind it all that much. Mannering realized it, too, of course.

6

At Kennedy International Airport in New York, I received $2,500 in cash (for which I signed) and a 1-cc booster shot of cholera vaccine (for which the Quarantine Officer signed). I also telephoned George Mannering at the office (for which I paid ten cents), and I had Scotch and soda (for which Air France paid). There was still an hour to wait.

The Air France flight from Mexico City spends an hour and a half in New York before going on to Paris. That is just long enough to make you want to stop right there. The secret of making a very long flight is to keep going, unless you are lucky enough to be able to break it in the middle for a day, which I never am. The thirty- or forty-five-minute refueling stops every few thousand miles don't hurt you, but anything longer breaks the trance which is the defense thrown up by the human organism against the indignities of long-distance air travel.

Having broken the trance in New York, I got all the newspapers and magazines and read them all the way to Paris to avoid thinking about the rest of the trip. It did not help. It was as though I were in one of those psychological states in which you think you detect your own name in the half-overheard conversations of complete strangers. Everything I read seemed to have to do with Vietnam. The *New York Times* had a long piece by Hedrick Smith on the private talks going on among the delegations in Paris. *Time* was talking about the success of the President's policy of troop withdrawals. *Newsweek* said Vietnam was the albatross around the President's neck. The *Wall Street Journal* analyzed the shortcomings of the Saigon regime. Even the *Village Voice* had a long article by someone from the Mobilization Committee to End the War in Vietnam, telling how much more reasonable the North Vietnamese negotiating position was than the American.

In Paris it was worse. We landed half an hour early, at 6:30 A.M. instead of 7 A.M., and the plane to Phnom Penh doesn't leave until 11:15. That meant the best part of five hours to kill. *Le Monde* of the day before carried the second of a three-part series on the bankruptcy of American policy in Vietnam. *Le Figaro* claimed the French Government was trying to act behind the scenes as an honest broker between the United States and North Vietnam. *Le Canard Enchaîné* had an unflattering cartoon of the President of the United States slipping money to the President of South Vietnam while, behind them, files of American troops boarded transports for home. "It is a point of honor to pay our hotel bill," the caption read.

Everything conspired to remind me of my ambiguous mission. By 8 A.M. I had checked in for the Phnom Penh flight, bought all the duty-free Scotch I could conveniently carry, drunk two cups of coffee and scanned most of the papers. I was trying to get Vietnam out of my mind by reading of the case of a thirteen-year-old girl who had been murdered in a peculiarly revolting fashion in the Bois de Boulogne, when a hand whacked me on the shoulder. It was a fellow I knew in our Paris Embassy. I couldn't think of his name.

"Bill," he said, "what are you doing here?"

"Just passing through," I said. "In transit. What brings you here at this ungodly hour? I didn't think you guys at the embassy ever got up this early."

"Had to put my wife on a plane for the South of France. I'm going to be a bachelor for a week. Too bad you aren't sticking around, we might have some fun. Where are you going, by the way?"

"East," I said.

"Vietnam again?"

"Yes, as a matter of fact. I practically commute."

"Never give them a sitting target, eh? Well, I'm glad you're going. It's very important."

"What's important?" I asked, because I thought I remembered this guy worked for the CIA.

"Vietnam, of course. Everything about Vietnam. We're getting close to some pretty delicate decisions, I can tell you, and we need someone out there who can make sense."

"Anything else?" I said. This character might be there to tell me something.

"No, no," he said. "I just wanted to say that what you're doing is very important. We need your help. The country needs your help, that is. Well, so long, Bill."

"So long," I said. "Nice to have run into you."

Rather cryptic, I thought. I had hoped for a moment that he was going to give me a message instead of a pep talk, and the message would have said they were reaching Nguyen Van Thanh through another channel and they didn't need me any more. But if he had told me anything, it was just the opposite. I decided he had been ordered to make a routine check to be sure I was on my way. The CIA is supposed to be very efficient in such matters.

I walked around the departure area of Orly for a while, mulling it over. Very important, he had said. I could wish it weren't. I didn't like the idea of getting mixed up in important things that were out of my line. The spy business, in particular. It seemed unethical somehow. It might also be dangerous.

It doesn't take long to exhaust the early-morning pleasures of an airport, even Orly. I browsed through the fake antiques, admired the ladies' scarves and fingered some neckties that cost only twice as much as they would have in town. By 9:30 I was looking at the day's entries at Longchamp and thinking how pleasant it would be to go to the races, when someone else I knew ran into me. His name escaped me, too, but I recognized him as a member of the South Vietnamese delegation to the peace talks.

"Monsieur Ben-sone," he said, a reasonable approximation of surprise in his tone, "how strange to meet you here. You are not going to Vietnam, by any chance?"

"Yes."

"Oh, yes. Not going to Vietnam. That's good."

"No. Yes, I am going to Vietnam." The affirmative answer to a negative question always confuses Orientals.

He looked at the red boarding pass sticking out of my breast pocket. "But this plane does not stop in Saigon."

"That's right. It goes to Phnom Penh, though. I thought I would stop off and see Angkor Wat again."

"That is not a good way to go to Saigon," he said earnestly. "Is it not dangerous for you to go to Cambodia, Monsieur Ben-sone? Sihanouk does not like foreign correspondents sneaking in to do funny business."

"I don't plan to do any funny business. Just ruins."

"Are you sure, no funny business, Monsieur Ben-sone?" he said archly. "I know you foreign correspondents. Be careful, Monsieur Ben-sone. Do not take unnecessary risks. A military axiom."

I laughed. "Of the South Vietnamese Army?"

He laughed, too. "No, we are doing much better now. I will tell you about it on the plane."

That surprised me. "I thought you said this was a bad way to go to Saigon."

"But I am not going to Saigon. I am going to Athens. We are on the same plane. That is how I knew it did not stop in Saigon."

"What are you going to do in Athens?" I asked this character who was getting more mysterious by the minute. "See some ruins yourself?"

"Only the Acropolis in the distance. This is an official mission. My government and the government in Greece have certain things in common. The same people who do not approve of us do not approve of them. We, therefore, have mutual sympathy. South Vietnam needs all the friends it can find these days, so we try to keep the Greek Government informed of the progress of the peace negotiations. That is my mission. Now, if you will excuse me, I will check in for the flight."

I watched him go, but he didn't head for Air France. The ticket counter was downstairs anyway. He went to the telephone and he talked for quite a while. Then he disappeared.

Even for a man less suspicious by nature than I, the snack bar at Orly in the morning is not the kind of place where one is likely to run into old acquaintances. In other words, it did not seem to me to be a coincidence that, first, an American from the CIA and, second, a South Vietnamese from their delegation should have bumped into me—and each with a message, if I was not mistaken. The American seemed to be spurring me on, the South Vietnamese to be warning me off—again, if I was not mistaken.

It might be all in my mind, of course. Amateur spies are doubtless given to delusions and fantasies. Nevertheless, although both had been elaborately casual, both had seemed to attach unusual importance to what ought to have appeared no more than a foreign correspondent's routine shuttling around the world.

I did not see him again until the flight was called, when he came up brandishing his boarding pass. "Where are you sitting, Monsieur Ben-sone?" he asked. "I am in 1B."

"Then we shall be sitting together," I said. "My seat is 1A. I am delighted.".

"We will have a good talk," he promised as we went aboard.

Whenever you are trying to get out of Paris on the ground, it seems to go on forever, but a plane from Orly gets you out over the smiling French countryside in minutes. The sun was out, and I was thinking that, whatever their faults, the French have an unerring instinct for creating beautiful landscape even when they aren't trying.

I was also placing my South Vietnamese friend. I had first met him in 1962, I remembered, when he had a job either in the Palace or the Foreign Ministry during the Diem Government. He must have switched sides at the time of the coup, because he still had a job in Big Minh's day. Then he chose the winning side again and became a part of Ky's entourage. He was a survivor. I'd think of his name in a moment —Buu, Bui something.

"You have not been covering our conversations here in Paris, Monsieur Ben-sone," he said. "You have been in Washington?"

"No, I've been away—" I remembered his name—"Monsieur Bui Van. I have been taking an extended leave in Mexico. I have not even been to Washington, so I am very ignorant. Have I missed a great deal?"

"On the surface, not a great deal. Below the surface things are going badly for us. Very badly. Even I am becoming discouraged, and I, as you know well, have always been a friend of the Americans."

"What are we doing wrong now?" I asked. "I gather your government feels we are trying to disengage too quickly."

"Yes, too quickly. But we are used to that by now. You Americans want to do everything too quickly. Do not misunderstand me, however. We are reconciled to your departure. We know the political pressures on your President. They have been explained to us many times and at great length," he said wryly. "But we cannot understand why, if you must leave, you will not leave things as they are. The Americans are a very meddlesome people."

He stopped as the steward backed up to us with a cart full of drinks. "*Coupe champagne,*" he said. I ordered a gin and tonic and reflected that it had not been many years ago that people like Bui Van had been begging for us to meddle in Vietnam.

"What is it that we are trying to change," I asked him, "besides reducing the level of fighting?"

"We are prepared to see your troops go home, I told you that. You are going too fast, but we can compensate for that, if we are allowed to. That does not frighten us so much. In a way, it is a challenge. The frightening thing is that you Americans seem determined to deprive us of the means of meeting the challenge."

"I am not sure I understand you, Monsieur Bui Van. I thought we were going to considerable lengths to re-equip and support the South Vietnamese armed forces."

"True," he said, "but it is not only soldiers who fight the Communists. The only force in South Vietnam capable of defeating the Communist threat is the present government, and the United States seems bent upon its destruction."

"Ah," I said, "you are disturbed by the talk of a coalition government?"

"The Americans do not call it that, of course, because that is what the North Vietnamese and the Vietcong call it, but it is the same thing. You want a government in South Vietnam which will pursue a policy of reconciliation, treat with the National Liberation Front as an equal and bring them back into political life. That cannot be the present government. They would never do such a thing. Therefore, the Americans wish to get rid of this government and replace it with one which is willing to deal with the Communists and will allow the Communists to participate in administering the country. It is madness. Quite madness."

D. — 4

"I am sure you exaggerate."

"Not at all. At this very moment the American CIA and State Department are engaged in a desperate search for alternatives to the present leaders of South Vietnam. Where you are going, Monsieur Ben-sone," he said with a quick sidelong glance at me, "where you are going, you will see this for yourself. You will discover it when you are in Vietnam."

"Oh, I suppose that there are some people in Washington who have doubts about your present leadership," I said offhandedly, "but I can't believe there is any serious American plot to supplant them. There might be a South Vietnamese plot. There usually is. I doubt if we would encourage that. It's too late in the day. What would we have to gain?"

"You could make peace with Hanoi. That's what your President seems to want to gain most. Monsieur Ben-sone, I speak to you with some knowledge when I say the United States is actively pursuing a campaign to change the present government in Saigon. There have been discussions with leading political figures who are opposed to the government. We know of approaches that have been made to personalities from former regimes who are living in Paris. We suspect that the CIA is talking with the Vietcong, at least through intermediaries. It would not surprise me if they had contacts in Hanoi."

I did not blink. "It would surprise me," I said.

He did not blink either. "It is not impossible."

This was a game that two could play. If I was not certain how much he knew, he could hardly be certain that I knew anything at all. There was no reason for me to volunteer anything. Let him make the next move. He did.

"How exciting it must be," he said, "for someone sitting back in Washington to play with the idea of introducing someone from the other side into our government."

"A Communist?" I said. "Not this Administration."

"I am sure he would not be a Communist. There are plenty

of people on the other side who claim they are not Communists. Even in Hanoi."

"I daresay you could simply refuse to give him a job."

"But if the United States backed him," he said, "if you supported him, urged him on us, claimed we were ungenerous in not accepting him, then it could result in a serious power struggle. The government might change at the very moment when continuity is needed most."

"Then all I can say, Monsieur Bui Van, is that your government must be very fragile if such a thing would endanger it."

"But of course it is fragile. You know South Vietnam well. Fragile governments are the curse of our history. We have not had great experience in government. It is difficult to make much progress in time of war, but we are learning. Our present government is the ablest and most effective we have had. It is the only hope of holding the country together. Now the Americans, because they are impatient, wish to sabotage it. I hope you will not encourage the undermining of our leadership."

I ignored his final innuendo and embarked with some relief upon a philosophical discussion of the problems of governing South Vietnam. Bui Van was a man of some subtlety of mind, and he discoursed in a very illuminating way upon the problems of factionalism, the lack of political tradition, the stubborn autonomy of village life and all the other factors which militate against responsible central government in South Vietnam. He always came back, though, to the need to sustain the present regime and protect it from the infection of disruptive elements from the other side.

We talked like this through lobster, the rack of lamb, the cheese, two wines, the coffee and brandy. I thought perhaps I had erased any doubts he may have had about the innocence of my expedition. But as we fastened our seat belts and put out our cigarettes for the descent to Athens, he brought it up again.

"You are in a position of great responsibility, Monsieur Ben-sone. There are those who may wish to use you in their scheme to do immeasurable damage to the future of South Vietnam. I believe you to be a friend of my country and to wish it well. I hope you will not allow yourself to be used against its best interests."

I replied with some formality, choosing my words with care. "I am, indeed, a friend of South Vietnam," I said. "I have both affection and admiration for its people. I wish nothing more than a peaceful settlement which will ensure its chance for an independent existence. I would not willingly do anything which would compromise that chance."

The airport bus dropped me first at the Transit Lounge, then took Bui Van on to the Customs and Immigration area. I did not see him again.

The souvenir stands in the Athens airport were running heavily to tinkling sheep bells and peasant embroidery this year. In anticipation of the summer's hippie invasion, I guessed, as I stretched my legs and thought over my encounter with Bui Van. What he had said could be read two ways, as a simple warning to a correspondent not to join in a campaign against the present government in Saigon or as a specific warning to me not to become associated with Nguyen Van Thanh's defection.

If he suspected the latter, it would imply a disclosure to the South Vietnamese. Unless, of course, they had their own sources in Hanoi and had put two and two together. Possible, but unlikely. I would have to take it up with the CIA man who was going to contact me in Phnom Penh. "Are you interested in archaeology?" he was going to say.

I brooded about the encounter with Bui Van all the way to Cairo. After Cairo, the numbness set in, as it always does on one of these interminable flights. You do not sleep, at least I don't, but things begin to blur and time passes because you have stopped looking at your watch. You have a drink when you take off from each stop, and they offer you food. Occasionally you eat it. Somewhere over India I took a sleeping pill. It didn't help much, although I may have dropped off for a bit after we left Karachi about 4 A.M.

We landed in Phnom Penh a little after ten. What with the pill and the drinks and the lack of sleep, I was so groggy that I had no difficulty at all in convincing the immigration man that I was just another tourist, too ignorant to have provided himself with a visa. I filled out a form, listing my occupation as "Professor," the purpose of my visit as "Tourism" and my address in Cambodia as the Hotel Royal. I paid a fee in dollars, and he gave me the visa then and there.

As far as I could see, there was no one at the airport waiting for me. I'd been a little worried that I might not even get into Cambodia. I'd half-expected that if I did, someone from the CIA would discreetly contact me. Instead, it was perfectly normal. Just as though I really were going to Angkor Wat. There was a lot about the spy business I didn't understand.

7

The old Hotel Royal in Phnom Penh has known good days and bad days. Right now it's in between, its decrepitude precariously kept in check by the profits from the rising tide of tourism. Out in back there is a swimming pool, bar and restaurant, with a few bungalows separated from the rest of the hotel. I wanted one of the bungalows for privacy. The thing I needed least right now was to be recognized by a lot of tourists who would tell the hotel who would tell the police that a well-known American correspondent was staying there masquerading as a professor. I'd be thrown out of the country before the ICC plane for Hanoi ever left.

The desk clerk was the same one who had always checked me in before. He didn't seem to recognize me. Not very flattering, but fine with me. He had the bungalow I wanted, the one farthest from the pool and farthest from the hotel. I changed my daily ten-dollar allowance at the good rate—any more and they're supposed to give you the official rate. Of course, you can get the best rate of all on the black market if you have green, but I didn't want to take any chances getting caught peddling dollars.

The hotel lobby always swarms with drivers offering their services to gullible tourists for a trip to Angkor Wat, or the Royal Palace, or some other beauty spot like a whorehouse, if that's how your tastes run. I picked out the one who looked the least piratical and made a deal with him to work for me as long as I was in Phnom Penh. His first job would be to come to my bungalow in half an hour and deliver a letter for me.

In the bungalow I typed out a letter on IBS letterhead to the Ambassador of the Democratic Republic of Vietnam in Phnom Penh. I informed him of my arrival, of my desire to visit North Vietnam and of my hope that a visa for that purpose would be granted me. I held myself at his disposal at the Hotel Royal. I wrote it in as formal French as I could muster and begged him to accept my sentiments the most distinguished and so on. The driver arrived as I was putting in the *accents aigus* that I had missed, and I sent it off with him.

I had them bring me lunch on the little veranda of the bungalow, and then I took a siesta. When I got up, I found the room boy squatting outside the door and sent him off for a gin and tonic with lots of ice. It was very hot. I've never been to Cambodia when it wasn't. I would have gone to the bar, which is air-conditioned, but I didn't want to be recognized.

It didn't matter. I was recognized anyway.

He came ambling along under the trees, a little man with slicked-down black hair and an iridescent summer suit. He looked like a salesman. Fuller Brushes, or maybe dope. He had a thick Bronx accent.

"Say," he said, "haven't I seen you on television back where I come from?"

"I don't know where you come from."

"New York," he said. "New York. I thought that was obvious."

It was, too.

"Say, Mac. I know I've seen you on television. Don't tell me, don't tell me. I've got it! You're Eric Sevareid."

"No."

"What's your name then?"

There's no escaping people like that, but sometimes you can play big shot and tell them you want to remain anonymous. I told him that and told him my name, too.

"So I was right!" he cried triumphantly. "William Benson of NBC. Don't worry, I'll keep your secret. What are you doing in Phnom Penh? Got a hot scoop? Can I write my family and tell them to catch you on the Cronkite Show?"

"Cronkite's with CBS. I'm with IBS. I work the other side of the street, but right now I'm not working. Just traveling."

"Say, if you're going to be here long, I could show you around. I know this town pretty good."

"Thanks, but I'm flying to Siem Reap tomorrow to see Angkor Wat, and then I'm moving on."

"Say, are you interested in archaeology?"

I was so anxious to brush him off I didn't even notice that that was Bailey's recognition line. A hell of a fine spy I'd make.

"A little. It's a hobby of mine," I said, getting up to go inside.

He grabbed me by the arm and gave me a card. "Say," he said, "I've got a few things at home I'd like to show you. What about dinner tonight?"

The card said "LOUIS PFEIFFER, ANTIQUES." There was an address.

Well, I had to admit that he was pretty good. But I didn't see the point in all the song and dance. As far as I could see, there wasn't anyone else around. He liked the cloak-and-dagger stuff, I guessed. Notes in hollow trees, knives in rubber heels, shaking off the tail. All that.

"Dinner's fine," I said. "I'll come by about eight-thirty."

Pfeiffer's house wasn't much to look at from the outside, but inside it was spectacular. He had more Khmer pieces than I'd ever seen outside a museum. One big Bodhisattva, almost life-size, was stunning.

"Absolutely authentic," he said. "The only piece in the room that is."

That surprised me and I said so because they all looked good to me.

"They ought to," he said proudly. "I'm the biggest dealer in fakes in Southeast Asia."

"I'll be Goddamned." I had forgotten all about his being a CIA man. "How do you get them out?"

"Oh, fakes are no trouble. Sihanouk only cares about the real thing. They know what I'm doing. As a matter of fact, they love me here. I not only encourage local handicrafts, but I bring in foreign currency. We make 'em here and ship 'em out to Bangkok or Hong Kong. Sell 'em to museums, collectors, dealers. All in dollars, of course."

He rubbed his hands in glee. "No," he said. "I run a very respected local industry."

"Good for your real job."

"Yes, we really ought to talk about that. But take a look at this little dancer. Isn't she beautiful? Would you ever suspect her? When I get through with the cover story on that one—oh, it will be romantic—right out of the private collection of a Prince of the Royal House—he needs the money for a French mistress, you see—when I document that, I'll get five thousand dollars for it from a museum. And the beauty of it is they'll never dare check. Oh, it's a marvelous gimmick."

He positively glowed with larceny.

"What was it you wanted to see me about?" I said. "Anything new?"

"No, I don't think so. Bailey told you about Jack Fan Tan, didn't he?"

I nodded.

"Well, all we have to do is to figure how you're going to get him out."

"How *I'm* going to get him out?"

"Yes, and, believe me, we're more than grateful to you for your willingness to undertake this great public service."

"Pfeiffer, you're crazy. I told Ned Bailey I would try to find out whether Nguyen Van Thanh *wants* to come out. That's all I said I would do, and it's all I'm going to do."

"Oh, he wants to come out, all right." The little man sighed a little sigh. "Bailey told me you might try to go back on your promise."

"There wasn't any promise, I tell you."

"Bailey thinks there was. He sent me this recording of your conversation with him."

Pfeiffer got up and put a white cassette into a black Sony tape recorder. He pushed a key. I heard Ned Bailey's voice.

"You think I'd be foolish enough to sign you up to work for the CIA?"

Then I heard my own voice: "If you think I can solve your problem."

I remembered that night in Puerto Secreto, and the conversation had not gone this way. Now on the tape Ned was saying, "There's something I want you to do while you're in Hanoi."

"What are you trying to do?"

"Nguyen Van Thanh," said Bailey's voice. "He wants to defect to the South."

You could hear me whistle. Then I said, "But then, of course, you've got to get him out?"

"Right."

"Ned, I'll do anything to help my country, but I'm just a poor working foreign correspondent. Now, from that point of view, what's in it for me?"

At this point I began to sweat. That bastard Bailey had had a tape recorder in his briefcase and had really done a job on the tape. I knew what came next. I had said I might sell my soul for a quarter of a million dollars. Sure enough, I heard it coming back to me.

"Let's say $250,000."

"That's a bargain," Ned Bailey said triumphantly.

Pfeiffer pressed the key and the tape stopped.

I just looked at him for a minute.

"You sons-of-bitches," I said. "You dirty sons-of-bitches. If you think you can blackmail me with a clumsy paste job on a piece of tape, you're out of your minds. What did you cut it with, a pair of toenail scissors? Any sound engineer in the world could spot those splices."

"Oh, no, they couldn't," he said gaily. "Oh, no, they couldn't. We do very good work at the Agency. You should have as good engineers at IBS as we have. But the beauty part is, it doesn't even have to be as good as it is. We aren't going to play it in court, after all."

"Who are you going to play it to, Le Duan or Pham Van Dong?"

"Oh, no, we want you in Hanoi. But if anything went wrong, we could play it to IBS."

"Come on. I've worked for them for nearly thirty years. Do you think they would believe that tape when I told them it was a put-up job?"

"Ah, but it would leave lingering doubts, wouldn't it? What kind of assignments do you think you would get after they heard that little negotiation with Ned Bailey?"

"Screw you," I said. "Just try it, you fake bastard. Fake sculpture, fake tapes, fake everything. I can work for any broadcasting network in the country, any newspaper, any magazine. I can free-lance. Don't try to blackmail me, you fraudulent jerk."

I was on my feet by now and started to get out of there. Pfeiffer went right on.

"We could run that tape for CBS and NBC. Do you think they would hire you? We could leak it to the *New York Times*. If you went to London, we'd play it for the British. If you went to France, how long do you think you'd stay if

Pompidou knew there was a man who had sold out to the CIA posing as a correspondent? Oh, we'd fix you, but good."

"You are a bastard, aren't you?" I said and sat down again. Pfeiffer was right. He could ruin me. A broadcaster, especially a news broadcaster, is in a very vulnerable position. His job security doesn't really depend on contracts. It doesn't even depend on his own abilities. It depends on a thread of public confidence, and that thread can be exceedingly tenuous. You could spend thirty years, as I had done, building that thread, strengthening it, nurturing it, trying to weave it into an unbreakable web, and then some little thing could come along and—snap—you were finished. It had happened a hundred times. An insignificant mannerism, a bad guess, a plausible story that turned out to be a phony, and a man who had commanded the attention of millions couldn't find anyone to listen to him. The worst is if they think you can be bought. I don't know how many good newsmen have been ruined by doing commercials. If the public once gets the idea that you will sell your opinion of a cigarette, they conclude you will sell your opinion of a news story.

"Have a drink," Lou Pfeiffer said and brought me a Scotch and soda.

I sat there drinking it and had another idea. Suppose I did help them get Jack Fan Tan out. It would be a hell of a story. I couldn't write it for a long time, but someday I could. Not the CIA part. Not the doctored tape. But I could write part of it. And just the surface aspect, just the outside of the inside story of how he got away, that would be a hell of a piece. It was history, too. I'm an amateur historian, and I like to watch it best from ringside.

I thought some more.

"Lou," I said. "The trouble with your proposition is that everything you threaten me with would hold true even if I did get your man out. Then there wouldn't be any doubt at all that I was working for the CIA. At least I can always claim that tape is a fake and, with the reputation your outfit has, at least half the people will believe me. What you're asking me to do is just to hang a label around my neck. I still say, the hell with it."

"You do us an injustice, kid. You don't think we want to advertise that we had anything to do with you, do you? Of course we don't. Believe me, when you get Jack Fan Tan out, no one will know you had anything to do with it."

"But someone already knows," I said.

"What makes you think so?"

I told him about Bui Van and his elaborate hints all the way from Paris to Athens. It didn't seem quite so convincing, the way I told it:

"You're jumping at shadows," he said. "You're nervous, apprehensive. Why on earth would anyone tell the South Vietnamese about Nguyen Van Thanh? No, Bui Van was just giving you their standard pitch. He's probably said the same thing to every American correspondent in Paris."

"It sounded different, it really did." As I said it, it seemed a little silly, and Paris seemed a long way away.

"Don't worry," Pfeiffer said. "Bui Van wouldn't know anything about Jack Fan Tan. Probably never heard of him. We wouldn't put you on a spot, kid. Now, can we count on you?"

"What's your plan?"

"We're working on it. Have no fear, we'll let you know."

I guess I'd already decided to give it a whirl, although I couldn't tell you why. Partly the tape, I suppose, partly the romance of the thing, partly Pfeiffer's ebullient confidence. I still knew a great deal less about it all than I would have liked, though.

"Have you got anybody in Hanoi?" I asked.

"What do you think we are? Of course we've got somebody in Hanoi."

"Does he know how you're going to extract Nguyen Van Thanh?"

"I told you, we're working it out now. When the time comes, he'll tell you. All you have to do is help him."

"Yes, but what is it exactly I'm supposed to do?"

"He'll tell you. Don't worry. It will be foolproof. You won't have to do anything you wouldn't do anyway."

"That's what Bailey said. Now look at what I've got into."

"Don't worry."

"Everybody says don't worry, but as far as I can see, the only one who is taking any risk is *me*."

"There won't be any real risk. If there was, we wouldn't ask you to do it. It's just that your going to North Vietnam is a break for us. It speeds up the timetable. With you, we can get him out the easy way instead of the hard way."

I gave in.

"Well, I don't like the smell of it," I said, "but you can tell your guy in Hanoi to get in touch with me and if it sounds all right, I'll try to help. How will I recognize him, by the way?"

"He'll come to you. You'll recognize him. There won't be any doubt."

I got up and started to go, but Pfeiffer stopped me and gave me a carefully wrapped package with a tag on it that said, "Work of Art. Genuine Antique Over 100 Years Old."

"What's that for?"

"You may have been followed, so it's better that it looks as though you bought something. You can mail it home from the hotel."

"What is it?"

"It's a Khmer warrior's head, chipped from a frieze at Angkor."

"Genuine?"

"Certainly not." He seemed offended.

"Thanks a lot," I said.

The next morning I checked for messages. There were none, so I took the driver and went off to the Royal Palace and the museum before it got too hot. There was some splendid stuff and an awful lot of junk. Everywhere in

Southeast Asia you encounter the most erratic variations in taste. Cambodia is no exception. The little girl dancers at the Royal Ballet School in the Palace grounds were enchanting, though. They were to anyone's taste.

Back at the hotel there were still no messages. I began to suspect the North Vietnamese weren't going to let me in after all. I went off to lunch at an inferior French restaurant recommended by my driver. By then it was getting very hot, and I went home for a nap. When I got up, there was a large, square envelope under my door. It was from the North Vietnamese Embassy and asked whether I would have the kindness to present myself at the embassy at 8:30 the next morning.

I was still partly on Mexican time, which meant I was sleepy at odd hours and wide-awake at equally odd ones. Anyway, it was no hardship to be up at 6:30 and breakfasting by seven, although that is by no means the usual time I prefer to greet the day. I put on my darkest suit and whitest shirt and left the hotel at 8:15. We got to the embassy at 8:28, but a Vietnamese in an equally dark suit was already in the courtyard of the modest bungalow, waiting to greet me.

He was the First Secretary, he explained, and would take me into the Ambassador's office, but the Ambassador came out, too, and we all went in together. The Ambassador wanted to know whether I had had a good flight and wasn't it an awfully long way? It was a very long way, I replied but I was getting adjusted to local time. After a few more such pleasantries, he got down to business.

"I understand you wish to go to Hanoi?"

"Yes. I hope it will be possible."

"Perhaps. My government is interested in what you would wish to see and do while there. Could you give me a list of the projects you have in mind so that I may forward it to Hanoi?"

I wasn't prepared for that. I thought I would just go

there, see what it was like and work out a program from there. It hadn't occurred to me that they would want to know in advance, but I began to improvise a plan of action as plausibly as I could.

"As I see the situation, Monsieur l'Ambassadeur, although we are still at war, we are hopefully approaching a peace settlement. I would like to be able to report on both these conditions. That is, I would like to show the present situation in North Vietnam, including the effects of the American bombing. But I am also anxious to show the progress that has been made in rebuilding and the plans that are being made for postwar reconstruction."

The Ambassador folded his hands and nodded enigmatically while the First Secretary busily took notes.

"To this end, I would like to film scenes of daily life in Hanoi and the countryside. I would like to show some of the damage caused by American bombing, which your government has frequently described and exhibited in still photographs but which has not been extensively filmed for television purposes. Needless to say, and without violating any security restrictions which might be imposed, I would like to show the efforts to repair the damage and maintain the national economy. Let me emphasize again my interest in the plans for rebuilding North Vietnam after the war. This, I think, is a moment when we should look to the future as well as the past.".

The Ambassador nodded again.

"Now in my business, television," I went on, "interviews are very important, and the most important interviews are with the most important people. Therefore, I would hope to be able to interview the President, General Vo Nguyen Giap, the Prime Minister, the Foreign Minister, the representative of the National Liberation Front and such other officials as your government might think it appropriate for me to see."

I didn't mention Nguyen Van Thanh, but otherwise it was as complete a list as I could think of at the moment. The First Secretary was writing it all down. It should give them quite a lot to chew on. I hoped it was enough.

"I understand you are an authority on our history?" the Ambassador asked.

"Not an authority, but I am very interested in it and would hope to learn more while in Hanoi."

"We have many museums devoted to our history. You would like to visit them?"

"Very much."

At that moment, a servant came in with a tray of Scotch, ice and soda. Nine o'clock in the morning is a little early for Scotch and soda, even for me. But when I saw it coming, I knew I was in. In the East, Scotch whisky has become a status symbol. It is a certificate of an Important Occasion. When they served it at nine in the morning, I knew I would get my visa. The Ambassador and the First Secretary consulted each other in Vietnamese.

"It has been decided to grant you a visa," said the Ambassador and mixed the drinks. He raised his. "To a successful visit to Hanoi."

"May it make some small contribution to the search for peace which I am confident both our countries wish," I replied.

They sipped theirs. I took a good gulp of mine. It was getting hot, and there was no air-conditioning in the Ambassador's office. That would be an unacceptable bourgeois luxury for a spartan Communist nation at war. The Scotch made me sweat.

"Could I have your passport?" the First Secretary asked. He leafed through it. "I see it is not valid for travel in the Democratic Republic of Vietnam. Would you like the visa on a separate sheet of paper or in the passport?"

"I did not consult with the State Department or ask

their permission," I said. "They do not know I am here. However, there will be no secret about it once I am in Hanoi. I will take my chances on re-entering the United States. Stamp the visa in the passport."

They seemed to think that was the proper attitude, and the First Secretary went into another office with my passport.

"You may not get all the interviews you requested," the Ambassador said. "Our leaders are very busy. However, I am sure you will be granted an interview with the Foreign Minister and that he will have something of importance to tell you."

"That would be very helpful for my program, and, as you are aware, the Foreign Minister and any other leaders who consent to be interviewed will be seen and heard by millions of people in the United States and other countries."

While I was getting that plug in, the First Secretary reappeared.

"Here is your visa. And here is a letter to the International Control Commission. It says that you have been officially invited to North Vietnam, hold a valid visa, and requests that they make available to you transportation to Hanoi. The next plane is Friday, the day after tomorrow. There will be time to make the arrangements, but I suggest you present the letter today."

"This morning," I said, "when I leave here."

There were some more toasts to the success of my visit. The Ambassador refilled my glass. They had barely touched theirs. What the hell, I thought, I'm on my way. I drank it down.

8   The International Control Commission is the vermiform appendix of the 1954 settlement of the Indochina War. It serves no useful purpose, but ordinarily does not do enough harm to make it worth removing. The ICC consists of Indians, Poles and Canadians, all neutrals but some more neutral than others. It was invented at Geneva to supervise the terms of the agreement to end the war between the French and the Vietminh. In this it has been conspicuously unsuccessful.

The one modest achievement of the ICC has been to run the world's strangest airline. Twice weekly its courier plane plies between the former capitals of French Indochina—Saigon, Phnom Penh, Vientiane and Hanoi. Thus it is the only link between Hanoi and the West. If you are a non-Communist journalist bound for Hanoi, the only way to go is on the ICC Courier Flight.

The plane is a Boeing 307, long forgotten by anyone except antique airplane buffs. A progenitor of the long obsolete Stratocruiser, only three or four 307s are supposed to have been built in 1943—according to legend, for FDR's Presidential flight. Two survive in the ICC's service, one to be repaired and the other, hopefully, to fly. It's easy to see why the 307 was abandoned. Awkward and ungainly, it carries few passengers in great discomfort at speeds which could hardly have been startling even in 1943.

I knew I'd be going in with the ICC, but, to show you how naïve I was, I thought I would just informally hitch a ride. You know, go up to an ICC officer and say, "Look here, old boy, would you do me a favor? I understand your Courier Flight is going to Hanoi Friday. Could you possibly give me a lift? Just tuck me in among the mail sacks or whatever." And he would say, "Nothing to it, old chap. Come along. Glad to have the company."

It wasn't like that at all. At the ICC office I was conducted to the noblest-looking Indian you ever saw. Looked like Ronald Colman with a sun tan. I thought he was an ambassador or something, but he was just the clerk in charge of transportation and he might as well have been working for Pan American. After checking my documents from the North Vietnamese he filled out a standard IATA ticket, gave me baggage checks and charged me $288 for the round trip. Just like a commercial airline, except that $288 seemed a little steeper than commercial rates.

Well, they had a monopoly.

The ICC even has a regular check-in counter at the Phnom Penh airport, where they treat you no better, but no worse, than at any regular airline desk. They weren't at all impressed that I was going to so mysterious a place as Hanoi. It wasn't mysterious to them. It was all in the hot day's work. Along with some Canadian officers and some Indian other ranks, I had my baggage weighed and was given a boarding pass.

You cannot understand what is meant by "The Teeming Orient" until you have been in a Southeast Asian airport. Any Southeast Asian airport. Travel is such an adventure that no Oriental departs without at least a dozen friends and family on hand to share in the excitement. When he returns, at least two dozen turn up to make sure he safely accomplished his journey. This creates a vivid scene, if

you are interested in local color. It also creates problems
if you are interested in moving in one direction or another.
Such as the direction of the bar.

The bar was over in one corner. It took no more than ten
minutes to get there, and I stepped on no more than three
sloe-eyed moppets and stumbled over no more than six
pieces of highly unorthodox luggage on the way. In the
bar, a toy air conditioner was waging an unequal struggle
against the temperature and the accumulated body heat of
a couple of hundred slowly dehydrating travelers and well-
wishers. I managed to get a gin and tonic and looked around.

I was looking for Pfeiffer. Perhaps he would show up to
tell me that plans had changed. Or at least to wish me
luck. In that case I would have to tell him that my own
plans had changed. I would tell him that I didn't care what
they did to me, I wasn't going through with it. I had no
business doing what I had said I would do. Let them get
Jack Fan Tan out, by all means, but let someone else do it.
I was the wrong man for a clandestine operation. I had done
a lot of foolish things in my life, but I had never sailed
under false colors. I had tried not to lie, or cheat, or pretend
I was anything I wasn't. They wanted me to do all these
things in Hanoi. It might be part of their business, but it
wasn't part of mine. I wouldn't do it.

I looked around for Lou Pfeiffer to tell him so, but he
was not there. The tiny piece of ice in my drink had melted.
The glass was nearly empty anyway. I might as well get
another.

"Excuse me, sir, but I recognize you from television.
You're Mr. Benson, aren't you?"

He was a tall, good-looking kid in his early twenties,
wearing an open shirt, khaki trousers and barefoot sandals.
He had an amulet on a leather thong around his neck and
an earnest expression on his face. I agreed that I was
Mr. Benson.

"You're a kind of hero of mine," he said shyly.

"There aren't many of us left who feel that way," I said. "Would you like a drink?"

"Well, I'd like one very much. I haven't been able to afford anything but one beer a day lately. Except, I ought to warn you that you *used* to be a hero of mine."

"That's all right. We all get found out sooner or later. What will you have? I'm having a gin and tonic."

"That would be great."

I got the drinks, and an extra fragment of ice in each, and asked him his name.

"William Makepeace."

"William Makepeace? As in Thackeray?" I had half-hoped he might have come from Pfeiffer, but this was going too far, even for him.

"Yes, sir. It was my father's idea. He's a Quaker and a pacifist. I was born on VE-Day, 1945, and he named me William Makepeace Simpson in honor of the occasion. Then, when I got involved in the Vietnam Peace Movement, I had it changed to just William Makepeace. It's appropriate, isn't it?"

"So that's how I disillusioned you, is it? Vietnam?"

"I used to think you were a liberal, Mr. Benson, but now you seem to be in favor of continuing the war." He said this not in anger but sadly.

"Oh, come on now, Makepeace. It's not as bad as all that. Ask the Pentagon whether they think I'm in favor of the war. Whatever gave you that idea?"

"Sir," he said gravely, "you have had many opportunities to demand an end to the war. You have never used them. All I can do is sign petitions, and march in demonstrations, and get arrested to draw attention to the urgency of the situation, and I do it. But you are on television all the time, and you don't do it."

"That's right, I don't. We work in different ways, Makepeace, we work in different ways. I don't suppose I like this war any more than you do. Rather less, I suspect. I've seen more of it. The difference between us is that you're obsessed by the principle of getting out and I'm obsessed by the mechanics of it. You think it's simple. Just get out. Right? I think it's complicated. How do you get out? Not so easy."

"I don't see that it's so hard. It should not be beyond a great nation to admit that we are wrong. Let us do so, and having done so, let us leave." He looked very young and rather noble.

"Makepeace, I wish I thought it was as simple as that. If I did, I'd be out with you on the picket line. But, without meaning to be rude, your idea that everything will be solved by taking half a million Americans out of Vietnam tomorrow doesn't make any more sense than some general's idea that everything will be solved if you put another half-million in. It's gone past that now."

"If it has, then it's due to consistent American escalation. It's our fault."

"Of course, it's our fault. It's also the fault of the other side. But assigning blame doesn't get you very far. It's just massaging your conscience. It's a form of self-indulgence. The important thing now is not to say that we've been wrong about Vietnam; most people agree to that by this time. The important thing is to try to understand and deal with the technical aspects of righting the wrong. That's what I'm trying to do."

I wondered whether Nguyen Van Thanh could be considered a "technical aspect." It occurred to me that I must sound very old and sententious to this young man.

"I'm sorry, Makepeace. Won't you have another drink?"

"No, sir. I'd like to talk with you more about Vietnam because I'd like to understand your point of view even though I don't agree with it, but I'd better find out about my plane. Do you know whether they announce the ICC flight on the public-address system?"

"I assume so. I'm going on it myself."

"You are? May I ask whether you're going to Vientiane or Hanoi?"

"Hanoi."

"Well, so am I, but I'm a little surprised they would invite you. I mean, it's obvious you don't look at the war the way they do."

"To tell the truth, I'm a little surprised, too. What about you, Makepeace, why are you going to Hanoi?"

"Actually, I'm on a sort of peace mission for a group I belong to. I guess it's a secret and I shouldn't tell you about it, but we've worked out a proposal. We took it to the State Department and they didn't think much of it, but they said it wouldn't do any harm to take it to Hanoi if we could get in. Our group could raise only enough money to send one person and I was selected. I've been waiting almost a month here in Phnom Penh for my North Vietnamese visa. That's why I'm so broke. I can't risk missing the plane now. I think I'd better go out and check on it. Excuse me, sir."

I watched him pushing gently through the crowd, getting farther and farther away. There was the generation gap, right there. Some curious chemistry in his growing-up process and my aging process seemed to have made it almost automatic that he would see the problem of Vietnam in one way and I would see it in another. I had no particular desire to convince him that I was right or he was wrong, but I wondered where the difference between us lay.

Perhaps it was nothing more than age—after all, I was old enough to be his father—but Makepeace's opinions seemed to have more than a glandular basis. They were based not only on a different view of the war in Vietnam, but on a different view of the world. That was perfectly natural; we had grown up in different worlds. What had I been doing when I was his age? The war, of course. Things had been so much clearer for my generation. We had had our doubts about World War II before we got into it, not after. Hitler had healed our conscience. We knew the war was awful, but we also knew, or thought we knew, that it was necessary and right. You couldn't blame Makepeace's generation for not seeing the war in Vietnam that way.

Nevertheless, there was a kind of softness, an unformed quality about Makepeace. Were we like that, twenty-five years ago? Probably; the young don't change that much from one generation to the next. Of course, we had grown up during the Depression, which probably was a stronger influence on us than the war. It taught us some hard lessons. One of them was that things usually get worse before they get better. Another was that you can't expect the world to do much for you; you have to do it yourself. The Depression had taught us to cope with a world that was imperfect, capricious and often hostile. If you didn't cope, you didn't survive.

People my age tended to see the war in Vietnam as a mistake, but a mistake which had to be coped with. The young saw it as a positive evil which had to be expunged at once. Our experience had indicated that evils didn't expunge easily, but nothing in their experience had proved that you had to put up with things that were wrong. It was a healthy enough point of view. Certainly my own pragmatic generation hadn't done much to convince them that we could cope with the problems we had so pragmatically saddled Makepeace's with.

Still, I was locked into my generation for better or worse and could probably never be convinced that protests and manifestoes were the best way to solve the problem in Vietnam. If that was the route they were going to go, though, his contemporaries couldn't have picked a better man to go to Hanoi than Makepeace.

The loudspeaker announced in four languages the ICC

Courier Flight was ready to leave from Gate 5. I finished the drink and started off. There was Makepeace, fighting his way through the crowd toward me, his big blond head looming over the little dark Cambodians, coming to make sure I didn't miss the plane. I was touched by that. If he had known how many planes I had managed to catch, he wouldn't have worried, but I liked his coming back just the same.

: There was a pile-up at the gate while an Indian officer counted off his men. We were four Canadian officers, one of whom was very drunk; the Indian contingent; two Polish officers, their uniforms buttoned right up to the neck in spite of the heat; Makepeace and me. I took one last look around for Pfeiffer, but there was no sign of him. We all filed out to the funny old 307, which looked incongruous among the big, sleek jets. The Indians sat by themselves, the Poles sat by themselves, the Canadians shepherded their drunken captain, and Makepeace and I sat up front.

The French crew had left the cabin door open and we could follow their whole conversation with the tower. When they cranked up the engines, they were very loud. One forgets how noisy planes used to be—inside anyway. All we've done since is exchange noise inside for noise outside. The 307 clattered out to the runway and took off in a crescendo of sound. Makepeace started talking, but I couldn't hear him. The pressurization didn't seem to be working either, and I had to keep popping my ears. Every now and then I could catch him saying, "Vietnam," "Pentagon" and things like that.

We must still be over Cambodia, I thought, looking down. Would we cross Thailand, which is on a straight line with Vientiane, or would we go up through Laos because the Thais and the Cambodians still don't like each other? I decided I wouldn't know the difference anyway. The French stewardess came by with a tray of drinks. I took a Scotch and soda. The Quaker kid was still talking.

"It really is a terrible problem," he said.

"Which one?"

"Vietnam, of course."

"Yes, it is a terrible problem. I hope we're finally getting close to solving it."

"Not the way we're going," he said positively. "There are too many people with a vested interest in continuing the war. Sometimes I'm amazed at the devices they can think up to keep it going. Look at the President; he's obviously in the hands of the generals. I read in the paper this morning that the President is going to make another speech on Vietnam. What do you want to bet that it's just another stall to buy him more time? Doesn't it make you sick every time he opens his mouth on Vietnam?"

"Well, I usually wait until after he's spoken, not before."

"I know I shouldn't prejudge him, but what has he done? He hasn't done anything for months and meanwhile thousands of guys are getting killed."

I hadn't even known the President was going to make a speech until Makepeace told me. It was about time. The Paris talks were deadlocked as usual, and the situation on the battlefield was as ambiguous as ever. Saigon kept saying we had the North Vietnamese on the run and it was only a matter of time before they caved in, but every time they said that, the North Vietnamese launched a new attack where we didn't expect it. The President told everyone privately that he wanted to get the troops out before the election campaigns got under way, but they were still there and the college kids were marching and the Young Turks in the Senate were getting restive. Perhaps the President was going to make a new proposal. It would make my trip to Hanoi more interesting if he did. That reminded me.

"Makepeace, you told me you're bringing a proposal of your own to Hanoi. What's it about, the Geneva Agreements, troop withdrawal, elections, that sort of thing?"

"Oh, we mention things like that in general, but, actually,

we didn't want to clutter it up with too many details. The whole point is that the United States should get out of Vietnam at once. In return for that, North Vietnam would guarantee civil liberties and democratic processes in South Vietnam after the war. Everybody can agree on that, don't you think?"

"Well, maybe," I said, "but it sounds a little vague to me. Wouldn't it be more effective if you laid out something more specific?"

"Actually, we aren't very interested in specifics," Makepeace said. "That's been the whole trouble in Paris, you see. They're bogged down in specifics. They've been going round and round for months on niggling little points while people are dying. What our group wants is to get everyone to put specifics aside for a while and look clearly at the problem. Then they would see how absolutely essential it is for us to leave Vietnam. Our statement is very eloquent about the absurdity of what we're doing there."

The generation gap yawned again. If there was one thing that older people couldn't understand about the young, it was their airy refusal to offer constructive alternatives to whatever they wanted to overthrow. It wasn't just Vietnam; they felt that way about everything they wished to change. I couldn't help prodding Makepeace a little on that, but it wasn't at all a sore point with him.

"We don't see it as our role to provide alternatives," he said politely. "The only real alternative is a whole new society. That's what we're after. Until we get that, there's no point in proposing solutions that are only a little better than what we have now. If we were to do that, we would pin ourselves down. We don't want to close doors, we want to open them and keep them open."

No wonder the State Department hadn't thought much of Makepeace's peace plan. But they were quite right in saying it wouldn't do any harm to take it to Hanoi. From what I had seen of the North Vietnamese in action in Paris, they would welcome Makepeace as another proof that American public opinion was with them and quietly change the subject when he brought up his peace plan. He might not care about specifics, but the North Vietnamese were the most specific-minded people I knew of.

"Well, good luck to you," I said, "but I suspect you're going to find the North Vietnamese more interested in providing alternatives than you are. They've got them by the dozen, all spelled out and mulled over. It's the way their minds work. They're very much nuts-and-bolts men."

Makepeace was very interested in the North Vietnamese. He'd never seen one in the flesh. I wasn't much help to him, having met only diplomats abroad and a few dazed prisoners and deserters on the battlefields of South Vietnam. I could only tell him that the prisoners were defiant, the deserters were usually sick, and the diplomats had been efficient, strait-laced and exceedingly uncommunicative outside their assigned brief. As for Hanoi, it was unknown territory for me. It was equally unknown to Makepeace, but he looked forward to it as a kind of Promised Land whose virtues were only enhanced by the abuse it had suffered.

The prospect was a good deal less inviting to me. Even with Makepeace to talk to, I hadn't been able to forget my role as a temporary CIA operative. Pfeiffer had sworn the CIA would have a foolproof plan to help Nguyen Van Thanh get away. In that case they probably wouldn't need me. The CIA was bound to have a very good man in Hanoi, and I would be able to leave it all to him, bowing out of the picture as gracefully as possible. But somehow I doubted that it was going to work out that way, and with every minute that drew us closer to Hanoi I became more apprehensive while Makepeace grew more eager.

After a while we started the descent for Vientiane. The pilot was taking it slow and easy, but the pressurization—or lack of it—made my ears hurt.

Tiny Lao immigration officials took our passports away.

There didn't seem to be any reason for that, since we were in transit. Maybe the CIA wanted to see who went in and out on the ICC plane. The CIA is supposed to run Laos. In that case perhaps I might get a message from Pfeiffer, or the Vientiane version of Pfeiffer. I even toyed with the idea of calling the embassy, asking for the CIA and telling them I said to tell Pfeiffer to go to hell. Instead, I took Makepeace to the bar for a beer, hoping someone would turn up.

No one turned up except the drunken Canadian captain from our plane. "You boys going on to Hanoi?" he asked.

When we said we were, he said, "Don't. Stay here. Far, far better place. Good bar in the hotel. Hanoi's a bloody awful place. Nothing to do, nothing to drink. They make some terrible vodka, don't drink it. I get the Polish stuff from my pals in the Commission. Better stay here."

It seemed to me very good advice, but Makepeace explained politely to him that we really had to go to Hanoi.

"Well, don't say I didn't warn you," the captain said and staggered off. Then he stopped and came back. "That vodka in Hanoi is called *lua moi*. It's poison. Avoid it like the plague."

We had to wait about three hours in Vientiane—something to do with not getting into Hanoi too early. The schedule and the course over North Vietnam had to be followed very precisely. We drank a lot of beer and sweated it right out of our systems. If anything, Vientiane was hotter and more humid than Phnom Penh. Finally, they checked us in again, gave us back our passports, and we took off on the leg for Hanoi. There was no sign from the CIA, although they must have known I was on the plane.

I dozed most of the way to Hanoi. So did Makepeace. In fact, he really slept. Indeed, he snored. I wished I were his age, not because he could sleep, but because, at his age, I would have had sense enough not to get mixed up in what I was mixed up in. If Makepeace had known I was involved with the CIA, he would have fainted. I hoped he would never find out. I'd rather he continued to think of me as just a middle-aged ex-hero with eccentric ideas about Vietnam.

The Hanoi leg was uneventful, except that we flew higher and it was even harder on the ears when we came down. As soon as we landed, a very correct young North Vietnamese officer in a trim uniform came aboard with two other officials and examined our passports. It took quite a long time, but these were my first moments in North Vietnam, and automatically I began to store up first impressions.

"North Vietnamese officials impersonally polite," I scribbled in my notebook. "All passports handled in order received. Contrast with Saigon where Americans get automatic priority. Other contrasts with Saigon—self-confidence, orderliness in Hanoi. Sense that these people clearly running own show. Civilian airliners on runway with Chinese markings. No other planes. Ground crew ragged but efficient as begin servicing our plane."

That might not make sense to anyone else, but I could decipher what I meant. Makepeace couldn't wait for our passports to be returned. We got them back too soon for me, and then there was nothing to do but disembark.

III

HANOI

9   It is not surprising that all airports have a
good deal in common. They serve a similar
function. Their internal organs are similar,
differing mainly in scale and convenience.
Thus the airport in Hanoi was not in the least exotic. Its
scale was modest, its convenience less than that. Indeed, it
seemed to pride itself on a utilitarian shabbiness, befitting a
People's Democracy at war. The principal decoration con-
sisted of strips of tape crisscrossing the windows, arranged
in imaginative cutout patterns. The purpose of these strips
was to prevent the glass from splintering when bombed, but
since these windows had never been broken by bombs, nor
were likely to be, the effect was rather like that of a combat
certificate showing that the place had been through the war.

There were also benches to sit on, a baggage counter,
customs officials, public health inspectors and the normal
appurtenances of a minor-league international airport. The
place was full of people, a plane from China having just
landed, and the usual proportion of greeters was on hand
to welcome them. There were also people there to greet
us.

Makepeace got off first and was gathered up by a smiling
delegation from some Peace Committee. They presented
him with a large bouquet of flowers encased in a transparent

plastic wrapping. He didn't quite know what to do with them. As he was swept off, he waved them despairingly in the air, and I called to him that I would see him later. Then a group came up to meet me. It was led by a small, neat Vietnamese and a large, thick European.

The European could only be the cameraman, Muller, whom we had had to take as part of the bargain to get me into Hanoi. IBS hadn't told me that he and I had worked together before, but we had and I remembered him. He was a thick-necked, thickheaded, self-important Kraut. We had had a very unpleasant row a long time ago, but he had a hide like an elephant and greeted me like a long-lost friend.

"Mr. Benson," he cried jovially, "we are a team again. Welcome to Hanoi."

"Hello, Muller," I said.

"This is Mr. Leng of the Foreign Office, who is going to look after you."

"Welcome to Hanoi," Mr. Leng said shyly and introduced me to three other Vietnamese, my interpreter, my driver and a grinning little fellow who presently brought us all warm beer and then went off to get my bags through customs. He was the general Dogberry, I guessed.

"You see," said Muller, "you have a team of four. That is good. Some people get more, but most people get less. Four is good. It shows you are important. Me, I have only one. But, of course, they know me."

"I'm grateful for the help," I told Mr. Leng. "There will be much to see and do. I hope to keep Mr. Muller and his camera very busy."

"Just like Mexico in the good old days," Muller said.

"I hope not." It was in Mexico that I had had to fire Muller off my crew. We had been filming a documentary on the Holy Week rites of the Penitentes in Taxco, a very grisly business where they march through the streets whipping themselves, dragging chains and staggering under great loads of thorns with the blood running down their naked backs.

Muller was a free-lance then as now, and we had taken him on as first cameraman because his credentials· were good. He had shot for Pabst in Germany and Eisenstein in Mexico and then stayed on, picking up what jobs he could get. He must have sought refuge in Mexico because he was a Communist—he certainly was one now or he wouldn't have been meeting me in Hanoi. I hadn't known it at the time, not that it would have made any difference.

Our difficulties had nothing to do with politics. Muller was an old-fashioned cameraman back in those days and insisted on shooting our little 16-mm documentary as though he were still working for Eisenstein with a 35-mm Mitchell when what we needed was someone who could shoot from the hip and keep moving, because the local people didn't like to have their gruesome ceremonies filmed. Muller gave us nothing but trouble, demanding all sorts of special privileges and generally antagonizing the whole town.

He capped it all by nearly getting us lynched. He held up the whole procession for fifteen minutes, leisurely lining up a shot, while the Penitentes relentlessly flogged themselves and the blood ran down their backs from the cactus thorns. He was making them suffer needlessly, and the crowd began to mutter and shove us. They have killed people in that part of Guerrero for less. I finally had to force Muller to make his shot, and that night I paid him off and told him I never wanted to see his ugly face again.

"You remember those days in Mexico?" he said. "Nineteen fifty-three or -four. We made a classic."

"I remember. I hope you can shoot 16-mm color. I've brought you a big batch of Eastman 7242 stock."

"Of course, my old friend. I know that 7242 so well I don't even have to use a light meter."

"Well, bring one along just for fun."

The customs formalities at Hanoi are perfunctory for VIPs. They asked apologetically whether I had any fire-arms. I said I was one imperialist American aggressor who was unarmed. That made them giggle. They asked about cameras, and I gave an airy wave of my hand and said loud enough for Muller to hear that I hired people to take my pictures for me.

Then we got into a car and drove into town across the Doumer Bridge, that we'd knocked out in 1965. Leng was telling me about the pontoon bridges they had rigged to keep the traffic moving across the Red River. He was prouder of that than of fixing up the iron bridge. The pontoons were Vietnamese, the big bridge was French.

They routed me by some American bomb damage, still carefully unrepaired. I didn't know what I was supposed to do. Apologize?

It wasn't a pleasant ride. Muller was sitting next to me and kept up a running commentary, mostly about his own exploits. How he had photographed the bomb damage while they were still dragging out the wounded. How he had been the first to film the pontoon bridges and the first to film the Doumer Bridge when it was repaired and the first to do God knows what. I didn't know how I was going to stand him day in and day out while I was in North Vietnam. But this time I couldn't fire him. He was part of the deal. And there wasn't anyone else anyway.

I tuned out his reminiscences by concentrating on the look of Hanoi. First impressions of a new place are always the most important. After a couple of days it becomes familiar and you stop noticing relevant detail.

Hanoi is a surprisingly handsome city. I suppose I had unconsciously expected something like Saigon, congested, teeming, loud with locust swarms of motor scooters and the air blue with their fumes. Instead, Hanoi seemed half-empty. As indeed it was, Leng explained. Because of the constant threat of renewed American bombing, the authorities had not yet permitted the people who had been evacuated to return.

"I don't think you need to worry," I said. "The United States is not likely to start bombing again."

"Perhaps not, but as President Ho Chi Minh said, 'We can never relax our vigilance until the last American aggressor has left Vietnamese soil.'"

Well, that was their business, I thought. Anyway, the very absence of people made Hanoi look even more spacious and graceful in comparison with crowded Saigon. The boulevards were broad and tree-lined. There were lakes and little parks. The façades of the villas the French had built were run-down and needed paint but were still imposing. After all, the French had always thought of Hanoi as their capital in Indochina. Saigon was a place for sailors.

The people did not fit their city. They were out of scale. Small, anonymous, they doggedly pedaled their bikes along the streets that were too broad for them, beneath the houses that were too high for them. Everyone seemed to be riding a bicycle. Now and then we would pass a convoy of dilapidated trucks, but mostly the traffic was bicycles, gliding noiselessly through the streets.

It was raining. The rain was not heavy, but rather a multitude of tiny droplets which kept the windshield wipers going and diffused the lights so it seemed we were passing through an aqueous landscape in which the bicycles swam like schools of fish. The riders kept their heads down and pedaled all at the same pace, wearing the same clothes, having the same faces. The very anonymity of the scene made it disquieting.

I looked in vain for a touch of color. I watched the faces that swam by the window in search of a smile. Everything was gray, the faces as expressionless as the dress. The uniformity made for a vaguely military air. It seemed to me that I had penetrated, by stealth and guile, into the heart of a fortress. It was utter madness to think that anyone could engineer an escape from it, could push his way through these faceless, purposeful battalions of bicyclists if they stood in his way.

I tried to shake myself out of this mood. It was the rain and the dark which made it seem so sinister, I told myself. These were only ordinary people, riding home on their bikes. Tomorrow, in the daylight, it would all seem normal. There was nothing to be afraid of. Hanoi was a city like any other city. The North Vietnamese were people like any other people. Tomorrow, I would see that. I would see that some girls were pretty and some were ugly, that some men laughed and others cursed. It would be all right.

I knew what had brought on all my nightmarish impressions of Hanoi. It was the Nguyen Van Thanh business. Well, that would be all right, too. Someone would come from the CIA and tell me what they had decided to do. It would be something simple and foolproof, as Pfeiffer had promised. My own part would be minor. They knew about these things. They wouldn't ask me to take any crazy risks in a place like this. I had nothing to worry about, I told myself, and, if I did, worrying wouldn't help.

We had come to a beautiful lake that seemed to be right in the center of the city. It was the Little Lake, Leng said, and he told me a tale of a magical sword found there by a legendary hero—a sort of Vietnamese Excalibur myth. There was a pagoda in the middle of the lake to commemorate it—now an anti-imperialist museum, Leng said—and along the banks were teahouses and vendors' stalls. Hanoi seemed attractive once again.

"We're almost there," Leng announced. "You are staying at the Thong Nhat Hotel. 'Thong Nhat' means 'Reunification.' You will hear the word often. We cannot offer you great luxury because we are at war, but you will have the best we can provide."

"I would not ask for anything more," I replied, realizing that this was the moment for a little Oriental formality. "I am grateful to be permitted to visit your country at all. I realize it is an unusual privilege to be here in time of war, and I hope you will convey my appreciation to those who have made it possible."

"You will have an opportunity to do that yourself. And while it is true, Mr. Benson, that your country has caused great suffering to Vietnam, you will meet with no personal antagonism. We Vietnamese draw a distinction between the warmongers and aggressive circles in the United States and the many peace-loving people who wish to end this war as much as we. We count you among the lovers of peace."

"Yes," I said, "I am anxious to see this war over on terms that are just and honorable for both our countries." I couldn't say less, but I was damned if I would say more.

"Here is the old Thong Nhat," said Muller heartily. "I live here, too. You will find it a melting pot. Chinese, Russians, French, Poles, Japanese—a real Noah's Ark. Even Americans.

"I have a surprise for you," he added archly. "An old friend. A very old friend. Another old friend from Mexico."

When we went in, there in the only miniskirt in North Vietnam, surrounded by the whole Noah's Ark looking at her legs, was Charlie La Bomba.

She ran up, threw her arms around me and kissed me hard. I had had a lot of surprises on this trip, but this was the biggest.

"For Christ's sake, Charlie," I said. "What are you doing here?"

"Mmmmm," she said, nuzzling at my cheek. Then she broke away happily. "I'm working in a hospital, teaching

English, and maybe next week I can do occupational therapy with American prisoners."

"Occupational therapy, that's a good word for it. How did you get here?"

"You know I always wanted to come, so I asked them and they said yes and here I am. Now I want you to meet some of these darling boys."

Charlie summoned up the Noah's Ark contingent, who I was glad to see were looking rather chagrined at our little scene. There was Nicole something-or-other from *L'Unità* in Rome, Jacques something from *Le Monde*, a man from Tass, Wilfred Burchett, the Australian, a Japanese novelist and I don't know who else. It was a real Noah's Ark, all right. One thing about Charlie, she made friends easily. I introduced her to Mr. Leng.

"*Enchanté, Mademoiselle,*" he said to her. And to me with an enigmatic little smile, "*Un bon accueil!*"

I started to introduce her to Muller, but he boomed, "Oh, I already have had the pleasure. We know each other very well, me and Miss O'Brien."

Miss O'Brien. It was the first time I'd ever heard anyone call Charlie by her last name.

"How long have you been here?"

"Only two weeks."

"Who paid?" I said, because she was always broke.

"What do you mean?"

"How did you get here? The airline ticket."

"Oh, that. Your friend, that nice man I met with you, lent me the money."

Ned Bailey. Now, what the devil was he up to? He couldn't have been stupid enough to have recruited Charlie as an agent. She was as incapable of guile as a babe in arms. Besides, she had a memory like a sieve. She couldn't keep a grocery list in her head as far as the corner store. Bailey had got her here for a purpose, though, and I had an uneasy feeling the purpose had to do with me.

Mr. Leng said I must be very tired and hadn't he better show me my room? Charlie said she had to go back to her quarters at the hospital. I said good-bye to the men from Noah's Ark and Leng, Muller and I went upstairs.

"This is the same room Mr. Harrison Salisbury lived in when he was here," Mr. Leng said, for all the world like the President putting me in the Lincoln Room at the White House.

"I'm very flattered. Salisbury's a good man and did a good job here. I hope I can do as well."

It was a big, high-ceilinged, old-fashioned bedroom. There was a mosquito canopy over the bed and a huge, three-bladed mahogany fan hanging from the ceiling. A desk in one corner, a peeling veneer armoire in the other. It was all a little shabby but clean. I'd stayed in worse.

Leng showed me the bathroom, almost as big as the bedroom. The toilet was on a sort of dais. Beside it was a container with sheets of toilet paper carefully folded and arranged like a bouquet of flowers. I felt one of the sheets and winced. If it had been blue, you could have had a suit made of it that would last a lifetime. I was glad I had brought my own.

Off the bedroom was a small sitting room. A low table, two easy chairs, two straight chairs and a small couch, all covered in plastic imitation leather. The table was laid with a plate of cold cuts, bread, a bottle of beer, a box of tea and a thermos jug of hot water.

"We are too late for dinner," said Mr. Leng, "so I had this sent up."

"Won't you join me? There's more than enough and we can talk."

"Ah, no. You have had a long trip and I am sure you are tired. We will have plenty of time to talk. Also, I must go to my office and make arrangements for tomorrow."

"Yes," I said, "tomorrow."

"Tomorrow you will sleep late because you are tired from your long journey. I will meet you here at nine. Then we will go to the Foreign Office to meet Mr. Ngo Xuan, who will give you a general briefing. After that you will be received by the President of the Supreme Court, who is also Chairman of the Commission for the Investigation of the U.S. Imperialists' War Crimes in Vietnam. He will give you a briefing on the war crimes. In the afternoon I hope to arrange a visit to a museum. Now I must confirm all this, so I hope you will excuse me."

We shook hands, and Mr. Leng withdrew ceremoniously. I unceremoniouly asked the odious Muller to stay and opened my bag and took out a bottle of Scotch.

"I have not seen a bottle of Black Label since I got here. You are smart to bring it."

"It's the only smart thing I've done on this exercise," I said. "Now tell me, what is Charlie—Miss O'Brien—doing in Hanoi?"

"Like she said." He looked surprised. "She is working in a hospital for children and doing other useful things. She adds to the scenery, no?"

"No," I said. "She has no business here. She's bound to get herself in trouble. I can't understand why they'd let her in."

"It is, I think, public relations. They are concerned that the antiwar movement in America has not been so active lately. They think that to have a typical American girl here helping them will be good for their image. If she is a success, they may invite many more."

"Well, she won't be a success because I'm going to get her out of here."

"How do you propose to do that, Mr. Benson?" he said blandly. "It is very difficult to get people out of the Democratic Republic of Vietnam if they do not want them to leave."

"What do you mean by that?" I said suspiciously.

"Only that it is not so easy to come in and it is not so easy to get out. Is that not obvious?"

"I suppose so. But I'm going to see that she leaves."

"Good luck, Mr. Benson."

"Oh, call me Bill, for heaven's sake. We're going to work together."

I was irritated both with him and with the fact that I was going to need more luck than Muller could possibly imagine.

"What have you done so far?" I said because he was supposed to have been shooting background material while waiting for me to arrive.

"Well, I have them repairing the bomb damage. Very pictorial. Hundreds of women carrying baskets of dirt. They are singing while they work. I have many close-ups and good sound. Then their leader speaks to them on the public-address system. They drop their tools and gather together while he reads them a quotation from Ho Chi Minh. They give three cheers and return to their work harder than ever. I have many good close-ups of this and a translation."

"Which quote from Uncle Ho—that they must strive even harder because of the false peace efforts of the Imperialist American Aggressors?"

"Something like that. I have it all in my dopesheet."

I groaned. It sounded like a 1920 Communist documentary. I could see it all. The smiling faces, the eager fingers clawing at the earth, the antlike labor of a willing people as each does his tiny mite to frustrate the designs of the Imperialists. It was the corniest kind of propaganda. I couldn't possibly use it.

"Did you just stumble on this inspiring scene," I asked, "or did they arrange it for you?"

"Well, it was explained to me what was going to happen so I could set up for it. But it goes on all the time, I was told."

"Who told you?"

"A man from the press office who was with me."

"Mr. Leng?"

"No, someone like Mr. Leng."

"Well, from now on, Muller, we don't film anything that is staged. Only what is actually going on. If we run into something like that, we'll take it as best we can, whether your angles are right or not, but no faking. That whole sequence is useless."

"Not useless, Bill," Muller said quietly. "You will find that you have to do here some things that they want if you are going to be able to do things that you want. You may want to do some unusual things. What I shot was an investment in goodwill. You will need goodwill here."

He was right. I was certainly going to do some unusual things and I would need what goodwill I could get.

"Well, I guess it won't do any harm. But let's not do any more of that sort of thing than we have to. Let's concentrate on things that will get on the air when I get back."

"You're the boss. What do you have in mind?"

"I want to show people what Hanoi is like. Get some street scenes. Make them quiet. I'll do a contrast between Hanoi and Saigon. We'll do some scenes of daily life. How do people get their food? What's rationed, what isn't? What do they do for recreation? Take the car and do a traveling shot showing some of the propaganda billboards. Then go back and get close-ups. Let's do a little piece on the loud-speakers they have everywhere. Get a translation of what they are saying. Propaganda, I suppose."

"Sometimes there's an air-raid alert if a reconnaissance plane comes close."

"Then stop everything and get that. See if people still go to shelters or if they pay no attention. It's a story either way. Let's go up to Haiphong and get foreign ships unloading military supplies. Do the Doumer Bridge with military convoys moving south. There are a thousand things to do."

"But, Bill, I did all that last year. We have it. I can get it sent to New York and they can start cutting right now."

"I don't care whether you shot it last year. I want to shoot it now. I want to give people a feel of what Hanoi is like now."

"But it hasn't changed. It looks the same way now as it did last year."

"All right, that's a point. Maybe it's a point we'll want to make. Maybe we can use a few feet from last year to show that, in spite of the Paris Peace Talks and the troop withdrawals, nothing has changed at all here. But we can only make that point if we see what things are like today. Get it through your head, Muller, I want people to see what I see and nothing else. I'm not a propagandist, and I'm not going to let them or you make me one."

"Okay, Bill, but I'll have to get permission."

"Even in Hanoi you ought to be able to get permission for those kinds of shots. See you tomorrow."

There are certain arrival routines that become as automatic to a roving correspondent as knee bends are to a boxer when he enters the ring. The first is to unpack at once. If you wait, things catch up with you and you never get out of your suitcase. The second is to seek out other correspondents who were on the ground before you. They can tell you a lot. So I unpacked and then went down to the lobby of the Thong Nhat to see who was in town.

The lobby smelled of disinfectant. A little man in a blue cotton tunic suit was mopping the floor out of a pail. It was not the woodsy, piny, tangy stuff you get from the neighborhood supermarket in the United States. It was disinfectant whose only purpose was to disinfect, and the place smelled like a men's room in the YMCA—a sort of puritan smell that might not be pleasant but, by God, showed the place was clean. They were always swabbing the Thong Nhat, and it always smelled like that.

Along the walls of the lobby stretched a row of plastic-covered leatherette couches and chairs with chipped tables in front of them. Most of the springs in the couches were sprung, and you had to move around in them to find a position that was comfortable. Down by the bar was a group of correspondents, some of whom I'd seen with Charlie. I got a drink from the bar, introduced myself and sat down with them.

"Aha," said the Tass man benevolently, "another imperialist saboteur. We have not had one for some time. Maybe we can get up a poker game. The American pacifists we usually see are worthy people, but they seldom play poker." He spoke excellent English, having been stationed in Washington for some years, he told me.

"I wouldn't mind a game," I told him, "as soon as I get my sabotage operation organized. How do you find out what's going on around here anyway?"

"That's a very good question. I have been trying to find the answer for six months." All the correspondents laughed loudly.

"No, seriously. Don't they talk to you?"

"They never stop, but they always say the same thing. You will find that out. Who is handling you?"

"I really don't know. A Mr. Leng of the Foreign Ministry met me at the airport tonight."

"The Foreign Ministry? Then that would be Ngo Xuan. He is in charge of the foreign press. You will find him as helpful as anyone. He is used to journalists. I do not say he thinks like us, but he understands how we think. That is already something."

"I am supposed to see him tomorrow. Anyone else I should see? Any North Vietnamese journalists who might give me some background?"

This was all standard procedure. There is a sort of freemasonry among correspondents, and one's colleagues will always help a newcomer, up to a point, whatever his political persuasion. If the Tass man had come to me in Washington, I would have told him what to expect from the State Department spokesman, how to file his cables and who might be useful for him to see. The Tass man probably wouldn't ask me, though. The Russians usually know those things already.

"Well," he said, "there is Phan Boi Chau. He is editor of one of the newspapers. He is not what you would call a newspaperman. He is the editor, not because he is a good journalist, but because he is an influential figure. He is a member of the Central Committee and will probably become a member of the Politburo when they hold another Party conference. That means he is involved in high policy. Nevertheless, he likes to be thought of as a journalist, and he likes our company. Sometimes he speaks more freely to us than others in his position. You ought to meet him. I am seeing him tomorrow morning, and, if you like, I will ask him whether he is free for lunch with you tomorrow."

I thanked him.

The other correspondents must have spoken English for they all seemed to be following our conversation. A Japanese suggested I might do my first story on the President of the United States' new peace proposal.

"That's right," I said. "I had forgotten he was speaking today. What did he say?"

"Same old stuff. Mutual troop withdrawals." He looked at his watch. "You want to hear it? We should get the Voice of America from Manila in a minute. I'll go up and get my radio."

"One is lost without a shortwave radio here," said the correspondent of Le Monde. "It is the only way to know what is going on outside, but if you do not have one, you can always depend on our Japanese friends. They have radios the way we have pencils. They also have pencils."

The Japanese came down the stairs, draped with radios,

tape recorders and cameras—a walking demonstration of the Japanese gift for electronics. He took our picture with a flashbulb attachment and switched on the radio. It squawked and screeched in a dozen languages as he ran through the dial, turning the set from side to side for the best reception. In a minute we got a time signal and then an announcer trying to sound like David Brinkley.

"The President of the United States has made what is officially described as an important contribution toward ending the war in Vietnam," the radio said. "In a major speech from the White House, the President today promised to withdraw by the end of next month important forces from I Corps, the northernmost zone of South Vietnam, in return for a pledge by North Vietnam to respect the status of the Demilitarized Zone, to cease further infiltration and to make corresponding withdrawals of their own forces in the area."

"You see," said the Japanese correspondent, "nothing new." I gestured that I wanted to hear the rest.

"The President further asserted," the announcer was saying, "that if this offer of de-escalation was accepted and the United States had reason to believe that North Vietnam was carrying out its part of the bargain, the withdrawal of substantial U.S. forces from other parts of South Vietnam would continue. The burden of defense would be assumed by the armed forces of the Republic of South Vietnam, who, the President said, are now fully capable of holding their own against indigenous military formations. If this offer is not accepted, the President warned, it will be clear who is obstructing peace in Vietnam. 'We have gone as far as we can go,' he said. A White House spokesman said the American units whose withdrawal is contemplated consist principally of remaining Marine units presently stationed in the I Corps area."

"Would you like to hear that again?" asked the Japanese. "I have recorded it on tape."

"No, thanks. I think I've got the gist of it. Actually, it seems to me he went a good deal farther than he has before. He's talking about a lot of men—maybe forty to fifty thousand—and all from one corps area. Won't that be tempting to the North Vietnamese?"

"Not tempting at all," said the Russian. "Your President is up to his old tricks. He offers with one hand and withdraws with the other. It is not a real offer when you know the other side cannot accept it. He must know by now that North Vietnam will never admit that it is withdrawing its own troops, and he must know they will never confirm the Demilitarized Zone. They want to get rid of it as a boundary, not accept it. So it all comes down to nothing."

"I don't know," I said. "I think the President is really trying to get out, but he's got to have something in return."

"Then this is the wrong way. He is asking too much."

"Anyway, it's a story for me. Where do I go to get some official reaction? My office will expect it."

Everyone laughed heartily at this.

"You go nowhere tonight," said the Russian. "It takes our Vietnamese friends a long time to react. Maybe in two or three days they will have an official statement, but not tonight. If you like, I will write your story for you: 'Well-informed North Vietnamese sources say they are awaiting the full text and translation of the President's remarks before offering any comment. Meanwhile, it was indicated in Hanoi that, at first glance, the President's proposal seemed merely another American trick to distract public opinion at home and abroad.'"

"Is that what all of you sent?" I looked around, and everyone nodded.

"Only stronger," said the Frenchman.

"Write it as I told you," said the man from Tass. "I will be your well-informed source. You will be quite safe. There will be nothing more for several days, in any event. Even the public will not be told."

"That is correct," the Japanese with the radio said. "The President's speech has not been mentioned on any North Vietnamese transmission."

"And there's nobody but you fellows I can talk to about this?" I asked. Everyone shook his head.

"Maybe Phan Boi Chau if he lunches with you tomorrow," the Russian said, "but he will only tell you what I have said."

"Funny place," I said. "I'd hate to be a spy here."

"Stick to journalism," someone said. "It's easier."

This seemed such good advice that I thanked them all for their help, shook hands all around and went upstairs to scratch my head over a cable:

URGENT PRESS IBSNEWS NEW YORK NORTH VIETNAM MADE NO REPEAT NO OFFICIAL ACKNOWLEDGMENT PRESIDENTS SPEECH TO-NIGHT STOP HIS DEESCALATION PROPOSAL UNMENTIONED LOCAL RADIO AND PUBLIC REMAINS IGNORANT ITS CONTENT STOP INFORMED SOURCES SAY OFFICIAL REACTION WILL BE DELAYED UNTIL COMPLETE TEXT TRANSLATED AND STUDIED WHICH LIKELY TAKE LEASTLY FORTY-EIGHT HOURS STOP FIRST UNOFFICIAL REACTION NOT REPEAT NOT GOVERNMENTAL SOURCE SUGGESTS PRESIDENTIAL OFFER APPEARS QUOTE JUST ANOTHER TRICK INFLUENCE PUBLIC OPINION UNQUOTE HINTS HANOI UNLIKELY AGREE PRESIDENTIAL CONDITIONS FOR TROOP WITHDRAWAL.

I didn't want to make the cable-ese too tight because these things can get garbled where there aren't many English-speaking operators. On the other hand, I had to keep it brief because cable tolls from out-of-the-way places are usually astronomical. This would probably get to New York via Moscow, and cables are expensive enough from there.

New York would want something else from me, if only to show they had a man on the spot. I batted out the standard piece about people working in spite of austerity, the signs of a nation at war and so forth. Pretty thin stuff, but there really wasn't much to write about yet. That never stopped the desk from wanting something, though.

Down in the lobby everyone had gone except the little man mopping the floor and my Vietnamese errand runner. He must have had extrasensory perception because he was expecting me and the cables.

"How much money will you need?" I asked him.

"It's all right. I will keep the receipts and you can pay when you leave."

"Okay, but I'd better have some dong, anyway. Can you change some for me?"

"I'll go to the National Bank tomorrow morning when it opens at six. The rate is like 3.50 to the dollar."

I gave him a hundred dollars and went to bed, wondering when I would meet Nguyen Van Thanh.

10 The next morning I sat around my room waiting. I had got up early, partly because of the noise, partly out of a sense of anticipation. I don't know what I was expecting. A note thrust beneath the door, an emissary, a concealed message, a sign of some sort, I suppose. There was nothing.

I made some tea with the water in the thermos bottle. It was still hot. I looked through the pile of propaganda literature thoughtfully provided for me. Perhaps there was a note in there. There were several issues of the *Vietnam Courier*, evidently a weekly newspaper, in French and English, copies of a glossy-paper magazine called *Vietnam*, a number of books put out by something called "Foreign Languages Publishing House, Hanoi." I leafed through them all, shook them. Nothing came out except little sheets titled "Errata." I even checked on those in case they represented a code of some kind. They were nothing but errata. No word from the vast network of the CIA or from Nguyen Van Thanh.

I decided to follow Ned Bailey's advice: When in doubt, go about your business as a correspondent. They were to call for me at nine. It was now nearly eight. It seemed an appropriate time for breakfast. It was not. Breakfast was over. The big dining room was empty except for the waiters and waitresses laying the tables for lunch. With what was either bad grace or normal Communist rejection of cast-off bourgeois concepts of servility, a waiter crossly indicated a table and then disappeared. Eventually he reappeared with coffee and somewhat later with two very good fried eggs and a thick piece of toast.

Five minutes before nine, Mr. Leng came in and courteously inquired whether I had slept well. I replied that I had slept so well that I was evidently late for breakfast. I apologized for putting the staff to extra trouble. He apologized for not having informed me more closely of the routine, which might possibly seem unusual to me.

"Since this way of life was first forced upon us by the murderous raids of the pirate planes of the U.S. imperialist aggressors," he said in a charming manner, "we have come to take it for granted. However, you need not breakfast before six, and you can come down as late as seven, or even seven-thirty." He mentioned these latter hours as though they were some extravagant concession to the eccentricity of indolence.

Precisely at nine, he said, "It is time to leave for our appointment with Dr. Pham Van Bach."

"I thought I was to see someone at the Foreign Office this morning."

"Perhaps later today. I will let you know."

In the car, he said, "You will find Dr. Pham Van Bach an interesting man. He is very intelligent. He is the President, what you call the Chief Justice, of the Supreme Court. He is also the Chairman of the Commission for the Investigation of the U.S. Imperialists' War Crimes in Vietnam. It is in that capacity that he is receiving you. He will give you a briefing. You have brought your notebook? Good. The briefing may be quite long, but it will be very important to your understanding of our struggle."

Dr. Pham Van Bach, beaming with smiles, was waiting for

us in the courtyard of his office, a former French villa. He was tiny, about four feet tall, with snow-white hair and an expression of great benignity. He clasped my hand enthusiastically in both of his and asked with interest whether I had slept well. I decided he was quite the dearest little man I had ever met.

We went inside and were served tea in delicate translucent cups. He explained that his briefing would consist of three parts. First, an analysis in terms of international law of the U.S. crime of genocide against the Vietnamese people. Second, factual examples and illustrations. Third, a complete chronology demonstrating the well-laid and systematic nature of U.S. imperialist designs on Vietnam.

The teacups were taken away and an aide brought a very large file of papers. He began to read in Vietnamese, pausing to beam at me while the interpreter translated. This will take forever, I thought. It very nearly did.

"The peoples the world over, including the American people, feel utter indignation at the unjust and horrible war," the translator was saying as Dr. Bach smiled and nodded. "To carry out their scheme of aggression, the U.S. imperialists do not stop at any savage and evil deed: day and night they kill and destroy. Even unborn babies still in the womb, children playing in the kindergartens, pupils on the school benches, women in labor, or elderly persons in the rest houses have not been spared by the criminal aggressors."

Dr. Pham Van Bach smiled and nodded like a little automaton in the intervals between his reading and the translator's rendering. It was the most extraordinary scene, this sweet little man, in his sweet old man's voice, making these dreadful accusations, smiling and bobbing his head in friendly enthusiasm as the translator told of "Mrs. Nguyen Thi Phen, eight months gone, cut in half, her unborn baby thrown off." He reeled off statistics, milked the thesaurus of every synonym for crime and cruelty.

"Sadistic, inhuman, barbarous, savage, cannibalistic," the translator droned on. "The American crime of genocide against Vietnam is worse than anything Hitler did in Germany."

"Do you really believe that?" I could not help saying.

Dr. Pham Van Bach said something, smiling and waving his notes. "Oh, yes," reported the interpreter. "It is all proved here. But you must not interrupt."

After about two hours we had got up to the chronology. The little doctor looked up from his notes and suggested that I might be tired and that we would take a break for tea.

"You found that informative?" he asked.

"Very."

"It is much the same brief I used before the Bertrand Russell War Crimes Tribunal in Stockholm."

"Perhaps, to a Westerner, the language is a little lurid."

"Do you find it so? My presentation has always been very successful with Westerners."

I suddenly realized that he had probably seldom talked to a Westerner who did not completely share his views. Nor, for that matter, had anyone I was likely to encounter in Hanoi. Except for the infrequent legitimate journalists, the only foreigners with whom they would come into contact would be fellow travelers, pacifists or professional sympathizers. I had better make it clear that I was none of these.

"You will understand, of course, that while, like you, there is nothing I more devoutly hope for than a just and honorable end to this war, there is much in your briefing with which I do not agree." A certain formality of address always goes down better anywhere in Asia.

"Really?" He seemed genuinely surprised. "With which part do you disagree?"

"Your central thesis, I am afraid. In spite of the death and destruction which my country has brought to yours, in spite of the many mistakes in the policies of my country's successive governments, I cannot accept that there has ever been any intention totally to destroy your country and its people. We Americans may be guilty of many things, but genocide is not one of them. If it were, we would not be sitting here now."

To my relief, he did not seem offended.

"But you are mistaken," he said, as though speaking to a very slow pupil. "Come. We will now take up the chronology and it will be clear to you."

I looked at my watch. It was nearly noon. "Alas, I have an urgent luncheon appointment. With Mr. Muller, my cameraman. It will be my first opportunity to make plans with him."

"Then come back this afternoon."

"I fear I cannot. Another meeting has been arranged for me." I looked to Mr. Leng for support. He was loyal.

"Yes," he said, "Mr. Benson has another meeting this afternoon."

"Another day then?" He seemed quite downcast. "You will find the chronology I have assembled most interesting."

"I am sure of it and look forward to your exposition of it at another time."

Finally we got away. I thought I caught on Leng's bland face the tiniest hint of the tiniest of smiles.

At the Thong Nhat, the Noah's Ark of correspondents were assembled at the bar as usual. I ordered a drink and made sure it was Russian vodka and not the local *lua moi*—the Canadian captain had been right about that. The man from Tass detached himself from his group and came over.

"I conveyed your invitation to Phan Boi Chau to lunch with you today. He was delighted and should be here any minute."

"How kind of you, and of him. I hope you will join us."

"I'd better not. They don't like us to sit at any table but

our own here. In any event, I think you would prefer to see him alone. We might have coffee later."

"Fine, and thanks again."

I saw Muller, who shared the table with me, and told him Phan Boi Chau was coming to lunch. If it was all the same with him, would he mind going in to eat early so that Phan Boi Chau and I could lunch alone?

"But I would like to know Phan Boi Chau better," he protested. "He is a very big shot here. I want very much to be friends with him. I can help you get acquainted with him."

"No thanks, Muller. I'm sorry to sound inhospitable. It's just that I think I'll get more out of him if we're by ourselves."

I'd have to make that up to Muller, but it really is easier to establish a new relationship without a third party present. I was debating whether to have another vodka when the Tass man brought up Phan Boi Chau. Phan Boi Chau was about fifty, very powerfully built, blocky and compact. He looked like an ex-prizefighter who still kept in shape. His face was broad and flat, and from the look of him there might be a lot of Chinese in his family tree. He was wearing a people's suit of the Ho Chi Minh type, which became him, and an expression of amiability, which did not. He seemed, in fact, a tough customer.

Muller had vacated the table. It was laid for two. One place was equipped with chopsticks, the other with knives and forks. Phan Boi Chau took the chair by the chopsticks. The waiter explained in pidgin French that I had my choice of European food or Vietnamese food. I looked around at the other tables. The European food looked as though it had all come out of cans. The Vietnamese food looked delicious. I said that was what I would have, and the waiter took the knives and forks away and brought me chopsticks, too.

"I hope you slept well," said Phan Boi Chau, in passable French, "and that you are finding your stay in Hanoi interesting."

I assured him that I had slept well, that everyone was being very helpful, and that I had passed a most interesting morning with Dr. Pham Van Bach.

"That did not put you back to sleep?" he grinned. "But he is a most charming man, is he not? And a very good lawyer. He travels a great deal in the West, presenting the case against American aggression. He makes a very good impression."

"He made a very good impression on me, but, perhaps because he has made his presentation so often abroad, it was not completely new to me."

"No, I suppose not. Still, facts are facts, and you should know them."

"Yes, I look forward to getting as many facts as possible while I am here. That is, facts in our Western sense."

"I understand your difficulty, but we are at war and cannot publish the kind of facts you are interested in for reasons of security. I imagine you want to know casualty figures, economic statistics, the size of the armed forces and matters of that kind?"

"Exactly."

Phan Boi Chau made no attempt to equivocate. "You will not get them. They exist. I know them. We use them as a basis for our judgments and decisions, but they would be too important to the intelligence services of the imperialist enemy for us to make public. I sympathize with you because, as an editor, I would also like to publish such information, but I cannot. It is not so easy being an editor in wartime."

"I suppose that, as an editor, you are waiting anxiously, as I am, for an official reaction to the President's latest offer of troop withdrawal?"

"Oh, not anxiously," he picked up my word. "It will come in two or three days. We are in no hurry to reply to such a transparent trick."

"You see it as a trick? I would have thought there might be

some substance there. The President was speaking of a good many troops in an important part of the combat area."

"It is a trick. Don't you see what he is trying to do? He is offering to withdraw troops which public opinion will force him to bring home anyway, in return for recognition of the Demilitarized Zone as a permanent boundary between North and South Vietnam."

"Then why does the government not reply at once instead of waiting for several days?"

"Ah, it must be discussed, you see. There are some who feel that maintaining the negotiations in Paris is very important. Others think there is little to be gained there. I daresay the reply will reflect both views. That is, it will reject the President's proposal, but will not completely close the door to further negotiation."

"You interest me, Mr. Phan Boi Chau. Is there a great deal of discussion within the government of such matters? We hear little of it in the West. In these discussions—let me think how to put this—is there usually the same group on one side and the same group on the other?"

"My dear Mr. Benson. Ever since the death of President Ho Chi Minh, you American correspondents have been pre-occupied with a mythical power struggle here in Hanoi. You want me to say that there is a Soviet faction, or a Chinese faction, or a Party faction, or an Army faction, or a bureau-cratic faction. I will not say that to you. I will say that it is as though I asked you to go with me to the teahouse on the other side of the lake. You say, 'Let us go around the lake in this direction,' and I say, 'No, let us go around the lake in the other direction.' We take a moment to decide, and then we go to our destination, in one direction or another, and we arrive still friends."

It seemed to me he was protesting too much. A journalist learns early that in talking to a source you must pay attention not only to what he is saying but also to how he is saying it, and, above all, to why he is saying it. Phan Boi Chau's manner was so intense and insistent that it was quite clear that there must indeed be a power struggle going on in Hanoi after Ho Chi Minh's death and that Phan Boi Chau was deeply involved in it but was anxious I not think so. I wondered where Nguyen Van Thanh stood in the competition. Probably not very well, if he was so anxious to leave.

There was no point in upsetting Phan Boi Chau, so I contented myself with observing that he had given an excellent description of the theory of collective leadership.

"It is not theory," he said. "It is the way matters are arranged here; we always go to the teahouse in the same direction and remain friends."

I was willing to leave it there, but he was still annoyed, or, at any rate, he had become very serious. He leaned forward and did not seem at all amiable.

"What is your true mission here, Mr. Benson?"

I was taken aback. "I don't understand. I thought I had made it all quite clear."

"Tell me."

"Well, as I informed your Ambassador in Phnom Penh, I want to see as much of North Vietnam as I can, and report it to the people of the United States as clearly as I can. It is as simple as that."

"I hope so. My country is at war with yours, you know, and perhaps we are overly suspicious. It would not be wise for you to become involved in anything outside the normal range of journalistic activities."

"I will bear that in mind, but I think it unlikely that I would stray very far afield. My program is arranged by the Press Department, and their representatives accompany me wherever I go."

"Yes. You have shown interest in our postwar plans."

"Is there anything wrong with that? The war will be over someday—I hope soon. It seemed natural to me to want to find out what you plan to do with the peace—without breaking any security regulations, of course."

He went doggedly ahead. "You will want to see the Minister for Postwar Reconstruction, Nguyen Van Thanh?"

"Is that his name? Forgive me, I have not been in Hanoi long enough to know the names of all your leaders. Yes, I suppose I ought to see him."

"He is an unusual man, Nguyen Van Thanh. Very intelligent. He has some highly original ideas." He started to say something more, then thought better of it. Finally he added, "Just confine yourself to postwar reconstruction when you see the Minister, Mr. Benson."

Another warning about Nguyen Van Thanh, but I couldn't be sure what it was he was warning me about. If Phan Boi Chau knew that I was going to try to get Nguyen Van Thanh out of the country, then the whole North Vietnamese intelligence community knew about it and both my life and Nguyen Van Thanh's were in imminent danger. But he had not sounded that threatening and, furthermore, if he was aware of the escape scheme. he would hardly go out of his way to tip me off.

I went back over our conversation. Phan Boi Chau had not begun to get testy until I had brought up the possibility of differences of opinion within the top leadership of Hanoi. Could it be that Nguyen Van Thanh was involved in those disputes and Phan Boi Chau was afraid he might expose them to me? That would fit with some of the things that Ned Bailey had told me about Nguyen Van Thanh's controversial role in Hanoi. That role would doubtless be even more controversial during the intrigue for power which must inevitably be following the passing of a charismatic leader like Ho Chi Minh. That must have been what Phan Boi Chau was getting at—don't probe into divisions over policy matters, particularly with Ngyuyen Van Thanh. I was relieved, but it meant that I would have to move even more carefully.

Muller and the Russian from Tass came up at this point to invite us to join them outside for coffee. It was a welcome interruption. The coffee was good. Years ago the French had started coffee plantations in North Vietnam, and there wasn't anywhere else in the world where it grew better.

Charlie came over then, looking cool and desirable in one of her abbreviated Puerto Secreto dresses.

"Hello, Bill," she said and gave me a big kiss. Next she gave Phan Boi Chau an affectionate pat on the arm.

"Hello, Boy," she said.

Phan Boi Chau looked black. He must have hated having an American girl calling him "Boy" in front of foreign correspondents. It hardly sat well with his position and dignity. Well, men were men to her, but I couldn't help wondering how that damned Charlie had got to know this fellow well enough to call him by a nickname—and she should have sense enough not to call him that in public.

"Excuse me, Mr. Benson. I was looking for you." It was Makepeace, still in his semi-hippie outfit. I made the introductions.

"Miss O'Brien, Mr. Makepeace, evidently the only man in Hanoi you haven't met. Mr. Phan Boi Chau, Mr. Makepeace. Mr. Muller." I paused because I never had got the Russian's name. He introduced himself.

"Mr. Makepeace," I explained, "is aptly named. He is here on behalf of an American peace organization."

"Good for you," cried Charlie. "And I hope you don't let Bill Benson give you any of his silly ideas. Peace is what we want. Right now. I'm on your side, Mr. Makepeace." I wished she would learn to keep her mouth shut.

"Mr. Makepeace can look after himself," I said.

"I came over to invite you all to a showing of Vietnamese documentary films on Monday night," Makepeace said. "The peace group here that is looking after me is going to put it on for me. There's a room right here in the hotel where they can show them. They have asked me to invite twenty people. I'd like you all to come."

We all mumbled something to the effect that we would if we could. We were quite a group by now and were soon made larger when Leng and my interpreter came up, making noises about our next appointment. That was a signal for us all to disperse, Charlie blowing kisses, the Russian shaking hands and Phan Boi Chau still looking black.

The afternoon schedule called for visits to two museums. The first was devoted mainly to the life and times of Ho Chi Minh, the second to the broader sweep of Vietnamese history. The procedure at each was the same. An English-speaking guide with a long pointer stepped forth, and off we went.

The theme was simple enough: how, from the dawn of time, the valiant Vietnamese had defeated all foreign attempts to subjugate them. Many parallels with the present situation were drawn. As history, much of it was highly suspect. As propaganda, it was brilliant. Some of the exhibits were ingenious, lighting up to show the strategy of some famous battle or great migration. Many of the precious objects, it was explained, had been evacuated for safekeeping and replicas put in their place. The replicas were marvelously well done. I thought of Lou Pfeiffer in Phnom Penh. He knew how to appreciate a good fake.

When we had made the last farewells, drunk the final cup of tea and paid the terminal compliment, I was tired and ready for a drink. But Leng said it was time to pay our call on Ngo Xuan, a Deputy Minister of Foreign Affairs and Press Director, the man overseeing my program in Hanoi.

Ngo Xuan was very well dressed, almost a dandy, if the standards of North Vietnamese tailoring could be said to permit such a thing. He made me glad I was wearing one of my dark suits. He had a thin, aristocratic face, rather sardonic in expression. He noticed the *Légion d'Honneur* in my buttonhole and asked whether I spoke French. I said I did, a little.

"Good, then we will speak in French. It is better than translation." He smiled, and added, "It is also quicker."

As he launched into his briefing, it was clear that his French was better than mine, very correct and with hardly a trace of accent. His account of the war, the iniquities of the Americans, the shortcomings of the Saigon Government and the course of the Paris Peace Talks was all pretty standard stuff. It differed from what I had been getting on every hand, however, in two respects. There was less of the quaint Communist jargon, and he was very tough. He was not exactly rude, but there were none of the elaborate courtesies or the frequent assurances that I was, of course, a friendly American as opposed to the wicked power structure.

Ngo Xuan made it quite clear that he regarded the United States as an enemy and that, while he had an open mind about me personally, I was in Hanoi on sufferance. It was his job to help me receive an accurate impression of his country, its policies, its suffering at the hands of the Americans, and the impossibility of its defeat, either by military force or diplomatic trickery. Within reason, and the requirements of security, he would do all in his power to assist me. This he would do, not out of any friendship for me, but because it had been decided that an objective picture of what was happening in North Vietnam would be helpful in offsetting the myths and lies that had been propagated in some quarters in the United States.

I found his bluntness refreshing. "I appreciate your frankness, Monsieur le Directeur, and am sure you will allow me to be equally frank."

He shrugged and lit a cigarette.

"I do not want to mislead you," I said. "I do not share all of your interpretations of this war and the efforts to find a solution to it. I am an American and I will tend to see things through American eyes. When I make my report on this visit, it may contain things with which you will disagree."

"We expect that. Reasonable men can disagree. I do not expect you to agree with me about everything. What I do expect is that you will be fair."

"That, I think, I can promise you. My report will be as fair, as objective and as complete as I can make it. After all, I am a professional journalist. It is my métier."

"I believe you. That is why you are here." He got out some notes. "Now, let us address ourselves to what you want to do while you are here. An interview with General Giap is possible, although he is not in Hanoi now. Certainly I can arrange to have you talk with an officer on his staff."

"What about seeing someone from the National Liberation Front?"

"I cannot speak for them. If you will write a letter requesting an interview, Mr. Leng will see that it reaches the proper quarters."

"I would like, of course, to see the Foreign Minister."

"That has already been arranged."

"Good. I trust he will be prepared to discuss the President's proposal about troop withdrawal and the DMZ?"

"He anticipates that you will be interested in that."

"I am, very. So are the American people, who regard the President's proposal as a major step forward."

"Do they? I am not sure the Foreign Minister will agree with them, but he will certainly comment on it. In fact, I think his fullest public comment will be in his interview with you."

"That's good. Can you give me any hint today as to what the official reaction will be?"

"No, it is still under study." He looked at me reflectively. "What do you think, as an American? Do you think the President is serious, or is he still playing games?"

"I think he's serious. I believe he is honestly trying to find a formula for disengagement. He is a politician, after all, and if he isn't able to show some progress toward ending the war pretty soon, he is acutely aware that the war in

Vietnam may become as great a handicap to him as it was to President Johnson."

"You think we should take this speech seriously, then?"

"I can only repeat that I think the President is sincerely trying to find a way to end this war which is becoming increasingly burdensome to the United States. However, it would be a mistake to believe that he is about to surrender or will soon offer concessions more sweeping than those he has already made."

"Very interesting. I will report your point of view. Now, Mr. Benson," he said, pointedly looking at his watch, "are there any other arrangements you wish to discuss?"

He hadn't even mentioned Nguyen Van Thanh or the Ministry of Postwar Reconstruction. That was curious because I had made such a point of it at the embassy in Phnom Penh, and even Phan Boi Chau had seemed to know I was interested. Was it an oversight, or was Ngo Xuan purposely avoiding the subject? It would have to be brought up, but delicately.

"Well, Monsieur le Directeur, besides the important interviews I requested, there are naturally other aspects of life here that I am anxious to film—public health, postwar reconstruction, street scenes in Hanoi and so forth." I gave him the list I had worked out with Muller.

"I see no objection to any of this," he said, "but I will have to take it up and let you know. Incidentally, why are you so interested in our plans for postwar reconstruction?"

I shrugged. "The end of the war seems to be in sight. The next step is obviously to look forward to what will happen when peace comes. Actually, I thought it would be one of the things you would rather like to have me cover. Of course, if there are questions of security involved or it is a sensitive issue, I will not pursue it."

There was no point in raising his suspicions by pressing the matter, so I tried to make it seem an unimportant item in a long list of potential subjects to film.

"It is a rather technical subject," said Ngo Xuan, "that is all, and our planning is not yet complete. However, since it interests you, I will raise the matter with the Minister, Mr. Nguyen Van Thanh. You know of him, I suppose?"

"Mr. Phan Boi Chau mentioned his name at lunch today."

"Ah, yes," he said. There was no way of telling what he was thinking. "I'll try to arrange a meeting. You will have an interesting discussion, I am sure."

Ngo Xuan rose abruptly and said good-bye in a manner that was neither friendly nor unfriendly, but distinctly reserved.

"How did you like Mr. Ngo Xuan?" asked Leng on the way back to the hotel.

"He's a very cool customer."

"I do not understand."

"That's an American expression. It means that he is calm and efficient."

"Oh, yes. Intelligent, too, and very well informed."

"I have no doubt of it."

It was disquieting that all the best-informed people were so curious about my interest in the Minister of Postwar Reconstruction. To ask to see him seemed a perfectly natural thing for a visiting correspondent, but I was getting the impression that this was delicate ground to tread on. Whether it was because they were dubious about him or about me, I couldn't tell. They were very secretive, these people. I found myself longing for the frank, open, straightforward encounters one has with Americans.

In the lobby of the Thong Nhat I walked into just such an encounter. Charlie was making a frank, open, straightforward play for Makepeace. Their chairs were close together, and she was leaning toward him, deploying an impressive amount of cleavage and her most inviting gaze. Makepeace had pressed himself back into the farthest corner of his chair, and was sitting up very straight and blinking rapidly. It was a very funny scene.

"Goddamn it, Makepeace," I said in a loud voice, "I

thought you were a friend, but I can't leave the hotel for a minute without finding you making a pass at my girl."

Makepeace leaped to his feet as though stung. "We were just talking," he started to explain.

"He wasn't making a pass at me," Charlie said comfortably. "I was making a pass at him. He's terribly handsome, you know."

Poor Makepeace blushed.

"Any progress?" I asked, sitting down beside Charlie.

"No," she sighed. "He thinks I'm an Older Woman. He doesn't find me in the least attractive."

Makepeace found it even more embarrassing to be looking down Charlie's dress, so he sat down as abruptly as he had risen. "It isn't that," he said.

"Actually, she's still not bad-looking," I said, "even though she must be pushing thirty."

"He's just shy, that's all," said Charlie, moving toward him in her chair again. "Don't be shy with me."

"I don't think I'm shy," Makepeace said. "It's only that I— well—I don't really know you very well."

"I gather Charlie wants to fix that," I said. "I think she wants to know you better."

"Well, sure, I hope to. I mean, we're all here together." He realized he was digging himself in. "What I mean is, we ought to be friends. Just friends. No, uh, no . . ."

"Sex?" Charlie supplied. "Don't knock sex. It'll do until something better comes along. What's the matter, Makepeace, don't you get along with girls?"

"Of course I do," he protested, "but I believe any relationship should be deeper than mere physical attraction. You ought to know someone really well and have a lot in common."

"I'm sure we have a lot in common," Charlie breathed.

"Charlie," I said, "you've struck out. You're going about it all the wrong way. Makepeace wants to put you on a pedestal and you keep falling off. What you've got to do is show him your finer side. She really does have a finer side, Makepeace. For instance, she's over here working with kids in a hospital while she might be lolling about the gilded salons of Puerto Secreto. She doesn't have to be here, you know."

"Oh, I realize that. I admire her very much. What she's doing is just tremendous. Please don't think I was being rude."

"You aren't rude at all," Charlie said. "You're darling. And we're going to get to know each other a lot better."

"Be careful, Makepeace," I warned him. "She means it."

"I know you're both teasing me," he said ruefully. "I guess I deserve it. I take everything so seriously."

"That's all right," said Charlie, patting his hand. "There's a lot to be serious about."

She was dead right about that. There had been a lot to be serious about ever since I'd seen Pfeiffer in Phnom Penh, and, putting the best possible interpretation on what they had said, my little colloquies with Ngo Xuan and Phan Boi Chau hadn't given me any reason to feel lighthearted. What made it worse was that there was no one to talk it all over with. The CIA man had not shown himself.

Muller came blundering along and man-handled a chair into the group, "You look gloomy, Bill. What's the matter?"

"Nothing," I said. "A little tired, maybe. Incidentally, I saw Ngo Xuan a while ago. He said he didn't see any objection to our shooting any of the things we wanted to but that he would have to check it out. He'll let us know later."

"Good, very good. It is a step ahead. How did you like my old friend Ngo Xuan? We have known each other a long time. Did he talk about me, I suppose?"

Muller seemed almost childishly anxious to know whether he stood well with important people like Ngo Xuan and Phan Boi Chau. In Muller's world, his whole livelihood depended on the whims of the mighty, and he must be constantly preoccupied with his place in the pecking order. As far as I could see, though, he was well entrenched.

He raised his hand and snapped his fingers. Muller knew the ropes or perhaps the ropes knew him, for the waiter came at once. I'd been trying to get his eye ever since I sat down, and he had looked right through me and gone off in the other direction. I didn't dare clap or call lest the gesture appear a relic of imperialist colonialism, but Muller, of course, didn't suffer from my compunction. There was the waiter. He brought the drinks quickly, too. No doubt about it, Muller knew how to operate in this topsy-turvy environment.

"I envy you the way you fit in here," I told him. "I feel like a fish out of water myself. I can't get the hang of the hours, or the customs, or anything. I can't even understand what they tell me; when they aren't giving a lecture, they talk in riddles. It defeats me."

"You will get used to it, Bill. For me, I have been used to it all my life. It has become natural for me to talk in riddles, too. It is safer that way for me, though I do not advise you to try it. You have always been so safe, you would not understand the need." He laughed ruefully. "You do not know what it is like to be underground, or hunted, or persecuted. I know these things—they have been my life—so it is not strange to me that these people are mysterious. There is also some mystery about me."

Muller did not seem mysterious; it is an advantage that very large men have, to be so tangibly there that one does not credit them with a secret life. Muller's life must have been full of secrets, though, secrets he couldn't impart even to other comrades. He hadn't been a Communist cameraman for all these years without mastering the art of evasion or understanding the uses of double meaning. His bulk made him seem guileless, but mystery comes in all shapes and sizes.

"Do not let Hanoi upset you, Bill. It is not really so different from other places. The people you see are also people. You are as cryptic to them, you know, as they are to you. While you are wondering about them, they are busy wondering what makes you click."

"I'll say they are. They've been wondering so damned much it makes me uncomfortable."

Muller shot me a quick glance and then laughed. "Enjoy it. To be a mystery gives you a great advantage. You are all mysteries, Miss O'Brien and Mr. Makepeace, too. You are rare birds in this zoo, so they want to look at you and learn something about the habits of these rare birds."

"They certainly look at Charlie," I said.

"Everybody does but Makepeace," she pouted.

Muller laughed uproariously. "Of course they look at her. I told you they are only people. People would look at her anywhere. Even me, an old worn-out man, I look at her every chance I get. It makes me feel young. Were I as young as Mr. Makepeace, you would not catch me looking in the other direction like he is."

Charlie gave Muller a glance so melting it must have taken twenty years off his age right there. Makepeace changed the subject.

"I know what Mr. Benson means," he said, "although I can't quite put it into words. Everybody here is very kind and courteous and appreciative of my point of view but—oh, I don't know—they don't really take you into their confidence at all, do they? I mean, if they were in the United States, we would have them in our homes and sit up all night and really do things together. Here they mainly make speeches to me about things I already agree with them about. It's strange. I guess they don't really trust you until they know you well."

"That's just the way you feel about girls, Makepeace," Charlie said primly, "so you have no reason to object. Personally, I think you and Bill are all wet. I adore the North Vietnamese and they adore me and now I'm going back to the hospital and put my kids to bed."

Off she went, with the Vietnamese looking at her every inch of the way just, as Muller said, like people anywhere.

"What a wonderful girl," said Makepeace.

11

The second day was Sunday. It was also Bomb Damage Day for us. I had read all the books by all the correspondents who had visited Hanoi before me, beginning with James Cameron and Harrison Salisbury. They had all been given extensive tours of the bombed areas and had reported them in meticulous detail and at great length. It was a good story then, but an old story now. Now that the bombing had stopped, I had rather hoped the conducted tours would have stopped, too. But in North Vietnam part of the program for Western correspondents had always been to see the bomb damage. They saw no reason to change it just because there were no more bombs.

Leng arrived at 6:30 in the morning to announce that we were to see some typical examples of unprovoked imperialist aggression against the civilian population of Hanoi. He had the interpreter with him and another man who apparently had something to do with the city administration. We all had a cup of coffee while Muller rounded up some help to bring down his camera gear and pack it in the trunk of the car. It wasn't a big job because Muller had stripped his equipment down to the absolute minimum. No frills and all sorts of labor-saving adaptations he had devised himself. I had to admit that, whatever else he was, he was a professional.

We had to drive a long way to find the damage. Leng and the city official pointed out places of interest along the way. Many of them were hospitals. When I asked whether they were military or civilian, they always turned out to be civilian. It came to a lot of hospital beds for the reduced civilian population of Hanoi. I decided they must be for the military casualties sent back from the South, but I contented myself with observing that the standard of medical care in Hanoi was obviously very high.

Twice we passed large walled enclosures protected by barbed wire. There were Army trucks inside, neatly piled crates and what looked like barracks. Each time we passed them, Leng pointed out something on the other side of the street. I asked about the second one, and Leng's companion said it was a center for building supplies to be used in reconstruction. They probably thought I didn't know a military installation when I saw one.

Perhaps they imagined I knew where we were. I hadn't the slightest idea. The streets were narrower now and the houses more congested. Finally we came to a broad avenue with streetcar tracks down the middle. It was full of people strolling, shopping and eating in little restaurants or from food carts on the sidewalk.

"This is Hué Street," Leng said, "named after our sister city in the South. It is an important thoroughfare. This is a popular quarter."

"It certainly seems popular," I said, looking at all the people. Then I understood that when he said "popular," he meant it was a People's Quarter, where workers lived.

"It is always crowded like this in the morning. People are having breakfast and doing their shopping. It was crowded like this when the bombs fell. Here is the place."

The place was an opening on the street front, like a missing tooth. It was about a hundred feet square and blank except for a billboard poster in the center which showed a soldier waving his rifle in defiance and, behind him, a woman with a wounded child in her arms. The interpreter translated the legend: "The American imperialist aggressors must pay for their crimes."

Two men in black plastic raincoats were waiting for us. It was raining, or trying to rain, and I was glad I had brought my own raincoat. The two men were introduced as the neighborhood commissar and his deputy. They smiled broadly, and the commissar took out a dog-eared notebook. He had obviously been through this before.

"You will now hear the details of this atrocity," said Leng. The commissar began a practiced drone in Vietnamese. The interpreter put more life into it.

"At 7:17 on the morning of August 22, 1967, two large bombs were dropped by American pirate planes." I looked at my watch. It was now 7:35. "There were many people in the streets, as you see now. In this small space were seven houses of three stories each. On the ground floor there were a drugstore, a small market, a restaurant and a bicycle repair shop. In the floors above lived 565 people. The bombs completely demolished three houses and so damaged the others that they had to be torn down. The bombs resulted in the death of thirteen persons and the injury of thirty-three." He read me their names and ages.

Muller was filming the empty space and the billboard. I tried to visualize how it must have looked before it was cleaned up. Five hundred and sixty-five people were an awful lot for seven small buildings.

"In this popular quarter," said the interpreter, "there are many small rooms and many people in each room."

"I am surprised the casualties were not heavier. The air-raid precautions must have been very good."

"Oh, yes. Everyone was very disciplined in those days. Here was a large underground shelter." He showed me where an opening in the ground had been sealed up. "And every few yards there are single-person shelters in the sidewalk."

There were, indeed. Round concrete tubs, sunk in the

earth. Some were open, and some had tops on them. I looked into one. It stank of urine and excrement and there was rain-soaked paper in it. I must have made a face.

"The discipline is not so good now," Leng said apologetically. "The people forget what might happen and do not always take shelter when there is an alert. Sometimes the shelters are misused."

"Let's film the shelter," I told Muller.

Leng gently steered him away from the one I had looked into. They investigated two or three until they found a clean one. Muller shot it and then ordered the commissar to get into it. The commissar was delighted to have his big chance in the movies. He stepped back and, at Muller's signal, leaped vigorously into the concrete-lined hole. It was shallow enough so that his head and shoulders remained above ground, like a character in a play by Beckett. The commissar pantomimed alarm, scanned the skies and then popped down, pulling the concrete cover into place over his head.

"That's the way it was done," said Leng. "Unfortunately, not everyone continues to obey the regulations, even when the imperialist reconnaissance planes come over."

We all congratulated the commissar on his performance. I told him he would certainly get the Academy Award. He indicated he was available for any other little acting jobs I might have, and shook my hand heartily when we left. He did not seem to bear this particular imperialist aggressor any ill will. But no one shook my hand at the next place Leng took us to.

It was a village seven or eight muddy kilometers outside of Hanoi, called Co Nhué. Although it had been attacked as long ago as February, 1968, they were still rebuilding, and many of the bombed-out houses had been left as wreckage to molder in the rain. They took me on a tour, the village chief explaining that 131 houses had been destroyed and many people killed and wounded. He also explained that I was the first American to visit Co Nhué and the people were curious to see what one of the race who had attacked them looked like.

It was not until then I realized we were being followed by an enormous silent crowd—a couple of hundred people—everywhere we went. They did not look curious to me. They looked angry. It was the first time since I had come to North Vietnam that I had encountered obvious hostility. They did not make a threatening gesture or any other kind of movement toward me; they just stared, with hard, level and accusing gaze. I thought, my God, I'd hate to come here alone. I'd hate to try to get Nguyen Van Thanh through a place like this.

Every time I thought about Nguyen Van Thanh—and I thought about him very often—I felt depressed all over again. It was hopeless. It was insane to think I could do anything for him in this country. They hated the very sight of me. I looked at Leng and the interpreter. They looked back politely but underneath I thought they probably hated me, too.

They took me into a house. A man was sitting on a bed. He had lost a leg in the bombing. He pulled back his trousers and raised the naked stump for me to examine. Everyone crowded around to see how I would react. The man looked at me with contempt. I felt ill.

"Tell him I'm very sorry," I said to the interpreter and stumbled out of the house.

"Shall I take the leg?" asked Muller. "It would be a good shot."

"Christ, no, you insensitive bastard," I said. "Leave him alone. Don't put him on exhibition."

"He wouldn't mind. He'd probably enjoy it." Muller made me feel even sicker.

We went into other houses, saw other scars. The people followed us everywhere, still staring at me in enmity. I could hardly blame them. They brought out a woman who told a long story about how her children had been killed in the raid. She began to weep when she said they found only part of the smallest one in a tree. She pointed out the tree. I felt like weeping, too. Muller shot the woman telling her story in close-up, with the interpreter holding the microphone and the woman's voice under his translation.

She finished by saying, "We thank you for coming to show your sympathy, but we always hold this hatred caused by the imperialist crimes and aggressions to my family."

Everyone looked at me. I knew I had to reply, but I didn't know what to say.

"Tell her," I said, "that my heart goes out to her in her tragic loss. War is a terrible thing. Nothing can bring back her children or those others who have died in Co Nhué, but I pray there will soon be peace between our countries so that more will not die."

It was not enough. I could see from the faces that it was not enough, but I could think of nothing more to say.

"Tell her again how sorry I am," I mumbled and we left. No one shook my hand.

After driving a long way in silence, Mr. Leng tried to make me feel better.

"You are the first American they have seen. It is natural that they still feel resentment for what your government did to them. However, you are quite safe when accompanied by me and my friends."

"I saw that and I was very glad that you were there. But what would have happened if I had wandered in there alone?"

"Nothing, I think. I mean they would not physically harm you. The orders are not to assault even American pilots who have parachuted to earth when their pirate planes have been destroyed. According to regulations they must be taken unharmed to the police or an Army post."

That was not an inviting prospect either.

"Just the same, Mr. Leng, I think I'll stick with you."

"It is best," he agreed.

All the way to the hotel I was haunted by those faces in Co Nhué, and the mutilated bodies, and the woman who had lost her children. I decided I couldn't face lunch. Nothing could spoil Muller's appetite, and he went into the dining room. I went straight to my room, poured myself half a tumbler of Scotch and lay down on the bed.

I felt sick at heart. Sick at what I had just been through and sick at what was to come, for I found myself relating everything I saw and did to Nguyen Van Thanh's escape. The more I saw of North Vietnam and its people, the more I despaired of bringing it off. There must be thousands of villages like Co Nhué, and if I stumbled into any one of them, I wouldn't have a chance. I remembered the look in the eyes of the villagers. If I tried to get Nguyen Van Thanh out and failed, I could expect no mercy in North Vietnam.

The whisky did not make me any more optimistic, but it made me sleepy. Just before I went to sleep I had an idea. I was still brooding over the impossibility of smuggling Nguyen Van Thanh through a hostile countryside when I thought, I obviously cannot do it. The only way is to let *them* do it. He could go out under government auspices. Perhaps I could arrange a meeting, a conference, outside the country that it would be imperative for him to attend. It was a thought anyway.

The telephone woke me up. I hadn't imagined that it even worked. Indeed, it didn't work very well. All I could make out from the faint voice on the other end was that there was someone in the lobby who wanted to see me. My watch said it was nearly four, time to get up in any event. I said I would be right down. My shirt was drenched in sweat, so I put on a clean one. It was probably Leng downstairs, ready to show me more American atrocities. I picked up my raincoat and went out.

It wasn't Leng waiting in the lobby; it was Charlie. The place is usually deserted in the afternoon, but she already had gathered a group of men around her. There must be some peculiar radiation that emanates from Charlie that men pick up like Geiger counters and come running toward like prospectors after a uranium lode.

"Darling," she said, "you've been neglecting me so I came over to see how you were."

"I'm sorry. They've been keeping me pretty busy. And you?"

"I've been busy, too. Those poor darling children in the hospital. They're so sick, some of them, and some of them were hurt in the bombing and have been there such a long time, but they're so grave. I like trying to make them happy."

"Good for you," I said, and I meant it. I was still thinking of the people of Co Nhué. "I'm glad there's some American they'll think well of."

I wanted to talk to her, but not in the lobby of the Thong Nhat, where she would bring every male in the place out of the woodwork.

"Let's go for a walk around the lake," I suggested.

"Goody," she said, clapping her hands in delight, "and we can stop at one of the little teahouses on the other side." She batted her eyes at the men around her and went out with me.

I gave her my raincoat, because she didn't have one. She had to roll up the sleeves and the bottom flapped around her ankles, but I thought she looked adorable. She put her hand in mine and we walked around the lake, avoiding the open manholes of the air-raid shelters and looking at the posters telling of victories in the South and threatening death to the imperialist aggressors. There were quite a few other couples, Vietnamese, holding hands, and some had their arms around each other. The regime hadn't stopped that, at least.

The teahouse was crowded, but we found a table. I felt conspicuous, but no one seemed to be paying any special attention to us. I hoped they took me for a Russian technician, though it would be hard to imagine Charlie as an Iron Curtain secretary. There was a bottle of *lua moi* on the bar and some pastel-colored bottles that looked like hair tonic. I ordered a beer instead, and Charlie ordered a café au lait.

I wanted to find out from her why Ned Bailey had sent her to Hanoi and what he expected her to do for him, but I didn't want to frighten her and I didn't want her to know what Bailey expected me to do. I tried to ease into the subject.

"How do you like it here, now that you've settled in?" I asked.

"Well, to tell you the truth, except for the children and a few friends I've made, I don't like it as much as I thought I would. Maybe you were right, Bill, when you told me that time that I shouldn't come."

"I know I was right," I said with feeling. "How did you ever persuade Ned Bailey to help you?"

"He didn't want me to come at first either. But I told him how much I wanted to help people here and how ashamed I was of what we had done to them. He said he understood that and wouldn't it be interesting to see what things were really like in North Vietnam? He was curious about that, he said."

"Of course, he was curious. Everybody is curious. That's why I'm here. But I'm a reporter. It's my job. You're just a girl."

"I know, but Ned said there were some things a girl would notice that a man wouldn't. He's very interested in Vietnam and knows a lot about it. He wants to know more, he said, and I promised to give him a full report when I got back."

"What sort of things did he want to know about?"

"Oh, like what they do about the casualties from the South, and how the people feel about them. I've found out some things already."

"I want you to tell me about that later. What other things was he interested in?"

"I don't know, things like public morale and whether there is a split in the government. There is, you know."

"So I've heard, but I still can't see him financing you just to provide him with dinner-table conversation when you get back."

"Well, it was really you, Bill, who turned the trick."

"Me?" I asked. Now we were getting somewhere.

"Yes. I wasn't supposed to say a word, but he told me your secret."

"My secret?" I said and took a gulp of beer to cover my surprise. "What secret?"

"That you were going to North Vietnam. He said you made him swear not to tell a soul."

"That's right," I said, silently cursing Ned Bailey for a dirty, deceitful son-of-a-bitch. "He shouldn't have told you. You can't trust him." By God, you couldn't. "I suppose he thought it would be a nice surprise for me to find you here."

"That's just what he said. Wasn't it a nice surprise?"

"Sure," I said. "It was a surprise, all right."

"Ned said I could help you, and I already have." She sounded proud of herself.

"And what have you done to help me?" I asked as casually as possible.

"Well, he told me of your plan to do a documentary on North Vietnam's plans for postwar reconstruction. I think it's a marvelous idea, Bill."

"Thanks. What did you do about that?" Getting something out of this girl was like pulling teeth.

"Well, he said they might naturally be a little suspicious of you, so I should try to meet Jack Fan Tan, that is, Nguyen Van Thanh, the Minister for Reconstruction, and I should bring your name up in some offhand way and tell him how important you are and that he could trust you."

"That was nice of him. What exactly did you say to Nguyen Van Thanh?"

"Just what Ned told me to say. I said, 'Uncle Sam says you can trust Bill Benson.' Ned told me to use exactly those words because Jack Fan Tan had been in the United States—that's where he got his nickname—and if I said, 'Uncle Sam says you can trust Bill Benson,' he would understand that the whole country trusted you. It's true, too, Bill," she said loyally, "they do trust you. So that's just what I told him."

Jesus Christ, I thought, if she's gone around Hanoi telling everyone she meets that I'm going to come to Hanoi and that they should trust me, I'm probably blown sky-high already.

"Whom else did you tell this to, honey?" I asked as calmly as I could.

"Nobody. Ned made a special point of that. He said your trip wasn't definite yet and that if I breathed a word to anyone but Jack Fan Tan, they might get cross with you and call it off. So I haven't mentioned it to anyone else. I've kept it a secret."

"Secrets?" said a familiar voice. I whirled around. It was Leng. "Lovers' secrets. I've found you out."

"Hello, Mr. Leng," I said. "Sit down." He had still been walking toward us when he first spoke, so I didn't think he had overheard anything. "How did you find us here?"

"It was not hard. Two Occidentals in the streets of Hanoi are not difficult to trace. One has only to ask. You could not even try to run away. It would be useless. You could never escape us."

I looked at him sharply and then decided it was his idea of a joke. "We weren't trying to run away," I told him. "I didn't think it was forbidden to walk around the lake and stop somewhere for a drink."

"Of course it is not forbidden. You may go anywhere you please. I merely thought I would find you because it is Sunday, and I'm sure you want to go to church. There is a six o'clock Mass at the Cathedral of St. Joseph." He looked at his watch. "It is twenty minutes before six. We can be there in time."

I suppressed a groan. The last thing I wanted to do was to go to church. I'm not much of a churchgoer to begin with, and I still had a hundred more questions for Charlie. She certainly wasn't interested in church.

"I'd love to see the cathedral, Mr. Leng," she said. I nearly fell off my chair. Charlie in a church? She was the least religious person I knew.

"What on earth for?" I asked.

"I've never been inside a church in Hanoi, and I want to see what it looks like."

So we went to the Cathedral of St. Joseph, where there were a surprising number of people. Obviously not all the Catholics had gone south in 1954. The service was in Vietnamese, of course, and I watched the others and crossed myself and knelt when they did. The cathedral itself looked old, but couldn't have been built before the nineteenth century. The pictures and decorations gave it a curiously Oriental look. I didn't pay much attention, though. I was too busy trying to put together what Charlie had told me.

So Ned Bailey had sent Charlie, of all people, in with a message to Nguyen Van Thanh. What had happened to his mysterious go-between who was supposed to pass the word that I was to be trusted? By now, of course, I was convinced Bailey had planned to have me bring out Nguyen Van Thanh all along. The Puerto Secreto approach was the first stage in his plan to trap me, and, by God, I had played right into his hands. Still, I couldn't make the pieces fit—especially Charlie. I'd have to pump Charlie some more, I thought as I hastily got down on my knees a good two seconds later than the rest of the congregation. The people I really should pump were the CIA, I thought as I got up again. Where was my CIA contact anyway? I didn't know much about espionage, but it seemed very unprofessional to send in an amateur like me and then just leave him to flounder about. It was worse to send in Charlie.

Charlie was following the Mass with what seemed to be rapt attention. O'Brien. She must have been brought up a Catholic and would know what was going on. She had a scarf on her head and looked very pretty. All at once, I felt very tender toward her. I made my only prayer in the church.

"Dear God," I prayed, "don't let anything happen to Charlie."

The priests and acolytes were filing out now. Even with their Vietnamese faces, they looked perfectly at home in their vestments. When the other worshipers got up to leave, we did too.

Outside, Charlie said, "It didn't seem all Catholic to me. I think they've added something."

"I am not Catholic myself," Leng said, "but I believe the Pope has granted certain special privileges to the Church in Vietnam."

"Well, it was very pretty anyway," said Charlie, "and I'm glad you took us. Mr. Leng, will you take me back to the Thong Nhat so I can get my bike?"

"Won't you have dinner with me?" I asked.

"No. I've promised a special treat to two of my children and I'm late already."

At the hotel, Leng had the driver tie her bike on the back of the car and take her to the hospital. I wanted to go along, but he indicated firmly that it would be better if she arrived by herself. "Not too many foreigners," he said cryptically: I didn't argue and suffered through a dinner alone with Muller.

I interrupted his endless anecdotes about his cinematographic exploits in various parts of the Communist world to ask him about all the hospitals we had passed. Were they all civilian? I wanted to know.

"That is what Mr. Leng said."

"What do they do about military casualties?" I asked.

"I do not know. One does not see them."

"That's what I meant. The only amputee I've seen was that civilian in Co Nhué."

"Perhaps there are military hospitals in the villages. Perhaps there are not so many casualties as the Americans suggest. I simply do not know."

There wasn't anything to be got out of Muller, so I went upstairs to type up my notes and send some cables before I went to bed. I might as well act like a correspondent anyway.

12

In the morning, the old anxiety settled in like the melancholy half-rain outside the window. It had become a companion I could not shake. I could hear its voice, muttering as constantly as the rain dripping off the gutter. It would not leave me nor cease its half-formed sentences.

The anxiety referred most often to Jack Fan Tan—I called him that in my head, although I hadn't even seen him yet. Then it switched to the CIA. I hadn't seen them either. Was that my fault? Had I been told to do something I hadn't done? I might have forgotten something. The anxiety moved on to Charlie. She was involved in this mess now, and the only reason was that she knew me. The anxiety blamed me for anything that might happen to her.

It did not stop. It made me remember the men I had met in the Paris airport. It repeated the enigmatic remarks of Ngo Xuan and Phan Boi Chau. People seemed suspicious of me before I had even done anything. Perhaps it was all in my mind. The anxiety said not. Then it jumped to IBS. I was working for IBS, wasn't I? What had I done for them? Nothing. I knew how to handle that line, though. I had had to deal with it many times before. There was a way to still that voice. Go to work. Cover the story.

The interpreter was in the lobby, sitting up straight in one

of the rump-sprung chairs. I asked him to bring the Vietnamese newspapers to my room and took notes while he translated them for me. Phan Boi Chau's paper had a long
editorial about the President's speech. That is, it was about
"the perfidious tricks and sly stratagems of the imperialist
camp which seeks to deceive world opinion into believing
that it desires peace in order to mask its true intention of
prolonging the war." The President's proposal itself was not
mentioned.

I sent a cable on that: "ALTHOUGH PRESIDENTIAL PROPOSAL
DEESCALATE WAR IN FIRST CORPS AREA STILL UNPUBLICIZED
HERE COMMA EDITORIAL APPARENTLY REFLECTING OFFICIAL
VIEWS COMMENTS TODAY QUOTE . . . ." I filled it out with the
liveliest selections from the editorial, which I assumed had
been written by Phan Boi Chau himself. It was hard to tell,
since everything in every paper was so cast in the official
jargon that it might all have been written by the same hand.

Leng came in while I was finishing another cable about
a complaint by the Party theoretician, Truong Chinh, that
capitalist tendencies were raising their ugly heads among
small farmers in the province of Vinh Phu. Leng and I
worked out a schedule for the day: a visit to another museum, a meeting with the Minister of Health, a further examination of bomb damage in Hanoi. And would I like to
resume the briefing with Dr. Pham Van Bach, who would
expose to me the chronology of events conclusively demonstrating the American crime of genocide in Vietnam? I said
I would rather postpone that, in order to work on my notes
and cables.

It was a busy morning, and if you want to know all about
the prehistoric pottery of Dong Son, or how North Vietnam
has conquered cholera and plague, or what happened when
an American rocket exploded at No. 46 Pho Nguyen Thiep
Street on December 13, 1967, well, it's all in the IBS files of
the broadcasts I made.

In the afternoon, alone in the big room with my notes, I was a captive audience for the old anxiety. It was telling me very clearly that I would never be able to do anything in this country they didn't want me to. In three days I hadn't made a single natural, normal human contact with a North Vietnamese. They were sealed off, which meant I was sealed in.

Outside the window, the bicyclists passed in streams. In any other country you see men who wear an index to their character on their faces. "This man is happy," the index reads. "This man is full of hate. Here is a man who dreams, here is one who would help you, another you could not trust." But in Hanoi there was no index I could read on any of the faces I had seen.

Here, if you were lost, no one would give you directions. If you were in flight, no one would give you shelter. If you were hurt, no one would bind up your wounds.

Nguyen Van Thanh's escape was what I was really thinking about. I tried to push it from my mind and lay down for a nap. Perhaps I slept, because evening came.

Charlie rode her bike over from the hospital to dine with me that night, and she was in the bar when I came down, surrounded by all the homeless correspondents and the diplomats too junior to rate a place of their own who lived there. She looked ten times more alive than anyone else in Hanoi, and it gave me a smug proprietary feeling to know she was dining with me.

I was so glad to see her that I wanted it to be a festive occasion, but there is nothing in the Thong Nhat to be festive with so it turned out to be rather like a family dinner in the neighborhood Chinese restaurant. Actually, Vietnamese food in the ordinary way is better than Chinese food —if you don't believe that, go to Paris, where they know what they are eating, and you will find the best Oriental restaurants are Vietnamese. The food was good, but the boardinghouse decorum was stifling, and we had to put up with Muller, who, according to house rules, shared our table.

Muller had improved since our Mexican days, but he was no Lucius Beebe in the conversational department, and the only light touch was Charlie's hand on my knee. Fortunately, the service in the Thong Nhat is quick, and when we finished dinner I started to spirit Charlie upstairs, where, among other things, I wanted to do a little more detective work on her brief life and times in Hanoi.

We were forestalled by Makepeace. We had forgotten this was the night he was supposed to bring his friends to a show of propaganda films. The peace group who was sponsoring him had rigged up a screen and set out chairs in a reception room off the lobby, but no one had turned up besides Makepeace. He was so embarrassed that there were tears in his eyes as he begged us to come in. His sponsors were all standing around waiting for his guests to show up, and we were the only ones he could lay his hands on. We couldn't let old Makepeace down so I said we were sorry to be late and Charlie and I went in to see the show.

On the screen a surgeon in a white mask was delivering a baby by Caesarean section amid shot and shell. The volume was up, and the sound effects of bombs, antiaircraft and jet noises were deafening. The mother was dead and the baby had a bomb fragment in its face. As the doctor worked, they intercut shots of American planes, bombs falling and antiaircraft gunners firing away. The aid station was hit, but the doctor worked on. Stretcher parties brought in fresh victims. Finally the all-clear sounded and the surgeon held up the bandaged child. Then, evidently some months later, they showed the child again, its scars healed except for a pucker around the mouth. This film ended with a montage of Robert S. McNamara, Lyndon Johnson and more American planes while a commentator in English told of the American campaign of genocide against the Vietnamese people.

The next film was the story of a young Vietnamese kinder-
garten teacher. Very pretty she was, too. She was teaching
a bunch of adorable little kids. The most adorable was her
favorite, or maybe it was her son—I couldn't quite make out.
The air siren sounded and all the little tykes rushed to the
shelter except the most adorable, who fell down. Outside, all
hell broke loose. Guns fired, planes swooped, things blew up.
Safe inside the shelter, the pretty teacher counted her flock.
They were all there except the most adorable one. Throwing
up her chin, the teacher started to go out into the maelstrom.
Hands clutched her, voices tried to dissuade her. Cut to
planes, machine-gun bullets ripping the earth, antiaircraft
guns firing, things blowing up. She goes out anyway. Where
to find the missing child? Distracted, she runs here, she runs
there. Machine-gun bullets follow her at every turn. Finally
she goes to the house. It has been bombed. On what is
left of the bed there is his little sweater. Hysterically, she
clutches it to her face. Then her eyes widen. She hears a
cry. In the corner, beneath the rubble, is the adorable child,
safe and sound. Gathering him up, she runs the gantlet of
machine-gun bullets once again and makes it back to the
shelter. Outside they shoot down an American plane. Everyone cheers. The all-clear sounds, and they all rush out and
start cleaning up the wreckage.

There were about four more of these short subjects. The
blood flowed and the camera dwelt on grisly rows of the
dead and wounded. One of the pieces had a shaky, obviously
hand-held sequence in which South Vietnamese soldiers tor-
tured and finally executed some bound Vietcong captives.
It was probably captured film and looked authentic. The
rest was so clearly contrived and the message so blatant that
it was sometimes funny and, oftener than that, tedious.

When the lights came on, I looked at my watch. It had
gone on for nearly two hours. Charlie was weeping like a
drain. Makepeace was pretty choked up, too.

"Ghastly, wasn't it?" he said.

"Ghastly," I agreed.

"I wish everyone in power in Washington could be forced to look at those pictures."

"I can imagine no Oriental torture more cruel or more subtle than to make the imperialist war criminals sit through a few hours of North Vietnamese documentary films."

"Bill," said Charlie, "you stop teasing Mr. Makepeace."

"My name is Bill, too," Makepeace said shyly.

"Well, they went on forever," I said. "And I hate to be talked down to for two hours. That's what I dislike about propaganda; it assumes you have the mind of a six-year-old child. It's too condescending."

"Well, thanks for coming anyway."

"Thank *you*, Bill," Charlies said to Makepeace, not to me.

"Come upstairs for a minute," I asked her.

"No, I want to buy this nice Bill a drink. And then I have to get back to the hospital."

"Okay, Makepeace, will you have a drink?"

"Thank you very much, sir. I'll be over as soon as I say good-bye to my friends."

"I don't understand you," she said when we had ordered the drinks. "I know you disapprove of what the United States is doing in Vietnam, yet you feel you have to criticize those films. Why won't you take sides?"

"It's what's known in the trade as Olympian objectivity, darling. It's what I get paid for."

"I know. 'There's something to be said for both sides,' said the famous television commentator Bill Benson as he returned from the war. Well, I'm not afraid to take sides."

"I envy you. I wish I could find a monopoly of virtue in one party or the other. I'd feel a lot better. But I can't. There's right and wrong, sense and nonsense, necessity and chance on both sides. Sit down, Makepeace. Here's your drink. We're having an interesting argument."

"I'm mad at Bill," Charlie explained. He insists on being so neutral it's sickening. Now, you just tell Mr. Makepeace and me—"

"Bill," said Makepeace.

"You just tell us why you won't say we've made a mistake in Vietnam and let's get out right now."

"I'd like to know that, too," said Makepeace.

"Because it won't work, that's why. Of course, it was a mistake to get mixed up in Vietnam. But life is full of mistakes. We have to live with them and make the best of them and try to straighten them out. I hope we can straighten this out by arranging to pull out of Vietnam. But when you make mistakes, you also acquire obligations. We've managed to acquire a lot of obligations in South Vietnam. That makes it more difficult."

"I don't see that at all," said Charlie. "I've made a lot of mistakes in my life and I'm not obligated to anyone."

"Right," said Makepeace.

"Well, you've both led sheltered lives, then. Look, Charlie. Suppose you and Makepeace here had an affair." She looked at him as though she thought that might be a good idea. "And suppose you got pregnant, and Makepeace came to you and said, 'It's all been a big mistake. I don't love you and you weren't that good a lay. I'm leaving town, good-bye.' What would you think of him if he did that?"

"That's what everybody who gets me in trouble does, leaves town."

"Well, Makepeace wouldn't and I wouldn't. We'd try to figure out some solution, something that would cause you the least harm, and him the least, and would be fairest to all concerned, including the unborn child. We sure as hell wouldn't run away."

"You've got an interesting point there, sir," said Makepeace.

"Well, it's the point of the Paris Peace Talks."

"You *wouldn't* run away, would you, Bill?" asked Charlie. "That's why I love you."

"I'm not sure it applies exactly," said Makepeace doubtfully.

"Maybe not, but I don't want my country to behave by any worse standards than my own."

"That's a lousy metaphor," said Charlie.

"Analogy," I said. "Excuse me, Makepeace. I want to have a private talk with Charlie. Thanks again for the movie show."

"I've got something for you," I told Charlie as we went upstairs.

"What?"

"What do you think?"

"Oh, darling, we can't do anything here."

"Charlie, you shock me! All I meant is that I have some Scotch in my room. Anyway, I want to talk to you, not make love to you."

"All right. But if we're going to talk, tell me why you're so mean to that nice boy."

"Makepeace? I'm not mean to him. I like him."

"I like him, too, and I think you're mean to him. You make fun of him all the time. Why don't you stop picking on him?"

"All right, I'll stop picking on him, but I don't think I'm doing him any harm. I may even be doing a little good." I made us a drink and sat her down in a chair for a serious talk. There was a lot more I needed to find out from her.

"Charlie," I said, "you certainly move in exalted circles. You told me you had met Nguyen Van Thanh. How did that happen?"

"Oh, there was a big party for some foreign mission and they invited me. I think they wanted to show off the American girl who had come to help them. He was there and we had a chat."

"You must have had other chats if you know him well enough to call him 'Jack Fan Tan.'"

"We've seen each other. Is there anything wrong in that?"

"I guess not. And Phan Boi Chau, you've met him, too, and know him well enough to call him 'Boy.'"

"He's around the hotel here all the time with the correspondents. That's how I met him. He's nice, but I don't think he and Jack Fan Tan get along."

"Charlie, tell me, how did you ever manage to get to Hanoi in the first place? It's not easy, you know. Makepeace and I are experts on how hard it is."

She looked at her watch. "Bill, I've got to get back to the hospital. I can't be late. They've been asking me questions."

"Who has been asking you questions?"

"Some men. I don't know who they are—the police, or immigration, or something like that. I guess they check up on all foreigners."

"What kind of questions?"

"The same kind you've been asking. Whom I've been seeing. Why I wanted to come here. How I got here."

"And what did you tell them, honey?"

"Just what I've told you. The truth. I said I've always wanted to come to North Vietnam to do something useful and show that there were some Americans who cared. I told them Ned Bailey had lent me the money. I said I went to the North Vietnamese Embassy in Phnom Penh and filled out a form. Then I met a man who introduced me to some North Vietnamese, and they invited me in. I didn't sneak in, for heaven's sake, I told them."

"Who was this man in Phnom Penh who introduced you to the Vietnamese?"

"I don't remember. A man called Piper, something like that."

"Pfeiffer," I said.

"That's the name. Do you know him?"

"I met him. He sells fakes."

"Oh, Bill, they looked all right to me. He has beautiful things."

"Fakes," I said. "All the way."

This was worse than I thought. I supposed it could have been a routine check. Even so, Charlie had told them a lot. Would they link Pfeiffer to Bailey, and Bailey to me? How *stupid* to send us both in the same way. They probably suspected me already. I wanted to ask Charlie whether she had mentioned her conversation with Nguyen Van Thanh about me. On second thought, I'd better not. I didn't want to make her suspicious, and I didn't want her to see how worried I was. I was worried sick.

"I guess you're right, Charlie," I said. "It *is* late and I guess we'd better get you back to the hospital. I'll work my wicked will on you another night."

"I've got my bike outside. I'll ride back. I do it all the time."

We went down to the lobby, to the ill-concealed interest of the Noah's Ark, not a man of whom would have believed I hadn't laid a hand on her up in the room. Charlie bade them all a radiant farewell. She couldn't just walk out of a place. It had to be an Exit.

I saw her off on her bicycle and lit a cigarette as she pedaled off along the empty avenue past the old French Governor General's mansion. She had just turned the corner when I heard the sound of the bike falling and a piercing scream.

I got there as fast as I could. Two Vietnamese in their anonymous, tattletale-gray Ho Chi Minh suits had her up against the wall. One had a knife. I couldn't tell whether they were trying to kill her or rape her. She was kicking and scratching and making gurgling noises because one of them had her by the throat. My cigarette was still in my hand. I jammed it into the face of the man with the knife, trying for the eye, and got his knife away before he kicked me in the crotch.

I doubled up in agony, and he hit me on the side of the

neck with some kind of karate blow. I thought I would pass out, but he must have missed the right spot, because I didn't. I landed one pretty good right on this guy's head and got in a kick against the other one still holding Charlie. Too low to hurt him much. The first one spun me up against the wall, and they both worked me over pretty thoroughly. It would have been worse, but one of them had to use a hand to hold Charlie. I didn't know there were so many parts of the body you could hit a man with. They hit me with their hands, their heads, their forearms, their elbows, their shoulders, their knees and their feet. Mostly in the stomach, where, after years of loose living, I do not take it so well any more.

After more of this than I thought I could stand, they picked up Charlie's bike, set it against the wall, mounted their own and rode off into the night. I just sat down on the sidewalk and, after a moment, vomited as close to the curb as I could get, trying to keep it off my clothes. I hurt all over, but nothing seemed to be broken and I wasn't bleeding much. Charlie had a knife scratch on one shoulder, and her dress was torn, but otherwise she looked all right.

"What the hell was that all about?" I said when I had enough breath back to speak.

"I don't know, but I'm afraid."

I realized I was afraid, too. The empty street was menacing. I could feel eyes in every window, but I knew there wasn't a soul who would have raised a hand to help even if they had dismembered us instead of just beating us up. There wasn't a soul in the whole country who cared whether we were alive or dead. They'd probably prefer us dead. The whole atmosphere suddenly oozed evil. I never felt so alone. Charlie must have felt the same way, for we clung to each other for a while on the sidewalk.

I wanted to throw up again, but I was damned if I was going to give the eyes behind the windows that much satisfaction. I got up, piece by piece, holding onto the wall. I saw the knife they had used on Charlie and got down again, piece by piece, picked it up and put it in my pocket. When I was upright once more, I started slowly pushing Charlie's bike.

"Let's go back to the hotel. I want to find out about this."

"Oh, Bill, darling Bill. You're so brave. You saved my life."

"Like hell. They could have killed us both. I think they damned near killed me."

"You were wonderful."

"Bloody marvelous, I was. Battling Benson. Beaten to a pulp by a couple of midgets, five feet high and half my weight."

"Poor Bill. They did hurt you, didn't they? I'm so proud of you."

I just grunted. I wasn't proud of myself, and my lips were puffing up so it was hard to speak anyway.

There were a couple of moments there when I wasn't sure I was going to make it the block and a half or so back to the Thong Nhat. But you get stronger after a while, and I was standing almost upright by the time we entered the lobby. I went straight to the desk.

"Get the police," I said. "I want to report an assault. Attempted murder."

The desk clerk's eyes widened with fear. I gathered the foreign honored guests of the Thong Nhat did not often turn up with multiple contusions and abrasions and vomit on their clothes. He was probably afraid they would blame him.

"Here in the hotel?" he asked anxiously.

"No, not in the hotel. Get the police here and get me Ngo Xuan at the Foreign Office. I want to talk to him."

Charlie had drawn a crowd as usual. Makepeace was there. He had lent her his comb and Charlie was combing her hair. Makepeace pulled out a fairly clean handkerchief and started dabbing at the blood on her shoulder. It was only a scratch. She took the handkerchief away from him and dried her eyes. Makepeace looked at me.

"What happened, sir?"

"I don't know. A couple of guys knocked Charlie off her bike. When I got there, they beat me up, too. I've had them call the police."

Most of the other correspondents had drifted away, I noticed. They were standing in groups at the other end of the lobby, looking at us and talking among themselves. Hanoi was just like any other big city, I reflected bitterly. Somebody gets hurt and no one wants to get involved. No one, that is, but good old Makepeace. He came up with a tumblerful of vodka for each of us. Russian vodka, at that. It helped.

"Shall I see about a room for Miss O'Brien?" he said. "She shouldn't go back to her own place tonight."

"I don't want a room," Charlie said firmly. "I'm going to stay with Bill. He needs me. He saved my life and they hurt him. They can just put another bed in his sitting room."

The police came almost at once. At least, they said they were police. I suspected they were hangers-on at the hotel. Probably the same thing. There was a whole room full of hangers-on down the corridor from the reception desk. Whenever I wanted to find someone from my entourage, he would be in there, along with people from other correspondents' entourages. Half of them were clearly from the secret police or intelligence, assigned to keep an eye on us. In any event, a round little man in a Western suit with an authoritative air and a notebook turned up so quickly he couldn't have been far away. He had my interpreter with him. We all sat down on the imitation-leather chairs in the lobby.

"Where did this take place?" he wanted to know, and we drew him a map. He sent someone off to the scene.

"Can you describe the assailants?" No, we couldn't, except that they were Vietnamese and dressed in the standard Ho Chi Minh getup. It was dark and, anyway, it's difficult for Westerners to recognize individual Vietnamese unless they have seen them often.

I gave him the knife, which seemed to me a valuable clue. He held it delicately at the precise point of balance and pursed his lips.

"There must be ten thousand knives like this in Hanoi. It is a standard item."

"I hope it is not standard to use them on visiting foreigners," I said bitterly.

He ignored that. "No other identification?"

"One of them will have a cigarette burn on his face. His cheek, I think. I missed the eye."

He wrote that down and turned to Charlie.

"What provocation did you offer?"

"Provocation!" she said. "I didn't offer any provocation. I was just riding my bike back to the hospital where I work when these two men jumped out of the shadows and knocked me down."

He gave an unpleasant giggle. "Perhaps, Mademoiselle, just the spectacle of you riding on a bicycle was provocation enough. Our ladies do not wear such short skirts. Those men might have found it intolerably stimulating. We Vietnamese are men like any others." He looked at her legs and the expanse of thigh on which a large purple bruise was beginning to spread.

Now, to be frank, the same idea had occurred to me. Charlie was an indubitably stimulating girl. I was damned, though, if I was going to let this punk cop, or secret policeman, or whatever he was, get away with any cheap cracks. I looked him in the eye, which was not hard because my neck was so stiff now I couldn't turn my head.

"I was not aware, Monsieur l'Inspecteur," I said in French, "that the notoriously far-reaching regulations of the Democratic Republic of Vietnam extend to the costumes worn by guests of the nation. Further, I must express my surprise and disappointment that the arrangements for public security in Hanoi are so lax as to permit an unprovoked assault upon a lady of another country who has, in effect, entrusted her safety to the local authorities. I will, as soon as possible, lodge a formal protest with the Foreign Ministry. Meanwhile, I count on you to explore every avenue and trust it is not beyond the resources of your department to apprehend the criminals and see that they are properly punished."

I was rather proud of all that, considering the shape I was in, and watched for the effect. His jaw tightened and his eyes narrowed, if that were possible, since they were pretty narrow to begin with. His whole expression proclaimed that he was not about to accept any instruction in his duty from an American pirate imperialist aggressor and that for the local equivalent of two cents he would take up with me where the two thugs left off. That was not what he said, though.

He got up and made a stiff little bow.

"I express my official regrets over the incident, particularly as it concerned the young lady. I will do my best to find those responsible. I promise nothing. Indeed, I doubt that they will be found."

I got up, too, although it was very painful. I had been sitting too long in one position and every muscle screamed. My head felt as though someone were twisting a knife in it. I tried to think of some parting shot, but nothing came. It was all I could do to stand up. I just watched him leave.

My man Leng materialized by my side.

"I also wish to express my regrets," he said. "I cannot understand how it could have happened. I have spoken to Mr. Ngo Xuan. He apologizes for not being able to come at once, but he is in an important meeting. He hopes you will be able to come to his office at eight o'clock tomorrow morning to discuss this unfortunate matter."

"I will be there," I said. "Mr. Leng, Miss O'Brien will stay in my quarters tonight. Would you be good enough to have a bed made up for me in my sitting room?"

"Would she not prefer to have her own room? I can arrange that."

"She has been through a very disturbing experience. I
think she would feel safer with me."

He bowed and went off. I saw that Muller was standing
beside me.

"Muller, could you get me another large vodka, please?
And one for Charlie. She needs it more than I do."

"Let us go to the bar," he said, and drew me away for
privacy.

"Do not discuss this with Charlie when you are upstairs,"
he said when we were out of earshot. "The room is bugged.
You and I will talk about it in the morning. I have something
to tell you."

The vodkas hit me hard, but not as hard as the implication
of what Muller had said. All I wanted to do was to stretch
out. Charlie was telling Makepeace what a tiger I was,
singlehandedly beating off a mob of villainous Vietnamese.
Tiger! I felt like a day-old kitten.

"Come on, Charlie, let's go upstairs," I said.

They had already made up a cot in the sitting room. I fell
on it.

"No, no," she said. "You must be in the big bed. It's more
comfortable. I'll sleep here."

"Oh, for Christ's sake, Charlie. I don't want to move. I
don't care what bed as long as it's a bed. Just let me stay
here."

"Well, you'll have to sit up so I can get those clothes off
you and get you cleaned up."

So, between us, we got me sitting up and somehow worked
my arms out of my jacket. That was the hardest part. The
shirt, trousers, shoes and etceteras came off easily enough.
Charlie got a towel and for her clean-up job used the hot
water in the thermos jug that's always there to make tea.
Either those thermos bottles are the best in the world or

the staff sneaks in every couple of hours to refill them, because the water is always hot enough to make tea, which meant I was nearly parboiled. But, finally, I was also clean.

"I don't think it was an accident," Charlie said. "They didn't act as though they wanted to rape me. I think there was a reason."

"I don't know, honey. I just don't know. Let's not talk about it now. I'm too tired." I raised my finger to my lips and gestured around the room. She got the message.

"Of course you don't. You've got to get some sleep. We'll talk about it tomorrow."

"There's some Scotch over there and some soda over there. Make me a drink and get me some aspirin and I'll see you in the morning."

13

Whenever I can remember a dream clearly, I'm never sure whether it was a real, honest-to-goodness dream, or a half-asleep half-dream that I half-consciously added some touches to because they were dramatically right. That night, I had such a dream.

Charlie and I were running away from something across a dark, smoky plain. The smoke didn't come from volcanoes or anything burning. It just sort of issued from pits in the ground. American bombs, I suppose I was thinking of. We kept running, but we were not tired. Then I saw what we were running from. Out of the smoke came a great horde, all dressed alike in smoke-colored Ho Chi Minh suits. They had no faces, or perhaps it was that their faces were also the color of smoke and I couldn't make them out. They were all around us. Then we were not on the plain at all, but in the streets of Hanoi. I saw an empty street, and, still running, we turned down it. There was Ned Bailey, standing alone, grinning, with a knife in his hand. I effortlessly struck him a tremendous blow and he fell aside. Behind him stood the police inspector. As I swung, he ducked. I swung again. He ducked. Then I saw a man I knew to be Nguyen Van Thanh. He beckoned us down another street, but Charlie had disappeared. I called to her and then realized she was running beside Nguyen Van Thanh. We came to a cliff. A gorge? A river bank? There was nothing to do but jump.

I woke to find Charlie bathing my forehead with the wet towel, which was cool now.

"Darling, you were calling me in your sleep," she said. "Is it all right now?"

"I don't know, Charlie. I don't know whether we made it or not."

"Try to go back to sleep."

"I will," I said, and I did. I must have slept very soundly. I had no other dream that I could remember, and the next thing I knew was that Charlie was gently stroking my shoulder and telling me it was almost seven and I had an appointment with Ngo Xuan at eight. I managed to get out of bed and into the bathroom, but I could hardly raise my arm to brush my teeth, and when I did I gagged. So I poured out another glass of drinking water from the carafe and took a Dexamyl and two aspirins to make me feel better.

After a shower and a halfhearted shave, I picked out my second-darkest suit and Charlie helped me dress. I could do most of it, but she had to button my shirt collar. My fingers wouldn't work. She had to comb my hair, too. When she stood me in front of the mirror, I was surprised to see I didn't look too bad. A little puffy here and there, but it was recognizably me. Those two boys the night before had done very good work. They had hurt me, but they hadn't marked me up much.

Charlie looked great. There was a little scratch on her shoulder where they had been careless with the knife and a big bruise on her right thigh, but that was all. I could make a complete inventory of Charlie because she wasn't wearing any clothes. As I said, she looked great. Charlie was made not to wear any clothes. I felt a distinct stirring of lust, which encouraged me to believe I was getting better. I put my arms around her.

"What are you trying to do?" she said, holding me so tight I didn't care whether it hurt.

"Just exploring for broken bones."

"Well, not *there*, idiot. There's nothing broken there."

"Thank God for that."

"Go on down and get some coffee or you'll be late. I'll be down in a minute."

Muller was already at our table when I arrived. I braced myself for some heavy Teutonic pleasantry about my pugilistic prowess, or lack of it, but he seemed genuinely concerned.

"You feel all right, Bill?"

"Better."

"You are going to see Ngo Xuan this morning?"

"Yes. There are some questions I want to ask him."

"You will find there are also some questions he wants to ask you, Bill." He leaned forward anxiously. "Bill, be very careful what you say. He may know more than you think he does. Do not let him think you are concealing anything. Remember, he has probably monitored everything you said in your room. To Charlie, to me, to anybody who has been in your room. Think back and do not try to hide these things from him."

"I have nothing to hide. I just want to know why they jumped Charlie last night."

"Bill, it is time I explained something to you," he began, and at that moment the inevitable Mr. Leng came up and Muller said no more.

"I trust you slept well, Mr. Benson," said Leng. In the morning all conversations in Vietnam invariably begin with an inquiry about the quality of your repose. In the afternoon they start by asking you whether you are enjoying your visit.

I said I had slept as well as might be expected.

"Then it will be possible for you to see Mr. Ngo Xuan? He is expecting us. We can leave whenever you are ready."

I finished my coffee, and Leng, the interpreter, the errand boy (whose name turned out to be Ba) and I all got into the rickety old car they had assigned to me and we drove off to the Foreign Office.

Ngo Xuan, in his neat black Western suit, his sparkling-white shirt and highly polished shoes, got up from his desk and asked whether I had slept well. We spoke in French, as we had before.

"I have known better nights," I told him.

"Allow me to express both my personal and official regrets over the unfortunate events of last night."

"Thank you. For the record, I wish to lodge a formal protest against the indignities to which Miss O'Brien and myself were subjected. If you like, I will deliver it to you in writing."

"That will not be necessary. I officially acknowledge receipt of your protest and will send you a formal apology on behalf of my government."

"Thank you. Now, Mr. Ngo Xuan, what I really want to discuss with you is the motive for the attack."

"Yes," he said, "that is the interesting thing, is it not?" He picked up a tortoise-shell letter opener on his desk and began to toy with it.

"The police believe that it is a case of attempted rape," he said. "Rape is not common in my country, but it is not unknown. Miss O'Brien is an unusually attractive woman. Moreover, she is a Westerner. We have not seen many Western women in Hanoi recently. To some they might seem particularly desirable. At the sight of Miss O'Brien on her bicycle, the two men may have simply given way to an outburst of unpremeditated passion. Is that not possible?"

"It is possible. I can only say that that is not the impression Miss O'Brien received. Nor does it seem consistent with the thorough and systematic way in which I was attacked when I arrived upon the scene. Would rapists not have fled at once upon being discovered? I had the feeling that they were waiting for me and knew exactly what they were going to do to me and how far they should go. In effect, it appeared to be planned."

"That is how it seemed to you?"

"Monsieur le Directeur, I hesitate to suggest this in view of all the thoughtfulness and courtesies which have been extended to me, but could it have been that we were attacked because we were Americans, representatives of a nation with whom your country is at war? Could the motive have been political?"

"Perhaps, in a sense, it could have been political." Ngo Xuan played with his letter opener again. "Mr. Benson, how well do you know Miss O'Brien?"

"Very well. She has lived in a place where I have lived in Mexico."

"Yes. She has told us that. In fact, it was there that you introduced her to a Mr. Edward Bailey."

"That is right." I was remembering what Muller had said at breakfast. Charlie and I could have been overheard discussing him. Besides, they had questioned Charlie, and she wouldn't lie about something like that.

"Mr. Edward Bailey provided the money for her voyage to Vietnam, did he not?"

"So she told me."

"Mr. Benson, how well do you know Mr. Edward Bailey?"

"I have known him a long time. We were in the war together. However, I have seen him only occasionally since, so I could not say I know him very well."

"You know, of course, that he is a notorious agent of the CIA."

"No, I do not know that, and I think it very unlikely. To the best of my knowledge he is in the insurance business."

"I assure you, he is an important member of the CIA. There is no doubt."

"You surprise me."

"Do I?" He held the letter opener up to the light and admired the grain of the tortoise shell.

"Miss O'Brien met a Mr. Louis Pfeiffer in Phnom Penh. It was he who introduced her to our representatives and recommended that we employ her as a symbol of the opposition of the great mass of the American people to their government's criminal and genocidal campaign against Vietnam."

"I believe she mentioned the name."

"We have had previous dealings with Mr. Pfeiffer. He has been useful to us in disposing of certain objects of art with which we acquired foreign currency to maintain some of our missions abroad."

I said nothing, not knowing whether he was aware of my own meeting with Pfeiffer.

"You also saw Mr. Pfeiffer when you were in Phnom Penh."

"As a matter of fact, I did. He tried to sell me some Khmer sculpture. They were not authentic."

"No, they seldom are. It is an interesting coincidence, is it not? You meet Mr. Edward Bailey in Mexico. You introduce him to Miss Charlotte O'Brien. Miss Charlotte O'Brien meets Mr. Louis Pfeiffer after arriving in Phnom Penh, her expenses paid by Mr. Edward Bailey. You also meet Mr. Louis Pfeiffer in Phnom Penh. Both Miss O'Brien and you come to Hanoi, where you are frequently in each other's company. Do you not find that an interesting coincidence?"

"Yes, but only a coincidence," I said, and added inanely, "It's a small world." I was beginning to sweat.

"It is very humid at this time of year in Hanoi; we call it the *crachin*," Ngo Xuan said pleasantly and made as if to reach for the handkerchief in his breast pocket. I took out my own and mopped my face. It hurt.

"Now, if you were in my position, Mr. Benson, what would you make of such a coincidence?"

"Very little. Miss O'Brien is a very idealistic person. She has often in the past expressed to me her desire to come to

North Vietnam and help its people as a gesture to show her disagreement with United States policy. She also wished to go to Cuba to offer her services to Señor Castro. I may say that I strenuously sought to discourage her. After last night's outrage I am sorrier than ever that I did not succeed."

"It may indeed have been best that she did not come. Let us return to this series of coincidences."

"Willingly. You appear to suggest that Miss O'Brien and I are somehow in league with Mr. Bailey, who you say works for the CIA, and imply that we are engaged in some sinister espionage operation. Now, that is absurd on the face of it. In the first place, she is working in a children's hospital, which cannot involve any important matters of security. I myself am under the control of your own department. I do not imagine that I have seen or am likely to see anything you do not wish me to. What possible espionage could we commit?"

"I do not know. I tell you that frankly. But still, there are the coincidences."

"I do not understand how you can think them sinister. When Ned Bailey took Charlie away from Mexico—took her away from me, if you must know, and for that I shall never forgive him—when he took her away, I did not even know I was coming to Hanoi. I don't suppose *you* knew, Monsieur le Directeur. It was three weeks later that my New York office told me of your government's invitation. By that time, Charlie—Miss O'Brien—was already here in Hanoi. It is quite impossible that we could be in collusion. I can assure you that no one was more surprised than I to find her here."

"I have considered all that, although I did not know that you resented Mr. Bailey's departure with Miss O'Brien. I believe that. You seem very fond of her."

"I am very fond of her."

"That may perhaps put a slightly different aspect on matters. Incidentally, Mr. Benson, I *did* know you would be permitted to visit Hanoi three weeks before you heard from your office. Indeed, it was I who recommended that you come."

"Well, I didn't know."

"No, I don't see how you could." He sighed deeply and played with his letter opener. "I suppose," he said, "I must give you the benefit of the doubt."

"You will forgive me if I fail to see any cause for doubt."

"I hope, for your sake and that of Miss O'Brien, that there is none. I will tell you one thing: my suspicions had nothing to do with your accident last night."

"What did?"

"I have my own theory."

He turned his chair and gazed, out of delicacy, at a lacquer picture in the very worst Vietnamese taste that was hanging on the wall.

"I do not mean to be indiscreet or personal, but would you say Miss O'Brien is a . . . ah . . . *promiscuous* person?"

I couldn't help but grin.

"Yes, I am afraid I must say that she is a promiscuous person."

"And yet you are fond of her?" he asked with genuine interest.

"Yes, I am fond of her. It is the way she is. I could wish she were otherwise. But I am very fond of her in spite of what you might call this failing of hers."

"It is as I thought. I have here a list of the men with whom she has been friendly since she came to Hanoi."

I looked across to see what I could make of the list. It was in Vietnamese, but, even so, I could see it was quite a list, considering the fact that Charlie had only been in Hanoi for a little more than two weeks. My God, she's incorrigible, I thought.

"I will summarize it for you," Ngo Xuan was saying. "I

will not give you the names. It is not necessary for you to know them."

He put on his glasses.

"A foreign correspondent at the Thong Nhat. He is not important. One doctor at the hospital. He is not important either. The editor of a Vietnamese newspaper. Very important. A member of the Party Central Committee. Most important of all. There are other names here, but we are not sure how well she knew them."

"Pretty well," I said, "knowing Charlie."

"We are not prudes. We are not concerned with such activities in themselves. What interests me in this list is that it might represent a pattern. If Miss O'Brien were an agent of the CIA, would she not . . . ah . . . ingratiate herself with precisely such people? Do you see?"

"Yes, I see. But I know Miss O'Brien. I can think of an alternative explanation. Round heels."

"Round heels?" He looked puzzled.

"It is an American expression. If one has round heels, it is more difficult to maintain an upright posture."

He thought about that for a minute and then permitted himself a wintry smile.

"Ah, yes. Very witty. We do not have such an expression in Vietnamese."

"It is your suggestion, then," I said, "that one of these men is jealous of another and decided to teach Charlie a lesson."

"It is an hypothesis."

"Then it would have to be one of the Vietnamese. From what I have seen of the way your country is organized, it would be impossible for a foreigner to arrange such an operation."

"That is equally my conclusion. It is reinforced by the fact that the two most important Vietnamese who have made the intimate acquaintance of Miss O'Brien do not like each other. I mean," he added hastily, "there is, of course, complete unanimity within the government on matters of policy. However, before policy is agreed upon, there are completely free and democratic discussions during which differences are expressed. In the course of these democratic discussions Miss O'Brien's two friends have been known to disagree. One of them might have expressed his disagreement through this retaliation upon Miss O'Brien."

"And me? Why would he want to retaliate against me?"

"You are known as a lover of Miss O'Brien. Perhaps he wished to strike two birds with the same stone. That is an American expression I *do* know. Perhaps it is simply that you arrived on the scene at the crucial moment, and what they did to you they would have done to anyone who discovered them. They would not have killed her, you know. They would have been very careful about that. Just as they were very careful not to injure you too severely. They were just instructed to teach a lesson."

"To Miss O'Brien or to her other friend?"

"Both, I would guess."

"Then it should not be too difficult for you to discover who was responsible."

"No, not difficult. Indeed, I think I know already. However, there is nothing I can do. They are both powerful men. The most I can do is to let the instigator know that we are aware of his identity and to hint that we would take a very grave view if it were to happen again. I can do that, and I think I can assure you that it will not happen again."

"I am grateful for that."

Ngo Xuan played with his letter opener some more, and looked at the saccharine picture on the wall, and stared up at the ceiling for a while.

"You know, Mr. Benson," he said finally, "you and your Miss O'Brien have greatly complicated my life. My government is in the midst of important negotiations with yours. We must give an appropriate reply to the impertinent proposal of your President. It is a delicate moment. A moment when friendly American guests might be useful, but unfriendly ones are an embarrassment. I really don't know what I should do about you and Miss O'Brien."

"If I were you, the first thing I would do would be to get Miss O'Brien out of here as quickly as possible. I would do this for her own safety, for the tranquillity of the upper echelons of your government and because you still seem to harbor suspicions that she is an enemy agent."

"I have thought of that. The difficulty is that there is no ICC flight this Friday. Nothing until next Tuesday and, since she is an American, we cannot send her out through China. Today is only Tuesday."

"Ah. Then the next best thing is to take her from the hospital, put her in the Thong Nhat and parole her to me. I am under your constant surveillance. You can arrange my schedule. Your men accompany me wherever I go. I will simply take her with me. She will never be out of your sight. In that way you can be sure neither of us will cause trouble."

"Parole her to you? An interesting idea. But what about you, Mr. Benson? Do you propose that I allow you to continue your work here as though nothing had happened?"

"I do not know what else you can do, short of putting me in jail or having me executed. You have no grounds for doing either and, without wishing to appear immodest, I am not unknown in the outside world. Any mysterious disappearance or sanctions against me would receive wide publicity and create very unfavorable repercussions for your government and its policies."

"If you were I, do you think I could trust you, Mr. Benson?"

"Only up to a point, Mr. Ngo Xuan. Only up to the point where you trusted me in the beginning. At that time you knew that I do not share many of the views of your government, about the war and about other things. Nevertheless, you trusted me to present a fair and objective account of what I saw and what was said to me. I think you may still trust me that far. I will not conceal from you that last night's incident may have impaired my objectivity in certain respects, but not, I think, in essential ones. I do not promise to suppress the incident. Too many people at the hotel know about it by now. On the other hand, I would not be likely to dwell upon it, lest it reflect upon Miss O'Brien. You have shown you can make a damaging case against her. I would not like that to happen. No, on balance and trying sincerely to look at it from your point of view, Monsieur le Directeur, I think you should trust me to carry on the journalistic work which you invited me to undertake."

"Perhaps you are right. Our minds seem to work in similar fashion. I have no desire for you to become an international *cause célèbre*. However, I must consult my Minister and other interested parties. Meanwhile, instead of the schedule I have arranged, we will substitute an interview with the Minister of Postwar Reconstruction, Mr. Nguyen Van Thanh. Then we will see."

I thought he looked at me closely when he mentioned Nguyen Van Thanh. If they had had a lie detector on me, the needle would have jumped a foot.

"This interview," I said. "May I film the Minister, or will it just be a briefing?"

"I think no filming until your status is decided."

"Well, then, may I have Muller make some background shots in the city? There is a great deal I would like him to do."

"I see no objection to that. We know Mr. Muller. I have the list of your requests, and they have been approved."

"If you have no other plans for me this morning, may I take Muller on a tour of the city and show him precisely what I want him to do?"

"We had planned an interview for you with a member of General Giap's staff. However, under the circumstances, I think it best that we cancel that. We will limit you to non-controversial subjects like postwar reconstruction and the War Crimes of the American Imperialist Aggressors. Yes, you may go off with Muller. I will tell Leng."

He looked at his watch. "I fear I am already late. We have had a long talk."

I stood up. "May I take Miss O'Brien with me from now on?"

"Yes, with Muller this morning. But not to see Mr. Nguyen Van Thanh this afternoon. They have already met. I will accept your suggestion and arrange a room for her at the Hotel Thong Nhat."

"Thank you, Monsieur le Directeur."

When I got out of there, the hot air of the street felt actually cool. Perhaps it was just the evaporation. I was wringing wet.

When Leng and Ba and I got back to the hotel, Muller bustled up to us.

"I think it is time that we have a talk about future projects, yes?" he said.

I told him Ngo Xuan had okayed a tour of the city.

Mr. Leng interrupted. "Perhaps you and Mr. Muller will excuse me," he said. "Mr. Ngo Xuan wishes me to attend an important meeting."

"About me?"

He looked unhappy. "I do not know the subject. Excuse me. I will meet you after lunch to take you to see Minister Nguyen Van Thanh."

Muller and I got into our car and told the driver where to go. He had shown no signs of understanding English and very little French, but I was beginning to think that in Hanoi you never know. We went to the Doumer Bridge and a kind of market area, and I went through the motions of telling Muller what I would like him to film. I threw in a site of bomb damage for good measure. When we came to the little lake in the center of town, I said we would get out and walk and told the driver in sign language to wait. There were quite a few people around, but it seemed safe enough for us to talk.

"I am on your side, you know," said Muller.

"Thanks."

"I don't mean that. I mean I am from Pfeiffer. I am the one he told you would identify myself."

"I wondered as much from our conversation at breakfast."

"You did?" He seemed crestfallen. "When did you suspect?"

"Not until last night when you were getting me that drink," I said truthfully, for Muller's double role really had surprised me.

"Ah, that is better. I did not like to think I was obvious."

To do him justice, Muller had not been obvious. Until he had warned me that the hotel room was bugged and then warned me about Ngo Xuan at breakfast, everything he had done had been in character. The warnings were not in character. Nothing in his relationship with me would have prompted them. The relationship itself was not unfamiliar, and I knew the ground rules.

There are perhaps fifty journalists in the world—Communists or fellow travelers—who have managed to maintain a foot in each camp. The foot in the Communist camp is more securely planted, but because they are good at their job and have retained some vestiges of objectivity, they also have access to the broader world of orthodox journalism. They perform a function which is valuable to both sides. They are the go-betweens.

If, for instance, you are covering the Paris Peace Talks and you want to know what the North Vietnamese or the National Liberation Front really think about an American proposal, you go to Wilfred Burchett, an Australian by origin and a correspondent of great ability, who has spent most of his life in the Communist world and enjoys their confidence. He will tell you what he thinks you ought to know. Not everything, but he won't lie to you and you will get more from him than from any official spokesman.

There is a reverse to the coin. It is not unknown that, in a private talk with an American official, he will let slip a piece of information and then say casually, "If you run into Burchett and want to tell him that, it's all right." It works both ways, you see.

It works both ways in other matters, too. If a non-Communist correspondent wants to get into one of the forbidden places of the Communist world—like North Vietnam, to put no finer point upon it—he works through or with one of this special breed of journalists. Muller was the one who had been picked to accompany me. The North Vietnamese knew him and they trusted him to tell me nothing important and to film things mainly from their point of view. We—IBS, that is —also knew him as someone with good contacts in Hanoi, and as a professional cameraman whom we could trust to produce usable film whose propaganda aspects I could balance with my commentary when I got out. Incidentally, we paid him very well.

So I understood Muller's role and what I might expect to get out of him and what I might not. It was no part of his job to produce any warnings about bugs or about the special knowledge of Mr. Ngo Xuan. Therefore, I knew that he couldn't be what he seemed and probably had been got at by Pfeiffer. What I couldn't figure out, though, was how the CIA had enlisted him. He looked embarrassed when I asked him.

"I am getting old, Bill, and tired. I have not had such a pleasant life, you know. After the war the West Germans took away my passport, so I cannot go where I want to go. I have lived in Mexico, Russia, China for a while, Bulgaria, Cuba and other places like that, but not in the West. I had my work to do and I did not miss it for a long time—but now I do. I want to give this up and go home."

"What did the CIA do? Offer to get you a passport?"

"Yes. You see, in my special position I have come to know some men from the CIA. It is natural. When I come out of a place like North Korea where they do not have many people, they arrange to make my acquaintance and they ask me questions. I do not tell them what they should not know, of course, and I report that I have been contacted and what was said. It is interesting for the North Koreans to find out what the Americans want to know. Anyway, I have these friends in the CIA, and one day one of them came to me and said he knew I would like my passport back and made me a proposition."

"Pfeiffer?" I asked.

"No, no, not Pfeiffer. He is such a crook, I did not suspect him of being an agent. It was another man. He said that if I did this one safe job for them—help you get Nguyen Van Thanh out of the country—he would get me a German passport and enough money to retire. I thought about it a long time. Then I said if it was really safe and no one would ever know, I would do it. That was when I was sent to Pfeiffer."

"Are you still a Communist, Muller?"

"I guess so. I still believe in it. But I have spent too much time with them, and I do not like many of them personally any more. But I have done so much for them for so many years that I think they would let me retire from active duty. I will be glad to go to some quiet place where everybody is not also a Comrade. Then, perhaps, I will again like better the ones who are."

I could understand now how they had got to Muller. I may even have sympathized a little, but not much. He had sold out. He was betraying everything he said he still believed in, not because he had had a change of heart but for money and comfort and personal convenience.

"You certainly took your time letting me know where you stood," I said.

"It was Pfeiffer's instructions. I was to tell you only when things became serious. Now they are very serious, I think."

"I think so, too. Damned serious."

"How did it go with Ngo Xuan this morning?"

"Pretty well, I think. As far as it went. As you warned me, he knows more than I thought. He doesn't seem to have put it all together, though. I think he wants to give me the benefit of the doubt, but I seem to be on a kind of probation until they make up their minds." I started to give him a blow-by-blow account of my talk with Ngo Xuan.

Muller interrupted to warn me that we must not appear to be plotting. He was right. So, from then on, while we walked around the lake, I would walk up to a propaganda poster, make a viewfinder out of my fingers, step back, mark a camera position and generally go through a pantomime of a big director, while I told him what Ngo Xuan had said.

"Did he mention me? Do you think he suspects me?" Muller asked.

"No, I don't think he suspects you at all. He seems to trust you. For instance, he won't let me interview Nguyen Van Thanh or anyone else on camera now, but he said it would be all right for you to film around town this afternoon."

"Yes, that sounds like a good sign. You are seeing Nguyen Van Thanh this afternoon?"

"Yes."

"I have heard from Pfeiffer. At a certain hour sometimes he sends me a very brief message in code. I can only transmit to him in the gravest emergency. I have never done so. Last night there was a message, but I do not understand it."

"What did he say?"

"He said, 'Try the Ben Hai Bridge.' Does that mean anything to you?"

I thought for a moment.

"I know the bridge," I said. "I've done stories from there. It's across the river that marks the Demilitarized Zone. On the 17th Parallel. It's where they used to send released prisoners across and that sort of thing. But that's all over. They couldn't mean that we should try to get Nguyen Van Thanh across there now. Each side mounts guard at its own end. They floodlight it at night. It's as public a place as you could think of. I can't imagine why he chose it. It's a crazy idea. I don't get it."

"Neither do I, but that is what he said."

I told him I'd have to think about it.

If it meant anything, Pfeiffer's suggestion of the Ben Hai Bridge must be connected with the President's proposal. Part of that deal was to get the North Vietnamese to respect the Demilitarized Zone. The Ben Hai Bridge was in the Demilitarized Zone. Somewhere in Pfeiffer's labyrinthine mind there must be a connection, but for the life of me I couldn't see it. Even if the North Vietnamese bought the package, which I doubted, it would be months before they agreed and months more before they opened up the DMZ. It didn't make any sense at all.

"I have done some detective work," said Muller importantly. "I know who was behind the beating up you got last night. Phan Boi Chau."

"I figured that out myself from what Ngo Xuan told me," and, just to forestall him, I added, "I know who the other man in the triangle is, too."

"Nguyen Van Thanh."

"I'm afraid so. It's going to make things more difficult. Our Charlie has an instinct for getting into trouble."

"Yes, it is so."

But I knew the problem went deeper than Charlie, and I wanted to get back to the hotel to think it out. Muller had one suggestion as we walked back to the car.

D.—10

"I think it's a good idea, Bill, if you will continue to act as though you can't stand me. It will throw them off the smell. You have been very convincing up to now."

"It's not hard, Muller. It's not hard."

Charlie was at the hotel bar, but, for once, she was not surrounded by the Noah's Ark Preprandial Drinking and Gossip Society. She was perched at one end, showing a lot of leg. The correspondents were clustered at the other end, covertly taking it in from a distance. I ordered a double vodka and managed to extract a piece of gray ice from the gap-toothed barmaid. The correspondents made way for me, but none of them said hello.

"Let's sit down at a table," I told Charlie. "We'll be more comfortable."

"Nobody will pay any attention to me today," Charlie said. "I don't like it."

I couldn't help laughing out loud. "Of course, you don't like it. You aren't used to it."

"It's not just that."

"I know it isn't, and I don't like it either. It means that after what happened last night, they smell trouble on us. We're bad news."

"Do they think it's going to happen again?"

"I hope not, but foreigners don't get beaten up for nothing in Hanoi. There's too much discipline here. It means there's something the matter with us. My colleagues over there don't know what it is, but, whatever is the matter, they don't want any of it to rub off on them. As a matter of fact," I said sternly, "we are in trouble, thanks to you."

"But, Bill," she said plaintively, "what have I done?"

I was deciding how much I ought to tell her when Jacques Delange, the correspondent of _Le Monde_, detached himself from the Noah's Ark and came over. He was in on a short assignment, as I was, and probably thought he had less to lose than the others by being seen with us. He was very handsome, which made Charlie perk up, and she gave him a big hello. He didn't sit down, however, but stayed on his feet beside the table.

"I heard about your fracas last night," he said to me. "Phan Boi Chau told me this morning."

"Did he, now? Does he have any idea who was behind it?"

"He thinks it may have been a matter of sex. You know, the beautiful Western girl who arouses ungovernable passion in the breast of the virile Oriental."

"I have just heard the same theory from Ngo Xuan," I said. "It's those Goddamned clothes she wears."

Delange looked at Charlie's dress, what there was of it, raised his glass in salute and sauntered back to the others at the bar.

"What's the matter with my clothes?" Charlie said defiantly. She was wearing her uniform, one of those little embroidered shifts that you see in every resort town in Mexico. She must have brought a dozen of them. They not only show a lot of uncovered flesh, but they make it clear that what's underneath is uncovered, too.

"They do not exactly resemble the traditional Vietnamese costume," I said, with what I hoped was heavy irony.

"They do, too," she said triumphantly. "The embroidery from Oaxaca has many affinities with the work done by the Moi tribes in the Highlands here. Vietnamese scholars are fascinated by my clothes."

"Oh, come off it, Charlie. Don't try to be intellectual with me. You know damned well that isn't why they're fascinated by your clothes, and it isn't why you wear them either. Let's go in and have lunch."

I was angry with her. Not about the clothes. About the whole thing. I didn't say much while we were eating our soup. Muller, who was already at the table, had sense enough to keep his mouth shut.

"Charlie," I said finally, "you have a great talent for making friends, don't you?"

"Thank you."

"For instance, Phan Boi Chau is a friend of yours, isn't he?"

"I've seen him a few times."

"Well, it seems to be the general impression that it's your friend 'Boy,' or your boy friend, or whatever he is, who got us beaten up last night."

"Oh, Bill, I can't believe it. Why would he do that?"

"One theory is that he was jealous of another friend of yours, Nguyen Van Thanh."

"That can't be it. He just wouldn't do a thing like that out of spite."

As a matter of fact, it didn't ring true to me either. The more I thought about it, the less likely it seemed to me that revenge or jealousy had anything to do with what had happened to me. If we had been in Sicily, maybe, but the Vietnamese are about four times as subtle as the Mafia. My guess was that it was meant as a warning and that the warning had to do with Nguyen Van Thanh. I couldn't say that to Charlie, though. I couldn't really stay cross with her either.

"Well, someone was trying to tell us something," I said. "So let's be more careful from now on. Also, our former friends of the press who are now avoiding us are not so far wrong. We are not in good odor at City Hall." I was breaking it to her gently, and I wasn't going to tell her more than she needed to know.

Charlie was shocked. "But what have we done? We haven't done anything."

"I know, but they seem to think it peculiar that we both started out in Puerto Secreto and ended up in Hanoi. They suspect we're up to no good. They think we're in cahoots."

"Poor Bill," said Charlie, and the tears welled up. "I've done nothing but cause you trouble. I wish I'd never come."

"It's too late to go into that now, and for God's sake, don't cry. It's not that bad, but I'm going to take you under my wing from now on. You're going to move into the Thong Nhat here. There will be a room for you. I've sprung you from the hospital. From now on you're going to be working for me."

"Very good," said Muller. "We'll make a sound man out of her. She'll look pretty with those earphones on her head. You should see some of the sound men I've had. They weren't pretty and they didn't know any more about sound than she does either."

"All right, we'll make her a sound man. Charlie, you're part of the crew now. No more bike rides at night. No more friends either. You stick with me. Get it?"

"That's all I want to do, Bill." And she sounded as though she meant it.

There was one more thing I had to say to her, and I couldn't think of any subtle way to put it.

"Charlie, don't ask me any questions about this, but never, under any circumstances, repeat to anyone your first conversation with Nguyen Van Thanh about Uncle Sam."

Both Charlie and Muller looked at me. Neither of them had what you would call a computer brain, but I could almost see the little lights flashing as the circuits connected and they both put things together. I was afraid I'd given too much away, but I had to warn her. Neither of them spoke, but Charlie looked frightened for the first time since they beat us up.

"Okay," I said as gaily as I could, "that's the lesson for today. Let us not be downcast, but, rather, present a serene and smiling countenance to the outside world. All will be well. As a demonstration of my own sangfroid, I am going up to take a nap. Muller, you tell the driver to take Charlie to the hospital. Charlie, you pack up your anthropologically fascinating collection of Mexican embroidery, say good-bye to the kids and move into the hotel."

I got up, still a little stiffly, I noticed, and made my way through the dining room. Everyone looked at me, but no one spoke. So I made a big point of saying hello to everyone I recognized. I was damned if I would let them see how frightened and discouraged I was.

I really meant to take a nap, but I couldn't. The wheels kept turning. I wondered whether Ngo Xuan knew more than he had told me. It was perfectly possible that he knew everything. I remembered the South Vietnamese diplomat who had met me at the airport in Paris. South Vietnamese security was as full of holes as a colander. The North undoubtedly had agents in the South's Paris Mission. But if Hanoi had known about me, they wouldn't have let me get farther than Phnom Penh. If Ngo Xuan knew, he wouldn't have let me near Nguyen Van Thanh. Ngo Xuan must still be in the dark.

But so was I. There had been nothing from Pfeiffer except a cryptic reference to the Ben Hai Bridge. It was beyond me. Could he really mean that was the escape route? There must be a dozen ways of getting someone out of North Vietnam. Over the mountains to Laos. By car. By plane. By helicopter. By boat. But you couldn't just walk a North Vietnamese cabinet minister across the Ben Hai Bridge. It would take a regiment to secure the thing, in the first place. And that would tear the already shredded Geneva Agreements into such small pieces they could never put them back together again. We kept demanding in Paris that the other side respect the DMZ the way we did. And now they wanted me to smuggle a high-grade defector across it. It really just didn't make sense.

Pretty soon, there was another discreet, tentative knock on the door. Mr. Leng. I had come to recognize his hand. It was time to meet Nguyen Van Thanh. I was slightly surprised to find I was looking forward to it.

14

The enemy of good reporting is preconception. We always seek to defend a prior notion and thus waste a great deal of time replacing it with something closer to the facts. One trains oneself not to begin anything with a fixed idea and to banish from the mind any premature impressions that may have taken shape unbidden.

I was surprised, therefore, to find that Nguyen Van Thanh was precisely as I had somehow allowed myself to imagine him to be. I was not aware that I had formed any mental image of him, but I would have recognized him anywhere. I even felt that we had met before. He was, of course, the man in my dream.

He looked younger than his age and carried himself with great self-confidence. He was slightly above middle height, on the tall side for a Vietnamese. His features were regular, his skin a light golden brown. His eyes were intelligent and even held a glint of humor, in itself the mark of a Southerner; in the North they prize gravity above wit. He had the air of a man who knows that he is good at his job, perhaps even a touch of arrogance.

I liked him at once and felt he liked me. I fear I shook his hand as warmly as I would that of an old acquaintance. That was neither good manners nor good policy. No one, even in retrospect, should be able to think they sensed anything more between us than his official duty to impart official information to me and mine to receive it.

As for Nguyen Van Thanh, he could not have been more formal or correct. Speaking in Vietnamese through the interpreter, he asked, as usual, whether I was enjoying my stay in Hanoi. I replied, as usual, that I was finding it very interesting. He inquired after my health, whether I was comfortable at the Thong Nhat, whom I had seen and so forth. I made the correct appreciative replies.

It was a very odd feeling to mince through the prescribed steps of the conversational minuet with this man for whom I had come so far to help betray his country and aid my own. Everything was all so normal and at arm's length. Of course, it could not be otherwise. He could not tip me a wink or give me a secret sign. I knew that, but I am not good at acting one way and thinking another—it is why I always lose at poker— and this man's life and mine had become inextricably intertwined. In some real sense, we held each other's lives in our hands. It did not seem to me that I was tense, but I had to stifle an impulse to laugh out loud. That is, of course, a sign of tension.

Nguyen Van Thanh unhurriedly wound up the courtesies and announced that he would now give the briefing he had prepared for me. I said I looked forward to it since it was my hope to make the work of his department an important part of my report on my visit to North Vietnam. I opened my notebook, and he took up his briefing papers.

"Properly to understand the enormous task of reconstruction which confronts the Democratic Republic of Vietnam," he commenced in a matter-of-fact voice, pausing every few sentences for the interpreter to translate, "you must be made aware of the extent of the destruction caused by the cruel and unprovoked aggression of the U.S. imperialists. The Vietnamese people, who are confronting that vicious and crafty aggressor, live on a stretch of land not larger than one-twentieth of the United States, with a population about one-sixth of the latter's. For the last twenty years this mainly agricultural country has been subjected to the ravages of war and latterly to a campaign of the systematic destruction of its very means of existence.

"Betraying such a sinister design, Curtis LeMay, ex-U.S. Air Force Chief of Staff, threatened completely to destroy North Vietnam by bombing it back into the Stone Age. But you did not succeed," he added, looking up from his papers and evidently ad-libbing. "The heroic efforts of an entire people frustrated the most fiendish instruments of destruction you were able to bring against us."

I scribbled away, as I knew I was supposed to do, but with a growing sense of surrealism. The man who was saying all this was the man I was to take out of North Vietnam. Was it an act? Perhaps not. Perhaps he had changed his mind. Perhaps Bailey and Pfeiffer had the wrong information. Maybe I could just stall until the next ICC flight and then they would throw Charlie and me out. Meanwhile, though, there was nothing to do but play out this little scene with Nguyen Van Thanh.

". . . medical installations," the interpreter was saying, "one of the prime targets of fierce, systematic and continuous U.S. attacks. According to still incomplete figures, 112 medical installations have been raided, some for dozens of times."

Nguyen Van Thanh was studying me while the interpreter translated. I wondered what he made of me. Probably that I was a very unlikely fellow to have been sent to him. Perhaps he was thinking he ought to call the whole thing off. I wanted to tell him the same idea had occurred to me.

"Attacks against agriculture," said the interpreter. "There are seventeen provinces in North Vietnam protected by dikes, and the dikes of all those seventeen provinces have been attacked. Most barbarous are the attacks that were concentrated during the high-tide season running from June to September."

I didn't believe that. If we had really gone after the dikes, half the damned country would still be under water. I tuned out the interpreter and looked at Nguyen Van Thanh. He was perfectly composed, waiting for the interpreter to complete the paragraph. Why doesn't he say it himself in English? I thought. He couldn't have forgotten all he learned at Cornell. It's not etiquette, of course. They always begin in Vietnamese. It's permissible to try them later in French or even English. If they pick up the cue, the conversation may be pursued in that language. If they don't, you are stuck with the interpreter. But you always begin in Vietnamese.

"Now that you realize the magnitude of the task," the interpreter translated, "we will take up in a general way the plans which are being elaborated in my department." He went on to speak of roads, electricity, water control, whole new towns, schools, universities, a vast new plan for Hanoi.

"It will take us many years, perhaps generations," he continued, "but we have had much experience in postwar reconstruction because we have had so many wars. Our greatest resource has always been the energy and dedication of our people. Today, thanks to the success of Socialism and People's Democracy, we are in a position to employ this great national resource more efficiently."

In due course we broke for tea and, as is proper, spoke of other things.

"We have something in common, Mr. Minister," I said.

He raised his eyebrows in inquiry.

"I believe you studied at Cornell University. So did I. Did you enjoy your stay in Ithaca?"

He replied through the interpreter that he had found it very interesting—he was using my lines now—and asked how matters were at Cornell now. I described the student disturbances there and elsewhere.

"The Minister says he is aware of these events," said the interpreter. "They are an outgrowth of popular unrest caused by opposition to the criminal acts of the U.S. imperialists in Vietnam. He was not aware that they had spread to the mountains overlooking the Sea of Cayuga."

"Far above Cayuga's waters," said Nguyen Van Thanh with a smile. It was the first time he had spoken in English.

"I hope, Mr. Minister, that you will choose some of the projects you have already under way as those we might film in order to show people in the United States what you are doing." I spoke in English, but again he replied, through the interpreter, in Vietnamese.

"There are many. I will consider the matter. They should be both important and pictorial, I assume. I will give you a list when we meet again."

"Perhaps tomorrow?"

"Yes, tomorrow. Why not?"

"Is there, by any chance, something here in Hanoi itself that we might start on at once? I want to keep my cameraman occupied."

He thought a moment. "There is the new park. You would find that very beautiful."

I looked at Mr. Leng. "Do you think I might look at it when we leave here?"

"I will take you myself," said Nguyen Van Thanh. "We can go now. I will continue my briefing when we meet tomorrow."

The park stretched around two lakes. It was a little seedy-looking now, but you could see that one day it might indeed be beautiful. We went in under an ornamental arch on which was spelled out "THONG NHAT." Nguyen Van Thanh began a formal speech in Vietnamese, which the interpreter translated.

"Like your hotel, this park is called Thong Nhat—'Reunification.' It symbolizes the urgent wish in every Vietnamese heart that our nation will be one again, that the imperialist aggressors will be driven from our soil and that the sacred task which history has given us to reunite our people will be successfully accomplished. Look at this flowerbed: the plants spell out the names 'HANOI—HUÉ—SAIGON,' the three sister cities which will one day be joined again in love and common purpose. That is the Vietnamese destiny, and no outside interference can divert it.

"So powerful is this spirit of unity among my countrymen, so deep is our sympathy for the torment of our brothers in the South, groaning under imperialist domination, that even amid the stress and preoccupation of war we have built this park. Everyone freely contributed his labor. President Ho Chi Minh himself planted several trees when the park was first begun. I myself have spent many hours of work here."

"And I, too," the interpreter added. "All of us."

. Nguyen Van Thanh then spoke to the interpreter in rapid Vietnamese.

"The Minister is going to do you the honor of conducting you through the park personally," the interpreter told me. "He understands you speak enough French to understand his explanations. We will stay here."

When the two of us were out of earshot, Nguyen Van Thanh said, in almost perfect English, "Now we can talk. How did you like my speech just now?"

"It was as good a statement of your government's official line as I have heard."

"I believe it, you know. Or almost all of it."

That did not sound like a defector, but it was a very Vietnamese way of broaching the subject. The Vietnamese, both North and South, delight in paradox, puns, wordplay and every form of verbal obfuscation. It is a legacy from their thousand years of Chinese occupation, during which, like the African slaves in the United States, they developed as a matter of survival a special kind of oblique discourse designed to confuse the master race. However, if they wish to be candid, they can suddenly become as straightforward as they had previously been cryptic. It seemed to me that Nguyen Van Thanh must want to be candid.

"I am sure you believe what you have told me, Mr. Minister," I said. "Why should I doubt it? But I was informed before I arrived here that you might wish to discuss with me other matters than postwar reconstruction." (It was a gambit that any Vietnamese would have disdained as being unconscionably blunt, but it worked.)

"I am told I can trust you," he said without further preamble. "I am told that Uncle Sam trusts you."

"Yes," I said, conjuring up the absurd picture of Charlie gushing it all out at some solemn North Vietnamese gathering. "You can trust me and so does Uncle Sam."

"I had suggested that, under certain circumstances . . ." He struggled between ellipsis and frankness, and settled for frankness. "I wanted to tell a responsible American that I am willing to leave North Vietnam and return to the South." It was an effort for him to say it so directly.

I nodded, to his great relief. He clearly felt he was taking an enormous risk speaking so bluntly to a stranger, however well recommended.

"I was quite prepared to hear you say that," I reassured him.

"It has not been an easy decision," he said, "but I am clear in my mind about it now. Since I have decided, I would be grateful if you would tell your friends as soon as possible and ask them to make the necessary arrangements. We should not wait too long. I have enemies here, and my position could become difficult."

It took a moment for it to register that he apparently did not know I was supposed to do anything more than receive a message from him. If I interpreted him correctly, he was not aware that I was to be the agent of his escape. It was curious that the CIA would go to such lengths to recruit me and then not tell him, but that was what it sounded like.

"Were you told anything else about me," I asked cautiously, "besides the Uncle Sam trusting me part?"

"No, just that." He smiled. "Oh, Miss O'Brien told me how famous you are, and how handsome, and how much she loves you, but nothing else important."

I didn't quite know how to play this. If no one had told him I was supposed to help engineer his departure, was I supposed to tell him? I hardly thought so. Somehow, the team of Muller, Charlie and me masquerading as dauntless, efficient agents of the all-powerful CIA did not seem calculated to inspire confidence in a potential defector. It would be better to wait for reinforcements, or a definite plan, or something more than a one-liner about the Ben Hai Bridge, before I told him we were in this thing together. Meanwhile, I tried to think of what a real secret agent would say if his only mission was to receive a message from this earnest Vietnamese walking beside me. A real agent would want to be convinced; he would take nothing for granted.

"Why do you want to go to the South, Mr. Nguyen Van Thanh?" I asked. "My friends will want to know."

"They already know I am not in sympathy with the government of North Vietnam. That is the important thing, is it not?"

"Yes, but they are interested in your motivation."

"Since you are an American, I suppose you want me to say that I am disillusioned with Communism. That happens to be true, but it also happens to be largely irrelevant. I am not greatly concerned with labels, as long as they do not interfere with what needs to be done. That is why I joined the Communist Party during our war against the French; it was doing what needed to be done. Since then—well—for all those years before he died Ho Chi Minh was a very old man, surrounded by other old men. They were together for a very long time and they became old-fashioned and doctrinaire. The old-timers still want to build a doctrinaire Communist state at any cost, and the cost has become too high. As for me, I don't care what you call the system; I just want it to work. I am like Dubcek in Czechoslovakia. But there is no room for a Dubcek here."

"Do you want to be a Dubcek in the South?" I asked.

"I am a Southerner," he said.

"I know, but there are many other Southerners here who hold important posts."

"Mr. Benson, you have been in both parts of my country now. Which do you like best, the North or the South?"

"The South," I said at once. "For all its faults, it is so much gayer, more free, more alive than the North. I must say, though, that if I were Vietnamese, I might prefer the more effective government in the North, however authoritarian, to the weak and divided one in the South. People need leadership in wartime, and there's not much of it in the South. Still, I personally find the South more agreeable."

"So do I," said Nguyen Van Thanh, "although I am not proposing to return out of anything so vulgar as nostalgia. You put your finger on the problem when you spoke of the inadequacy of the present regime in Saigon. They do not know how to govern. This is a very ancient fault of my people: Throughout our history we Vietnamese have been so busy fighting that we never mastered the arts of government. The only hope for the South is a strong and effective government to harness the energies and resources of the land to productive purposes. I can help them."

Nguyen Van Thanh was saying almost exactly the same thing that Bui Van had said to me on the long flight from Paris. Weak government is the historic curse of Vietnam. Of course, he and Bui Van had different ideas of what kind of strong government South Vietnam should have. Bui Van had argued that the proper course was to strengthen the only government they had. Nguyen Van Thanh seemed to want to start afresh. I was going to ask him to spell that out, but he had started into the kind of historical analysis the Vietnamese love so much.

He was telling of Vietnam's millennium of Chinese rule, and how they had finally shaken off the Chinese yoke, repelled the Mongol hordes and driven out the armies of the warlike Ming Dynasty. Then, freed from the burden of China, though not its example, the Vietnamese became an expansionist people themselves and embarked upon their Great March South, the Vietnamese equivalent of the American conquest of the West.

He told how, led by geography, their migration funneled by the mountains, the Vietnamese expanded South along the coastal plain. They swept aside those who stood in their way as ruthlessly as the Americans swept aside the Indians. The Vietnamese destroyed the great Cham nation, pushed the Khmer out of the Mekong Delta and, by the middle of the eighteenth century, stood on the tip of the Camau Peninsula.

I was beginning to wonder when he would get back to his defection, but Nguyen Van Thanh would not be stopped.

"I am making a point," he said when I tried to interrupt him, "a crucial point. If you want to understand why I wish to cast my lot with the South, you must understand what I am telling you. Everything in modern Vietnamese history follows from the basic fact of the Great March South. It explains why my country is divided and why it has proved so difficult to govern."

I let him go on. It was a very big lake we were walking around, and there was plenty of time. A ray of sun came out. The flowers brightened, a pair of lovers held each other more closely, a pair of ducks rustled their feathers, and Nguyen Van Thanh talked on.

"You see," he said, "as long as my people were huddled

around the Red River Delta here in the North, the administrative techniques we inherited from the Chinese were adequate—the old mandarin system. Then we moved south, but while we could stretch the country, we couldn't stretch the institutions. Hanoi was too far away. There weren't enough administrators. Communications weren't good enough. The writ of the central government did not run to the frontier, and the inevitable happened. The nation was divided. Vietnam entered upon a period of four hundred years of civil war, a period which has not yet ended. This present war is part of the same series, altered only slightly by colonialist intervention."

Nguyen Van Thanh was talking about a very different war than most Americans thought of. To us, it had seemed at first a war about Communism and China, which happened, by geographical and political accident, to take place in Vietnam. Then it had become a war for American prestige and the sanctity of American commitments. By now we were willing to measure our prestige by other yardsticks; we were fighting in Vietnam for a decent way out. It was a curious thing, and the source of much disaffection, that for most Americans the war had never been really about Vietnam.

For Nguyen Van Thanh it had never been about anything else. He saw it as part of a four-hundred-year-old struggle for the soul of Vietnam, fought largely by Vietnamese, occasionally helped or hindered by outside powers. He thought in terms of centuries. Americans, whose longest war had never lasted more than a few years, found a few years in Vietnam endless. But in Nguyen Van Thanh's view, the whole vast expenditure of American lives and effort in Vietnam would prove to be no more than an incident in the long and troubled political evolution of his country.

On the face of it, it would appear that tiny, backward North Vietnam had stood off the mighty panoply ranged by the United States in support of South Vietnam. Yet Nguyen

Van Thanh, at the very nadir of Southern fortunes, had elected to abandon the North and take up the cause of the South. He was not an adventurer, nor did he appear quixotic.

"Who won those civil wars?" I asked him. I knew the answer, but I hoped it would bring him back to his own case.

"The South," he said. "The South won them all."

"And you must think that the South will win this one."

"I do," he said. "You are grasping my point. In the long run the South will win. It is inevitable. I speak not only as a patriot, but as a professional economist. When Vietnam is reunified, as it must be, the South will become the dominant partner. Every factor of history, geography and economics points to this. It may or may not happen in my lifetime, but as a patriot I would like to live to see it. That is why I wish to help them in the South."

It was not a point that you hear very often, even in South Vietnam. As in most countries, the North Vietnamese are looked on as go-getters, those from the center of Vietnam as the politicians, and the Southerners are regarded as indolent rustics. Hanoi is the ancient capital, Saigon the upstart metropolis. In our day, at least, the North had proved itself in war, while the South floundered in disunity. The cards of the future seemed stacked in favor of the North.

Nguyen Van Thanh laughed at that. "You Americans," he said. "You are prisoners of your own frustrations. You have come to look upon your clients in the South with contempt, while you make giants of those in the North. It is how you explain your own failures, by blaming your allies and magnifying the genius of your enemies."

"You must admit," I said, "that in the American experience the North has had the better of it so far."

"Certainly, but it is a matter of government, not economics or national character. From an economic point of view the South has all the advantages. It is not overpopulated, like the North; there are still wide-open spaces. The land is richer. You Americans will leave the people with a whole modern system of ports, airfields, communications and utilities. You will leave them with many new skills and an understanding of modern technology. Here in the North everything is worn-out, patched together and old-fashioned. Not only the industrial base is out of date, but the economic and financial thinking of those who rule us is hidebound and a generation behind the times. Believe me, it is my business to know these things. The South will emerge from this war stronger economically, if not politically. It is there that the future of the nation will lie in time of peace."

I thought of that puzzling, beautiful country I had never known in time of peace. It was the same country as this one in the North and the same people, yet there was a difference. Whether the difference went back as far as the Great March South, or only as far back as the Vietminh, Nguyen Van Thanh would know better than I. I only knew that South Vietnam touched me in the same way that Mexico had touched me, and I would like it to have such peace as it was able to sustain for as long as it could sustain it. A dominant role in a reunited Vietnam was something else again.

"When I was in your country, Mr. Benson," said Nguyen Van Thanh, "I came to the conclusion that the source of its strength lies no longer in the Eastern cradles of your history, but may be found in the newer and exuberant West. Boston and Philadelphia may be mirrors of the past, but Los Angeles is the mirror of the future. So in my own country: Hanoi will be its Boston, Saigon its Los Angeles. That this will happen one day, I have no doubt. Whether it will happen normally and without further bloodshed depends on the ability of South Vietnam to govern itself effectively in the difficult days of transition."

"As effectively as North Vietnam is governed," I offered.

"Precisely. We have learned something about governing

Vietnam in the North. That was Ho Chi Minh's great achievement. He will be remembered not as an ideologue but as the man who taught us to govern ourselves. He will also be remembered as one in the long line of those who have liberated us from foreign invaders, but that would have happened anyway. His historic accomplishment was that he liberated us from our own antique ideas of government. What is necessary now is to transplant to the South this new capacity to govern without also transplanting the Communist trappings in which it is clothed."

"If you feel this way, Mr. Nguyen Van Thanh, why do you want to defect to the government side in South Vietnam? Why don't you offer your services to the National Liberation Front? Your old sponsor, Pham Hung, is there. He would welcome you with open arms."

"Yes, Pham Hung is there, but if I were to join him, it would only be to leave him to go to the other side. My honor would not permit that. I owe him too much. However, the National Liberation Front can never be the instrument of Southern salvation. It is too heavily mortgaged to the North. It will make the same mistakes that have been made here. The baggage of Communism is too heavy for the South to carry, just as the baggage of the Chinese mandarin system was too heavy."

"Then what makes you think the present government of South Vietnam will prove a responsible alternative?" I asked. "It carries its own baggage of corruption, inefficiency and disunity."

"Oh, I'm not talking about the present government. The present government will not survive the peace. I am thinking about the next government, and the government after that. I can play a part. I can help them. They will need my help."

"Are you quite sure they will want it?" I asked. I was thinking of Bui Van on the plane to Athens. The last thing.

those he represented would want would be to get any help from Nguyen Van Thanh. "The power structure in South Vietnam has many vested interests in the status quo. They are likely to be hostile both to you and to your ideas."

"But the United States will be behind me," he said with surprise. "Having been responsible for my arrival, the United States will support me with its great influence in South Vietnam."

I shook my head. That was exactly what Bui Van intended to prevent. "The leaders of South Vietnam are not such puppets as they may appear to be in Hanoi. The United States does not control them as completely as you seem to think. Sometimes I wonder whether it controls them any more than the Russians or the Chinese control the leaders in Hanoi. If you get to the South, you will find many obstacles in your way."

"Then I will surmount them," he said cheerfully. "But first I must get there. I count on you, Mr. Benson, to tell your friends that I am ready to leave as soon as possible."

"I will tell them that."

"Do you think it will be soon?"

"It is my impression," I said carefully, "that they would like to get you out of here as soon as possible but that they have not yet fixed upon the method."

Nguyen Van Thanh seemed keyed up. "Please emphasize the need for haste. I will tell you frankly that I am getting a little nervous. In my position one becomes sensitive to very small changes in the atmosphere. I have noticed certain differences in the behavior of some of my colleagues toward me that are disturbing. It may only be that I am once more in disfavor for speaking too frankly. I hope that is all it is."

"You haven't spoken frankly to anyone else about wanting to defect, have you? If so, you had better tell me at once."

"Of course not. I have spoken frankly to no one about leaving the country. Not directly, that is. However, I confess that I have not always been discreet in pressing my points. It is possible that in contrasting the advantages of the South with our situation here in the North, I caused some of my opponents to suspect my interest in joining the South. You would not credit the amount of suspicion that has existed among us since the death of Ho Chi Minh. However, it would only be a guess. I have mentioned it directly to no one."

Nguyen Van Thanh stopped short and looked at me. "To no one," he repeated, "except the man to whom I confided my wish to speak directly with an American. He would know why I wanted to see an American. Do you think *he* could have betrayed me? He is not even a Vietnamese, and he is my friend. Long ago he told me he had undertaken missions for the Americans in search of peace. He has told me since then that he is still in touch with them. We have often discussed it, and it was this that gave me the idea of approaching you through him. Could he have betrayed me?"

The possibility of betrayal had been troubling me ever since I left Paris. Nguyen Van Thanh's fears only confirmed my own. I told him so.

"I don't even know the man you're talking about, but I know this: if he has betrayed you, he has also betrayed me, and that would explain a great many things."

I described Ngo Xuan's frank suspicions of both me and Charlie, and the links with the CIA they had uncovered. I spread out the whole pattern of suspicion and how often his own name had cropped up in the ambiguous hints that had been dropped about my secret purposes in Hanoi.

"For instance," I said, "last night Miss O'Brien and I were attacked and beaten in the street. When I made a formal protest, Ngo Xuan indicated that it was due to a rivalry over Miss O'Brien between two men who could only be you and Phan Boi Chau. Do you know anything about that?"

"No, I have not been informed." He was clearly startled and upset. "It is one of those changes in atmosphere I mentioned. A month ago I would have been told of such a thing at once, and now they hide these matters from me. I am very sorry to hear it for your sake—and I am more worried than ever. Whatever was behind that encounter, I can assure you it had nothing to do with any competition for Miss O'Brien, attractive as she is. She does not love me, nor I her, and even if she did, Phan Boi Chau would never retaliate in such a way. It is not his style. He is too subtle and too controlled for that. I do not doubt that he was behind it, though, and I suspect it has something to do with your intelligence connections and quite possibly something to do with me. That makes it worse. He is an enemy of mine. We do not agree on policy, nor do we like each other personally. He is quite unscrupulous. He may have arranged this thing to precipitate action against both of us."

His alarm was contagious. The net was tightening, no doubt about that. Panic has a taste, and I could taste it as I thought of what might happen to us if the net was sprung. But panic is a poor guide. I must not let myself follow it. I took a deep breath and told myself the question was not what would happen to us if we were exposed, but why we had not already been exposed. This more reasoned version of the question prompted a less alarming and obvious answer: they still did not know the real reason I had come to Hanoi.

"It may not be as bad as you think," I told Nguyen Van Thanh. "They may suspect you of being a dissident and me of being a spy, but they do not seem to have connected us yet. You are almost the only person in authority I am still allowed to see. Ngo Xuan has put the Army off limits, other ministers, anything to do with security, but he still lets me see you. He said you were not controversial. Now, would they have permitted our meeting if they suspected you of wanting to defect and me of wanting to help you by passing on your intention?"

"Who knows? Perhaps they want to lead us on, to see how

far we will go, whom else we will compromise. That is an old trick. But even if you are right and they have not yet connected us with each other, they soon will. They do not give up, these people. They will get to the bottom of it. We are in terrible danger, you and I."

He did not need to tell me that. Danger had been in the air from the beginning. Now it stalked us, and North Vietnam is a bad place to have danger on your trail; the things that might happen did not bear imagining. What would they do with spies, or defectors? Then once again I groped for reality. What did they really have to go on? Coincidence and perhaps some tip-off from the CIA's courier to Nguyen Van Thanh, that was all. We weren't caught yet.

"I don't think they know everything," I said to Nguyen Van Thanh.

"Probably not," he replied gloomily. "Not yet. But they will. It is only a matter of time. How much time I do not know. We must make the best use of whatever time we have. Obviously your friends do not know how desperate things have become. If they did, they would rescue us. Can you get a message to them?"

"I think so. A brief one."

"Then tell them it is a matter of the utmost urgency that we leave at once. They must not delay."

"But what can they do? I can send the message, but then what? How do you get out of this damned country? I've never been in such a place. Maybe you could disguise yourself, but I'm a marked man. I'm too visible. It might be best for you to disappear and make for the border alone. I'll brazen it out here."

"Hopeless. They would pick me up as quickly as they would you. If that were possible, I would have done it long ago. No, our help has to come from the outside. You must arrange it."

"But I can arrange nothing. I can only send a distress

signal, and I do not know what my friends are prepared to do. Certainly they can do nothing here in Hanoi. I have a little money. Could you bribe someone to give you a car or a boat?"

"Not now. Not if I am being watched. If I tried to bargain for an auto or even a fisherman's boat, it would be reported. I have nothing but my official transportation."

"Could we use that? Could we drive to the Laos border?"

"It would do no good. North Vietnam holds all the areas on the other side of the border. If you and I went into Laos, it would only be to deliver ourselves to the North Vietnamese Army or the Pathet Lao. However," he said suddenly, "however, we might get to the coast. I might be able to arrange an official inspection trip to some project or other of my department. An out-of-the-way place. They could meet us there and take us away."

"I don't know whether they could get to us," I said. "We would have to know exactly when we would be there. It would have to be synchronized with great precision."

"In this country such trips, if they are made at all, are synchronized with precision. That is the trouble. Our intelligence will know exactly where we are at any moment. Nevertheless, I cannot think of anything better."

Neither could I, though the hazards seemed overwhelming. "Choose a place to go that is as far south as possible," I suggested. "The closer we are to the 17th Parallel, the easier it will be for them to come and get us."

It was the 17th Parallel itself I was thinking of, and the Ben Hai Bridge across it. Pfeiffer's message about the bridge was all there was to go on. Surely, some preparations had been made there. If Nguyen Van Thanh could be got within striking distance of the bridge, there might be a chance of getting him out.

Why I didn't tell him about Pfeiffer and the bridge message then and there, I do not know. Partly because it seemed so inadequate, I suppose, and partly because I hadn't mentioned it earlier and had been silent about my own assignment to help him escape. In retrospect it was silly not to have done it because we were both in this up to our necks now, and if we got out at all, it would have to be together. I should have told him, but I didn't. I just said again that it would be a good idea to go as far south as we could.

"I agree," he said. "My department has many projects south of the 19th Parallel because the American bombing went on longer there. We might even get as far as Dong Hoi, which is almost to the Demilitarized Zone, and there are many beaches there. Shall we try?"

"Let's try. At least it will give us a head start. And it will get us out of this place. I am beginning to find Hanoi terribly depressing."

"All right then, we will try. This is what we will do: I will prepare a memorandum at once endorsing your request for filming privileges in the area so brutally devastated by American imperialist bombardment in the neighborhood of Dong Hoi. You will also have to make a formal request to that effect to Ngo Xuan at the Foreign Ministry."

That reminded me of something. "But Ngo Xuan intimated that Miss O'Brien and I might have to leave on the ICC flight next Tuesday. In that case, there won't be time."

"There is a week. That would be time enough if Ngo Xuan agrees to it. If he does not agree to it, I do not know what will happen. A week from now you and Miss O'Brien may or may not be aboard that plane—they may have other plans for you, unpleasant ones—and, as for me, if I do not leave very soon, there is no other chance for me. We must try it. You have to get a message to your friends at once."

By now I had formulated the necessary information in my own mind.

"I will tell them we may have been discovered and that we are trying to move south. There's no point in saying anything more until we know where we're going—if, indeed, we are allowed to go anywhere at all. Meanwhile, what do we do now? Avoid each other?"

"No, that would be the worst thing to do," he said, shocked by my naïveté. "I understand the mental processes of an investigation. If I were to say I was too busy to see you any more, or if you were to say that you were no longer interested in postwar reconstruction, it would only confirm their suspicions. The secret is to show no fear and behave normally. I have had much practice in this. As for you, I would accept all invitations, make all the proper calls, have drinks at the bar and go about your regular work. It would be a good idea. if you smiled a great deal."

I tried, but it didn't work. "Wouldn't the serious, preoccupied air of an earnest searcher after truth do just as well? It's more my line just now."

"No," he said. "You must smile, and you may begin now since we are approaching the others. Imagine that I have just said something amusing. Meanwhile I will tell you about this park so that you may make suitable comments when we return."

I smiled broadly as we reached the others and complimented them on the beauties of the park. They smiled back.

"If you would like to hear more about the work of my department," said Nguyen Van Thanh, "perhaps you will call on me again tomorrow morning."

"I would like that very much," I said with a smile.

15 It had now become desperately important to find Muller and get word to Pfeiffer. Back in Phnom Penh Pfeiffer had not seemed to think there was any particular urgency about removing Nguyen Van Thanh. He would have to be told that it had come down to a matter of days. There was no way of knowing what he had in mind, but "Try the Ben Hai Bridge" wasn't enough.

Muller was not in the bar, only a group of correspondents who made no move to ask me to join them. That meant they still smelled trouble. I realized I was frowning and gave them a cheery smile as I went up to Muller's room. No one locks his door at the Thong Nhat—it would be insulting to Socialist standards of honesty—so, when I got no answer to my knock, I went in. It was a cameraman's room, strewn with boxes of equipment, one of which must have contained his transmitter. It would take a real expert to know what all that junk was for, and Muller stood so well in Hanoi that it was unlikely they had put any real experts to work going through his gear. I wouldn't know how to operate the thing if I found it, so I went back to my own room to compose a letter to Ngo Xuan.

The meeting with the Minister of Postwar Reconstruction had revealed interesting film possibilities, I wrote, and I

had proposed to the Minister that we document some photo-
genic example of work in progress. Since the final phase of
the American bombardment of North Vietnam had taken
place in the area below the 19th Parallel, it would be
particularly meaningful if we were able to visit a suitable
project there. I put the request in the most matter-of-fact
terms and enclosed a copy in another envelope with an
equally matter-of-fact covering note to Nguyen Van Thanh.
I did not seal either envelope.

Ba and the driver were in the back room with the security
people. I smiled and apologized for disturbing them and
asked them to deliver the letters at once. Turning them over,
they noticed they had been left unsealed, which would save
someone the trouble of steaming them open to read before
they went off to their destination. They seemed grateful for
that and said they would run the errands at once.

The man at the desk said Muller had gone out about an
hour ago, leaving no message, so I took Nguyen Van Thanh's
advice and went into the bar for a drink, not forgetting to
fix a broad smile on my face. No one smiled back except
Charlie, who was sitting by herself again. I gave her a big,
confident buss on the cheek because I was anxious that she
think everything was all right.

"Still in Coventry, eh?" I said. "Charlie, how long has it
been since you sat alone in a bar without someone trying to
pick you up?"

"Aren't they silly!" she said contemptuously. "Well, we'll
show them. I've got us invited to a party tonight that I'll
bet they can't get into."

"Oh, Lord, let's not go anywhere tonight. It's been a tough
day. I mean I've been working hard. Let's stay here and make
an early night of it. Besides, I've got to see Muller about some
shooting plans."

"But this is a very important party, Bill. It's the official
reception for the Hungarian Day of Liberation. Everybody

will be there from the Prime Minister down. I had to wangle the invitations from a man I know in the embassy: It wasn't easy. We've got to go. And it will show all these creeps that we still mean something around here."

I was tired, nervous, and I wanted to see Muller, but Charlie had a point. If one was bid to such an affair, the natural thing would be to show up, and naturalness was our word for the day. It would demonstrate to one and all that we were not frightened and show the Noah's Ark at the bar that we were not yet beyond the pale. Anyway, Charlie liked parties, any kind of party. She might as well have a little fun before the roof fell in.

"Okay," I said, "when do we go?"

She looked at the invitation. "It says half-past seven, which means you ought to get dressed now. I'll come up with you. I don't want to sit here alone. It looks funny for a girl to be alone."

Feminine logic. It didn't occur to her that it might look funny to be going upstairs to a man's room. I showered, changed my clothes and took a Dexamyl to fortify myself for what had to be a dull occasion. Outside the hotel, the car was back from delivering my letters, and we set forth, I to beard the lions in their den and Charlie to enjoy herself. To her it was just another party, and all the way there she kept asking me whether she looked all right.

We needn't have worried. It was not exactly a glittering throng, but everyone was there, all right. The Prime Minister rather ostentatiously wore a Ho Chi Minh–style worker's suit. Nearly everyone else was dressed in the dark Western business suits which pass for formal attire in Communist countries. The ladies were in flowing *ao dai* instead of the black sateen trousers and white shirts which are the normal female uniform in Hanoi. No one seemed to be having a particularly good time.

The hall was decked out in bunting in the colors of Hungary and North Vietnam, rather like a high school gymnasium decorated for the Junior Prom, and the flags of the two countries flanked the speaker's platform, which also bore portraits of Ho Chi Minh and János Kádar. Long tables held trays of national delicacies, running largely to sausages and ham. There were also a number of bottles of wine, including several of champagne, and a great many sugary cakes and pastries. It was not precisely what one would have ordered oneself, but then this was a country at war—a fact which had already been brought to my attention in less subtle ways.

Everyone stood around rather stiffly, waiting for the formalities to begin. Everyone, that is, except Charlie, who was flitting around as though it were a Greenwich Village cocktail party. She seemed to feel the party wasn't going very well and that it was her duty to liven things up. I saw her talking to Nguyen Van Thanh and began moving to break that up when I saw that Phan Boi Chau was between us. He was the last person I wanted to run into, so I changed direction and found myself beside Ngo Xuan.

We shook hands formally, and he reached over to the table and handed me a glass of yellow wine. I sipped it. It was very sweet.

"You will need it for the toasts."

"Yes, of course," I said, wondering whether it had been a breach of etiquette to have tasted it before the ceremonies started. I was getting so jittery after what I had been through that I was sure now everything I did was wrong.

"I have good news for you," Ngo Xuan said. "In spite of the unusual circumstances surrounding your visit, it has been decided to continue with the original plan. In other words, when the government issues its official reply to the recent statement of the President of the United States, the Foreign Minister will read it for your camera. I hope you are pleased."

"I am very pleased, indeed, Monsieur le Directeur. Not only because of the opportunity to film the Foreign Minister, but because I take it your own confidence in me has been restored."

Ngo Xuan looked at me speculatively and sipped his wine. I was absurdly relieved to see him drink. It meant that was one misstep I hadn't taken.

"I wouldn't say completely restored," he said. "Our investigations are continuing. We are not at all happy about you, Mr. Benson, but you are here. Since you are here, it seems reasonable to allow you to perform such of your professional functions as do not jeopardize the security of the state. I do not think the dissemination of our official position involves a security issue."

Clearly, I wasn't out of the woods yet. My impulse was to protest my innocence again, but that would be what a guilty man would do. The impulse to defend myself stemmed from guilt, of course. What would an innocent man do? He would take his position for granted and explore the mechanics of handling the North Vietnamese reply.

"May I ask when you expect the Foreign Minister to respond to the President's proposal, Monsieur le Directeur?"

"Perhaps tomorrow or the next day. No, it will be the next day, I am sure."

"That means Thursday," I said. "I cannot get my film out until the ICC flight on the following Tuesday. I assume you will release the Foreign Minister's reply as soon as it is issued?"

"Of course. It is a matter of international importance. It will be released at once."

"Well, I don't want to bother you with my problems, Monsieur le Directeur, but you see what that means? It means my film of the Foreign Minister will not be seen on American television until the content is at least five days old. I am afraid that unless the Foreign Minister is willing to elaborate on the official statement, the film will be of historical interest only. Not that that is not also important," I added hastily.

"We have thought of that," he said with a hint of condescension. "We have handled such things before, as I am sure you are aware. You will be permitted to ask the Minister three questions to allow him to add further detail to his statement. I assure you that his answers to your questions will be as important as the original statement. After five days of world-wide speculation, you may be sure that the Foreign Minister's clarifying remarks to you will make news."

"That is just what I had hoped for. Thank you, Monsieur le Directeur."

"If you will come to my office at eight o'clock tomorrow morning, we will discuss the questions so that I may submit them to the Foreign Minister."

"I have another meeting tomorrow morning with the Minister of Postwar Reconstruction. I will arrange to postpone that. Thank you again." I had started to move off when Ngo Xuan said something which relieved me greatly.

"It goes without saying, Mr. Benson, that you and Miss O'Brien will depart on the ICC flight with your film next Tuesday."

"If that is still your wish, Monsieur le Directeur, there is nothing I can do but comply." Then, not wanting to sound brusque, for I certainly didn't feel that way, I added, "I can't thank you enough for what you have done."

Nor could I, for Ngo Xuan had just given me as welcome a reprieve as any condemned man ever got from the Governor. If I was to interview the Foreign Minister on Thursday, there was certainly not going to be enough time to get Nguyen Van Thanh to the Ben Hai Bridge or anywhere near it. Even if the wheels of North Vietnamese bureaucracy moved faster than they had shown any signs of doing and permission was granted, it was simply not possible for me to travel that far and back in that many days.

As for Nguyen Van Thanh, well, I would just have to disappoint him. He was still on the other side of the room, talking earnestly with a Slavic type in a gray suit. He caught my eye and I started over, but Charlie interrupted me.

"Bill, there's someone I want you to meet."

Nguyen Van Thanh beckoned me urgently with his head. "Can't it wait, Charlie?" I asked. "I've got something important to tell Nguyen Van Thanh."

"It's the French Ambassador, Bill. You ought to know him. *Monsieur l'Ambassadeur, je vous présente Monsieur Benson. Madame, Monsieur Benson.*"

The French Ambassador was a calm, shrewd professional of the kind in which the Quai d'Orsay specializes. His wife was a real character. She was handsome, in a careless sort of way, with unruly white hair, a deep, booming voice and the assured manner of one who has successfully gotten away with a thousand outrageous remarks.

"An American with the *Légion d'Honneur!*" she bellowed. "It is impossible. You are an impostor. I will tear it off."

"My dear," sighed the Ambassador, who was evidently used to such outbursts and guessed that I, too, was aware of the twinkle in her wild blue eyes.

"I came by it honestly, Madame," I protested. "During the war I was a premature Gaullist, and it was given to me in a fit of absent-mindedness before either the General or I had discovered the true nature of our sentiments."

"You bombed my house, you Americans! Right here in Hanoi! The bomb fell in the street outside and broke all the windows. What a shambles you made! If you had been here then, I would have killed you with my own hands, *Légion d'Honneur* or no."

There is something about the French language and French women that brings out the Cyrano de Bergerac in all of us. I bowed.

"I congratulate myself on a fortunate escape. But, believe me, dear Madame, I would have died more happily by your hand than those of others here who might have been seized with the same impulse."

"You must dine with us one evening," said the Ambassador. "It is not like Paris, but I can offer you better food than you will find anywhere else in Hanoi."

"Better wine, too," said his wife, and then shouted in her stentorian voice, "My God, we are going to have the speeches!"

The Prime Minister and the Hungarian Ambassador had mounted the platform. We all turned toward them and applauded. They applauded back. The speeches took a long time, since they had to be translated into several languages.

The Prime Minister thanked the Ambassador for the valuable assistance of Hungary in the struggle against the imperialist aggressors, which would not end until the last one was driven from the soil of Vietnam. The Ambassador told the Prime Minister that the ties of the Socialist countries would never be severed and that Hungary was proud to help in a cause whose justice was recognized throughout the world. Finally the toasts were drunk, and I started off again to find Nguyen Van Thanh.

He found me first and led me outside into a small garden. "You did not tell me!" he said angrily. "You did not tell me that *you* are empowered to take me out. That is not fair. I have confided in you. You have not confided in me. Why did you not speak frankly of what you have in mind?"

I stared at him, stupefied. He had known nothing of this earlier in the afternoon. How could he know now? Who could have told him? As far as I was aware, no one in Hanoi knew of my commitment actually to try to get him across the border except Muller. Muller must have told him.

"Who told you?" I asked.

"It does not matter. A friend. He told me you have a plan for my escape. I am, naturally, glad. But why do I hear it from someone else? Why do I not hear it from you, if you have the plan?"

"There is no plan," I said helplessly. "You did not hear it

from me because there is none. It is true that I promised to do what I could to help you get away. I was to receive further instructions. I have heard nothing. There is no plan."

"I do not believe you." He spoke softly, but his grip on my arm was hard. "You are still not telling me the truth. Why did you agree to the trip to the bombed areas farther south if you had no plan? Tell me now, is that not part of your scheme?"

"It was all I could think of. It was just as I told you. I thought that perhaps if we could get you closer to the 17th Parallel, and I let my friends know where we were, then they might find a way. But it was no more than that. Believe me, I hate to tell you this, but if an operation has been organized to get you out, I do not know of it. Moreover, even our trip below the 19th Parallel is impossible now."

· I told him of my talk with Ngo Xuan, including the fact that I was under orders to leave with the ICC on Tuesday because I had come under suspicion.

"I do not understand it," he said. "I simply do not understand it. I was told this very night that you were the man from the CIA who was to take me out. Everyone knows how powerful and well organized the CIA is, but you say you have mounted no operation. And you have the whole CIA behind you."

"A long way behind me, I am afraid."

"I do not know whether you are lying to me or not. I hope you are lying for your own reasons. There may be some things you cannot tell me. I hope that is it." He clutched my arm again. "You must take me away."

"Monsieur Benson," said a loud voice from the door, "you must not take Monsieur Nguyen Van Thanh away."

My heart stopped. Nguyen Van Thanh's hand dropped from my arm. The game is up now, I thought.

"The ladies have no one to talk to," the voice said. It was

only the French Ambassadress. "Monsieur Nguyen Van Thanh is the only amusing person here."

"Of course, Mr. Benson can take him away," said another voice. "He is a journalist in search of news." It was Phan Boi Chau. "However, he will also give him up. You take Nguyen Van Thanh, Madame, and Mr. Benson can talk to me."

I didn't want to talk to him. There were a number of things I would have liked to say, but, under the circumstances, none of them seemed politic.

I stopped Nguyen Van Thanh as he went inside. "Do we still have an appointment tomorrow, Mr. Minister?"

"Yes, of course. At what time would you like to come?"

"Would two o'clock be convenient? I must see Mr. Ngo Xuan in the morning."

He nodded and left me alone with Phan Boi Chau. They had not spoken to each other. I braced myself for this encounter. I didn't like Phan Boi Chau and had good reason to think he did not like me. As it turned out, he could not have been more charming.

"These official receptions are very boring, are they not?" he said sympathetically. "At least you do not have to carry the complete text of the speeches, as my paper does. My paper is not always light reading, I fear. Journalism is different in the West."

I conceded that there were certain differences, and we chatted for a while, agreeably enough, about other Western correspondents he had met, and a trip he had made to Paris, and places he would like to visit when the war was over. I couldn't fathom his motives for this affability. Last night he had had his thugs give me a going-over from which I was still aching. Tonight he was almost fawning. It made no sense at all.

He must have read my mind, for he suddenly said, "I am sorry about your accident last night, Mr. Benson."

"Was it an accident?" I said coolly. " I didn't think so."

"Let us say it was a mistake. A regrettable mistake." He shook his head in annoyance. "It should not have happened."

Now, what was this? An apology? I decided to say nothing and just let it lie.

"I hope you will not allow it to color your impressions of North Vietnam," he went on. "I can assure you that no one here wishes you any harm or has any doubts about the value of your visit."

This surprised me more than anything else he had said. As nearly as I could see, practically everyone I had met in Hanoi, including Phan Boi Chau, had had the gravest doubts about the value of my visit.

"Really?" I said. "I was given to understand only a few minutes ago that there were still serious reservations about me, and about Miss O'Brien as well."

Phan Boi Chau looked pained. "Please accept my word that that is all a thing of the past. No one suspects you any more. No one wishes to hinder your work. You will be quite free to do what you came here to do."

I suppose I was getting jumpy, because when anyone said something about my doing what I had come to do, it was like touching a raw nerve, even though I knew they were thinking of one thing and I was thinking of another.

"I hope so," was all I said. "It would make things easier."

"Things will be made easy for you. You will see. I promise you that."

The raw nerve jumped again.

"It's beginning to rain," he said. "Shall we go inside?"

Inside the hall, the party seemed to be breaking up. "Ah, here is someone you should meet," said Phan Boi Chau and introduced me to a man in a gray suit. I had noticed him talking to Nguyen Van Thanh earlier and remembered him because of the way his clothes were cut—neither old-fashioned enough to be up to date nor up to date enough not to look old-fashioned. They only make a suit like that in certain countries behind the Iron Curtain. I didn't catch his name, but Phan Boi Chau said he had just arrived that evening on the ICC flight.

"Do your ears still hurt?" I asked the new arrival, remembering my own descent to Hanoi.

"Yes, they do. They really must do something about the pressure in those old planes."

My ear wasn't good enough to place his accent, but, like his clothes, it came from somewhere in Eastern Europe. I was looking around for Charlie so that we could leave. The man was asking whether I was a journalist. Then he asked my opinion of the President's speech.

"I really don't know," I said, still trying to spot Charlie. "One doesn't get the full version here, but it sounded as though he was really trying to make a deal."

"I think so, too," the man said. "I think he wants it quiet along the banks of the Ben Hai River."

The nerve twitched again. Good Lord, I thought, I'm getting to the point where I read sinister meanings into everything I hear. Why shouldn't the man mention the Ben Hai River? I'd better go to bed.

I spotted Charlie at last and said good-bye to the man. It took some minutes to propel her to the door. Taking her away from a party is like taking a syringe from a drug addict. When I finally got her out, found the driver and returned to the hotel, I told her to go to her room and went to see Muller in his. He was taking his camera apart and putting it back together again, the way all cameramen do.

"Let's go for a walk," I said.

Outside, it was still trying to rain. We walked in silence until we were a safe distance from the hotel. In spite of Phan Boi Chau's assurances, I found myself looking into the shadows for potential eavesdroppers or assailants. Finally I burst out to Muller, "For Christ's sake, where have you been? I've been looking for you since afternoon."

"I was out shooting the bridge, like you asked me. What's the matter?"

"We've got to get a message to Pfeiffer. A lot has been happening. It's important."

"So? What is the message?"

"Well, first I wanted you to tell Pfeiffer that it was urgent that we move at once. Nguyen Van Thanh is in trouble. But now—" I hesitated because it was going to sound foolish— "now we must tell him we can't move at all. They have other plans for us that will make it impossible to help Nguyen Van Thanh. Pfeiffer has to know."

"You think so? I think it must be lucky you didn't find me sooner. Then we would have said one thing to Pfeiffer first and another thing next, and he would not like that. You are too excited, Bill. Maybe everything will change again tomorrow. You better tell me what has got you so excited, and then we will decide if we have anything to say to Pfeiffer."

That made me furious. What business did Muller have telling me what we would say to Pfeiffer and what we wouldn't? He hadn't talked to anyone. He couldn't know what was going on. All he did was fool around with his Goddamn camera and act wise. My impulse was strong to tell him nothing, but that was stupid; he was the only link with Pfeiffer and he had to be kept up to date.

So I began with Jack Fan Tan's fear that someone had betrayed him, possibly the CIA's courier, and his proposal that we try to get down to the DMZ as soon as possible. Certainly Pfeiffer had to know about that. Muller nodded and then asked what had caused me to change my mind.

"Because Ngo Xuan changed his mind," I told him, and then filled him in on the schedule for the Foreign Minister's announcement. "You can see it's hopeless, Muller. We could never make it even if they did let us go south because Charlie and I are being thrown out of here on the Tuesday ICC flight. I couldn't possibly get back to Hanoi by then, so we've got to tell Lou Pfeiffer to lay on a different rescue operation for Nguyen Van Thanh. He had better do it fast, if they want to get him out. He doesn't think he has much time left. Now do you understand why I wanted to send two messages?"

He didn't answer that. "I suppose you have told Nguyen Van Thanh about this?" he asked.

"Yes, and he was sore as hell. Said we had to think of something. And by the way, Muller, he was sore about something else, too, and I don't understand it either. Someone must have told him this evening that I had been assigned to help him defect. I didn't tell him when I saw him this afternoon, but he knew tonight. Someone got to him in between, and you're the only other person who knows. Did you tip him off?"

"Not me, Bill. I haven't seen him, and I wouldn't tell him if I had. If anybody here thinks I know such things, even him, I am a dead bird. The least hint and they would start on me with the electricity. It is extremely painful. After they had broken me, they would kill me, also painfully. So you don't have to worry about me saying anything even in my sleep."

"Well, it's damned funny that Jack Fan Tan knows now and he didn't know this afternoon. Until tonight he thought I was just delivering messages."

Muller was thinking. "Yes, messages. That must be it. There is someone else who may know about you. It is the man who brings messages to Nguyen Van Thanh from Pfeiffer. He has acted as a courier for a long time. Maybe he is back in Hanoi now. Maybe he saw Nguyen Van Thanh and told him."

"Then why the hell didn't he bring a message for me? Why didn't Pfeiffer use him for us, too? Who is this man anyway?"

"I do not know, Bill. They do not tell people like me these

things. It is always best if one agent does not know the identity of others. Only the man who is handling them should know. I do not like the way this man sounds, though. If Nguyen Van Thanh is right and this fellow *has* betrayed him, he may be a double agent. In that case he will tell the intelligence people here about you and maybe about me. Then we are in the soup."

."But tonight at the party everyone was acting just the other way. Even Phan Boi Chau was falling all·over me. He practically apologized for having Charlie and me mauled last night. Come to think of it, he as good as told me that I was no longer under suspicion. Everyone says he knows everything that goes on, but he certainly didn't act as though he thought I was in trouble."

Muller looked very unhappy, as well he might. If we had been fingered by a double agent, Charlie and I might beat the rap somehow, but he and Jack Fan Tan wouldn't have a chance; they'd be dealt with as traitors. It was time to make a decision.

"Muller, we're going to have to give up on Jack Fan Tan. It's our only option now. We're locked into Ngo Xuan's shooting schedule for the Foreign Minister interview, which eliminates any possibility of a trip south. Maybe Charlie and I have been rehabilitated for the time being, but·we are still under orders to leave with the ICC next Tuesday. And believe me, I can't wait. I never thought that old 307 would look good to me! You haven't been under suspicion, I guess, but you'd better get out, too. I'll arrange to take you with us— I'll say you're the only one who can cut the film—and don't worry, I'll see you get your passport. You've done all you could. Let's quit while we're ahead."

That should have made Muller happy, but it didn't. "What about Nguyen Van Thanh?" he objected. "He is hanging by his fingernails. How can we leave him in the lurch?"

"I feel guilty as hell about him, but I don't think he's in immediate danger. He ought to be safe for a little while yet. In fact, if we leave, it may even take some of the heat off him. The best we can do for him now is to emphasize to Pfeiffer that he's got to organize something else to get him out. Let's draft a signal to Pfeiffer, something like: 'Being expelled Tuesday without Fan Tan but he's hot and it's urgent you make alternate flight plan.' Maybe we can tighten that up a bit, but that's the line."

Muller shook his head.

"Sorry, Bill, but it's too late. I've already heard from Pfeiffer."

I stood stock-still and glared at him. "Now why the hell didn't you tell me that before? What's the matter with you, Muller?"

"You were talking so much, you didn't give me a chance to tell you."

"Well, I'm not talking now, damn it. What did he say?"

Muller was still defiant. "He said the same thing: 'Repeat try bridge.' That's all he said, but it means his plans have not changed."

"It means he's out of his bloody mind, that's all it means. He doesn't know what is happening here, he hasn't had a word from us, the bridge is out of the question and he needs to be told. Let's pare down that message for you to send."

"I can't, Bill," Muller said uncomfortably, "I just can't send it."

"What do you mean, you can't? I'm telling you to send it."

"I don't take orders from you about this, Bill. I only take orders from Pfeiffer, and he has told me it's too dangerous to transmit progress reports. This is only a progress report. I have direct orders from Pfeiffer to contact him only in an extremity."

"Listen, Muller, if the failure of an operation is not an extremity, I don't know what would be one."

"No, Bill," he said in his stubborn Teutonic way. "This is a problem. It is a difficulty. A setback. It is not yet a failure and it is not an extremity."

We argued absurdly about the definition of an extremity. He refused to concede that this was an impasse and kept repeating that we still had a week to do something in. I finally put a stop to it by saying, "Have it your way, then. We'll just leave Pfeiffer in the dark. God knows, he's left us in the dark long enough."

"But, Bill, he has not left us completely in the dark. We have had two messages that say the same thing. There is still the bridge."

"The bridge! You know where Pfeiffer can put that bridge! If Nguyen Van Thanh ever gets out of here, it won't be by the Ben Hai Bridge. I think you ought to tell Pfeiffer that. You don't. All right, I leave it up to you. It's no longer my affair. I wash my hands of the whole business. My work with the CIA is finished. I'll do the Foreign Minister, and Charlie and I will leave on Tuesday. You can tell Pfeiffer or not, as you please."

It relieved me to say that. I had been willing to give it my best try, but events had taken Jack Fan Tan out of my hands. Stalking back to the hotel with Muller lumbering along to keep up, I felt lightheaded at the thought that the worst was over. I even half-forgave Muller his mulishness.

"I'll book you passage on the Tuesday ICC flight," I told him.

Charlie was in my room. She had folded the mosquito netting over the top of the big bed and was stretched out on it as naked as an odalisque. I understood her. She was trying to make up for all the trouble she thought she had caused. Nothing had been her fault, but the trouble was over now and I felt like celebrating myself.

I do not want to go into it, but Charlie is very good in bed. If that room was really bugged, the security men in the back room downstairs got themselves a hell of a set of tapes that night.

I didn't think of the Ben Hai Bridge once.

16 I entertained the warmest feelings for Ngo
Xuan as I climbed the stairs to his office the
next morning. I was very grateful. After all,
he had solved my problem for me. He had
made it impossible for me to do anything about Nguyen Van
Thanh. He had delivered me from the hands of the CIA.
He had given me back my proper job. From now until Tuesday there would be nothing to do but the only thing I really
knew how to do, reporting. I had told Nguyen Van Thanh it
was all off. I had told Muller. I could explain to Ned Bailey.
The whole crazy extracurricular escapade was finished. I was
almost giddy with relief and, for the first time since I arrived
in Hanoi, I could look Ngo Xuan in the eye with a clear
conscience.

"I trust you slept well, Mr. Benson?" he said.

I was so happy I decided to tell him the truth. They would
play last night's tapes for him anyway.

"My dear Monsieur le Directeur," I said gaily, "I hardly
slept at all. Miss O'Brien spent the night with me. You may
add my name to your list."

He shook his head in admiration, or perhaps it was pity.

"Well, at any rate, it is better that she sleep with you than
some of her other friends." He fiddled with his letter opener
again.

"Mr. Benson, as you know, I have taken your advice. I have decided to trust you. In general. I am about to go further and trust you in particular. I am going to show you the text of the official statement my government will make tomorrow in reply to the President's address. Do I have your word that you will not attempt to cable this information or otherwise divulge the contents of this document until its official release?"

"You have my word. It should go without saying."

"Yes. I do not think I am taking a great risk. I see your cables before they are sent. I am going to let you read the text at this time, however, only because the Foreign Minister is very meticulous and wants the questions you will address him well in advance so that he may prepare his replies and memorize them. That is best for television, is it not, if he memorizes them?"

"Of course. And if you can say to him without offense that when he says what he feels it proper to say, if he should say it with as great an appearance of spontaneity as possible, that will be better still. It makes it easier for the large audience he will command to follow his thought. You might tell the interpreter the same thing."

"That is good advice, Mr. Benson. Where your profession is concerned, at least, you seem a practical man."

With that, he passed across to me two pages of text, already mimeographed on thick, coarse brown paper. It was just like the toilet paper in the Thong Nhat. I read through it quickly. It was all the customary gobbledygook, save for two paragraphs. They were reasonably straightforward and clear.

"What is the matter, Mr. Benson? Is it not clear? Do you not grasp the implications?"

"I think I do, Monsieur le Directeur. Let me just read it again."

The text was headed:

STATEMENT

Government of the Democratic Republic of Vietnam on U.S. violations of the 1954 Geneva Agreements.

For over ten years now, the U.S. imperialists have been blatantly violating the 1954 agreements on Vietnam, strenuously carrying out a policy of intervention and aggression, and waging war against the Vietnamese people.

I skimmed down the page:

The heroic South Vietnamese people, under the skilled leadership of the National Front of Liberation . . .

The valiant North Vietnamese people . . . meted out welldeserved punishment to the U.S. aggressors. . . .

Oh, God! I wish they didn't feel they had to talk like that, I thought as I read. It is so boring. Now came the real part, though, almost at the end:

The Government of the Democratic Republic of Vietnam categorically rejects the specious proposal of the President of the United States. It is not the Democratic Republic of Vietnam which violates the integrity of the Demilitarized Zone but rather the United States which has often and flagrantly violated the Demilitarized Zone and thus shown its contempt for the Geneva Agreements of 1954.

Next came a long passage analyzing the Geneva Agreements, a reference to the President's proposal as a "perfidious trick to perpetuate the division of Vietnam," and the usual bit about the "just stand for peace as expressed in the Four Points of the DRV and the Political Program of the National Liberation Front." Then the statement got down to business again:

However, in accordance with its goodwill attitude and sincere desire for peace, the Government of the Democratic Republic of Vietnam announces its readiness to discuss acceptable international verification of the status of the Demilitarized Zone when the United States has made clear its intention unconditionally to withdraw all U.S. and satellite forces from South Vietnam. Such a demonstration of clear intention would also make progress possible toward a political settlement in South Vietnam based on the Political Program of the National Liberation Front.

I looked up at Ngo Xuan. "Clear intention. Not actual withdrawal."

"That's it."

I was thinking hard, trying to put the pieces together. Somewhere in here was the clue to the Ben Hai Bridge and how I could get Jack Fan Tan across it. Pfeiffer must have had the President's speech in mind when he sent Muller the message. I couldn't put the two together yet.

"It may be a step forward," I said cautiously.

"It is meant to be. How do you think it will be received by your government and public opinion?"

Actually, it was a very large step forward. It vastly narrowed the difference between the United States and the North Vietnamese bargaining positions. If they wanted to, they could accept almost anything as a "clear intention" of ultimate withdrawal. But, whatever the long-term implications, it didn't help me with my Jack Fan Tan problem. I decided to play down the whole thing while I looked for an opening that would take me south.

"Oh, the government will be interested. The State Department is full of experts who love to chew over these things. If you are trying to influence public opinion, though, I don't think it will help you much. It's a pretty subtle point, after all. What the public is going to notice is that the President has made a generous offer and has received a pettifogging and ungenerous refusal. Even your friends in the United States will think that."

"Perhaps the Foreign Minister can provide some clarification when he answers your questions."

"What do I have, three questions?"

"Yes. What would you like to ask?"

"Well, first of all, I suppose I must ask him what is the significance of his new formulation—'clear intention' of withdrawal instead of complete withdrawal as a precondition."

"You know he can't go into that."

"But if I don't ask it, I'll look like a fool, as though I had missed the whole point."

"The most he can say is that you must draw your own conclusions."

"That's quite a lot. It recognizes that the formulation is new. I'll be satisfied with that."

"And your second question?"

"I think I would have to say something to this effect: You say that 'when the United States has made clear its intention . . . to withdraw all [its] forces,' you are ready to discuss international supervision of the DMZ. The President spoke of withdrawing other U.S. forces in 'due course.' Could not that be interpreted as a clear intention ultimately to withdraw all U.S. forces?"

"We will make that your second question. I cannot, of course, speak for the Foreign Minister, but I suspect he would reply in this vein: We demand the unconditional withdrawal of all U.S. and satellite forces. The President, however, unfortunately persists in making conditions. Nevertheless, we have noted with interest the passage in his speech to which you referred. We would welcome more specific indications from the President that he intends a complete and unconditional withdrawal."

"Then I would ask whether, if the President were to be more specific, you would be willing to agree to respect the Demilitarized Zone and allow international inspection to confirm it."

"Fair enough. The answer would be: in principle, yes. We have nothing to conceal in the DMZ. Any forces fighting the imperialist aggressors south of the Ben Hai River are fighting for the National Liberation Front. Moreover, the Foreign Minister will say, there are no important North Vietnamese military elements in that part of the DMZ north of the Ben Hái River. So we have nothing to conceal from inspection. However, our willingness to allow inspection would in no way modify the provisional character of the DMZ. We resolutely refuse to fall into the American trap to permanently fix the Demilitarized Zone as the demarcation line and thus sanctify and perpetuate the division of our nation."

There was the clue. Halfway through the answer to my third question, I saw the loophole that might get us into the DMZ. It was a very long shot. If I were Ngo Xuan or his bosses, I wouldn't agree to it. I had to try, but I would have to play it very carefully.

"Will he really say that?" I asked. "Will he really say you don't have any troops in the DMZ?"

"No important military elements, I think I said. Yes, the Foreign Minister will confirm that. That will give you an important story, will it not, Mr. Benson? That should calm any doubts about the significance of our gesture."

"I am not sure, Monsieur le Directeur. It will certainly make the story more important, but I am not sure that it will have the impact on public opinion you seem to expect."

"You surprise me. Why not?"

"For the simple reason that no one will believe you. Since the Paris Peace Talks began, your government has developed its own credibility gap. You have never admitted your forces are in the South. Now you say they aren't in the DMZ. People just won't believe you. The U.S. Government won't believe you and the man in the street won't believe you. They will say you are once more evading the issue in order to distract attention from your rejection of the President's offer."

"But we have no important military elements in the DMZ. I give you my assurance of that."

"I will so report it. I will say that an important official in the North Vietnamese Foreign Ministry gave me his personal assurance. Do you think that will be more convincing than what the Foreign Minister says on film?"

"Perhaps I can persuade the Foreign Minister to say to you that we have already, unilaterally, scrupulously fulfilled our engagements regarding the DMZ. Unilaterally. Do you know what that means?"

"Well, it doesn't mean very much since you have never admitted being in the DMZ in the first place. It's proof, my dear sir, proof, evidence, that you must present along with the Foreign Minister's statement."

"Ah, but your government and your military are very suspicious people." He smiled sarcastically.

"I have an idea, Monsieur le Directeur." This was what I had been leading up to. "You are using the Foreign Minister's interview with me as the principal vehicle to publicize the new factors in your response to the President's proposal?"

"Yes."

"An interview with a friendly journalist—usually one friendlier than I—is a frequent technique of yours on such occasions."

"True."

"Except that it is to be on television, would you say my interview will be any different from those previously conducted with, say, Burchett, Green and others?"

"Not really. It is our first experience with television, of course."

"Exactly, and you are using it like print. Television is a very different medium. There is a cliché, which I think was coined in China, that one picture is worth a thousand words."

"You will have pictures of the Foreign Minister."

"Yes, a talking text."

"What do you suggest?"

"Well, I have been thinking. Suppose Muller and I went to the DMZ with our camera. We could see for ourselves that there are no military installations there, if, as you say, there are none, or will be none when we get there. It would be visual evidence.'"

"An interesting idea, but I have already undertaken to our security people that you will leave on Tuesday's ICC flight. There will not be time."

"I have an even better idea then. Suppose I leave across the DMZ itself. Go right from North Vietnam to South Vietnam. I suppose the bridge over the Ben Hai River is still intact. Listen," I said, warming to my theme, "Muller could film me walking across from the Northern side. I could get one of our crews from Saigon to be on the other side to shoot me walking into the South. What could be more dramatic evidence that you are telling the truth? A correspondent and cameraman can safely walk right across! People all over the world will see it with their own eyes. That's television, Monsieur le Directeur, that's television!"

I leaned back, feeling like a huckster who had finished a pitch. Unless you are actually a huckster by profession, it is not particularly pleasant to feel like one. I would rather have felt like a journalist. As a journalist, I knew I was selling Ngo Xuan and myself a bill of goods. It would be perfectly easy for the North Vietnamese to pull their troops out of the little part of the DMZ I would go through. I would see nothing, but the rest of the Zone could be thick with troops, for all I knew. I was offering to assist in the perpetration of a fraud. I was not cynical enough to enjoy it, but cynical enough to go through with it, if it was the only way to get Jack Fan Tan out.

"It would be very dramatic," he admitted. "Would it also be useful? Perhaps. I do not know. Certainly it is not our way of doing things."

"Why not? You have released captured American pilots through Laos and Cambodia. What is so different in permitting an American correspondent to leave across the Demilitarized Zone?"

"Hm," he mused, and then said, "Then there is the security angle. If you are, indeed, connected with the CIA, a supposition we cannot dismiss, would this not be precisely what you would want to do? Spy about for any DRV activity in the Zone, assess bombing damage, the results of your operations there and so forth? I do not think our security people would permit it."

"Oh, Monsieur le Directeur, if you still think I am a spy, let us forget the whole thing. I would only point out that if, as you tell me, you have nothing to hide, then what could I spy upon? Indeed, if you have nothing there, what would be better than to have a spy report it? As for assessing bomb damage, our reconnaissance planes see more than I ever could."

"Hm," he said again. "Of course, there would be no time for you thoroughly to explore the Zone. Moreover, you would be accompanied."

"Monsieur le Directeur, that gives me another idea. I proposed to the Minister of Postwar Reconstruction that Muller and I be permitted to visit the area below the 19th Parallel where the bombing went on the longest and was most concentrated. He felt I should see that and even offered to show me himself the remarkable work of reconstruction which is taking place. Could we not combine the two, the trip down there and then the crossing of the DMZ?"

"Your request to visit the area below the 19th Parallel was, indeed, under consideration. Favorable consideration, I may say, since the ruthless and unnecessary damage done by American bombers during the partial bombing halt is still very clear in that part of the country. Also, we are proud of what we have done there since the U.S. imperialists were forced to accept the complete and unconditional cessation of the bombing. Except for the necessity of your early departure, that trip would be possible."

"Why not, then, combine the two? We would be almost to the DMZ anyway, and could simply continue and make the crossing. It would give me much of the material I need for the documentary I hope to produce after my visit, and it would serve your purposes by dramatizing your inactivity in the DMZ."

He was not yet convinced. "Logistically it would be possible. Artistically," he smiled, "it has merits. I can see them. Whether I can persuade others to see them, I cannot say. We do not like to make rapid decisions here. I doubt if there is time to arrange it. As you know, I have undertaken that you and Miss O'Brien will leave the country on Tuesday. That cannot be extended."

"If we were able to leave promptly," I said, "we could cross the bridge on Tuesday. I could take Miss O'Brien with me. Muller is training her to operate the sound equipment of the camera."

"I do not know. I cannot give you an answer. I do not think there is time."

"Will you, at least, Monsieur le Directeur, present my proposal in the proper quarters?"

"Yes, I will do that."

"When do you think you can let me know the decision?"

"I cannot say. Probably never. It will simply not happen."

"When will my interview with the Foreign Minister take place?"

"Perhaps tomorrow. Yes, tomorrow. Since you have already seen our reply to your President, there is no reason to wait until the release."

"And, now that the ban on my interviews has been lifted, may I interview other important personalities? The Prime Minister, for instance? I do not want to return empty-handed."

"I will try to arrange that."

That was all I got out of Ngo Xuan that day. It could be nothing, it could be everything. I left his office as depressed as I had entered it exhilarated. For I was back with the CIA now. Back in the Bailey–Pfeiffer–Muller–Nguyen Van Thanh web of deception and intrigue. It made me sick. Literally. Right there in the courtyard of the Foreign Ministry.

In spite of everything, I still had my job to do. At the hotel, I read through the morning handouts and the latest edition of the *Vietnam Courier*. There was another story warning about spies, disloyal elements and apathy in general. I wrote out a cable quoting it verbatim, but adding no comment of my own. I wrote two other news cables, one a mood piece, the other on Nguyen Van Thanh's postwar plans. I did not hint at any impending official reply to the President's speech, although it occurred to me that that would be the easiest way to get out of the whole crazy scheme I had elaborated to Ngo Xuan. He wouldn't trust me with a box of matches if I even implied there was something afoot.

I read a batch of cables that had come in from my New York office, begging me for more material and asking what interviews I had made. I sent them back a placatory service message, promising more news cables and saying I was hopeful of important interviews before I left Tuesday.

I found Ba and gave him the cables to be sent and ran into Muller in the bar. We went outside.

"I understand now about the Ben Hai Bridge," I told him. "There is an outside chance."

"Tell me about it."

"I can't now. We will film an interview with the Foreign Minister tomorrow. You'll get the idea then."

We went back to the bar, where, as usual, I needed a drink. I knew I was drinking a lot on this assignment. It didn't make my mind work any better, but it made me feel less miserable.

Charlie came in, looking radiant. She had a dashing fellow from the Cuban Embassy with her. The Cubans had an enormous delegation in Hanoi. Learning about guerrilla warfare, probably. They were all handsome. The ones who didn't look like Castro looked like Che Guevara. I don't know whether they picked them that way or whether it was their barber.

"Bill, it's so exciting!" Charlie said. "I'm learning how to operate the equipment."

"His?" I said, indicating the Cuban.

"No, you idiot. He's just a friend. I mean the *sound* equipment. Muller's teaching me."

"Good. Keep at it."

"I hear you're going to see Jack Fan Tan this afternoon."

"Who told you that?"

"He did."

"I thought I told you to stay away from friends like that."

"I couldn't help it. I just ran into him here at the hotel. He was meeting someone, I guess."

"Did he go up to your room?"

"No, he didn't."

"Well, thank God for that." I knew Charlie was telling the truth. She had a lot of vices, but not the ordinary ones. She didn't lie.

That afternoon, Nguyen Van Thanh found another excuse for us to be alone. I had gone to his office and received another standard briefing. At the end, he announced that we would drive to the suburbs, where a whole new town was to be created after the war.

"I think the Minister likes you very much," said my interpreter admiringly.

"I'm glad. He's very impressive and has given me much useful material."

"He does not usually spend so much time with correspondents. Perhaps it is that you both attended the University of Corhell."

"Cornell," I said.

"It is like the Sorbonne?"

"Not very." And then, not wishing to make Nguyen Van Thanh lose face, I added, "You might say it is like an *American* Sorbonne. We even have our own little *événements* from time to time."

We drove out to a large swamp on the outskirts of Hanoi. There was a banana grove and several ponds of open water covered with green scum which they skimmed off and used for fertilizer. Nguyen Van Thanh unrolled a map.

"Here, there and here, there will be two hundred houses. Here a school. Here the community center and town hall. All this will be fields where the people will grow vegetables for the Hanoi market. The land will be very fertile when it is drained. Way up here there will be a dam to control the water. Come, I will show you. Wait here," he told the others.

We picked our way along a muddy causeway between two slime-covered ponds.

"Well?" he said interrogatively.

"I apologize for not telling you at once that I had been asked to help you escape to the South. There was only one reason I did not inform you and that was that I did not then have the faintest idea of how it could be done. It seemed unfair to raise false hopes when there were none."

"And now? Perhaps you will confide in me now."

"I will tell you everything I know and everything I have done. However, I must be completely frank and say that there is still not much hope."

"Then why did they send you here?"

"It is as much a mystery to me as it is to you. I have had exactly two messages from the CIA. The first said, 'Try the Ben Hai Bridge.' The second said, 'Repeat try bridge.' I can only assume some sort of preparations have been made there."

"But that is ridiculous," he protested. "When I told you we might be able to get to the coast around Dong Hoi, I meant that we might be picked up there. It did not occur to me that we would go as far as the Ben Hai River. It is in the Demilitarized Zone, which is still an important area of operations. Under no circumstances would you and I be permitted there. I do not think your friends can be serious when they talk about the Ben Hai Bridge."

"I must assume that they are serious because that is all I have heard from them. Believe me, I have shared your reservations from the beginning. It seems very unlikely that we would be allowed to get so close to the border. However, I have made certain suggestions."

I told him of my latest conversation with Ngo Xuan and how I had proposed that we combine the inspection of the southern provinces below the 19th Parallel with my own crossing of the line via the Ben Hai Bridge.

"They will never agree," he said.

"They just might, because of the propaganda value of having a Western correspondent demonstrate that the DMZ is as free of military activity as they claim it to be—not that it would be much of a demonstration."

"But what about me? I don't care how you get out; I care how I am to get out. They would never allow me near the bridge."

"Well, my idea was that you go with me as far as the DMZ and, once we are there, I would then suggest, on the spur of the moment, as it were, that you come with me to the bridge and say good-bye there. The North Vietnamese Minister of Postwar Reconstruction himself sees the American correspondent off across the DMZ. Very good television, I told Ngo Xuan." It sounded lame to me and lamer still to Nguyen Van Thanh.

"And what am I supposed to do then, run for it?"

"Maybe. It's not a very long bridge, as I remember. I hope, though, that our people will have made some arrangements down there. That is, if we ever get there."

"We won't. Do you call that a plan? Is that the best the mighty CIA can come up with?"

"No. It's the best that I could come up with. If you don't want to try it, I certainly don't blame you. From your point of view, it would be better not to try it at all than to fail. The CIA will certainly send someone else in for you with more elaborate operational instructions. I agree with you completely that my idea is rather unconvincing. If you like, I can ask Ngo Xuan to forget the whole thing. Indeed, it would take a great load off my shoulders."

"You do not want to do it yourself? You do not think it would work?"

"I think it's about a thousand-to-one shot."

"My friend, it is a million-to-one shot. However, let us continue to discuss it."

We talked it over while the mud seeped into my shoes and my best dark suit got covered with it. Once I slipped into a pond. I went over every detail of my talk with Ngo Xuan and even told him of the indications from Phan Boi Chau that I had been restored to favor. We weighed all the pros and cons. They were mostly con. Nguyen Van Thanh found it impossible to believe the CIA was not more enterprising.

After a while it sounded to me as if he would refuse to participate in any dash across the DMZ. It was very chancy, I agreed. If he preferred, I would tell Ngo Xuan at once that I had changed my mind and would rather take the ICC flight after all.

He did not reply and we walked on in silence for some time before turning back. Then Nguyen Van Thanh looked down at my muddy shoes.

"If we go into the DMZ," he said, "you will need heavier shoes."

"Do you mean you want to try it after all?"

"You are disappointed, my friend, I know. It will be more dangerous for you, too, with me along. It is not a good bet, but I think I must take that one chance in a million."

"We may not even have that chance. They may turn it down."

"They probably will. But you told me something important when you told me of Phan Boi Chau's friendly attitude toward you. He is a good barometer. It means that you are now well thought of. In that case you may be able to accomplish much. Ours is a curious society; there is still an aspect of the court about it, something left from the days of the emperors and mandarins when a court favorite would be denied nothing. If you are truly in favor at the court now, then nothing is impossible. It will depend on that, my friend."

We walked along some more. "It's strange," he said suddenly. "I do think of you as my friend. Do you know what my friends called me at Cornell?"

"Jack Fan Tan. Did you like it?"

"Yes, I liked it in those days. No one here calls me that except our friend Miss O'Brien."

"She told me."

"She is not discreet."

"No."

"Fan-tan is the name of a card game."

"I have played it."

"We are playing another game now, you and I. A very dangerous game. A million to one. The odds are bad. But since we are playing it together, when you and I are alone, perhaps you will call me Jack Fan Tan?"

"Good. And you will call me Bill."

And then we came up to the others.

17

Once you have embarked upon something it becomes increasingly difficult to disembark—even if you wish you had never decided to go in the first place. Things pick up speed until there comes a point when it is easier to keep going than it is to get off. That is the story of the American involvement in Vietnam. It is also the story of my own involvement in the defection of Nguyen Van Thanh.

Matters now began to move very quickly. The timetable was still against our ever making the Ben Hai Bridge. Both logistically and in terms of the psychology of North Vietnamese officialdom, it remained a million-to-one shot. Nevertheless, on this Thursday the momentum of events began to pick up at an ominous rate—ominous because fundamentally I still clung to the hope that, after all, we would still be ushered out on schedule aboard the next ICC flight.

The street cleaners woke us early in the morning, and Charlie snuggled over and made a grab at me. She was sharing my bed, of course—the camouflage of a separate room for her was a pretense that fooled no one.

"Please, Charlie," I said. "Stop. I've got to interview the Foreign Minister this morning, and you're going to come along and do the sound. Let's stay fresh and eager for the .fray."

Well, she nuzzled around for a while and I began to think, the hell with the Foreign Minister. Charlie could always arouse me—and anyone else, for that matter. But there's a faint streak of practicality in her, because pretty soon she got up and started cleaning the mud off my shoes, like a good squaw, and brushing it off my good suit. We got down to breakfast bright and early.

I never got used to meetings with cabinet officials at eight o'clock in the morning, but we had finished breakfast and Muller was giving Charlie a final check-out on the sound gear when Leng came to fetch us. He was all done up in his best, too, and so was the interpreter and so was Ba. We were obviously hitting the big time today.

We drove to a small pavilion on the grounds of the Presidential Palace. The pavilion was evidently used for formal occasions, receiving ambassadors and the like, for it was very well furnished and well adapted to a small reception. Muller decided where the Foreign Minister would sit and where I would sit. He put the camera in position and was still setting up his lights when the Foreign Minister came in.

He was a craggy little man of peasant origins and no pretension. He looked like a North Vietnamese country lawyer, if they have country lawyers in North Vietnam. To be more precise, he looked like a rural prosecuting attorney confronting the accused. Me.

I realized that he knew everything about me that Ngo Xuan knew and probably more. He scrutinized me without haste, and everything he saw seemed to confirm his impression that I was the guilty party. When he asked me whether I had slept well, it was in the tone of a warden asking a condemned man whether he had enjoyed his dinner.

This was unsettling, but it was also, paradoxically, reassuring. For if the Foreign Minister found me so untrustworthy a character, he was certainly not going to let me go off into the blue with the Minister of Postwar Reconstruction. I was perfectly content to forgo his friendship in return for his veto on that project. I was as ambivalent as ever.

While Muller finished setting his lights, I tried to make small talk. The Foreign Minister had no small talk. He looked at me with the knowledge of all prosecuting attorneys that guilty men tend to talk too much. We fell into a long silence, and I lit a foul-tasting North Vietnamese cigarette from the coffee table. He did not seem to approve of that either. I decided I would not like to meet him in a courtroom.

Ngo Xuan came in and passed out copies of the Foreign Minister's statement in Vietnamese and English, complete with my questions and his answers. Muller was finally ready. I slated the roll, "Interview with Foreign Minister. Take One."

"Rolling," said Muller.

"Speed," said Charlie, just as though she'd been doing sound all her life, and the Foreign Minister started.

He made one fluff and we had to do another take, but otherwise he had it all memorized, just as Ngo Xuan said he would. His manner was stiff and conventional, and I decided while he was still speaking that all we could possibly use would be the paragraph about the DMZ and part of the questions and answers.

"That was splendid, Monsieur le Ministre," I said. There was no point in asking him to do it again; not a single intonation would be changed. My only hope lay in the interpreter. The interpreter, at least, tried to put a little life into his translation and you could understand his English. Still, not much of an interview, except for the content.

Tea was brought while Muller packed up the camera and lights.

"I am sure your statement will be very well received in many quarters, Monsieur le Ministre," I said.

"I hope so," he said bleakly, "especially in the United States. That is the purpose." He had one sip of tea and then took his leave with the air of a man who had more important things to do than talk with enemies of the state. The whole thing had taken less than an hour.

Outside, Ngo Xuan looked at his watch and said, "You will come back here at noon to see the Prime Minister. He wants to meet you."

"Wonderful! May we film it?"

"The Prime Minister will have a statement which you may film. But no questions. He is a very busy man and will not have time."

"I will be delighted to have him on film at all," I said. The Prime Minister was not as much of a mystery to the outside world as the rest of the hierarchy in Hanoi; he often saw foreign correspondents, for instance, while his rival, Le Duan, the Party head, never did. Nevertheless, he was reputed to be a man of parts and he certainly wielded great authority. Just a look at the Prime Minister would be something.

Muller, Charlie, Leng and I went back to the hotel and drank beer to kill time until noon. She was bubbling over at the prospect of meeting the Prime Minister.

"Everyone says he has enormous sex appeal," she said. "Do you think he'll notice me?"

"Charlie," I said, "he'll notice you. You're very noticeable. But keep your damned bedroom eyes on the sound box, will you? This is important."

Muller had been playing back the tape of the Foreign Minister. It was clean and the levels were consistent.

"Don't be hard on our Charlie," he said. "She did very good. She's going to be a good sound man."

"Well, I'm glad we've equipped her for a new profession. I was beginning to think she was only equipped for the oldest."

"Bill, you owe me a vodka for that."

So we each had a Russian vodka, and then Leng said it was time to go.

The Prime Minister was quite a different proposition from the Foreign Minister—indeed, from anyone else I had met in Hanoi. He was tall and powerfully built, with a poet's face that was both rugged and sensitive—a little lopsided, the face asymmetrical. He radiated not just the impression of command but command itself. He was the man in charge, and he wore this as casually as he wore his blue Ho Chi Minh–style tunic.

He began to speak at once in French, not Vietnamese, and he did not ask me whether I had slept well or whether I was enjoying my stay in Hanoi. He asked me what books I had been reading. I told him, and he said they probably hadn't been translated yet into French and embarked on a discussion of recent trends in French literature. He spoke of books I hadn't read, and I observed to him that they probably hadn't yet been translated into English. He threw back his head and laughed.

Phan Boi Chau was there as well as Ngo Xuan and several people I had not seen before. Phan Boi Chau explained that this was an important journalistic occasion and that, as an editor, he wanted to take notes on what the Prime Minister said.

"It's just a formal statement," I said.

"No, I think he wants to talk to you and I will learn from what he says."

I saw Ngo Xuan looking significantly at his watch, so I said, "I know how busy you must be, Mr. Prime Minister. Perhaps we should record your statement. It will take less time if we stand outside and let the sun be our light instead of Mr. Muller's battery of bulbs."

"Of course," he said. "Let us get it over with as quickly as possible. I hate these things. And then we can talk."

We went outside into a little garden and he delivered a "Message to the American People." It was innocuous enough, hoping that North Vietnam's latest peace initiative would cause the scales to fall from the eyes of those still clouded by mistrust, and would be supported by all peace-loving elements. He read it very well, though. I was getting more warning looks from Ngo Xuân, so I thanked him and made as if to leave. Not at all. He seized me by the arm and led me back into the pavilion, where tea was laid.

"Do you want tea?" he said. "Or would you rather have whisky?"

"Whisky, please," I said, and they wheeled in a tray full of Scotch, ice and glasses.

"Now," he said, "you have been in the South, I understand. I am a Southerner myself. Tell me what it's like."

Well, what the hell, I thought. So I told him. The good and the bad, the vitality and the corruption, the exuberance and the prevalence of Americans. I suppose I made it clear that, in spite of all its faults, I enjoyed the South more than the North.

"Ah," he said, "I miss it. I can't get used to the climate here. But we will have it, we will have it."

"First there must be peace," I said.

"Oh, there will be. Wars always end. This one will, too. You Americans are making slow work of it, though."

"Do you mean on the battlefield or at the Paris talks?"

"The battlefield we don't worry about. Oh, we are aware that your large country has it in its power to destroy our small one. But we don't think you will. Too many things restrain you—domestic opinion, world opinion, politics, economics. You are already beginning to withdraw your forces. For a while, in 1965 and 1966, we were really afraid of what you might do to us. I tell you that honestly. Now we are no longer afraid. We can cope with anything you are able to bring yourselves to do on the battlefield for as long as you want to go on. We have more patience than you. No, it is in Paris that you are wasting time."

"That is true of your side as well, Monsieur le Président,

if I may say so. You have not made many concessions."

"We do not have to." Then he laughed. "But you are right, of course. I know your President has his problems. I have my problems, too. When you are driving along a road, you cannot make a 180-degree turn." He gestured as though holding a steering wheel. "If you do, you go into the ditch and break your neck. You must turn slowly. That is what we are doing and what you are doing. It will be all right. There will be peace."

"It still seems a long way away, Monsieur le Président. Your Foreign Minister has been good enough to discuss with me his reply to the latest offer of the President of the United States. It doesn't seem to get us much further."

"Well, Monsieur Benson, your President didn't go much further. This is not much of an offer, this latest proposal of your President. He has made such offers before. He makes an enormous point of pretending to withdraw troops, but the killing and destruction have not stopped in the South and your support of the gangster clique in power there has not lessened. Indeed, each time your President makes a token reduction of American forces, he augments his help to the puppet regime. He even goes to Saigon and holds up their hands and puts his arm around them and tells the world that he will not abandon them. I do not understand him. Can't he see that the two things must go together, the complete withdrawal of American forces and an end to your backing of the renegades in Saigon?"

"No," I said, "I think he sees them as two problems. His first priority is to de-escalate the war. He thinks he has made a start and is now waiting for a signal from you that you are willing to reciprocate. Then I think he expects the processes of political evolution to alter the government in Saigon."

"Signals! Reciprocity! Evolution!" The Prime Minister threw up his hands and laughed. "If that is what he expects, he will wait a long time. He is not promoting evolution in

Saigon, he is preserving those scoundrels like fossils, like flies in amber. He may think he is protecting them with his amber, but look at them! They cannot move. If they speak, no one hears them. If they are spoken to, they cannot listen. Above all, they cannot change. The only possible evolution is to break the amber and let them turn to dust. If your President will not do it, then he must wait for us to smash them. We will make the evolution in Saigon for him. Meanwhile he can admire his specimens on the shelf."

"Well, they might fall off the shelf, and I don't know whether the President would try very hard to catch them," I answered, "but you can hardly expect the President of the United States to take a hammer and smash the amber in Saigon."

"Then he must wait for them to fall off the shelf. Perhaps we can give them a little push." The Prime Minister moved his hand as though jiggling a shelf. "We can wait. It is not pleasant for us; you have seen for yourself that our life is hard, but I think we can wait longer than you. Then, when the moment is ripe, the Americans will discover that it is not impossible, after all, to make peace with us."

"How will that happen, Monsieur le Président?"

"I am told you know something about our history."

"A little."

"Then you will remember that when the greatest Vietnamese soldier, Tran Hung Dao, defeated the Mongols in 1287, he did not kill them to the last man, but allowed them to return to their homes. And when Le Loi drove out the Ming in 1427, he let the defeated remnant of their force go back to Kwangsi. It has always been thus in our history. Once we have repelled the would-be foreign conqueror, we make it easy for him to leave. We have even given them boats to help them home. Of course, today we do not have the boats and the United States does not need them."

"But you are suggesting that, like Le Loi, you will make it easy for the Americans to leave?"

"That is what I am trying to tell you. We will find a formula, a device, and then you Americans will discover that it is not so hard to leave after all."

"With honor?"

"Honor! Honor means much to you, I know. It also means much to us. But it may not mean the same thing to both of us."

"To us, it has to do with the obligations we have undertaken to South Vietnam."

"Oh, the South. There is no hurry about the South. The South will come to us in time, but not at once. The people there have undergone a different development. There must be time for re-education. Do not worry, we are not about to swallow up the South. There must be contacts, yes. Trade, yes. Opportunities for people to go back and forth. People like me who were born in the South. But we do not plan for unification at once. That will come in due course."

The Prime Minister looked around the room at his advisers and laughed. "They want me to go," he said. "They think I have talked to you too much. There are people waiting. They know I do not like interviews or journalists, but I like talking to you. We will have another talk one day."

"I would like very much to meet you again. Perhaps in Paris when the peace is signed."

"Why not Saigon? Let us meet in Saigon." He gave my arm a friendly squeeze, and I took my leave.

Ngo Xuan came out to see me into the car. "You made a great hit with the Prime Minister," he said approvingly. As we left, I noticed that he and Phan Boi Chau were talking with the Prime Minister.

"I was so proud of you, Bill," Charlie said. "He talked to you like an equal."

"Well, he said quite a lot."

"He did, from what I could understand. I liked the part about the car. He's very masculine, isn't he? Do you think he noticed me? I thought he did."

"I'm sure he did. Thát's probably why he talked so much. He was trying to impress you. The next thing will be that he'll want to make a date."

The Prime Minister didn't want to make a date, but Phan Boi Chau did. He came up to our table when we were half-way through a late lunch.

"I want to invite you all to dinner tonight," he said. "It will be a very special dinner. Here in the hotel at six. You will come?"

"Of course," I said, though Phan Boi Chau was the last person in Hanoi from whom I would expect a social invitation.

"The Prime Minister liked you a great deal," he said. "It will be a very special dinner."

The dinner was in a private room and it was special, all right. To begin with, the principal dish was dog.

"How do you like your dinner, Miss O'Brien?" said Phan Boi Chau.

"Delicious," said Charlie.

"It is dog," he said, watching her closely. "We consider it a great delicacy."

It was obviously a kind of test. They knew how Westerners feel about dogs and wanted to see how we would react. To do Charlie credit, she didn't turn a hair.

"Really?" she said. "I've never eaten it before. It's excellent. If I don't do it justice, it's because we had a very late lunch after our interview with the Prime Minister."

Now it was my turn. Phan Boi Chau reached across the table with his chopsticks and filled my bowl from several dishes. He gave me an immense amount.

"It is all dog," he said with a wicked grin. "Prepared in different ways. How do you like it?"

"It's very good." I looked at the heaping bowl and thought of all the dogs I ever knew, especially a black poodle I once owned called Beauregard. It was clear I was going to have to eat it all. Then I remembered that the ancient Mexicans also used to eat dog and I fixed my mind on a red pre-Columbian effigy of a dog I have from Colima. That somehow made it better and I attacked my dish. It really was quite good as long as you didn't think of an actual dog.

They sat there watching us eat. Nearly everyone I had met in Hanoi seemed to be there—Nguyen Van Thanh, I was relieved to see, Ngo Xuan, a man from the Prime Minister's office, even tiny little Dr. Pham Van Bach. Phan Boi Chau got up to propose a toast.

"It is an honor for me as a fellow journalist to be allowed to offer this dinner as a way of welcoming and saying farewell to our new friends." He paid a number of ritual compliments and ended by saying, "I propose this toast to Mr. Benson and his friends: that they take away with them nothing that will not contribute to the cause of peace."

I wondered whether I was reading too much into this. I'll give him something to read, too, I thought as I rose to reply.

"First," I said, "let me thank Editor Phan Boi Chau for the exciting reception to Hanoi that he and his friends arranged for us." Let him chew on that, I thought, remembering the way we were beaten up. Then I thanked one and all for the courtesies extended to us, the privilege of meeting the Prime Minister and the Foreign Minister, the opportunity of seeing at firsthand developments in North Vietnam, and wound up by assuring Phan Boi Chau that I intended to take nothing with me that would not contribute to peace.

Next, Ngo Xuan stood up. He apologized for the Foreign Minister's absence but emphasized that what he was about to say was on the Foreign Minister's authority.

"As everyone in this room is aware, the Democratic Republic of Vietnam will issue an important statement tomorrow concerning the status of the Demilitarized Zone. In order to impress upon the world the seriousness of our intentions, it has been decided to accept Mr. Benson's suggestion that he leave the Democratic Republic of Vietnam by way of the Demilitarized Zone, crossing into South Vietnam over the Ben Hai Bridge. He will be the first journalist to do so in fifteen years. It is hoped that this gesture will symbolize both our true desire for peace and the essential unity of Vietnam.

"Minister Nguyen Van Thanh has already agreed to show Mr. Benson some of the projects of his Ministry in the region devastated by American bombs below the 19th Parallel. Mr. Benson's party will then continue on through the Demilitarized Zone and reach the bridge across the Ben Hai River at twelve noon on Tuesday. In order to maintain this schedule, it will be necessary for you to leave tomorrow morning, Mr. Benson. I will discuss arrangements with you after dinner."

I was dazed. They had bought it all. The entire plan. Everyone stood up and clapped. Jack Fan Tan was clapping with the rest, but no more vigorously than anyone else. His face showed nothing but polite congratulation. I guessed that he had had his surprise earlier. I got to my feet and thanked Ngo Xuan, thanked Phan Boi Chau for the dinner, made some more appropriate remarks about peace and said I supposed we ought to start packing.

Phan Boi Chau shook my hand. "Congratulations," he said. "It will be a great journalistic coup. I hope everything goes well."

I shook hands all around. Then Ngo Xuan led me to a corner as the others left.

"You should leave as early in the morning as possible," he said. "It will be a hard four-day trip. The roads are still very bad in places. Instructions have been given to assemble the most roadworthy vehicles possible. You will have a security guard and carry your own gasoline and water. It will not be easy."

"I want to arrange to have a camera crew meet us at the other side," I said. "May I send a cable tonight?"

"No. Not until the official announcement is made. If you will give me your cables tomorrow morning, I will see that they are given priority as soon as the official statement is released."

"Ngo Xuan, I must thank you very much for your help in all this."

He shrugged. "It wasn't me. The Foreign Minister didn't like the idea. He is my superior, of course. It was the Prime Minister. He wanted to make his own judgment of you. You made a very good impression on him. He said to allow you to do anything you wanted."

"Then thank the Prime Minister for me."

"Phan Boi Chau also helped."

"Honestly?" I was really surprised.

Ngo Xuan shrugged again. "He admired your journalistic enterprise, I suppose. Now you have much to do. I will see you in the morning."

Upstairs, I started knocking out cables to IBS. The first was a news story on the DMZ announcement. The wire services would carry the text, but, if Ngo Xuan was going to give my cables priority, we might get a small head start, so I quoted liberally from the official statement. I added some interpretation of my own and threw in some of the things the Prime Minister had told me, attributing them to "a high government official." I slugged it "Urgent Press."

Then I knocked out a service message:

URGENT PRESS IBSNEWS NEW YORK MANNERING EYES ONLY THERES POSSIBILITY EYELL BE PERMITTED LEAVE NORTH VIETNAM VIA DMZ AND BEN HAI BRIDGE STOP THIS OBVIOUSLY RELATES DRVS NEW PROPOSAL AND COULD BE MAJOR ELEMENT IN WHOLE STORY STOP PLEASE HAVE BEST SAIGON CREW AT SOUTHERN END BRIDGE TWELVE NOON TUESDAY TO FILM CROSSING MULLER COVERING OTHER END STOP UTMOST SECRECY ESSENTIAL MUST BE NO REPEAT NO PRIOR DISCLOSURE

SINCE ANY PREMATURE PUBLICITY COULD WRECK WHOLE OPERATION CANT EMPHASIZE TOO STRONGLY NEED FOR SECRECY STOP CEASE MESSAGING ME HERE FROM NOW SINCE WILL BE IN FIELD BENSON

Reading it over, I realized about a hundred people at IBS would read the cable if I sent it to the office. I was crossing out "IBSNEWS NEW YORK" and substituting Mannering's home address when Muller came in.

"You did it, Bill," he said. "You did it. I knew you would."

I held a finger to my lips. "Want some fresh air, Muller? I'm tired of typing."

Outside where we could talk, Muller was terribly excited. "I don't know how you did it," he kept saying. "I'm very proud of you."

He had picked that up from Charlie. She was always saying she was proud of me. I didn't feel proud of myself. Lies and tricks and subterfuge are not my way of doing things. In fact, if you want to know, I was ashamed of myself. Everyone in Hanoi, even the ones I didn't like, had played straight with me, and I was playing it crooked with them. If I hadn't believed in Jack Fan Tan, I wouldn't have gone through with it.

"Well, it isn't over yet," I said. "Not by a long shot. Have you told Pfeiffer?"

"Yes." Muller looked scared. "My God, I hope they didn't pick it up here. It was only three words. Do you think they would pick up three words, Bill?"

"What did you say?"

"Just three words, 'Bridge noon Tuesday.' Do you think they'll pick that up?"

"The question is whether Pfeiffer will pick it up."

"I sent it at the proper time—the time he always monitors. I don't dare send it again."

"No, don't send it again. They'll figure it out anyway when we try to get a crew up there from Saigon."

"You mean I didn't need to send it at all?"

"No. You were right to send it. Let's go back to the hotel.

We've got to pack."

"Bill," Muller said on the way back. "This all happened so fast. They don't do things so quick here. Has it struck you that it might be some kind of trick?"

"What kind of trick could it be?"

"I don't know. This is just not like them, Bill. I've known them too long. It's not like them to let us go to the DMZ in such a hurry. They don't hurry here. It's not like them to let us take Nguyen Van Thanh with us. Maybe they want to get us out of town and then we have a convenient accident." He drew a finger across his throat. "Do you think it is possible they have discovered what Nguyen Van Thanh wants to do?"

"Good God, Muller. I don't know. They know a lot already. Maybe they've guessed the rest. Maybe they know everything. I don't think so, but there's nothing we can do about it anyway. We're committed."

"I guess so. But there are some things I don't like about it."

"There's a lot I don't like about it. The whole damned thing."

Muller's suspicious afterthought didn't improve my mood a bit. I was even snappish with gentle little Mr. Leng when I met him in the hotel lobby.

"Mr. Leng, I'd like you to get my hotel bill ready and a list of all the other charges I've incurred."

"I don't think there will be any charges, Mr. Benson. Just the cables, perhaps."

"Oh, yes, there will be, Mr. Leng. Other visitors may have their expenses paid by your government, but I pay my own way. I don't ever want it said that the Democratic Republic of Vietnam picked up the tab for my visit. Please get the hotel bill, my bar chits, the cable charges, and prepare a list of what I owe for the car, the driver, the interpreter and everything else. I want to pay for everything. IBS can afford it."

Leng and Ba came to my room with the bills while I was

packing. The cables were fantastically expensive. Everything else was ridiculously cheap. The hotel, with meals, came to about five dollars a day. The car and driver were about the same, with some overtime for the driver when he worked at night. The interpreter got about $1.50 a day. One more country, I thought, where a cab driver makes more than a civil servant.

We added it all up and converted it into dollars. I remembered the cables I had just written, and we estimated what they would cost and added it on. I counted out a sum in dollars for Ba to get changed at the bank in the morning.

"It's more than enough," he protested. "There will be some left over."

"Use it to buy me a couple of bottles of Russian vodka from the bar." I only had part of a bottle of Scotch left.

"There will still be some left over."

"Well, give it to charity." I knew you weren't supposed to tip in North Vietnam—very unsocialist—but I thought Ba could probably use the money.

"There is a fund for the victims of American aggression," said Leng, "but I don't know whether your contribution would be approved. You would have to write a letter."

So I wrote a letter saying that I hoped that any excess North Vietnamese currency I left behind would be used to help those who had suffered during the war or to assist any cultural activity that might be thought appropriate. When Mr. Leng said, "That is very generous, Mr. Benson," I knew it had been the right thing to do.

I had everything packed except the file of propaganda material I had collected when Charlie came in.

"All packed?" I asked.

"Almost. I'm tired, though. Let's go to bed."

It seemed a good idea at the time and got better as we went along.

"Better than eating dog," Charlie said, as she rolled over to go to sleep.

IV

AFTER
HANOI

18

"It was 1956," Jack Fan Tan told me. "Nineteen fifty-six was the year I became disillusioned with Communism. That was a terrible year."

"A long time ago," I said. "Why didn't you do something about it before?"

"I did. Like the Abbé Sieyès, I survived."

We were in Thanh Hoa, or what was left of it, a provincial capital where we spent the first night on the road. It was quite a caravan that had started off from the Thong Nhat Hotel in Hanoi that morning. Ngo Xuan had managed to assemble one truck for the gasoline and provisions, three Russian-version jeeps and one reasonably serviceable-looking civilian sedan. The sedan was obviously in deference to Jack Fan Tan's ministerial rank. There were sixteen of us in all. My own little party made six, Charlie and Muller, of course, plus Leng, Ba and the interpreter. Nguyen Van Thanh brought along his *chef du cabinet*, which made eight. Then there were the five drivers and three unidentified characters, whom I correctly took to be security guards. The leader of these was a squat, ill-favored bully for whom I felt an instant dislike which was obviously reciprocated. He and his men were all armed, as were the drivers. If there was an accident to be arranged, these were the babies to arrange it.

We got off more or less on schedule. Charlie was only half an hour late and Muller not much more. It took him a lot of time to get the camera gear stowed to his satisfaction so that nothing would be damaged on bad roads. Ba turned up with three bottles of vodka. They had only let him have one bottle of the Russian, so he got two more of the Vietnamese on the grounds, he said, that it is only half as good. That was an exaggeration.

Ngo Xuan was on hand with a present for me. It was a little palm tree, each frond painstakingly carved from buffalo horn. It probably took a lot of work to make, but it was quite hideous. I told him it was what I had always wanted.

"The palm tree," he explained, "is, as you know, more common in South Vietnam than it is in the North. Therefore, it is to us a symbol and reminder of our duty to unify our country."

"Very appropriate," I said, thinking that these people could invent more parables than Norman Vincent Peale.

I had to think of something to give him in return. My briefcase was Italian, made of supple leather and almost new. I quickly emptied it and presented it to him with a little speech of thanks and the hope that, in his hands, it might one day carry the details of a just solution to the war. All very Oriental.

Makepeace came down the hotel steps to see us off, all very American.

"I wish I were going with you," he said regretfully. "They're going to take me to a place called Phu Ly next week, but I've still got to listen to a lot more briefings here. They come on pretty strong, don't they?"

"They come on pretty strong," I agreed.

"Still," he said, looking at Ngo Xuan and Nguyen Van Thanh, "they're fundamentally right, of course, and we're fundamentally wrong. You can't forget that."

"How's your peace plan coming along?" I asked.

"Well, they haven't really said much, but they seem to appreciate our interest. I must say you were right, Mr. Benson. Now that I'm here, making peace doesn't seem as easy as I had hoped."

"No, it's not easy," I said. "Well, good-bye, Makepeace."

"Good-bye, Makepeace," said Charlie and gave him a big kiss which made him blush. "Good luck."

"Good luck," he said. "*Bon voyage.*"

And we left him there, standing a little forlornly on the steps of the Thong Nhat, doing his best to live up to his name.

Charlie, Jack Fan Tan and I got into his sedan, with the head gorilla in the front seat with the driver. The others spread out into the Russian jeeps and the truck, Muller cradling his Bell & Howell silent camera in his lap in case we encountered any targets of opportunity. The big Arriflex was so carefully swathed in blankets in the truck that it would take half an hour to get it out and an earthquake to damage it.

Charlie was wearing one of her Mexican shifts. Her legs were bare, and there was nothing on her feet but a pair of flimsy Puerto Secreto sandals.

"For Christ's sake, Charlie," I said, "haven't you got a pair of shoes? We may get into some rough country."

"The Vietnamese don't wear anything but sandals. I guess I can go anywhere they can go." It was unanswerable.

The marks of American bombing were evident as soon as we got out of Hanoi. The road had been resurfaced and was in pretty good shape, but on either side hardly a building was left standing, and they were only just beginning to rebuild, mostly with mud huts. Very little brick and mortar were going in.

The road from Hanoi to Nam Dinh is the Pilgrim's Route, along which nearly all of the odd little trickle of Western visitors to North Vietnam are required to travel in order to see for themselves the American penchant for bombing nonmilitary targets. We passed through Phu Ly, a long town strung along the railroad, which had been devastated in 1966. No attempt had been made to restore it. It sprawled in ruins, with vines beginning to grow in the rubble, a memorial to American frightfulness, a sort of Potemkin village in reverse from which the pilgrims could draw an easy moral.

We had lunch at the House of the People in Nam Dinh, an ugly city, once the third largest in North Vietnam. A textile center, it had been much knocked about, but the cloth mills, we were proudly told, had never stopped working. They were harder-working than ever now, having been extensively repaired.

At Leng's insistence, we made a detour to Phat Diem to see the Catholic churches which had been destroyed. Leng seemed to have a thing about churches. Evidently he labored under the impression that all Westerners were devout Roman Catholics who would be shocked and horrified at the sacrilege. To be fair, he also pointed out Buddhist pagodas which had been damaged. Perhaps he was a pious man at heart.

On the road between Nam Dinh and Thanh Hoa, where we were to spend the night, we had our first trouble with the security guards. I'd never liked the look of the chief thug, whose name was Minh. We had got ourselves in the middle of a long military convoy, mostly supplies and very few soldiers, and were making slow going. At one point we came to a dead stop, and Muller ran up ahead to film the line of trucks. This infuriated Minh, who raced up to Muller, brandishing his gun, and tried to knock the camera out of his hands.

"Military, military," he screamed in his bad French. "You must not film military or we go back. You are spying on us."

Muller, whose long years in Communist countries had taught him respect for authority, especially when it is carrying a gun, protested feebly that he had been allowed to film the same sort of thing in Hanoi, but Minh wasn't having any of that. He insisted that Muller destroy his film, which contained many stirring shots of the textile factories in Nam Dinh and overturned crucifixes in Phat Diem as well as the offending pictures of the convoy.

I didn't like that bit about "spying." I had thought that was all over with. Clearly we were going to have trouble with Mr. Minh. He evidently decided the same thing about us, for he abandoned his seat in the sedan and thereafter rode beside Muller in the jeep, ostentatiously fondling his gun.

We were getting into good rice country now, and it was very beautiful. The fields were wide and wet and green, with peasants bending over and water buffalo pulling. In the distance there rose, here and there, those improbable miniature mountains which you see in Chinese paintings and are not at all the artist's fancy. They really grow like that in the Far East.

Thanh Hoa Province, Jack Fan Tan's aide explained, is one of the granaries of North Vietnam. He said they were getting five tons per hectare now as against two in the days of the French and landlordism.

"What made the difference?" I asked.

"We have made better use of water, more fertilizer and new strains of rice. But above all, it is organization. In every village the women have joined in the 'Five Ton Valiant Fighter Movement.' It has spurred everyone."

I watched the Five Ton Valiant Fighters for a while, bending endlessly in the rice fields. Most of them were women and old men. The war must have taken the young men. Even so, it was clear they were growing a lot of rice.

At Thanh Hoa the first thing they showed me was

another ruined Catholic church. There were a great many other ruins, for Thanh Hoa had been hard hit, but it still had the aspect of a pleasant town. A great deal of reconstruction was under way, and, for the first time since we had left Hanoi, I had the impression of being in a place that was thriving.

"It's very impressive," I told Jack Fan Tan. "There's an awful lot of work going on."

"Oh, yes. I told you we know how to organize. The people are still working hard, pushed by the government and by the momentum of your bombing. You don't know how much the bombing helped the Party fasten its control on the people. The bombing united people. It was an excuse for everything the Party wanted to do, good or bad. It wasn't always that way, and it won't be that way when peace comes. That's why some people don't really want to stop the war."

"When did you become disillusioned with the Communist Party, Jack?"

"It was in 1956. That was the year of agrarian reform. Agrarian reform! That wasn't what they were after. They wanted absolute political control of the population. They wanted to eliminate every kind of potential opposition, every class that might stand in their way. Their instrument was terror. You cannot imagine what went on. They probably killed a hundred thousand people that year. It was sickening."

"My God! Why didn't people revolt?"

"They did. They rebelled in Nghe An, Ho Chi Minh's home province. We're going there tomorrow. They had to send troops in to massacre the farmers. It had nothing to do with land reform. It was just a device to establish the Party's control. Of course, it worked."

I could not see how.

"Why, they just turned off the terror. Just like that! Ho

Chi Minh and Vo Nguyen Giap admitted that 'errors' had been made. Excesses. And everyone was so grateful to them for stopping the killing that they became bigger heroes than ever. For them, I admit, it was a master stroke. I was very young and very idealistic, and for me it was a betrayal of everything I believed in, everything I had run away from home to fight for. Perhaps I should have left then, but it seemed to me then the only thing to do was to carry on as best I could. I have been doing it ever since. I am glad it is almost over now."

Muller came out to report that dinner was ready. I asked him if he'd like a drink, and, while I was making it, he whispered, "I don't like this fellow Minh."

"I don't like him either. What's the matter? Is he giving you a bad time?"

"He follows me around with that gun all the time. I think he's bad trouble. I smell trouble."

It came the next day on the road to Vinh. We had stopped and Muller had got out to make some shots of the rice paddies and the Five Ton Valiant Fighters. Suddenly Minh pulled his gun and fired two shots at his feet. The other two security men moved in on either side of Muller and tore the Bell & Howell out of his hands. Minh was shouting and pointing the gun at Muller. We all came running up.

"What's the matter?" I asked the interpreter.

"He says you are photographing a military installation."

"What military installation?" All I could see were the pale-green rice fields and the Five Ton Valiant Fighters, who were now looking up to see what the shooting was about.

"Over there," he gestured way off to the left, quite outside the pan shot that Muller had been making. "There is a missile site over there."

Then I could see it, the long, ugly snout of a SAM sticking up from the rice field about a quarter of a mile off the road.

"Mr. Minister," I said to Jack Fan Tan, "please tell this man that the SAM wasn't in the shot. It's so far away you couldn't tell what it is anyway. I'm sure Mr. Muller didn't even see it."

They jabbered away in angry Vietnamese. "He says you have been making persistent efforts to photograph military objectives," said Jack Fan Tan. "For security reasons, he demands that the trip be canceled and that we return to Hanoi. I have said no and that I will be responsible. He insists. He says that there is a telephone in the next village and that he will call Hanoi and have us ordered to return."

"What a nasty man," said Charlie when we all got back into our cars. "He tried to feel me, you know."

"You mean like this?" I said, feeling her.

"Like that. But I wouldn't let him. He's ugly."

"Be careful. He's got the gun."

Still, we didn't kid around much on the way to the next village. Jack Fan Tan and I were both pretty glum. We didn't dare say much in front of Charlie and his *chef du cabinet.*

"I'll be very disappointed if we have to go back," I said finally.

"We won't go back," was all Jack Fan Tan said.

There was indeed a telephone at the next village, and Minh brushed through the crowd of officials anxious to do honor to the great Minister of Postwar Reconstruction and put in his call. He talked for quite a while and then beckoned triumphantly to Jack Fan Tan to take the instrument. Jack had what seemed like a few crisp exchanges, hung up and put in a call of his own. This took quite a while, and his conversation took longer. Then he, in turn, put Minh on the phone. As Minh listened, his manner became more and more respectful. He ventured a few remarks of which all I could catch were our own names, "O'Brien" and "Benson." Then he listened in silence, murmured something obsequious and sullenly returned the phone to Jack Fan Tan. Jack sounded courteous but by no means fawning as he wound up the conversation and hung up. Minh put in another call.

"We will go on," Jack Fan Tan said. "Unfortunately, our friend here will continue to accompany us. He is explaining now why his orders have been revoked. Be careful what you film, though."

"How did you do it?" Charlie wanted to know.

"The Prime Minister's office. I'm not a minister for nothing. There'll be an unholy row back in Hanoi, though. Let's go."

We had wasted a lot of time with the telephone and didn't make Vinh until almost dark. Now, even in the dusk, we really began to see what bomb damage was like. Vinh is around the 19th Parallel, and we had been bombing that far north until the end.

"Wait until we get south of Vinh," Jack Fan Tan said. "Then it begins to get really bad."

They wanted to put us up for the night in Vinh—at least the local people and Minh, much subdued now, wanted us to stay. But Jack Fan Tan wanted to push on to Ha Tinh, where he had a reconstruction project going which we had agreed to film the next day.

So we had dinner in Vinh, scrounged some gas and set off again. Though there had been no bombing here since November, 1968, regulations still prescribed no more than a pinpoint of light from the headlights. The road was now very bad. It did not follow a fixed course but meandered, twisting and turning like a stream finding weak spots in the terrain. These meanders were the remnants of the daily detours imposed when the bombing was at its height. Much work had been done on the road, but they hadn't got it straightened yet.

The lack of illumination added to the eeriness of the landscape. When we swerved or reared up over a bump, our little, pencil-thin rays of lights would briefly reveal a slice of desolation—bare mounds and gullies of damp earth on which no blade of grass grew, only now and then the shattered skeleton of a tree. It was a blasted heath, a place for witches' brew. We saw no animals, no people.

"Where are the people?" I asked.

"In villages. Over there." Jack Fan Tan gestured to the right, toward the foothills.

"Many casualties around here?"

"Not so many as you would think. We moved the people away from the road years ago to relatively safe villages many kilometers off the road. During the bombing it was not permitted to drive to the villages lest the wheels leave marks that would attract the bombers. The people walked to work, and even the wounded had to be carried on foot to the hospitals in the villages."

"Is it better now?"

"A little better. Discipline is not so strict now and people are filtering back to their old homes, but along here there is nothing yet to come back to."

In Ha Tinh the bombed cathedral loomed up like some ghostly monument in the night. There were quite a few people living in Ha Tinh and some evidence of building and restoring. Although it was late, our caravan was soon surrounded when we stopped in the middle of town. We had been expected. The North Vietnamese staff work is very good. Someone in authority was brought up to Jack Fan Tan, and, after introductions all around, we were conducted to our accommodations. They were in some sort of official building. Beds were set up in offices for us according to rank. The drivers and the security people slept on benches in a meeting room. There was even some food laid out, but we were too tired to eat. Charlie, Muller and I went to bed, Charlie in an office by herself, Muller and I sharing another one. Jack Fan Tan said he was tired, too, but that protocol demanded he go off and have a conference with the town leaders. By the time he got back we were asleep.

The next morning we visited Jack Fan Tan's big project outside of town. It was a huge dam and hydraulic complex, which had been pretty well knocked out. Over a thousand people were working on it, I was told. Originally it provided water for a million and a half hectares and now when completed would take care of two million hectares. Already over a hundred thousand man-days had been expended on the job. The man from Jack Fan Tan's office read off those statistics and a lot more for me.

Then the local commissar, or whatever he was, stepped forward to relate the history of the imperialist aggressors' attacks on the dam, "clearly and transparently designed to bring starvation to the province," he said. He gave the usual details and names of victims who were the sole support of large families but no figures on numbers killed.

During all the speeches, Muller was having the time of his life shooting the work on the dam, which was spectacular to film. A thousand people with baskets of dirt and picks swarmed over the sloping side of the great earthwork. A couple of bulldozers and trucks were taking out some wrecked steel and concrete bastions, but most of the work was being done by hand. Cecil B. De Mille could have used the project for a scene of the Egyptians building the Pyramids. Muller got down low and made his shot up the slope so it would look as though they *were* building a pyramid. The Vietnamese are all natural actors, and Muller was putting them to work here and putting them to work there, wherever he could get the angles and backgrounds he wanted. They loved it. Even Ugly Minh left him alone. From time to time the workers would burst into song, and Charlie faithfully got all that in natural sound.

When the commissar finished giving me the gory details, he told me that the Minister of Postwar Reconstruction would now make a speech to the workers, who would respond with loyal cheers. It would make a very good scene for me, he was sure. I was not so sure, but Jack Fan Tan whispered in English, "We have to do it."

I gave Muller a wry salute, remembering his warning about things like this. I started to tell him how I wanted it shot, but he took over in his bossy way and told the commissar where he wanted the people to stand and when he wanted them to cheer and then, on cue, to cheer again for close-ups.

It all went according to plan, which is to say that it was the most unconvincing, unspontaneous sequence you could imagine. But the ceremony would have been the same whether we had been there with the camera or not—just as unspontaneous, just as unconvincing. To these people, propaganda was now a way of life, a ritual as automatic and meaningless as spinning a prayer wheel.

"A hundred thousand man-days on that pile of dirt," I said as we left.

"It is not remarkable," Jack Fan Tan said indifferently. "It took 500,000 to build. It may take 500,000 more to finish. There are plenty of man-days available. It is simply a matter of organization, of administration. You do not see things like this in the South these days because there is no organization and no administration, but that is the only reason. The human material is just as good. Better."

All along the road now we passed crews working, filling in the holes, straightening the path back to where it used to be, repairing bridges. We had to make many detours. Once or twice we stopped so Muller could get some shots of the road building. Other times, Jack Fan Tan told us not to stop because the workers were soldiers and we would get Ugly Minh on our backs again. Charlie had got us both calling him Ugly Minh. We passed a good deal of traffic going both ways. All of it looked military to me, but I saw no signs of encampments or military installations.

"You wouldn't expect to see them along the roadside, would you?" Jack Fan Tan said when I asked him about it. "They're around here, though. You can be sure of that."

What with the truck convoys, the road repairing and the bridge building, our progress was slow.

"I knew we'd never make Dong Hoi today," Jack Fan Tan said. "I only hope we get to the village where I told them last night we might stay. It is not too far off the road and we can drive in most of the way. If we have to stay anywhere else, it will be a long walk and they will not expect us."

Our drive all day took us through the worst bomb damage I had ever seen. I had seen the aftermath of B-52 strikes, and I had seen what the concentrated use of air power could do in World War II, but this stretched on and on for miles. The road, of course, had been the target, and the damage did not reach very far on either side, which is why the villages off the road were safe, but along the road a gangplow could not have torn it up more.

In the late afternoon, Jack Fan Tan's *chef du cabinet*, who had been studying the map, said, "We'll make the village. It should be only about fifteen more kilometers." Then we came to a milestone, miraculously still standing, which gave the distance from Hanoi. Jack Fan Tan took the map and worked it out. "About ten kilometers to go," he said. Sure enough, ten kilometers farther on, there was a barely discernible track leading off to the right.

We turned in, although Minh didn't look very happy about it—no wheeled vehicles were supposed to go to villages even now—and drove half a mile or so. Then we pulled up under some cover, and the drivers cut brush and palm fronds to camouflage the transport. It seemed pretty silly to me—the Americans weren't going to start bombing tomorrow morning—and I said so.

"One does not have confidence in you Americans," said Ugly Minh sourly in bad French.

The drivers made packs for everyone of blankets, food and drinking water. I put the bottle of Russian vodka in mine, and, thus laden, we set out for the village.

It was not, I suppose, more than half a mile away, but it was hard going if you weren't in shape. The village, really a collection of hamlets, was like any other Vietnamese village —perhaps spread out a little more against detection and bombing from the air. The houses had thatched roofs and mud floors, were fenced around with wattle and connected by dusty lanes. Each house had an air-raid shelter. Except for the shelters, it reminded me of a Mexican village.

The elders came out to greet us, and people took the packs from our shoulders and laid them out in three houses which had been set aside for us. It had all been well arranged. They knew in advance where everyone was to go. They had even hung a curtain screen across one room where Charlie was to sleep in deference to her presumed modesty. The villagers had obviously never seen anything like Charlie before. They gathered around her in frank curiosity. The women fingered her Mexican embroidery, and one little boy put his fingers around her wrist. He couldn't make his fingers meet, although Charlie's wrist is really quite delicate. Then, to show that he meant no rudeness, he put her fingers around his wrist to show the difference in size. Emboldened, another little boy stroked the hair on my arm in wonderment. Like the Mexicans, and, indeed, all Asiatic peoples, the Vietnamese carry little body hair. I could not decide whether my own foliage was repellent or attractive to them.

Jack Fan Tan showed all the city-dweller's suspicion of the countryside. They were preparing a meal for us. He took me aside to tell me what to eat.

"The soup is the safest. They boil it a long time. Go easy on the vegetables, do not eat the meat, and under no circumstances drink any water we did not bring ourselves. Intestinal parasites abound," he said ominously. "We will open some cans, and I will explain that we do not want to be a burden on their food supply."

When the time came, I ate everything, including some delicious crab from the murky-looking river. So did Charlie, who, after years of living in Mexico, would eat anything. Jack Fan Tan stuck to the soup and the canned goods. I must say I didn't drink the water, but they produced beer anyway. There were no noticeable ill effects from the meal.

After dinner, Jack Fan Tan and I walked around the village and met a lot of dignitaries. He told me what they all did. There were the village elders, who no longer had much power but represented tradition. There were the government men, who really ran the town. The government ministries were well represented. There was a man from the Interior Ministry, another from the Health Ministry, a Culture and Propaganda man, people in charge of the Women's League, the Farmers' League, the Youth Group and all the rest. There was a security man and even someone from Jack Fan Tan's own Ministry.

All that organization seemed impressive to me, but Jack Fan Tan said it was not a good village. "The rot has set in," he said. I asked him what he meant.

"Look at the machinery," he said. "It is broken and not repaired. The cadre in charge of farmers told me he is having difficulty getting the communal tasks performed and can do nothing about it. There is a black market, which they did not even bother to conceal from me. The spirit is not good and you can feel it."

What was the reason, I wanted to know, the attitude of the people or the quality of the government representatives, the cadres?

"Both," he said. "The people are tired, and the cadres are not giving them leadership. This war has been very hard, and ever since the death of Ho Chi Minh there has been a loss of vigor among the people. He was for them a powerful talisman, and they felt a sense of protection from his presence. Now that he is gone, the people sense there is trouble at the top, and there is a falling off of their enthusiasm. The little men in the government, they feel that way, too, I think." ·

"Do you think there will be trouble?" I asked him.

"Not yet. Not until after the war. After the war, unless the leaders remember what Ho Chi Minh taught them about government, then there may be trouble."

"I wonder whether after the war the people of the South will remember what the Americans tried to teach them about government."

"I hope not," Jack Fan Tan said. "You tried to get them to adopt the institutions of good American government. That is not at all the same thing as institutions of good Vietnamese government. Furthermore, you think everything can be solved with money. Does money really solve things even in the United States? I don't think so. In South Vietnam it only provides more opportunities for corruption. What the South needs is not American money but a good civil service. Not a good American civil service, a good Vietnamese civil service. I am going to see they get one."

"Jack, what makes you so sure you'll have the chance? To begin with, even if you do get into the South, they may not give you a job."

"Oh, they will have to. I will be the first important political defector from the North. Of course, there will undoubtedly be an attempt by my colleagues here to discredit me when—if—I reach South Vietnam. They will say all sorts of things about me, but I hope you and your people will not believe them."

"I have no doubts about you," I assured him.

"I know you don't," he smiled. "But they will try to sow doubts, and when that time comes, I hope you will help me convince anyone who is taken in. Then the South Vietnamese will have to use me. Surely the Americans still have enough influence in Saigon to get me a job."

"I honestly don't know whether they do. They will want to help you, but there are people in the government of South Vietnam who aren't going to like it."

"There are also people in the South Vietnamese Government who aren't going to be there long. Peace will bring about many changes. Of course there will be a place for me. Your people realize it, which is why you are helping me. Soon all South Vietnam will realize it."

We left early the next morning, the villagers carrying our packs down to our motor pool under the trees. The drivers took the camouflage off the vehicles, and we eased down the path to the main road. Ugly Minh grumbled that we had left tracks and ordered the villagers to rake them out.

All the way to Dong Hoi we passed labor crews working on the road. Clearly, a work force of thousands had been deployed to get the road back into shape. Some of the groups we passed were a couple of hundred strong, and we went by a lot of groups. Whatever they said in Washington, manpower did not seem to be a problem in North Vietnam. The bomb damage was concentrated on the road, but Leng, who was riding up front on this leg of the trip, assured me that traffic had been going through right up to the end of the bombing.

Leng had a pocket transistor radio which he turned on from time to time for the news, at one point translating for me: "Peace-loving elements throughout the world endorse the firm answer of the Democratic Republic of Vietnam to the transparent peace trick of the President of the United States." There followed laudatory quotations from *Pravda* and *Izvestia* and lengthy excerpts from commentaries in other Communist papers.

Toward the end, the announcer referred contemptuously to a statement by the spokesman for the U.S. delegation in

Paris. The American spokesman had expressed regret that the President's proposal had been turned down and once more challenged North Vietnam to respect the neutrality of the Demilitarized Zone. "The whole world laughs at this stale contention," said the Hanoi commentator. "It is well known that the imperialist forces continually violate the Demilitarized Zone while the Democratic Republic of Vietnam upholds the Geneva Agreements of 1954."

"The Foreign Minister puts it better in my interview," I said.

"Yes," said Leng, turning off the radio, "that is why you are being allowed to cross into the South over the Ben Hai Bridge. It will confirm all the truth of what we say."

It came over me that we were almost to Dong Hoi, our jumping-off place for the DMZ. That was where the official schedule called for Jack Fan Tan to leave us. Time was running short. Without disclosing our intentions prematurely, I wanted to lay the groundwork for his going as far as the bridge.

"Mr. Leng," I said, "it's important that we make my departure as dramatic as possible. Perhaps we can arrange some sort of ceremony at the bridge. Do you have any suggestions?"

Leng seemed doubtful. "There will be no one there to make a ceremony with," he said. "Only two or three guards at the bridge. If you wish, you may shake hands with the guards as you leave."

"I do not wish," I said. "No offense, Mr. Leng, but it would hardly be appropriate for me to clasp the hands of soldiers of your country who may tomorrow be shooting at soldiers of my country. Why don't I bid an elaborate farewell to you, a high official of the Foreign Ministry come to see me off?"

Now it was Leng's turn to be shocked. "That would not be appropriate for me," he protested, "not appropriate at all. My rank is much too modest for such a responsibility. Others would think I was putting myself forward."

"Nevertheless," I said, "I would like to make my leave-taking as impressive as possible."

Jack Fan Tan said warningly, "I am sure it will be impressive by its very nature."

Having planted the seed, I took his hint and left it there in the hope it would take root.

There was still plenty of light when we got to Dong Hoi, and you could see how much punishment it had taken. It was the first place we had bombed in North Vietnam. On February 7, 1965, forty-five planes from the *Coral Sea* and the *Hancock* had hit it in reprisal for the attack that morning on Pleiku which killed 8 Americans and wounded 109. Dong Hoi was also one of the last places we bombed in 1968, so it got it all. There wasn't much left intact, but by now there were boats back in the harbor and some of the buildings had been repaired.

After the usual briefing and the usual statistics (over eight hundred attacks on Dong Hoi) and the usual speech by Jack Fan Tan, I said that I would like to see the famous walls nearby. These two walls had been built in the seventeenth century by the Nguyen, Lords of the South, as fortifications in their civil war against the Lords of the North, the Trinh. They were never breached by the North, and when that particular North-South civil war ended in a truce, the Trinh of the North respected them as a demarcation line for a hundred years. It's an interesting fact that they lie just above the 17th Parallel, which is the present demarcation line. So I wanted to see them and film them.

This was Jack Fan Tan's first visit to Dong Hoi, and he had no idea where they were. The town leaders said they had heard of such old walls but couldn't say precisely where they lay. Perhaps they didn't think this was an appropriate moment to remind people that there had once been a time when North and South Vietnam were peacefully separated for a hundred years just about where they are separated now. I persisted. Surely someone must remember where the walls were. Finally an old man said he thought he could find them.

We drove a little way out of town and there they were, not so much walls now as broad mounds running from the sea to the foothills. Even after the erosion of time and, probably, American bombs, one could see that the Dong Hoi walls had been a formidable military obstacle in their day. One was eleven miles long and had been twenty feet high when it was built. Not comparable to the Great Wall of China, of course, or Hadrian's Wall, but a lot of man-days must have gone into constructing them. Still, as Jack Fan Tan had said, there is no shortage of available man-days in Vietnam.

I asked Muller to film them, and Ugly Minh immediately intervened. He had been getting difficult again. I demanded to know why we couldn't film them. "Because they are military," he said. I didn't know whether to laugh or get angry. I did both.

"But these were built three hundred years ago," I said. "Look at them. You could drive a jeep across."

"Military," he said. And that was that. This didn't seem a good time for another row with Ugly Minh.

Jack Fan Tan and I took another of our little walks.

"I gather you think we should wait until tomorrow," I said, "before I suggest that you go with me to the bridge."

"That is best. The last possible moment.".

Then we drove back to Dong Hoi, and after dinner I repacked my bags. When we went across tomorrow, I could take only one bag with me, if that. I put in two good suits, two shirts, a pair of decent shoes, my shaving gear, all the notes I had made in North Vietnam, and filled up the bag with as much of the propaganda material showered on me as might be helpful to quote from when I got out. Muller placed all the film he had made into four film cans and carefully taped them together with his dopesheets on top. Charlie didn't pack at all.

The next morning after breakfast we loaded the cars, and

I exchanged farewell gifts with my little entourage. I gave Leng a little traveling clock I had with me, explaining in a little speech that it was fitting because he was always so prompt. It was a Movado, and he was fascinated that it was wound by sliding the case back and forth. To the interpreter, I gave my typewriter. It seemed appropriate to his line of work. For poor old faithful Ba, the only thing I could think of was a fountain pen. To add up the next correspondent's bills, I told him.

The things they presented to me in return reflected the austerity of wartime life in North Vietnam. From Leng, a carved tortoise-shell hair ornament—"for your wife." From the interpreter, a comb made from the metal of a shot-down American plane. From Ba, a ring made of bone. I gave Jack Fan Tan a leather cigarette case, and he gave me a paperback copy of *Ho Chi Minh on Revolution*. It was a nice touch— exactly the sort of farewell present a loyal Minister should give an ambiguous American correspondent.

"Mr. Minister," I said formally, through the interpreter, "I want to thank you for being so gracious and informative a host during this difficult trip. I realize that you had planned to leave us here and return to your duties in Hanoi, but I have a suggestion to make. My proposal is that the purpose of our expedition would be better accomplished if you were to accompany me to the Ben Hai Bridge. As I suggested yesterday, some ceremony would make my crossing more dramatic. You could bid me adieu in full view of the cameras. Think of it, a full minister of the Democratic Republic of Vietnam saying good-bye to an American correspondent in the DMZ. It would be very impressive and would show the sincerity of your government's intentions."

"I'm afraid it would be in contravention of the Geneva Accords," said Leng.

Jack Fan Tan pretended to consider. "I don't know," he said. "I am a civilian. It might be possible."

Suddenly Ugly Minh, who was not the fastest thinker in

the world, got the drift of our conversation and all hell broke loose.

"I forbid it," he screamed. "I will not allow it. I am responsible for your security, and you may not go any farther with these people. It is dangerous."

"Isn't that for the Minister to decide?" I said.

At that, he turned on me in fury. The interpreter was mumbling a running translation for me.

"I have no confidence in you and Miss O'Brien," he shouted. "It is not safe for the Minister to be with you. You may be American agents."

At that, one of his underlings stepped up and put a gun in my stomach. He wanted to use it, too. He was a mean-looking little bastard. The other one leveled his gun at Charlie. We both stood very still. Was this going to be the accident that had been arranged for us?

Jack Fan Tan rose to the occasion. He was pale with anger. He began to speak to Minh in hard, level tones of authority.

"He asks Mr. Minh," the interpreter said out of the side of his mouth, "whether he has forgotten the telephone call. He has only to make one more such telephone call and Mr. Minh will lose his rank and be working on the road. He says, how dare Mr. Minh give him orders and forbid him to go anywhere? He will give the orders, and he now forbids Mr. Minh to accompany you to the bridge. The Minister will go with you, but Mr. Minh and his men will stay. If he wants to know why, it is because it would be a direct violation of the Geneva Agreements to introduce armed men into the Demilitarized Zone. 'Stay here. That is an order,'" the interpreter finished.

Minh glared at Jack Fan Tan silently, after this peremptory speech, and then turned to bark an order to his men. They lowered their weapons and got into one of the jeeps and drove off.

"Let's go," said Jack Fan Tan.

We headed south toward the DMZ. "That was a close one," he said. "He has gone to telephone, I am sure—but I think we will be all right."

"What's the matter with those men?" asked Charlie. "They scared me. Do they really think we're spies?"

"Something like that," I said.

"How ridiculous."

The road from Dong Hoi started out well and got progressively worse as we approached the Demilitarized Zone, but there was little traffic and we went past the abandoned ICC headquarters about eleven o'clock. A little later a dilapidated sign in French and Vietnamese announced we had entered the Zone itself. Now the road grew much worse. So much work had been done everywhere else that I asked Leng why they hadn't fixed up this part.

"Every time we send a repair crew, the Americans bomb them," he said bitterly. "The next day they issue a communiqué announcing that an enemy concentration was attacked in the DMZ and at least thirty-five North Vietnamese troops were killed. They were only laborers, but the communiqué says this was the 147th North Vietnamese violation of the Demilitarized Zone. It is all absurd, but I suppose it impresses the imperialist warmongers in the Pentagon."

There were no North Vietnamese troops to be seen in the DMZ. I hadn't expected any, but at one point, where the road twisted and turned through the mud, it was clear where they had once been. A B-52 strike—no one remembered when—had splintered the trees and mangled the earth. Though vegetation was already beginning to cover the mounds and craters, the timbers and sandbags of what must have been a big underground tunnel-and-bunker complex could still be seen. It would easily have sheltered several hundred men.

Perhaps a tortuous mile past this, we came over the brow of a hill and there beneath us was the Ben Hai Valley. It was spectacularly green and beautiful and, after the desolation we had journeyed through, strangely peaceful. There were no people to be seen, but the rice fields were clearly still being cultivated and water buffalo lay contentedly in the mud. It was hard to believe this pastoral scene was the goal which had drawn us so inexorably through all the confusion and tensions of the past week.

Around a bend, the bridge came into view—no longer an abstract symbol, but a real bridge, and not much of a bridge at that. It was drab and weather-beaten, but the two great flagpoles still stood at either end where once North and South Vietnam had each competed to raise its flag higher than the other. The flags flew brightly still—in our honor, I supposed—but the bridge itself was a sorry affair. It had been bombed since I had been there last and only partially repaired. You could no longer drive a truck across it, as someone escaping from the North had done in 1962, but as nearly as I could tell, it looked safe enough to cross on foot, which was all I had in mind.

The bridge over the Ben Hai is flat and narrow, supported by groups of vertical piles. It is perhaps 150 yards long. In the old days it had been brightly painted—red at the northern end, green at the southern, and white in the middle to mark the 17th Parallel. Now there were only traces of paint left, though you could still see what the colors had been. My last visit—to the southern side, of course—had been in 1965. In those days the bridge had been a colorful place—loudspeakers bawled insults from each side and sometimes theatrical troupes would perform propaganda shows for the enlightenment of the unbelievers across the river. There was no sign of any of that now, only the flags waving above the decrepit bridge.

At our end we were stopped by six North Vietnamese soldiers with AK-47s slung on their shoulders, mounting guard before a dilapidated sign in French: "LIGNE DE

DÉMARCATION MILITAIRE PROVISOIRE." Underneath, the same thing was repeated in Vietnamese. At the other end there seemed to be quite a large welcoming committee assembled to receive us, including, to my relief, a camera crew already set up and ready to shoot.

It was only 11:35. We had said we would cross at noon but Jack Fan Tan was anxious to start at once. He was worried about Ugly Minh. I told Muller to break out the big Arriflex and get organized as soon as he could.

Jack Fan Tan sent Leng over to inform the soldiers that we would be going onto the bridge. I was measuring it with my eye. It was too Goddamned long. Whenever I had seen it before, I had marveled at how so short a span could separate these two warring countries. Now it seemed to stretch to an impossible length. If anything went wrong, I hated to think of having to run Jack Fan Tan across that long expanse of rickety bridge.

"I'd like to shoot in the white part of the bridge," I told Jack Fan Tan. "Let's get as close to the other side as we can. Tell Leng it's because I want the camera on the southern end to be able to get us as well as Muller."

The North Vietnamese guards evidently had orders to let us on the bridge, but I didn't know how far. They lifted the red-and-white barrier to let Muller and Charlie through. Muller had the tripod balanced on his shoulder and was lugging the camera and the cans of film we had already shot. Charlie had the sound box. Jack Fan Tan wanted to go with them, but I said no. I didn't want us standing in the middle of the bridge for five minutes while the camera was being mounted.

Muller got to where the bridge used to be painted white and looked back. I waved him on authoritatively. He walked right to the middle and unlimbered his tripod. The North Vietnamese soldiers became restless at that, talking among themselves and looking at us. One of them took the AK-47 off his shoulder and called Leng over. He made threatening sounds in Vietnamese, and Leng ran back to where we were standing.

"The soldiers are concerned," he said. He sounded concerned himself. "They say no one, not even the ICC, has been allowed to go so far onto the bridge. They insist that Mr. Muller come back closer to us."

"Certainly not," I said firmly. "It is essential for him to go as far as he has because of the requirements of the camera." If you tell an amateur that a camera needs a certain distance, he is always impressed. Complex machinery is awe-inspiring. Leng went back and told the soldiers about the camera. They seemed impressed, too, and the soldier slung the rifle back on his shoulder.

At last Muller made a go-ahead signal with his thumb and forefinger in a circle. I shook hands with Leng, the interpreter and Ba. I even gave the soldiers a cheery wave. Since Jack Fan Tan was supposed to be coming back, he merely nodded to everyone.

The barrier was still up and the entrance to the bridge open. I picked up my bag and we walked onto the bridge.

19

We had made it to the bridge. God knows how we'd done it, but there we were, Jack Fan Tan and I—the bridge under our feet, the North behind us, and the safety of the South no farther than a man could throw a stone. Nothing could stop us now.

All the while we walked toward the south and the group gathered there to meet us, this bridge we had sought so long seemed like an old and comforting friend. Then we passed Muller's camera and turned to take our places in front of it, once more facing the north. I could see the North Vietnamese soldiers and two of our drivers strung out in a line across the entrance to the bridge, their weapons in their hands. They looked like a firing squad and my euphoria vanished; the bridge suddenly became a place of peril.

"Hurry up," I told Muller. "Let's get this thing over with. Quickly."

Charlie passed me the microphone. Muller started his camera. Charlie looked at the dials in her sound box, nodded, and said, "Rolling."

But no words came from me. I had nothing to say. We had been so nervous waiting at the northern end that Jack Fan Tan and I hadn't worked out any dialogue.

"Well, Mr. Minister," I fumbled, because I had to say something, "we have crossed the Demilitarized Zone."

"Yes," he replied calmly, "and now you are going to South Vietnam. I think I will go with you."

At that, we turned. I carefully laid down the microphone, picked up my suitcase, and we started walking toward the other side. We covered about fifty feet in utter silence. We got almost to where the green paint of South Vietnam began. Then the first shot was fired. It came from the north. It was answered at once by a crackle of fire from the south.

My instinct was to run for it, but Jack Fan Tan only walked a little faster. He wanted to show that he wasn't running away from North Vietnam, but leaving of his own free will with his head high. It was very brave. It was also very foolish, for the firing had increased to a fusillade now, coming in automatic bursts instead of single rounds. You could hear the bullets ping and ricochet off the steel girders of the bridge. They didn't seem to be missing us by much. What frightened me most was that they would get Jack Fan Tan. At that moment I didn't care about myself, but I couldn't bear the thought that we might lose Jack Fan Tan after having got him so close.

The firing grew more intense now and seemed to be coming at us from several directions. Jack Fan Tan and I were well into the green part of the bridge and had broken into a shuffling trot when Muller dashed up beside me. He was carrying the four cans of film he had taped together. I dropped my suitcase as he shoved them into my arms. Then he turned around and started running back toward his camera. He's out of his mind, I thought. Why doesn't he keep going? I looked back after him as he zigzagged toward the northern end of the bridge.

That was when I saw Charlie. She was stretched out by the sound kit, her earphones still on her head. She had been hit.

"Jack Fan Tan," I yelled over the sound of gunfire. "Catch!"

He was running in a crouch now toward the southern end of the bridge, but he caught the heavy package of film like a tight end taking in a pass and kept going without breaking stride. I turned around and raced back toward Charlie. Muller was fiddling with his camera. He was trying to unload the damned thing, paying no attention to Charlie. Once a cameraman, always a cameraman, I thought savagely. Who the hell cares about the film now?

A machine gun had opened up a hundred yards downstream on the southern bank and the weight of fire was now coming from our side. The North Vietnamese riflemen had had to disperse and take cover, but they were still firing. Their bullets were striking the bridge girders all around us. Muller was standing up in the middle of it, trying to unthread his film, when I reached him and Charlie. I had just enough breath left to shout at him to help me with her, but it didn't penetrate his single-track mind.

Charlie was alive but unconscious. The right earphone was smashed and blood was trickling out beneath it. I carefully removed the earphones from her head and the blood gushed out, so I couldn't see the wound.

I reached down and picked her up as gently as I could. She was a big girl and all dead weight. As I straightened up with her limp body in my arms, I heard a groan and a crash. Muller had toppled into the camera tripod and knocked it over. The whole front of his face had been blown away. Since he had been standing between us and the North Vietnamese, the bullet that killed him might well have got one of us instead.

There was nothing I could do for Muller, so I staggered back across the bridge with Charlie. My God, we made a big target, and a slow one. I didn't see how they could miss us. I had less than a hundred yards to go. It seemed a hundred miles. I wasn't even sure I could carry her that far. She kept slipping out of my arms, and I had to pause and get a good grip on her again. The firing from the north had slackened, but the bullets still pinged off the girders of the bridge.

They were what saved us, the girders. The sides of the Ben Hai Bridge are almost man-high, and the girders which form them are set in a continuous W pattern, with straight beams running vertically through the inverted Vs. At the beginning, when the North Vietnamese were still grouped at the open end of the bridge, we were as easy targets as tenpins in a bowling alley. That was probably when they got Charlie. But when the North Vietnamese had to scatter under the suppressing fire from the south bank, they were forced to fire at us from an angle and there was a lot of metal in the way. At least, that was the way I figured it out afterward.

I had made it with Charlie about halfway into the green end of the bridge when two GIs in flak vests came running up and took her from me. I don't know whether I could have carried her much farther, but with the weight gone I had enough strength left to get to the end. There is quite a steep slope at the southern approach to the bridge and, finding myself going downhill with my legs like rubber, I stumbled on the incline and would have fallen if someone had not come out of nowhere to catch me. I looked into his face. It was Ned Bailey.

Bailey trotted us to a deserted house a little distance away, and we took shelter behind it. I knew the house. I had used it twice to film from in the old days because, if you went in from the blind side and stayed well back from the windows, you could get a shot of the northern bank without drawing too much attention to yourself. It provided cover for us then, and it was providing cover for us now.

I sat down and gasped for breath. I was shaking like a leaf, whether from fear or exhaustion I couldn't tell. Probably both. We still had quite a gun battle going on, which didn't help.

When I got my breath back and my heart was pounding

less, I looked around for Jack Fan Tan. He was standing off to one side with Pfeiffer, of all people. Jesus, Old Home Week. He looked all right. That is, Jack Fan Tan looked all right. Pfeiffer looked just the same, although rather morose. Behind the house, a doctor was crouched over Charlie, dressing her wound and giving her a shot. I'd go over there in a minute, when I was up to it. Ned Bailey was sitting beside me, and I saw a camera crew packing up its gear.

"All right, Bailey," I said. "Where's my crew?"

"They were filming," he said. "They got it all."

"They aren't my men. I know every IBS man in Vietnam. What the hell happened to my crew? What's going on here?"

"Well, we couldn't let them come, actually. Things didn't work out quite the way we had thought, so I had to stop your people and bring our own."

I was in a rage, out of terror and exhaustion.

"I'll say things didn't work out, you bastard. You may have killed Charlie. Why did you send her to Hanoi in the first place? This is all your doing. Ned, you used to be a friend of mine, but if you have killed her, I swear before God I'll kill you. I don't care about the CIA, the FBI, the laws of the United States or anything. If she dies, I'll track you down wherever you are, and I'll kill you."

"Don't be melodramatic, Bill. The doctor says she won't die."

I pulled myself up and went over to see for myself. Ned came along. She still lay on the ground unconscious, and the doctor was working on her. He had fixed a tube in her arm and a corpsman was holding up a bag of plasma. I crouched down beside her.

"She'll be all right," the doctor told me. "The headphone saved her. If the bullet hadn't hit that first, she'd probably be dead. As it is, it's mostly concussion, although there are some fragments of metal and plastic that are imbedded fairly deeply. We'll get them out at the hospital."

I wanted to kiss her, but didn't dare. It might be bad for her. Germs, or something. I stroked her hand for a minute and then turned to Bailey.

"What went wrong?" I asked him. "You said something had gone wrong."

"There isn't time now. I'll tell you later. Just one thing you better know right away. Nguyen Van Thanh isn't what we thought he was. He's a plant, a double agent. They were trying to plant him on us. That's why we couldn't let your crew come. It's not the kind of thing you want to publicize."

I could not believe my ears.

"Ned, you're either lying or you're crazy. It just isn't true. I know him. He's okay."

"We have absolute proof that he's not," Bailey said. "But don't worry, Bill, I'll fill you in later, and you did a hell of a job in getting him out. We want him anyway, don't worry about that."

"I'm not worrying about that. I'm worrying about him." Jack Fan Tan was still standing off to the side with Pfeiffer and a couple of Americans I didn't know. CIA men, I supposed. It looked as though they were guarding him. They kept intercepting a nervous little South Vietnamese major who was trying to join the group. They shouldered the major away, and he stood on the fringe glaring at Jack Fan Tan. I went over to them.

"You all right, my friend?" I asked Jack Fan Tan.

"I'm not wounded, if that's what you mean," he said. "But something is wrong, Bill. This is not the treatment I expected."

"I know something is wrong. I don't know what it is, but I'm going to find out and I'm going to fix it. Don't worry." I hoped I was being reassuring.

There was still a certain amount of shooting going on, mostly from our side. A U.S. Marine captain came up to Bailey. "Sir," he said urgently, "please get your party out of here. We've got them pinned down on the other side for the time being, but they'll bring up mortars pretty soon and this will be a bad place to be. I'd appreciate it if you'd get out of here as soon as you can."

The CIA travels in style. A dozen vehicles were lined up behind the house, more or less out of the line of fire, and twice as many as should have been there. I doubted if it was the Marine captain who had thought of that. The Marines were always short of transport. They had rigged up a stretcher for Charlie in one of the vehicles and were lifting her onto it. I tried to ride with her, but the doctor wouldn't let me. I got into a jeep with Ned Bailey instead and put in the four cans of film and my bag, which someone had rescued. Jack Fan Tan went with Pfeiffer and the two CIA men, with a Nung guard riding shotgun at the back. They made the South Vietnamese major ride in a different jeep.

All this took quite a lot of organizing, but eventually we got moving. The Marines laid down a heavy blanket of fire as we moved out of the protection of the house and into the road leading out of the Ben Hai Valley. There were only a few incoming rounds and they were wild. The road was almost as bad on this side as on the other. I doubted whether we fooled around much in the DMZ ourselves, beyond patrols.

Ned Bailey said, "I'm sorry about all this. I really am."

"You should be," I told him. "You got us into it. I can understand, I suppose, why you lied to me. I'm expendable, I guess, and I can take care of myself. But I can't understand why you brought Charlie into it. That was the most reckless, underhanded, dangerous thing to do to an innocent, helpless girl that I ever heard of. I didn't think you were capable of it."

"I know," he said and shook his head against the thought of it. "It's just that there wasn't anyone else and she kept pestering me about wanting to go to North Vietnam. You're right. I really shouldn't have let her go, but time was running short. Do you want to know how it happened?"

I nodded and he went on. According to him, their problem

has been to get word to Nguyen Van Thanh that I was coming and that he could speak freely to me. Jack Fan Tan had insisted that he would only talk to a responsible American and had himself suggested the identifying phrase, "Uncle Sam." The CIA had planned to send in the word about me by the same emissary who had brought out the original hint from Jack Fan Tan that he might be getting ready to defect.

The trouble was that the emissary was already in Hanoi and showed no sign of coming out in time to collect a new message and return. That meant they had to find someone else to go into Hanoi and let Nguyen Van Thanh know it was all right to talk to me. There were no other journalists—apart from me—in the pipeline, so they ran a check on the New Left, the SDS and every antiwar group on their list—hundreds of them, Bailey said—to see whether any of them had been invited. They even knew about Makepeace waiting in Phnom Penh, but they doubted his visa would be granted. Bailey explained that it was not unusual for the government to ask favors from such a quarter. On more than one occasion they had been instrumental in getting American prisoners released. He thought the CIA could frame a message to Nguyen Van Thanh innocuous enough for one of them to carry. But no one at all was going to Hanoi from the Left; and meanwhile Charlie kept talking to Bailey about how much she wanted to go to North Vietnam, time was passing, and I was due to start off at any moment.

So, Bailey said, he did the easy thing. He got her fixed up with some of the peace outfits in California, where they abound. They recognized a fellow spirit at once, applauded her idea of trying to work with the war victims and urged her to try to get admitted. Some of the big shots in the peace campaign who had been to Hanoi themselves even wrote her letters of recommendation. With those credentials, they sent her off, leaving the rest to Pfeiffer.

"Well, she got through and delivered the message," I said.

"But it was still a crazy thing to do. She damned near got killed."

"Quit it, will you?" he said. "She didn't get killed and she did deliver the message. She has had a very interesting experience and probably loved every minute of it."

I could have slugged him and it must have shown, but he went right on. "Incidentally, Bill, I did not lie to you down there in Mexico. We weren't sure then that Nguyen Van Thanh wanted to come out, or that there was anything phony about him. I told you exactly what we knew, and all we wanted then was to have you find out whether he was serious about defecting."

"What about that tape recording then?" I demanded. "And that conversation you steered so carefully? You were setting me up for blackmail and you know it."

Ned Bailey just grinned. "Oh, that," he said, as offhand as you please, "that was a dirty trick, wasn't it? It's a bad habit of mine, taping conversations. I won't say that somewhere in the back of my mind there didn't lurk the thought that this operation might develop into something in which you might be persuaded to play a larger role if the opportunity arose. But truthfully, it wasn't my first thought. What the hell, you always knew I was a no-good bastard, didn't you?"

What the hell, my mind echoed, he was a no-good bastard all right, but the important thing now was Jack Fan Tan. I started to tell him why he was wrong about Jack Fan Tan, but we had pulled up inside the perimeter of a Special Forces Landing Zone and everyone was getting out.

This LZ was a miniature fortress. It had to be, for it was frequently the target of North Vietnamese attacks, and when they struck, the defenders would have to hold out for as much as twenty-four hours before help came on the ground. Air support got there quicker, of course. The LZ was protected by barbed wire, ditches, redoubts commanding a

360-degree field of fire, and little South Vietnamese CIDGs in tiger suits. The landing pad was protected by sandbags, and three helicopters sat on it.

A very tough-looking and very nonchalant major in a green beret strolled up to Bailey and said, "From what I hear, you'd better leave as soon as you can. It doesn't matter to us, but the chopper pilots are getting nervous."

Bailey worked out the seating arrangements. Charlie was strapped into a stretcher which had been slung in one helicopter. That was where I went, along with the four cans of film and my bag. The pilots kept talking on the radio, and yelling to us to hurry up. The Vietnamese major, who was carrying an attaché case, insisted he must ride with Nguyen Van Thanh.

"No, you will not," said Bailey firmly. "He is my prisoner. He rides with my men and you do not."

"I have my orders," the major said miserably. "I must accompany him."

"Sorry," Bailey said, but the Vietnamese major climbed in anyway.

"Get this man out of here," Bailey told the CIA men. He got out himself, and he and one of the spooks grabbed the major and took him bodily out of the chopper. The major had left his attaché case inside with Jack Fan Tan. He reached back in, picked it up for a moment as though to take it with him, and then left it behind.

They brought him over and shoved him into the helicopter where Lou Pfeiffer and I were sitting opposite Charlie's stretcher. Ned Bailey started to get in with him, but there wasn't room—Charlie took up one whole side, and Pfeiffer, the major and I took up the other. The pilots were making hurry-up noises, so Bailey clambered into the third ship. Then the blades began to turn and one after the other we took off, Bailey's chopper first, ours second and Jack Fan Tan's last. We leaped up to cruising altitude and headed south in echelon.

I leaned over and shouted in Pfeiffer's ear, "Okay, Lou, tell me what happened."

"Not now." He looked meaningfully at the major. "Wait until we get to Danang. It wasn't your fault," he shouted. "You did fine."

At that moment there was a flash and a great shock wave struck us. We tilted violently and slid sideways. The pilot and the co-pilot fought with the controls. I was not familiar with these birds, but I knew they do not fly on their backs and we were very nearly on our back. You could hear the blades thrashing to find the air as the pilots struggled to right us. I was sure we were going to crash and I thought, what a hell of an anticlimax, to make it all the way through North Vietnam and across the bridge, only to die in an American helicopter in South Vietnam.

We did not crash, but another helicopter did. My first thought was ground fire—at our altitude it would have to be antiaircraft—but when I looked out the window to see whether there were any more bursts, because they wouldn't have fired just one, there were none to be seen. But there was only one other helicopter in our formation instead of two.

The pilots had gotten our chopper on an even keel again and we came around. Looking down, I could see some pieces of the missing aircraft still falling—not falling exactly, but sailing. The heavy solid parts had already hit the ground. The helicopter had evidently exploded in mid-air. I realized it was the one carrying Jack Fan Tan. I knew then what had happened.

We banked once more and came down just over the trees to circle the wreckage. It was spread out all over the place. No one could possibly have survived. I couldn't remember whether four or five people had climbed aboard, but one of them had been Jack Fan Tan.

The pilot, who had been talking on the radio the whole time, turned his head and shouted back at us, "There's nothing we can do. All dead. The Medivacs are on the way. We'll have to go on to Danang. Fuel," and he pointed to the indicator. We rose up to altitude and throbbed on toward Danang.

I am not strong in the face of the death of friends. It comes hard, even when they die in their beds a long way off. I took this which had happened before my eyes very hard and was sick inside because it had been pointless as well. It was unnecessary and cruel that those people should be dead, down there in the wreckage among the trees. Being given to a sense of guilt, I couldn't help feeling I was somehow to blame for it. I had brought Jack Fan Tan out of North Vietnam and had delivered him into the hands of his enemies. Clearly, I was in some way responsible for what had happened to him.

I also felt responsible for what had happened to Charlie. I looked over at her. She was either unconscious or asleep. At least she didn't know what had happened. I didn't want her to know what was going to happen next either.

The South Vietnamese major was gray with fear and gibbering to himself in Vietnamese.

"Do you have a gun?" I asked Pfeiffer.

"Yes," he said and took it out of a shoulder holster inside the bush jacket he was wearing.

"Kill this man," I said, looking at the Vietnamese major. "He blew up that helicopter. He put a bomb aboard it in his attaché case. I saw him do it."

The major understood English all right, for he shrank back in his seat when he saw the gun and heard what I said. "They were my orders!" he cried. "I was ordered to kill him. He was a traitor."

"Who was a traitor?" asked Pfeiffer.

"Nguyen Van Thanh!" screamed the major. "He was a dangerous man. He would have destroyed our government. He wanted to rule over South Vietnam. You Americans are mad.

You brought him here to give him a free hand. You do not understand us. All you want to do is to leave us—and to leave us with a man who is no better than a Communist. I was ordered to kill him before he reached Saigon. I should have been on that plane with him. I tried to go, but you would not allow me." He was shaking with passion.

Lou Pfeiffer looked at me. In that instant, and without hesitation, the major seized the gun from Pfeiffer's hands and shot himself through the temple.

The pilot and co-pilot whirled around at the sound of the explosion. I gestured to them not to panic and pointed ahead toward Danang. Pfeiffer reached under the seat, got a Mae West jacket, took it out of its case and wrapped it around the major's head so at least we wouldn't have to look at it.

Charlie stirred. I unbuckled my seat belt and went over to her. "What's happening?" she said.

"Nothing," I told her. "It's all right. Just lie still. Everything's all right."

"Are you all right?"

"Yes, I'm fine. You will be, too. Just a scratch, the doctor says. We'll have you in a hospital in a few minutes."

She made a kiss with her lips and went back to sleep, or maybe she passed out again. It was a while before we got to Danang, but she didn't come to until we had landed.

They are used to emergencies at Danang, and they know how to cope with them. When we had come in on the helicopter approach pattern and set down, about a hundred people swarmed around us. They had to take the Vietnamese major's body out first before they could get to Charlie. An ambulance was waiting, and they lifted her in with great delicacy.

I went along in the ambulance with her to the base hospital. She was awake now.

"What happened, Bill?" she asked.

"I don't know, baby. I just don't know. It was kind of a

mess. I'm going to find out and then I'll tell you all about it."

"How's Jack Fan Tan?"

"He's dead."

"Oh, poor Jack Fan Tan. I liked him so much."

"So did I."

"And Muller?"

"He's dead, too."

"I *am* sorry. I was almost beginning to like him."

"Yes."

"And me? Am I going to die, Bill?"

"No, baby. You're not going to die. Just a couple of days and you'll be fine."

"I don't feel very fine now."

"Of course you don't, but you'll be all right."

"Bill, if I don't die, can we go back to Puerto Secreto?"

"That's what we'll do. And when we get back there, we'll get married."

"Oh, Bill, you don't want to marry me. You know how I am. I'd be an awful wife for you. I'm not made to be a wife."

"Well, somebody's got to take care of you."

A big tear trickled out of her unbandaged eye. She was still crying when we got to the hospital.

A lieutenant colonel in a doctor's coat took charge of her. I was glad of that. With that much rank, he ought to be a good doctor, and I wanted her to have the best they had. He acted like a good doctor, too, because he told me to get the hell out.

"When can I see her?" I asked him.

"When I say it's all right," he said. "Maybe tomorrow."

"I want to see her tonight when you've finished with her."

"I'll have to see what kind of shape she's in," he said, reading the description of her injuries that had been taped to the stretcher they brought her in on. "It doesn't look too bad."

"Then I'll wait."

Pfeiffer had come out of nowhere to stand beside the doctor and say, "I'm afraid you can't, Bill. There's someone waiting to talk to you."

"This is more important," I said. "I'll wait."

"No, you can't. You've got to come with me now. Listen, Doc, try to let Mr. Benson see her tonight, will you? And when you're ready for him, call him on this extension." He wrote down a number on a piece of paper.

"You're the television correspondent?" asked the doctor. I nodded. "This girl means something to you?" I nodded again. "All right," the doctor said. "I'll try to fix it. I promise to call you anyway."

I thanked him, and Pfeiffer took me off.

"I'm glad she's going to be all right," said Pfeiffer as we walked along. "It's about the only good thing that's happened so far. My God, what a mess."

I didn't answer him because it seemed to me that Pfeiffer himself had had a good deal to do with making it a mess.

"I'm blown, you know," he said unhappily.

"That's no surprise. One of the things that made them suspicious about Charlie and me in Hanoi was that they could trace us both back to you. Naturally, I told them it was just coincidence, but they made such a point about it that I figured you were uncovered. Maybe I was clumsy, but I did my best to steer them away from you."

"No, you weren't clumsy," he said. "I was clumsy. I was ordered to be."

"That's funny. I thought you were wonderfully devious at the time."

"Kid stuff," he said contemptuously. "I as good as left them a paper trail when you and I saw each other. I was so amateurish I stunk out the joint. I was ashamed of myself. Look, if I'd wanted to talk to you privately, I could have fixed it so God himself wouldn't know that I'd seen you. They never learned in Hanoi that I'd got to Muller, did they?"

Looking back on it, I realized they never had worried about Muller in Hanoi. They had let him go everywhere unescorted, they hadn't even searched for his transmitter. But they had certainly worried about Charlie and me, and one reason for that was Pfeiffer. I wondered whether someone had turned him in.

"I just told you," he said crossly. "I turned myself in. I was ordered to be so conspicuous with you that they couldn't miss our connection. I was also ordered to make it clear that I had been an undercover agent all the time. God knows how many contacts have gone up in smoke by now. Guys I'd worked with for years."

I didn't give a damn about his contacts. I was thinking about Charlie and me, a couple of innocents abroad, already betrayed as we wandered in a strange and unfriendly country. We had nearly gone up in smoke ourselves and all because someone had instructed Pfeiffer to put the finger on us. It was the most cold-blooded thing I'd ever heard of. I hadn't thought anyone in the world hated us that much.

"Whose idea was this?" I demanded.

"Washington's," said Pfeiffer bitterly. "Who the hell do you think? It was all part of the master plan."

I snorted. Our little escapade had lacked a great many things, of which the most apparent was a master plan. It had all been improvised from the beginning, with the inevitable result that it had ended in a debacle. I didn't think there had ever been a master plan, and I doubted whether Pfeiffer did either.

"What did the great brains in Washington have in mind?" I asked him.

"Better let Ned Bailey tell you. He was in on more of it than I was. We're going to see him now."

I didn't want Bailey to tell me. I wanted to hear it from Pfeiffer, who didn't seem to like the whole setup any more than I did and who might at least give me a straight story.

I was beginning to develop a certain sympathy for Pfeiffer, which was a lot more than I could say about Bailey.

"Let's stop right here, Lou, and you fill me in," I told him. "I don't want to see Ned Bailey now. If I do, I'm likely to hit him right in his handsome bloody face."

"Well, I'm a little sore myself," he said, "so I've probably made it sound worse than it is. There was some method in the madness. They were trying to protect you."

"Protect me!" I shouted. "By advertising to Hanoi that I was an enemy agent? They were sending me up there with three strikes against me."

"No. The idea was to get them to give you an intentional walk. Bailey's going to claim it worked, too. After all, you're here, aren't you?"

"Just barely," I said acidly, while I worked over what he had just said about an intentional walk. Bailey had already told me the CIA believed Jack Fan Tan was a North Vietnamese double agent. Double agents are no use unless they are in place. The only reason for the North Vietnamese to have given me an intentional walk to the Ben Hai River would be because they *wanted* me to get Jack Fan Tan across, and into the welcoming arms of the CIA. That must be what Ned Bailey was about to tell me. I asked Pfeiffer.

"Sure," he said. "Our whole scheme was based on the calculation that Hanoi was trying to insert Fan Tan into South Vietnam. In that case, anyone going in after him—especially an amateur like you—would have a safe passage. They would want you to bring him out, don't you see? You've got to give our outfit credit; they made damned sure Hanoi would realize you'd come for him. They not only tipped off those blabbermouths in Saigon; they made me stick my neck out, too."

"Does Bailey believe all this?" I asked.

"Sure."

"Then he's crazy."

"I agree. They went and screwed me out of the best job

I ever had. There were a lot of simpler ways to handle it."

"That's not what I meant," I said. "Bailey's crazy because Jack Fan Tan wasn't a double agent at all. He wasn't any kind of agent. The poor bastard just happened to believe in South Vietnam and wanted to get out of the North. If you guys based your plan, such as it was, on the theory that there was something funny about Fan Tan, it's no wonder it came apart."

But Pfeiffer wasn't buying that.

"That isn't why it came apart," he said. "Of course he was a double agent. That's one thing Bailey and the rest were right about. Listen, if he hadn't been a double agent, if Hanoi hadn't wanted to get him into our line-up, you wouldn't have lasted for one day in Hanoi, let alone got across that bridge. You don't really think, do you, that the North Vietnamese, of all people, were going to let you go around their border provinces with a cabinet minister in tow unless they had a Goddamn good reason? Well, they had a reason all right. It was because they wanted you to. It was because that way they could con you into arranging a hairbreadth escape for Brother Fan Tan. Nearly worked, too."

Now, it would have been much more flattering to think it had been my own resourcefulness that had got us down to the Ben Hai River and across it. This was certainly what I had believed all along. But I had to admit, in retrospect, that somewhere along the way our exodus to the South had become ridiculously easy. Even the rougher moments had not been all that rough. Muller had spotted it early in the game, and I suppose that subconsciously I had, too. All of a sudden they had picked up my lame excuse to take Jack Fan Tan on a tour to the south and had virtually escorted us to the border. Hell, they had even pulled off that simple-minded oaf, Ugly Minh, when he got troublesome. I hated to think that I'd been played for a sucker by both sides, but maybe that's the way it had been.

But they were not right about Jack Fan Tan, and there was

still the fact that the whole thing had gone wrong at the end.

"Why did they shoot us on the bridge, then?" I asked Pfeiffer.

"Who knows? Maybe a trigger-happy guard. Maybe the guards had been told to let two guys go across the bridge and then when they saw you all out there and all of us on the other side, someone panicked and started to shoot. That's the way these things usually happen."

"I don't know about that," I said. "It looked to me as though they knew what they were doing. They were lined up there like executioners."

"Well, you can't blame our people for that," he said. "I blame them for other things."

"Like what?"

"Why, the whole thing was overdone, overstaffed, overelaborate. We violated a cardinal principle. We put too many people into the act. There was you, and that girl, and Muller, and the courier we used, and me, and the whole damned what is laughingly called South Vietnamese Intelligence Service. Let me tell you, something *always* goes wrong when that many people are in the know—especially if any of them are Vietnamese. Seen it happen a hundred times. Now, if they'd just left it to me, I could have managed the whole thing with maybe one other guy. Instead, those ignorant sons-of-bitches from Saigon blow up the helicopter and we wind up losing not only Jack Fan Tan but all those others guys as well. Our guys. That's what comes of trying to run a simple operation with a cast of thousands."

"Did Ned Bailey mastermind this thing?" I asked.

"No. He's too much of a pro to screw it up this way. He was in on some of the planning, I guess, and I know he was in on the operation itself, but the Rube Goldberg part was dreamed up on a higher level."

"He must be feeling pretty lousy about it too, then."

"Like hell he is," said Pfeiffer. "I just saw him before I came to get you. He's sitting on Cloud Nine. He's got something up his sleeve—I don't know what it is, but it better be good. For everybody's sake. Especially mine."

"Why?" I asked. "Nothing that happened was your fault."

"I've got a selfish interest, kid. I'm thinking of Number One. They've finished me out here now, and what I get to do next is going to depend a lot on how this operation is evaluated back in Washington. The CIA's like any other big business, no different: once you're involved in a disaster, you never live it down. It doesn't matter whether it's your fault or not—the black mark sticks to you. No, if old Ned can paper over this one so the cracks don't show, it'll be a lot better for me."

We started walking toward Bailey's quarters again. It was time to have it out with him. I had a vested interest in seeing that it didn't get papered over too well. I was grateful to Pfeiffer for leveling with me, though clearly he didn't know all the answers. A lot was still missing, and it had to do with Jack Fan Tan. Bailey and Pfeiffer were obviously convinced that he had been a double agent, and I could see some aspects that might make it look that way, but every instinct told me they were wrong.

"I'm going to miss Phnom Penh," Pfeiffer said gloomily. "It took me a long time to get established there and I came to like the place. It grows on you. I'm kind of an expert on Southeast Asian stuff by now. Goddamn it, if they give me some crummy job after this, I think I'll just quit and open a gallery somewhere. I've managed to get out some good Khmer stuff of my own—I mean the genuine article, not fakes—and I could start with that. Do you see any reason why I couldn't run an art gallery, Bill?"

"Not a reason in the world, Lou. You'd be a great success. In fact, I'll be your first customer."

The thought of becoming an art dealer seemed to cheer him greatly.

20

Ned Bailey had established himself in a general's office for our meeting. It was not quite his kind of place, being austere and leathery, but he had made it more homelike by ordering in a tray of bottles and glasses. I made straight for the improvised bar. Bailey hadn't waited for us and was already well into his drink. He seemed chipper as a flea as he came around from the big desk with the flags behind it.

"That was a close one," he said. "I suppose you guys realize that any one of us might have been on that chopper that went down."

"The idea had crossed my mind," I said. "Why the hell didn't you take that attaché case away from the Vietnamese major? What did you think he had in it, sandwiches?"

That was unfair and I knew it, but I needed to blame somebody for letting the South Vietnamese kill Fan Tan.

"He did make me nervous," said Bailey. "That's why I pulled him away from Fan Tan. I couldn't figure out why he kept horning in all the time. Still can't. But why should I have taken his attaché case away from him? I didn't think the South Vietnamese wanted to kill him. He's no good to them dead."

"He'd be worse than no good to them alive, you dumb bastard." Obtuse people annoy me, and Bailey was being obtuse. "The South Vietnamese knew he was no double agent, even if you were too thickheaded to see it. They could tell he was the real thing—and the real thing represented a threat to them. If a man like Fan Tan ever got a foothold in South Vietnamese politics, he'd run the present crowd out of business. They didn't dare let him live an hour after he got across the river. He had too much class for them—and you were so stupid you not only couldn't see this, you tipped them off so they could make sure he'd never get to Saigon alive."

"They were wrong, Bill," said Bailey seriously, "absolutely wrong. Just as you are. There is no doubt whatever that Jack Fan Tan was a double agent and was being sent here for that purpose. We not only have documentary proof of that, but the way Hanoi let you bring him out clinches the case." And then, almost in afterthought, he added, "But thank God, it isn't really important."

That enraged me. Here he had run me all over North Vietnam getting Fan Tan out, Charlie had been wounded, a lot of people killed—some of his own men among them—Jack Fan Tan himself eliminated, and still Ned Bailey could stand there and tell me it really wasn't important. I left no doubt in his mind about what I thought of his concept of what was important.

He gave me his most apologetic and disarming look. "I'm sorry. I didn't mean that the way it sounded to you, Bill. Of course it was important, and I am genuinely sorry we had to put you and Charlie through so much. Sure, we would have liked to have had Jack Fan Tan. What I meant was that this little operation of ours has turned into something much bigger and the net result is a plus for our side. We wind up ahead of the game."

A plus for our side. Pfeiffer had been right: Bailey did think he had something up his sleeve. Smug bastard.

"Sorry," I said to him, "you lost me there. Maybe you'd better spell that out for me."

"I wish I could, Billy boy," he said regretfully, "I really

wish I could—but I can't. It's dynamite. Very high-level stuff. I'm not even able to tell Pfeiffer here about it."

Pfeiffer looked surprised at that, but he also looked as if he didn't want to make waves. He was still working for the outfit, after all, and if the outfit wanted to keep him in the dark, that was their business. It wasn't mine, though. I didn't mind making waves. I had been an innocent bystander until these same two people I was drinking with here had roped me into a high-stakes game. I was entitled to know what the deal was. To hell with Bailey.

"Okay, Neddie boy," I said amiably. "If that's all you can tell me, I guess I'll have to accept it. Let's just make sure I have it straight. You say Jack Fan Tan was a double agent whom the North Vietnamese were trying to palm off on us. However, the CIA, which never sleeps, tumbled to their little game and, realizing that Hanoi wanted us to have him in the worst way, sent me in as the escorting committee. The North Vietnamese generously cooperated, and—except for a few unfortunate accidents at the end—everything went according to the master plan. Is that about the gist of it?"

"You've got it exactly right," he said, pleased.

"You've got it exactly upside down," I answered. "Nevertheless, I want you to know that I plan to do full justice to your point of view when I write this story. As it happens, I don't agree with you, but I'm a large-minded man and I will make it clear that representatives of the Central Intelligence Agency believe they apprehended an important Communist double agent when Nguyen Van Thanh, North Vietnam's Minister of Postwar Reconstruction, was caught crossing the Ben Hai Bridge with me. Naturally, objectivity will compel me to say that my own acquaintance with Mr. Nguyen Van Thanh leads me to believe he was a genuine defector. And that, I'm afraid, will have to be the burden of the piece."

I watched Bailey for a reaction, but he was coolly lighting

a cigarette. "When do you plan to write this?" he asked.

"Just as soon as I finish this drink and get out of here," I said cheerfully.

"I can understand how you feel, Bill, but you can't. It would upset the most delicate arrangements."

"I can't see why not," I answered. "There's no security involved. You had a lot of Marines there on the other side of the bridge when we came across, and you know how Marines talk to reporters. It's probably all over the Press Camp in Danang already. Furthermore, they'll know soon enough in Hanoi that Fan Tan was killed, so I could hardly be giving away secrets to them. Frankly, Ned, on the basis of what you've told me, I see no reason not to write the story."

He leaned back and you could see the wheels going round, like a poker player who has just been raised and is trying to work out how good his hand really is. The room was quiet. I went over and made myself another drink.

"You will probably have to say something," he admitted at last. "Something about crossing the bridge. A lot of people were involved and they'll talk. You're right about that. But I'm afraid I'll have to ask you to say nothing, absolutely nothing, about Jack Fan Tan. You may not mention him at all."

"Sorry, Ned. You'll have to do better than that. I'm not going to cover up for you. The whole thing stinks, and unless you give me a very good reason, I'm going to write everything I know about Jack Fan Tan."

Bailey thought that over as Pfeiffer and I watched him. He seemed to be trying to decide where to begin—or whether to begin at all. Finally he nodded.

"All right. The kernel of the situation is this: Although it wasn't what we had in mind when all this first began—you know, when I talked to you in Puerto Secreto—this whole operation has acquired for us someone in Hanoi whom we know to be reliable. He is really well placed, much better placed than Jack Fan Tan. That's why I say we're ahead of the game, even though Jack Fan Tan turned out to be a lemon. We now have a real pipeline into Hanoi at last. It's probably the single most important intelligence breakthrough of the war. Now can you understand why I can't talk much about it and why you can't write *anything* about it?"

"Interesting," I answered, "but not enough. Where does this mysterious man in Hanoi of yours fit into what I was doing in North Vietnam?"

He sighed. "I shouldn't be telling you anything at all. Okay, perhaps this much. Remember when I told you in Mexico that a minister wanted to defect and showed you Jack Fan Tan's dossier? Well, this information came to us from one of our very few contacts in Hanoi—an Iron Curtain diplomat who occasionally helps us. Usually all you get from people like him is atmosphere, gossip, that sort of thing, but this man sometimes gives us something interesting. And he's the one who passed along the word that Fan Tan might want to defect."

He was trying to lead me astray. "How did he learn that? From Fan Tan himself?"

"Yes, and it was confirmed by another North Vietnamese source."

"And then a little later," I said, "this same North Vietnamese source persuaded you that it was all a mistake and that Jack Fan Tan was really being groomed as a double agent?"

Bailey was surprised. "Yes, that's right."

"Very accommodating fellow," I said.

"Well, that's what he's paid for," answered Bailey, for whom this seemed sufficient explanation. "He's given us information before and we pay him. Nobody gives you anything for nothing in this business. I suppose he wants to get out to the West someday with enough money to live on. They all do it for money."

And he went on, explaining that the revelation from the

usually reliable North Vietnamese source that Fan Tan was a double agent had sent the Big Spook House into a crisis. Did they want to encourage him in his duplicity or not?

It was finally decided that they did want him to come over, however suspect his motives, on the principle that it's no bad thing to have a double agent on the premises as long as you're onto his game. You can get a good deal of information from such an agent by judicious interrogation, and he's also on hand to be traded for some of your own people who have been picked up by the other side. And it followed, or was assumed to follow, that since the enemy wanted Fan Tan inserted, no obstacle would be put in the way of anyone assigned to bring him out. That was where I came in again. Good old Benson, about to appear on the scene. Let *him* shepherd Fan Tan through the lines. It would be a snap. All the CIA had to do was to let Hanoi, eager to plant their double agent, know that I was coming for him and we'd coast right through.

From the CIA's point of view it must have looked clever as hell: Hanoi would think its plot had succeeded, while in reality the CIA would have put one over on Hanoi.

And there was a bonus. That highly placed North Vietnamese informant, after all, was almost too good to be true. Everyone would breathe easier if he were to pass some conclusive test of his reliability. The Fan Tan–Benson experiment would be the test. If we really had no difficulty escaping, it would prove that Jack Fan Tan was indeed a double agent and that the North Vietnamese who had fingered him was a true friend of the CIA. Chalk up one more coup for the master spies.

It did not seem in the least reprehensible to Bailey to send amateurs like Charlie and me—*friends,* for Christ's sake—on a fishing expedition to test the reliability of some vague informant in enemy territory. I let him know how I felt about that.

"Well, hell, Bill," he said defensively, "we were virtually certain it would work out the way it did. There's some risk in everything, even crossing the street. But you made it, which shows we were right. The North Vietnamese didn't really want to harm you or Charlie."

"In that case," I said bitterly, "why did they beat us up as soon as I got there?"

He hadn't known about that, but he wasn't greatly disturbed. "Probably didn't want you to think it was going to be too easy," he said with a shrug. "Actually, I can guess what must have happened. We had a slight failure of communications for the first few days you were there. Our diplomatic go-between was supposed to come in with you to pass the word of your mission to the right people in Hanoi, but he couldn't make that flight. I imagine the North Vietnamese may have had some doubts about the real purpose of your visit until he came in on the next ICC flight. When was the next flight, by the way?"

"It would have been on a Tuesday," I said. "I came in the Friday before."

"Well, then, they might have been a little unfriendly until Tuesday, but I'll bet things went more smoothly after that. They did, didn't they?"

I thought about Tuesday for a while. Tuesday had been the night of the Hungarian reception. That was when someone had let Jack Fan Tan know I was the man who was going to bring him out. It was the night Phan Boi Chau had suddenly turned all smiles and Ngo Xuan had said I could interview the Foreign Minister after all.

"Yes, things got better after Tuesday," I said.

I kept thinking about Tuesday. Beaten up on Monday, lionized on Tuesday. I remembered the French Ambassador's wife and how she had interrupted Jack Fan Tan and me in the garden. Phan Boi Chau assuring me everything would be all right now. Trying to get Charlie to leave the party. Making polite conversation with the little man in the gray suit. The little man in the gray suit.

Suddenly the final piece fell into place.

I said, "Ned, if you think you can count on Phan Boi Chau, you're making the mistake of your life."

The slightest shock tremor crossed Bailey's face. Only a poker player would have noticed it. "Never heard of him," he said.

"You always were a lousy poker player," I told him.

"What makes you think we ever had anything to do with Phan whatever his name is?" he said, and I knew he was bluffing.

"Everything," I answered. "He's the only one who fits."

I wasn't bluffing. Phan Boi Chau was their man, all right. And the little man in the gray suit who had come in on the Tuesday ICC flight was their diplomatic courier.

"You're wrong," Bailey said firmly. "So forget about this little theory of yours. It's all in your head. You can't mention it any more than you can mention Nguyen Van Thanh. Forget you ever met Phan Boi Chau."

I was frightened for the first time since the bridge. Bailey's anxiety to steer me away from Phan Boi Chau only confirmed my certainty that the CIA had accepted him. The terrifying part was that if our government thought they had scored a great coup, if they really believed in Phan Boi Chau, then they'd pinned the whole outcome of the war to the word of an enemy agent. We would base our policy on what he told us.

"Ned, you never met either Nguyen Van Thanh or Phan Boi Chau," I said in a final effort at persuasion. "I knew them both, and I know that Phan Boi Chau is the real double agent in this affair. My God, isn't it clear? Hanoi cooked up the whole thing to convince you of his reliability. You said yourself this would be the test. If you think now that he has passed it, you're asking for terrible trouble."

I tried to explain it as best I could. It was easy enough to see how they had fallen for it. First Phan Boi Chau had peddled a few interesting and probably authentic bits of information to the CIA. He made them pay for it, too, which at once prejudiced them in his favor. Once the CIA was attracted, Hanoi contrived a bolder plan. With one master stroke they could liquidate Jack Fan Tan, whose willingness to defect they had smelled out, and at the same time consolidate Phan Boi Chau's position with the CIA.

Obviously, Jack Fan Tan and I were never meant to reach South Vietnam alive. We were to have been gunned down on the bridge. In case that failed, they had a back-up plan. The South Vietnamese would do us in. It was child's play to plant suspicion about Fan Tan in the minds of the South Vietnamese; Hanoi had agents aplenty in Saigon who would get the word to the right people that Fan Tan was a menace to the status quo. It had worked, too. Jack Fan Tan had been eliminated and Phan Boi Chau now had the field to himself.

Bailey told me I was a lunatic, spinning a fantasy out of thin air, out of my depth in areas where I had no business and no experience. Nothing I could say seemed likely to shake his conviction that the CIA had scored a breakthrough, but I made one last try.

I pleaded with him. "Listen, Ned, I'm not making this up. Fan Tan warned me there would be an attempt to discredit him and—oh, Christ, what's the use!" I felt helpless. They wanted to believe in Phan Boi Chau. They had acquired a vested interest in him.

One more try. "Look," I said, "do you realize the power over us that this guy will have now? Suppose we're trying to get a commitment out of the other side in Paris and they won't say yes and they won't say no. All Phan Boi Chau has to do is to slip us the word that they really mean yes, and we'll buy it. We'll buy anything he tells us. If I'm right about him and you're wrong, he could change the whole pattern of the peace settlement. The amount of harm he could do is incalculable."

"No, it isn't," Bailey snapped. "Once in a while we get fooled, but not often and not for long. We'd catch up with him sooner or later."

"But we're running out of time, Ned. You know the situation as well as I do—no progress in Paris, the pressure to pull out more troops building up all the time, elections coming up, more and more people in Washington ready to grasp at straws. We're terribly vulnerable to a plausible liar with good credentials like Phan Boi Chau. My God, give him a six months' run and he could scuttle whatever chances are left for a decent peace settlement."

Bailey looked at me coldly. "Forget it, Bill," he said, "and stop worrying. I'm sorry you feel this way, but you have done your bit—for which we're grateful—and now you are finished and can get back to your job. You can write and talk about your visit to North Vietnam, use your film and all that, but you'll have to leave Jack Fan Tan and Phan Boi Chau out of it. Don't mess with things you don't understand. The shooting at the bridge was just a mistake by nervous border guards. The helicopter was shot down by enemy fire. Got it? Charlie will have to keep quiet, too—and if she doesn't, I'll hold you responsible: I'm not kidding. There's too much at stake."

I knew I had lost. I hadn't convinced Bailey and I wasn't going to write the story. It wasn't his implied threat that would stop me. A correspondent has certain privileges, including the right to call things as he sees them. He also has certain responsibilities, one of which is not to try to play God. As long as there was an outside chance Bailey was right, I could not take into my own hands the responsibility for tampering with the possible fate of men and of my country.

"All right, Ned," I said slowly. "I won't write about it, not now, anyway—unless, of course, somebody stumbles on the story or the South Vietnamese leak it. Then I might have to say something about Jack Fan Tan, I'll go along with you, though, and not speculate about Phan Boi Chau."

"Good," said Bailey.

"Just one thing in return," I said. "I assume you're going to file a report on this business. I want your promise that you will include in it my own strenuous objections to the official version of what took place. If I'm not going to write the story, I want to be on record somewhere as having foreseen what is going to happen. This is very important to me."

Lou Pfeiffer, who had been silent for a long time, cleared his throat. "I guess you'd better associate me with that, Ned," he said awkwardly: "I don't know that I agree with everything Bill thinks, but I have my own doubts about Phan Boi Chau." His voice grew firmer. "You can make it more formal if you feel like it—that I voiced serious doubts about the wisdom of an uncritical acceptance of any intelligence we get from Phan Boi Chau—something like that."

Bailey was completely taken aback. Pfeiffer's independence nonplused him. "You don't realize what you're saying, Lou," he said. "You're up for reassignment, you know. Can't you see what this could do to you? Bill's right; Washington will go along with our estimate. A comment like that from you is going to look like hell on your record, and I'd hate to see you wreck your career. Don't you want me to forget what you just said?"

"No," said Pfeiffer carefully. "I don't think so. I don't care that much about my career any more; I'm washed up out here anyway. I've been listening and I've been thinking and now I've decided I have to go along with Bill that it's risky to rely on Phan Boi Chau. You can quote me."

I don't know how Bailey felt as we both looked at Pfeiffer, but I admire a man who will stick his neck out for what he believes when he doesn't have to.

I said, "I hope I haven't got you into trouble, Lou."

He shrugged his shoulders. "I don't have that much to lose. There's always the art business."

The telephone rang then and Bailey handed it over to me. It was the doctor.

"Benson," he said, "you'll be glad to know your girl isn't hurt badly at all. We've got her cleaned up and I don't foresee any complications. If it will make you feel any better to see her tonight, you can—but get over here right away. I want her to get some rest."

"Thanks, Colonel. I'll be there."

I knocked my drink back and shook hands with Lou Pfeiffer. "See you in the gallery, friend," I said.

Bailey shook my hand and said I'd done a great job and that we'd keep in touch. "If there's anything we can do for you," he said, "not just me, I mean the Agency too, let us know."

"You've done enough already," I said. "More than enough."

On the way over to the hospital, I thought that was God's own truth. More than enough. It had been a long way from Puerto Secreto. The whole long expedition had been a kind of microcosm of the war in Vietnam. First my being talked into getting a little involved. Then deeper, and once on the ground, there was nothing to do but keep going. And when, finally, we crossed the last river, it turned out that what I thought I had been doing wasn't what I was doing at all. And Ned Bailey and all the professionals, they weren't doing what they thought they were doing either. The only ones who knew what they were doing were sitting back in Hanoi, ruthless, cunning, bending everything to their long-term design. Maybe. I wasn't even sure about that, come to think of it. Maybe Jack Fan Tan was right and they didn't know what they were doing in Hanoi either.

All that was certain right now was that I wanted to see Charlie.

Charlie had a big new bandage on the right side of her head. It went beneath her chin and around her head so she looked like a damaged nun. They had cranked up her bed until she was half-sitting, but she looked asleep—at least, her good eye was closed. I put myself where she could see me when she opened it and stroked her hand. The eye opened slowly and she smiled.

"I thought you'd never come," she said sleepily.

"Just as soon as the doctor let me. He says you're in great shape."

"He told me that, too. I'm glad. I was afraid I'd die. I was worried that if I died it would be a big bother for you."

"Worse than that, kid," I said, "but the question didn't arise. You're going to be the same old La Bomba in a couple of days. They'll have to put a guard on the door to keep the other patients out."

She tried to make a face at me, but it hurt. "How's the sound?" she said.

"You sound just fine, just like my girl."

"I mean the sound on the film. I hope it comes out all right. I tried to remember everything."

"The sound was perfect. You're a great sound man. Everything is going to come out all right."

Her eye shut and I thought she was asleep, but she said, "Are things really all right? You sound upset."

"Well, Ned Bailey's a little confused. He thinks Jack Fan Tan was a phony."

"That's silly. I don't think he was. Do you?"

"No. He was as good as they come. He might have made a difference here."

She didn't answer at first, and I thought she had dozed off. Then she said, "Really? Do you think one man could make a difference?"

"Yes, I think so."

"Well," said Charlie, speaking very slowly through the fog of drowsiness, "it has been my experience that one man more or less doesn't make any difference."

I waited for her to add "except you, darling," or something like that, but she said nothing. She must have been asleep.

The Devil's Lieutenant

M. FAGYAS

Amidst the decadence of the waning Austro-Hungarian Empire the officers of the army's General Staff stood out – an *élite* corps. But death stalked the *élite*, like some grim spectre of the Great War looming over Europe.

A dashing young officer passed over for promotion, is accused of mailing poisoned "aphrodisiac" capsules to ten members of the General Staff. The sudden death of one of the officers triggers an investigation that plunges imperial Vienna into a scandal, shattering the élan of the proud, patrician army and shaking the foundations of Europe's oldest royal house.

A Sphere Book   50p

Ghost Dance

JOHN NORMAN

It was the year of the Ghost Dance and on the Standing Rock reservation Sitting Bull's Sioux warriors readied themselves for the last great fight against the white men whose carbines had slaughtered the buffalo and the pony soldiers.

The Ghost Dance would make the Sioux immortal, its magic deflect the bluecoats' bullets. They rode off the reservation into the Bad Lands and at a place called Wounded Knee they met the United States Army. . . .

That meeting went down in history as THE MASSACRE AT WOUNDED KNEE

A Sphere Book   40p